The Night of the Scourge

Also by Lars Mytting in English translation

FICTION

The Sixteen Trees of the Somme (2017)
The Bell in the Lake: The Sister Bells Trilogy I (2020)
The Reindeer Hunters: The Sister Bells Trilogy II (2022)

NON-FICTION

Norwegian Wood: Chopping, Stacking, and Drying Wood the Scandinavian Way (2015)
The Norwegian Wood Activity Book (2016)

Lars Mytting

The Night of the Scourge

*Translated from the Norwegian
by Deborah Dawkin*

THE OVERLOOK PRESS, NEW YORK

This edition first published in hardcover in 2025 by
The Overlook Press, an imprint of ABRAMS

Abrams books are available at special discounts when purchased in quantity
for premiums and promotions as well as fundraising or educational use.
Special editions can also be created to specification. For details,
contact specialsales@abramsbooks.com or the address above.

Copyright © Gyldendal Norsk Forlag AS, Oslo 2023
English translation copyright © 2025 by Deborah Dawkin
Jacket © 2025 Abrams

This translation has been published with the financial support of NORLA.

All rights reserved. No part of this publication may be reproduced
or transmitted in any form or by any means, electronic or mechanical, including
photocopy, recording, or any information storage and retrieval system
now known or to be invented, without permission in writing from the publisher,
except by a reviewer who wishes to quote brief passages in connection
with a review written for inclusion in a magazine, newspaper, or broadcast.

Library of Congress Control Number: 2024941011

Printed and bound in the United States
1 3 5 7 9 10 8 6 4 2

ISBN: 978-1-4197-6093-8
eISBN: 978-1-64700-634-1

ABRAMS The Art of Books
195 Broadway, New York, NY 10007
abramsbooks.com

"All that ye sow in earthly life ye shall reap in the hereafter. Therefore I say: Go, ye! Come, ye!"
INSCRIPTION IN RINGEBU
STAVE CHURCH, REMOVED 1600

"Nothing disappears."
ASTRID HEKNE

Contents

A TALE REDISCOVERED: STIGMA DIABOLICUM // 1

A Winter Lamb — The Will of the Yarn

FIRST STORY: I SHALLNA' BE
CONTENT WITH LESS // 37

The Wedding Ring — A Map of a Seter Road — Over This Smell, the Smell of the Pastor's Pipe — There'll Always Be a Use for Dynamite — Von der Maas bis an die Memel — We All Turned Crazy — A Hungover Scientist — Metron, Temperantia — A Sketchbook Comes Home — The Law of Nature's Many Paragraphs — Evil Earth, Evil Rock, Evil Cross — A Stave Church of Stone — No Electric Light at Such Time — Time Is Running Out — A Pale Yellow Fokker Universal — Winter Seters — Was It Something You Bore? — A Swarm of Wasps He Could Not Be Stung By — Die Brüder und das Volk — Gifts of the Mountain — Consecrated Floodwaters from the Breia — Only until May 1940, Pastor Schweigaard! — A Pastor's Departure

SECOND STORY: RUNES AND WARPLANES // 205

An Ordinary Tuesday in April — Our Lord's Decommissioned Warship — The Ice on Daukulpen — Major Sprockhoff — An Unmarried Hekne Woman — His Right Hand — We Too Must

Draw Strength from Nothing — A Suitable Job for a Pensioner — Four Trusted Men — The Poor Souls who Languish in Paganism — The Simplified War Liturgy — Six Dead Pheasants — The Fly in a Clenched Fist — The Second Most Powerful Man in the World — Farewell to Svarten — A Layer of Grease in the Milk Churns — Sunbeam's Martyrdom — A Bible and a Kicksled Stand — The Past Demands No Interest — Death is Quick for the One who Dies — Dead Woman's Will — Not a Word to Yer Father — Eighteen Cassocks to Helgøya — Greetings to Fru Ro — Firebirds — Old Mother Reindeer

THIRD STORY: NIGHT OF NIGHTS // 435

Altar Candles for a Farewell Mass — Eight Hundred Years to the End — The Last Pastor in Butangen — You Were in the Church When the Church Burned Down — A Final Task for an Unloved Church — He Could Bear Death No More — Arrests — Necropolis Dresden — I Thought It Was the May Wind — The Last Piece on the Sledge — The Dead Say *Come* — Wishing the World Goodnight

FINAL STORY: WHERE THE ANCESTORS TREAD // 507

A Profusion of Thistles and Brambles — The Promise

Those who Lived and Those who Live On // 521

Acknowledgements // 535

A Tale Rediscovered

Stigma Diabolicum

A Winter Lamb

HE COULD NOT UNDERSTAND HOW SHE COULD HAVE nurtured it out here in the snow. Much less who, or what, she had mated with.

The year was 1613, the place, the mountains above Butangen, the man, Eirik Hekne. He had come on his skis that morning to lay grouse snares, travelling between the twisted birch trees and scattered spruces along the treeline.

A raven took off before him.

A raven, surely it had to be? Blinded by the light, all Eirik could see was the flap of black wings and a string of entrails dangling from a beak. So sharp was the sun that the snow looked pale blue. The bird vanished over the mountains and Eirik trudged on.

In his path lay a dead sheep, its wool so torn and frozen it was one with the windblown snow. Her eyeballs were gouged out, and the bird prints around her head indicated how the raven had feasted upon her. From her eye sockets came a wisp of steam. She must have died that morning.

It happened sometimes that sheep lost their way, wandered around until the snow settled and were taken by a wolverine, mostly sooner rather than later.

But this was later. Much later. It was February, for pity's sake.

He turned to look around the snow-covered slopes. So different from the landscape he knew in the summer and autumn, where sheep and cows grazed, and trout and char filled his nets.

This was another world. Blinding and deceptive. Anything small was gone, anything big was bigger. Rocks and streams, thickets and landmarks were hidden beneath snow that was high or deep, all according to the creature you were. The mountains stood white against a blue sky and lied about their distance: *Come here, mortal, you shan't freeze to death on the way.*

Behind him the dead sheep bleated.

Eirik stopped still, then turned slowly. The ewe threw back her head, scattering droplets of blood over the snow. She seemed to be trying to kick, but her legs were frozen fast. She looked at him with empty eye sockets, uncertain, perhaps, if he was raven or human. What difference would it make anyhow?

That it will soon be over for you. That's the difference.

He got out his knife to free her from life. Dug his hands in between the frozen wool and her ribs to find her heart. Eirik Hekne always felt distaste at killing in cold blood, but death was undeniably whole. Where life was a half or quarter present, it might be made whole again, but not when it was so close to nothing, as it was here.

Then he felt another kind of movement in her. Something seemed to come loose from behind her, a little creature came up in a rush of snow, and the animal that looked up at him now looked at him through two good eyes. Curious and quick.

A lamb. A skinny lamb with big ears.

Eirik pulled it out. In that moment he thought that the shine of its wool was an optical illusion, but later he and his daughters would conclude that its topcoat was as shiny and glittery as it had first seemed. As long as a goat's beard, it gleamed like silver, the undercoat soft as a hare's fur. The lamb kicked and seemed healthy.

The lamb must have come into the world as winter lambs do. Its mother had probably been one of the year's younger ewes that were described as "springtime empty" and reckoned to be

A Winter Lamb

"debt-ewes". Put out to graze with the rest of the herd, she had come into heat later that summer. A ram had doubtless caught her scent and come to her, perhaps from as far away as a farm on the other side of the mountain.

These things happened.

Not often. But more often than not.

So, the lamb had come into the world in late autumn, a sad season in which to be small and newborn, when the rain was cold and the wind raged, as if the mountain itself gave forth a warning: *Leave me, go down to the village, I shall soon be another.*

Eirik changed his mind. He put his knife in its sheath, dug the ewe free and tried to squeeze some milk from her teats, but whatever milk she must have had, she had already given.

He stood up with the lamb in his arms. Looking around and over at the spruce tree nearby, he could see how they had survived. The bark was peeled off and the lowest twigs had been eaten to the height a sheep can reach when it stands on two legs. Round its trunk was a black wreath of trodden-down dung. The ewe and her lamb had stood under these spruce trees, with the snow falling around them. And when everything was eaten, they had gone on to the next tree. But this being the young mother's first winter, she had not yet learned the ways of snow – it is in no hurry like the rain, but settles in ever higher layers – so that the two sank deeper each time they ventured further. After the last heavy snowfall, hunger must have forced them out into the white snowdrifts again, but by then they were too malnourished and the snow was too deep. Unable to reach the next tree, they got stuck, and the single and last thing she could do was to protect the creature she had birthed.

Eirik Hekne had seen, over several long days, what could be demanded of a woman to bring children into the world, and his wife's prolonged torment as she died in childbirth had instilled something contrary in him: a promptness in decisions, total trust in the worth of a first impulse – swiftness of action that might end in disaster or be richly rewarded. It was a characteristic that would run through future generations of the Hekne family, and which the villagers called "the Hekne Way". They made a decision, and that was that, whether it led them into a dungeon or up onto a throne.

And so it was today. He saw what the lamb was destined for, and in that same instant he saw his twin daughters. He tucked the lamb inside his coat, gripped the ewe by her legs and heaved her onto his shoulders, emaciated but caked with so much snow that she was as big as a small bear.

He pushed steadily on through the snow to the Hekne seter, the upland farm where there was a cabin in which he could spend the night. Clumps of snow melted in the warmth under his clothes, and the water ran down over his front. It was as though the lamb was growing smaller and smaller, and when all the snow was gone it felt like a bag of bones against his chest, while the ewe on his shoulders was the same heavy clump of ice.

In those days the family did not use their seter exclusively in the summer for its rich pastures, but wintered the cows there too. This was because the path down to their farm was so long and arduous, leading through narrow passes where loose rocks tumbled down with each step, through treacherous fords, before finally crossing a rickety footbridge high over the Breia, the river that ran down from the mountain to the village. That was simply how the terrain was, and the terrain could not be controlled. So, instead of transporting load upon load of mountain moss and marsh grass down to the Hekne farm for winter fodder, they stored it in large barns up on the seter, where they housed the cows until well after the frost set in. Only when all the fodder had been eaten sometime after Christmas were the herd driven through the snow, across the now frozen marshes and rivers, and down to the village.

A Winter Lamb

Eirik had recently had a new cabin built on the seter. It was handsome and spacious, as money was plentiful at Hekne now. His twin daughters, Halfrid and Gunhild, who were conjoined at the hip and whom the villagers simply called the Hekne sisters, had recently finished their apprenticeship in Dovre, and were now among the finest weavers in Gudbrandsdalen. In exchange for a weave depicting the Three Kings, Eirik had been given some fine, block-cut soapstone. He had built a fireplace at the seter with it, and the soft, buff-coloured stone emitted an even warmth all the night through.

Eirik laid the ewe and her lamb in front of the hearth and fed them with hay and cow's milk. The lumps of snow in the sheep's fleece melted and ran into pools on the dirt floor. And still he wondered over the silver-coloured lamb. It was impossible to tell what type of ram this ewe had met. Not a ram from Butangen, at least.

If it was a ram at all.

He sat there into the evening until the pitch pine burned out. The ewe had no need of her eyes to do what she must, and the last thing Eirik saw as he fell asleep was her licking and tending her scrawny little lamb.

When he awoke the lamb was standing and nudging its mother. She was dead, and this big farmer felt tears in his eyes. Perhaps the ewe had sensed what was happening. Thought as mortally ill mothers often do when they know that others will care for their child: You are safe, you shall live, I can die.

An idea flashed into his mind, engendered by an idea he had had once long ago. When Astrid had died in childbirth, he had cut three lengths of her hair, without thought of what they might be used for. Now he carried the ewe outside, clipped off her fleece and gathered it into a sack. Then he laid her body on the edge of the seter, and the raven took what the raven was due.

7

Stigma Diabolicum

Eirik Hekne brushed the snow from the slaughter stone in the field. Sat down and thought. Then he crossed the marshes and the footbridge over the Breia with what would prove to be the most valuable burden the mountain had ever given him.

Down on the farm he gave the lamb to his daughters and said, *What we mun thank for this lamb's survival, as wi' yer life and survival, is the strength o' a mother.*

From this lamb's wool the Hekne Weave was woven. The weave that would be the sisters' life's work. They set up a separate upright loom for its creation and did not finish it until the day they died. It was made in accordance with the old Norse traditions, with mysterious figures of beasts and human beings and shapeshifters. The sisters wove some motifs with the blind ewe's wool, others with the lamb's topcoat that glinted like silver thread. And – so it was said – one depicted Astrid Hekne's sacrifice, and into this they wove some of their mother's hair.

The hand-reared lamb grew into a long-haired ram with curly horns. He liked to reach up and eat the leaves of the rowan and willow, and would stand with his front hooves on their trunks, and the sisters called him Leaf Drifter. Like the other breeds of sheep reared here in Butangen for generations, Leaf Drifter had a two-layered fleece, and stayed outside all the year round. The rain ran off his topcoat, while his undercoat kept him warm. He followed the seasons and moulted when the new leaves sprang. Then the sisters took him on their laps and tugged off his wool, and while they sorted the fine, gleaming topcoat, Leaf Drifter leaped happily about, naked and free of his winter coat.

In the summer he accompanied the sisters on their regular trips down from Hekne to the tar-smelling stave church, as they humped along in waltz-like rhythm and sat in the sun with their backs against the cemetery wall, embroidering or sewing, looking out over the unconsecrated graves of those who had either ended their own lives or been executed. It was here that Halfrid had scattered thistle seeds in remembrance of her bygone love, the Scottish soldier who had had to leave her because she and her sister could never be separated. There weren't many who knew anything of this. Most just saw the ram grazing among the unmarked graves, and many imagined that its fleece absorbed the wisdom unique to those in purgatory, who, finding no rest in unconsecrated ground, spent so much time thinking.

A man stood within the cemetery walls. His name was Sigvard C. Krafft, and he had been Butangen's pastor since 1591. He had, in his time, buried the Hekne sisters' mother and baptised her daughters in a ceremony the villagers would never forget. Village gossip had raged since their birth. There was much whispering in corners; some said the girls' mother must have succumbed to witchcraft since she had met such a terrible end.

Pastor Krafft had a hard job tempering the village's unrest. He had seen the twin girls soon after their birth and had pinched the thick fold of skin that joined them. It appeared to be numb.

Witchcraft was the usual charge when babies were sickly or deformed. Folk often said they had been switched with the children of underground spirits, and their own human offspring were alive elsewhere. This explanation eased these parents' pain, as it meant the dribbling, ogle-eyed infant on the floor was not theirs, and did not need the same care, or maybe none. It still happened that newborns vanished without ever being entered in the church register. They were left in the forest, where their cries lured the fox and the wolf, but if the animals were occupied elsewhere, the night frost needed no cries to find its way to a naked babe.

His fellow priests, most of whom followed Martin Luther's teachings to the letter, did not oppose this custom. After all, Luther had said in his *Tischreden* that changelings and monstrous creatures were put in the cradles of rightful babes by Satan as a torment to the people.

Krafft accepted the commonly held Lutheran belief that a decisive battle was being fought, right now, between God and Satan. A war in which humankind found itself confused on the battlefield and was easily led therefore by Evil. But being so close to his congregation, he was ashamed of the priests and officials who waged this war with an unerring brutishness that seemed more allied with the Devil himself.

As a student in Copenhagen, Krafft had been fascinated by the works of Aristotle. Now, as a priest, he felt increasingly alone as he watched the Church adopt more and more extreme and rigid opinions. Any unusual event was now considered an act of God or Satan, and as such demanded interpretation. If a newborn had six fingers or a crooked back, this might be passed off as God's chastisement for irregular behaviour or loose morals. But the Bishop – who was several days' journey away in Oslo – was likely to view the birth in Butangen in a far more dramatic light. Scholars might well be tempted to come and investigate these two baby girls, and even transport them to Copenhagen where their existence could be interpreted by the Church's wisest clergymen.

Without a doubt, these scholars would declare that greater powers – if not the Devil himself – had sent nothing short of a *monstrum* to Earth.

This was a word used only in the rarest and most alarming cases. *Monstrum* did not just denote a horrifying creature. Those who read Latin knew it meant "a divine warning". In Copenhagen the young Krafft had discovered that, for more than a century, pamphlets had been circulating on how the birth of a deformed child should be interpreted. Conjoined twins were, according to church scholars, the darkest of all warnings, for they heralded doomsday and the Apocalypse.

The very next day after their birth, Pastor Krafft made his choice. He took Jesus' side in what he knew would be a battle against rumour-mongering and authority. The birth of the sisters was, he concluded, not some dreadful omen. On the contrary. Astrid's daughters were among Our Lord's rarest gifts. He let nobody beyond the secluded village know about the sisters, and he baptised them in all haste to give them God's protection. The church was filled to the rafters, and after pronouncing their names Halfrid and Gunhild Hekne, Krafft turned to his congregation and said:

"The Good Lord hath chosen to fuse these babes together as one. We humans are too lowly to grasp all His purposes. But Holy Scripture commands that no man shall put asunder what God hath joined. Therefore, let them walk in friendship among us, as two sisters. Two ordinary sisters."

The Hekne sisters grew up. Always curtsied in unison and looked folk in the eyes. They found it hard to get around in the winter, but their father made a wide sledge so they could play with the other bairns, speeding down the slopes and across the ice on Lake Løsnes. From the age of twelve they showed signs of being tall and fair-faced, at fifteen they were half a head taller than girls of the same age, and being two and very alike, they made a dazzling impression. Their hair was always set up in beautiful, elaborate plaits, and any man could confirm that, were it not for their deformity, the sisters might have attracted suitors from the grandest farms.

But there were no proposals of marriage. It was unthinkable for two girls who had to walk sideways through doors, and to whom a question could never be asked of just one on her own. They were always a plural and a half of a whole, and they could also share sensations and predict the opinions or thoughts of the other, so that their quarrels were desperate and exhausting,

Stigma Diabolicum

because no escape was possible. Halfrid generally started their sentences and Gunhild finished them. If they disagreed, they talked over each other, and it sounded as if they were both contradicting themselves and trying to persuade themselves, making it impossible to know what they really thought. They were often forced to come to an abrupt truce, sealed with a rhyme that summed up the immutability of life: *Thus 'twas, thus 'tis, and thus it shalt be.* The order in which they said these words was unchanging, with Halfrid saying *thus 'twas*, and Gunhild saying *thus 'tis*, before they said the rest in unison.

Their artistry grew finer with each weave they wove. They plucked the patterns out of the threads with their fingers, each motif, each figure, in a unique, uneven rhythm. Leaf Drifter's shining wool was carded and spun. They collected plants to make dyes, among them heather, witch hazel and devil's-bit scabious. The bark of the mountain willow created a yellow as strong as the sunrise, and in the kitchen garden at Hekne they planted rose madder and woad; the first offered a red as vivid as human blood, the second a blue like a summer sky. The yarns were so beautiful that simple-minded farm folk used the word *magic* when describing the dyes. The sisters would never impart their methods, and some folk grew envious and said there was something occult about the week-long process in which plants were fermented and dried. Nobody knew that the sisters were simply shy because they had to soak the wode leaves in their own urine to extract the exquisite blue dye known as pot-blue.

Eirik Hekne rarely let strangers into the farmhouse. His greatest fear was that Church scholars might get wind of his daughters' condition, or that the two of them might be kidnapped, for it was said that certain royal households had collections of human freaks.

Which was why he was suspicious when a man in unusual apparel turned up at Hekne, leaving a leather pouch with a red wax seal around the drawstrings. The purse was meant for the sisters, but nobody dared give it to them for fear its contents were bewitched. Eirik set off on horseback and caught up with the stranger at the end of the Løsnes Marshes. The man was a pedlar from the Møre coast and the pouch had been handed to him by a Scottish merchant some months earlier. He had no other message or explanation except that he had been paid handsomely to make the detour to Butangen, and that he was an honest man.

The pouch contained gifts from the Scottish lad with whom Halfrid had fallen in love in Dovre. Eirik remembered with horror the time when the sisters tried to hack themselves free from each other, so that Halfrid might accompany this boy, and he also recalled Pastor Krafft's words: *What God has joined . . .*

But he gave his daughters the leather pouch, and from that day on they each wore a silver ring. Gunhild's ring was chased with a motif that posterity would recognise as Celtic. Halfrid's was wider and bore a pattern that only she understood.

The notion that silver could heal wounds, both visible and invisible, was not unknown to Sigvard Krafft. As a pastor he encountered a myriad unbridled cultural mores, for Butangen was not governed by Christianity alone, but also by what remained of the ancient Norse faith and countless weird creatures, benign and malevolent. Folk had absolute belief in these, they had done so since they were small, for a child's mind was a white canvas, and whatever the grown-ups painted there, remained. Some of these superstitions could, Kraft had to admit, be useful. His wife often told their bairns of the fearsome *kvernknurr* who hid in the millstream, the monster whose terrible groans they could hear, for it was impossible to mind them the whole time, and this story kept them from danger.

So, the villagers were allowed to continue with their fancies. They gave life a certain framework. Difficulties had named

Stigma Diabolicum

sources, making it possible to identify a remedy, whether that was to draw a cross over the buttermilk or slather butter on the log walls of the farm *stabbur* – where a family would store vital grain and food supplies – to hasten the arrival of spring. Krafft had also learned to be sparing with notions of *sin*, for when he was too rigid, it led to a sense of guilt and apathy that trapped the villagers in a world they did not understand, and even less control.

Krafft had tried, with gentleness and guile, to row the Lord's boat across the murky waters of faith. For a long time life in Butangen was largely gentle and forgiving, until 1617 when he received a scroll with the king's seal. It was one of the land's first printed laws. When he unrolled it, he found it was entitled *Forording om Troldfolk*. It was an ordinance on witches and their accomplices. Having read this new law, Pastor Krafft slumped down on a bench.

From now on he and all Norway's officials were to follow a new directive: they must pursue witches with full force. If a person communed with the Devil, they must face death. Execution without mercy. The following month, Krafft received a new directive. The population's lust for ornamentation must be stamped out. Any unnecessary expenditure on weddings and funerals must cease. Away with precious stones and pearls.

And . . . silver adornments.

Krafft could guess why these laws were being instituted now. The centenary of Martin Luther's *Theses* was being celebrated in the cities, and in Copenhagen the king wanted to distinguish himself as a true Protestant.

Witchcraft had undoubtedly been feared since time immemorial, but now Krafft felt that whole communities were being poisoned by this obsession with so-called accomplices of the Devil. These extensive new powers were popular among his colleagues, who enforced them with whips and iron and fire. In

1618, three girls in the nearby village of Fron were burned alive. Two families had their farms seized and were exiled. They were said to have visited a local wisewoman to get help for their sick children. The following year, Fron's pastor testified against two more girls and had them sent to the stake.

Krafft knew how hard it was to act with reason when disease struck. He and his wife had lost two little ones to illness. But he was even more helpless in this new battle. The craziest ideas were now valid suspicions, and their expression was increasingly vicious. Safer to find some prohibition and cling to it, then you could discredit anyone who did not follow suit. Gossip had always been a problem in the village; now it was doubly dangerous and difficult for him to extinguish. A finger was always pointed at somebody for any mishap or sickness these days. Another villager must have cast a spell on the barn when the cows escaped, or used witchcraft when a young wife was childless, and there were constant rumours that some person or other had taken scrapings from the walls of the stave church to use in a pact with the Devil.

The new law also kindled another flame: envy. In 1619 Krafft got wind of some very dark rumours. Like a man who prepares his farm before a storm, he made three trips to nearby villages. Concealing his identity as a pastor, he chatted with both humble and lofty folk, sat near noisy tables in taverns and inns and listened. And as he turned back home, he knew who in Butangen would be envy's first target: two deformed weavers, whose skills surpassed understanding.

The Will of the Yarn

They came the next year.

One stuffy day. Before Pentecost.

Over the pastor's cottage loomed a sky that could not make up its mind. Heavy clouds pressed the air down in the valley so that the womenfolk had headaches and menfolk were cranky.

A fire crackled in the fireplace in the centre of this large, low-ceilinged room, the smoke rising lazily up through the hole in the roof. The Breia roared outside with the rushing water of the spring melt. This familiar yet exaggerated sound outside gave Pastor Krafft the feeling that his hearing and other senses were heightened.

It was then that Pastor Krafft spied a large group of men on horseback on the other side of Lake Løsnes, distorted through his tiny, buckled windowpane.

He stepped outside.

Even from a distance their clothes pronounced them men of rank. Humble folk wore clothes of undyed wool that blended into the landscape, but two of the horsemen wore long, dark suits, and were followed by well-dressed soldiers.

Soon they were standing on the grass forecourt of the pastor's cottage, surrounded by strong horses in harnesses from foreign saddleries. The soldiers' scabbards held long swords and battle axes. Krafft recognised the two men in black. One was Bailiff Nielssøn, the chief law enforcer in Gudbrandsdal, appointed the previous year, after his predecessor was beaten senseless while collecting taxes in Brekkom. The other, a man with a sinewy long neck, was Pastor Mortensen from the village of Fron.

They were dressed much like Krafft himself, both wearing the official garb of the day of long black coats, with a neat row of buttons from top to bottom. But where Krafft still wore a plain

The Will of the Yarn

ruff, these men wore the flat linen collars trimmed with delicate lace that were the latest court fashion in Copenhagen. They were clearly here on an errand of modern times. And the similarity of the Fron pastor's outfit to the bailiff's was as troubling as his reputation as a witch hunter.

Pastor Krafft's farmhands walked towards them with hay and water. Being rather portly, the bailiff had to be helped from his horse. To anyone who did not know better, he seemed timid and harmless. With small eyes and a small mouth, his facial expressions never changed, irrespective of what he said or heard.

Pastor Krafft sent the farmhands away.

"Our errand concerns accusations against two sisters from Hokne Farmstead," said the bailiff.

"Hekne – it's Hekne," Krafft said.

"Hekne, hmm. But first, might Pastor Krafft explain why he did not, as obliged by law, investigate these obviously depraved women?"

Skirting the question, Krafft asked why he and the pastor had turned up with no warning.

"My gaze is upon you too, Herr Pastor," Pastor Mortensen said. "You are to be reported to the bishop for neglect of your duty."

"Which duty? I have many."

"Your duty *to observe, to investigate and to pursue*. You, sir, are obliged to root out all forms of witchcraft. And to keep the bailiff notified of your actions. The creatures we are come to investigate put the larger flock in peril. There are innumerable stories circulating about them. Or about *it*."

Krafft replied that he had indeed undertaken a thorough investigation, but having found nothing evil about the sisters, he had seen no need to report on the matter.

"Aha!" said the bailiff. "So you do admit to possessing information. Oughtn't you to have handed that over to me? It is conceivable that these sisters exercise a witchcraft so strong that you yourself have fallen under its power. That is why I have with me our most learned Pastor Mortensen from the village of Fron. A man who has seen the Devil in the eyes of five women."

"What are the accusations brought against the sisters?" Krafft asked.

"That will be yours to know when the time is right. The accused – are their names Gjertrud and Henrikke?"

"Halfrid and Gunhild. I shall bring you to them."

"Nobody accompanies my men," the bailiff said, waving over four stout aides.

Pastor Mortensen stood with his hands at his side and gazed around. Krafft looked skywards. The clouds were darkening. They know where to find Hekne, he thought to himself. Despite never having been there. These accusations must have been spread by locals.

"The hearing will take place here, in the pastor's residence," said the bailiff. "It must be unpolluted. Sacred. Put more logs on," he said, pointing at the hearth in the centre of the room, "and light some pitch pine torches so we may see clearly. I shall decide afterwards whether this case should be brought before the magistrate."

"Prepare the equipment," the bailiff shouted to his men.

Two soldiers lifted a stretcher down from a packhorse, and a large, heavy crate.

"What is that?" Krafft said.

"Lead," said the bailiff. "Four plates of lead."

One of the men took Pastor Krafft by the arm and led him inside. The man exuded a particularly bad odour. Three other men disappeared up to Hekne.

Not long afterwards, screams could be heard outside. Later Krafft would learn that Eirik Hekne had not been in the farmhouse when the men arrived. The sisters had been at their loom as usual when the three men barged in. They went straight to where the girls were. The men spoke in a strange dialect, and blindfolded the girls and bound their wrists. It was essential their eyes be covered lest they bewitch the men with their gaze. Dragged out screaming, they writhed against the ropes *like serpents*. The farmfolk were threatened with axes and shown a document bearing a red wax seal, and the two sisters were flung over the packhorse like chattels seized in lieu of a debt.

They were carried into the pastor's cottage, where Bailiff Nielssøn and Pastor Mortensen were seated on a bench behind the long table. The guards could barely get through the door, as they held the sisters high off the ground, for fear they might send spells through the earth to soften the hearts of their interrogators.

Pastor Krafft was put in a corner with the malodorous man as guard. The lead plates had been laid out on the dirt floor, and all around them Pastor Mortensen had drawn crosses in powdered chalk. The girls were placed on the lead plates and their blindfolds removed. Their captors took a hasty step back.

Mortensen leaned forward.

"Is this – this *thing* – of this world?" he said.

"I thought at first it was an enormous beast squeezed into clothes," said the bailiff.

Mortensen shook his head.

"There can be no doubt at all," he said. "This is Satan's work. And this you have baptised in the name of Our Father, Pastor Krafft, sir?"

"Remove their apron," the bailiff said.

The girls were so terrified they couldn't speak. When their apron was torn off, it was revealed that they each had a separate undertunic. Gunhild's was red and Halfrid's green, both exquisitely embroidered. Then the pastor observed that – no – these tunics were in fact one, with a single waistband, laced high above both their hips. *Off with this tunic!*

Stigma Diabolicum

One of the men cut through the laces with a knife and began to pull the garment down, while another yanked at the girls' shoulders, as though trying to part two logs that had not been properly split. The sisters screamed, and Pastor Krafft yelled that this was *enough*. Only in a court trial could suspects be stripped naked, and surely this was merely a hearing, an investigation?

Everybody stopped. The sisters sobbed and crumpled on the lead plates. The men gripped them by their armpits to pull them up again, while they struggled to hold their tunics and stop them slipping down.

Once again, Krafft interrupted, saying it could not possibly be an offence to be born conjoined.

"Perhaps not," said Mortensen. "But this is a *monstrum*."

"You shall call them no such thing," Krafft said.

"Are you not versed, sir?" Mortensen said. "A *monstrum* is precisely what they are. An omen. The only question is of what. Whether it is God's punishment or the End Times."

"The laws about witches did not exist when these two were born," Krafft replied.

"Correct," said Pastor Mortensen. "In this, our investigation pertains to *you*, Pastor Krafft. It is now clear to us that you, as any good Lutheran, should have let this creature be seen by scholars immediately after its birth. So it might be ascertained what its arrival here on Earth meant. Now, it is sadly too late. The Devil has got a hold of them, and the omen is rendered unclear."

"You, Pastor Mortensen, sir, are confusing your disciplines!" Krafft said. "The notion that a deformed person is an omen may be extant in the Christian faith. But the two of you are come as representatives of the *law*. So, Herr Bailiff, I must ask you now to lay out your charge!"

The bailiff slammed his fist into the table and demanded silence. The flames rose high from the logs in the hearth.

"Listen here, there are two charges," he said. "One against

you, Pastor Krafft, and the other against these sisters. But yes, this is a preliminary hearing. An interrogation. The creature may keep its tunic on."

The sisters gazed over in desperation at Krafft. He nodded towards them.

"Tell us," the bailiff continued, "you are – Gunhild and Halfrid Hekne. Correct?"

Gunhild mumbled something. Halfrid trembled.

"You are weavers, is that correct?"

Both trembled. They did not answer.

"*You are weavers?*"

"Aye, sir," Gunhild muttered. "Weavers both."

The bailiff laid out his case.

Two years ago, a man who ran a guesthouse near Fåvang church had accepted a pillow as payment from a guest unable to pay his bill. The pillow's cover was woven by the Hekne sisters. A traveller had slept on the pillow one night and complained next morning of a headache and stomach pains. The same happened to the next two guests, both of whom refused to pay. A fourth guest vomited during supper, and in the following week two more were robbed of their money. Whereupon the lodge-keeper placed the pillow on the cemetery wall and burned it. From then on, all his visitors were hale and hearty and satisfied.

A further allegation had come from the Heidal municipality. The sisters had been commissioned to weave a bedspread depicting the five wise and five foolish virgins. In the centre of the weave was a narrow band filled with cunning symbols that looked like farm emblems, but none of which matched any emblems in the village. The bedspread had been given as a wedding gift to a farmer and his young, healthy bride. Years passed, but she bore no children. Eventually, neighbours testified that the man who had given the couple the bedspread had been besotted with the woman. He had asked for her hand, but been spurned. In revenge he had ordered a bedspread with spells that made her barren. When the couple learned of this, they removed the bedspread from their farmhouse, and the woman immediately fell pregnant. This was doubly sinful, for the weave showed events from the holy scriptures, at the same time as being imbued with witchcraft and spells.

The bailiff offered yet more testimonies.

A family with scant experience of raising cattle, who had recently moved to the village, had ordered a weave that depicted a bull. Pretty soon they were breeding fine cows that produced large quantities of milk, while their neighbour's herd, which had always been one of the finest, wandered astray while they were out grazing.

Another case hailed from the municipality of Gausdal. It was here that one of the first weaves by the Hekne sisters could be found. Made for a cradle, it showed three virgins with jet black hair. The woman who had bought it gave birth to one, then two, then three fine daughters all with dark tresses, despite her and her husband having flaxen hair. Meanwhile, her older sister, who possessed no such coverlet, bore just one squint-eyed son.

The bailiff had received reports of weaves ordered in secrecy and bought for much greater prices than normal, or for vast quantities of silver or livestock. These were the prices the sisters demanded to imbue their weaves with spells. He had heard that the Hekne farm now owned several fine herds and a chest full of silver. And – had the sisters not begun work on a large weave that nobody was allowed to see?

The bailiff paused. Then he presented what was his final allegation, but also the most devastating, and now Pastor Krafft knew for certain that the informants were from Butangen.

The sisters were, it was said, keen to spin yarn on the summer and winter solstice, two days of the year when it was forbidden to work any device that turned. The girls had flouted this rule,

The Will of the Yarn

and thus allowed evil powers to enter their yarn. But worse still, the bailiff said, the sisters were protected by a strange creature with large, crooked horns, one that was neither sheep nor goat. And was it true that Pastor Krafft allowed it to graze among the unconsecrated graves? Did nobody realise that this might be the Cloven-Hoofed Beast himself? And where, he demanded, was this creature now?

The sisters' reaction was disastrous to their cause. They talked at and over each other, in a battle of incomprehensible words. They could easily be taken for speaking in tongues, and with every clumsy word uttered, Krafft noticed a faint smile grow in the corner of the bailiff's mouth.

"We are not unkind," the bailiff said. "Hark, my unhappy children. We believe there are human souls within you. You must wrest yourselves free from the abominable powers that have possessed you. Suffering will help in your liberation."

Pastor Mortensen interjected that the burden of proof was on the accused. The twin sisters must *prove* their innocence. And any confessions could not be retracted, for when the Devil had time to reflect, he always found something crafty to muddy the truth.

"Confess now," said the bailiff, "and you will be saved from later humiliation. You will avoid being disrobed during your trial, and—"

Pastor Krafft interrupted. "If they confess, the stake awaits! You want to burn these girls alive – for nursing an orphaned lamb!"

The sisters said nothing. They were well aware of the punishment that might await them and could not be more frightened than they were.

Pastor Mortensen described how he had exposed the five witches in Fron, and how they had been "helped over" on the purifying pyre, and the bailiff said that the same procedure would be followed now. There would be a speedy trial if the girls did not confess; until then they would be held under arrest. The sisters would be stripped naked during the hearing and shaved from top to toe, to see if the Devil's mark was hidden under any hair growth. With blindfolds over their eyes, they would be pricked with needles to determine whether areas of their body lacked sensation. In particular, he added, they were interested in the mass that connected their bodies. This would be subjected to especially precise tests with needles and knives. If they did not react with pain, that would be proof that the body bore a *stigma diabolicum*, the mark of the Devil. If nothing was found, there would still be the water test. They would be thrown from a boat to see if they floated or sank. Preferably here on Lake Løsnes, so that the whole village might see. If they floated, they were guilty.

All this they could avoid if they confessed.

The girls stood quaking on the lead plates. Then they suddenly grew calm, and Krafft was alarmed at the firmness of their words. It was as if an external authority had come to their rescue.

"It would be an untruth if we said we be evil," said Gunhild. "And if we utter untruths, we shall never enter the Kingdom o' Heaven. Thus 'tis better we speak true and that ye torment us. Lies will at least not pass our lips."

Pastor Krafft demanded a break in the hearing.

Pastor Mortensen refused. "You have been blinded, Krafft. Can you not see that this grotesque creature is captured by the Devil? It was sent to us here as a *monstrum*, but captured by the Devil."

"We could have done much more for the Devil were we divided int' two and nay trussed t'gether," Gunhild said.

Pastor Mortensen got up and shouted: *"Do not mock!"*

"No, wait!" the bailiff said. "Hark these words! The thought of conferring with the Devil is not unfamiliar to them!"

The pastor agreed. The girls must have known, he said, from an early age that they would never be married. They would therefore experience strong, unsated desires, and these would draw the Devil to them for gratification. Such desires were to be found in all womenfolk, but married women were not such easy targets for Satan, because their children gave them an outlet for their carnal inclinations.

"We were simply born thus," Gunhild said, and together with her sister she chanted, "*Thus 'twas, thus 'tis, and thus it shalt be.* The Lord Our God, she did want us jus' as we be."

The room fell silent.

"*She? God as female?* You're making a mockery again."

"That's how they say it up here, it's their dialect," Pastor Krafft said.

The accusers now gave a worryingly calm statement in which *diabolism*, *maleficium* and *casting spells* were all mentioned. And, while he remembered, what of the silver rings they wore? These rings with their strange, occult patterns? The 1617 directive stipulated that all unnecessary jewellery was forbidden. What power did these patterns possess? Had they been given to them by the Devil himself? Gunhild sobbed that they were very ordinary rings, but that they held them dear.

Pastor Mortensen shook his head and said the rings must be cut off with pliers and thrown into the sea. The bailiff continued to interrogate them about *maleficium* and the use of spells.

Halfrid managed to steady herself.

"It be true, Herr Bailiff, that folks come to our farm and ask if we might put certain powers in our weaves. To weave sommat that may make sommat happen. But our father, he be an honourable man in business. And whenever folks ask such terrible things of us, he shews them the door and tells them never to come back."

The bailiff revealed now that he had in fact tracked down one of their creations. It showed a half-naked woman being disrobed by spiders. Was this not a glorification of the harlot? Of beasts that crawl. A mockery of God's word?

"'Tis nay disrobed but enrobed she be by the spider," Halfrid said. "Spiders be called *vevkjerringa* here in t' valley – the old wives of the weave. We wanted to say how 'tis women's work, dainty work, like that of the spiders, which clothes us and keeps us warm. We weave as it comes t'us. We have woven many a story from the Good Book, and then we follow the old patterns. There be a large pious weave hangs in t' church up at Dovre. 'Twas a gift from us in gratitude for all we learned up there. We weave swiftly cos there be two of us and we hold our yarns wi' four hands. Sometimes we weave what we have dreamed in t' night. What we have *both* dreamed. And then it just takes shape as we work, as though the sheep's wool wills it."

"And this wool comes from this – this beast that follows you about?"

"'Tis a ram with a long topcoat," Gunhild said. "We walks with him outside the cemetery wall, for the grass there be tall – and sweet."

She could say no more, and once again Pastor Krafft demanded a pause in the hearing. But Pastor Mortensen was in a near frenzy now and started muttering: "We must go on! Without vacillation! They are on the brink of confessing! They said themselves that they were subject to other powers. That they *weave what the wool wishes*. The wool that comes from the very beast that roams with them. The beast to which we must send our men in all haste, to put a rope around its neck. What they have said here, for all to hear, is that they are in the power of this Beast! We must slay this crea—"

It was Halfrid who shook her fist and shouted.

"Never! Ye mustna' slay Leaf Drifter. Better far ye slay us!"

The pastor grew yet more fervent.

"Behold! These sisters *are* in the service of the Beast. Hark how they are willing to die for him! A Devil's pact! This is a Devil's pact! A pact with this goat with twisted horns that devours the residue of murderers and criminals through the grass on this unconsecrated ground! This is *so* clear to see, Herr Pastor, that you must have been led very much astray. You, sir, have allowed the Beast to graze near your church!"

The bailiff raised his hand to interrupt.

"Do not think us inhuman. Let me repeat, we wish these children well. We are here because people in our villages walk in fear. Death at the stake will purify these young girls' souls and save them from eternal torment in hell. The pain in the roaring flames shall not be *their* pain. It will be the Devil's agonies the crowd beholds."

There was a loud ruckus outside. Eirik Hekne burst in with a knife in his fist, so angry that the men guarding his daughters backed off. Two others rushed in, the tenant farmer from Norddølum and another from Flyen who had heard that Eirik Hekne needed help. Fierce hand-to-hand fighting ensued. More villagers burst in, and only when Krafft stepped between them was an all-out brawl averted, but, by then, Eirik had almost killed a man right in the middle of the parsonage, and pressed in a corner was gasping for breath.

Pastor Krafft got the bailiff to himself and led him outside.

"Perhaps, sir, you will let me speak now," he said. "Without our being bombarded by the screams of the accused and their raging father. I know that you've paved the way in case I too am prey to sorcery, and thus part of the Devil's game. I would have done the same. Now that you have made your preliminary enquiries with such admirable rectitude and intelligence, I ask you for time to lay out the facts I have gathered. I have, of course, been aware of the rumours circulating about these sisters. The reason I have never raised concerns is, as I tried to explain, that I have investigated each case most thoroughly."

The bailiff brushed a speck from his sleeve and glared at him.

Pastor Krafft continued:

"Take the first story – the one concerning the pillow. Every complaint can be traced to a short period when the lodge-keeper served rotten food because he had nothing else to offer. Fearing for his reputation, he exonerated himself by saying that the pillow had been cursed. He then claimed that the pillow had been burned, and that it was, from then on, safe to spend the night at the lodge. But the pillow was never burned. He still has it. I myself have slept on it without falling ill, and the food I was served was excellent.

"As to the bedspread and the childless couple. It is true that the woman removed the bedspread for fear of witchcraft. But it was another two years before she finally gave birth to a child – a little boy. And when you compare the boy's face with his father's, well, the similarities are few. Naturally they need an explanation that shifts the blame, since these miserable folk are guilty of an immorality – the childless woman, the man who impregnated her, and the two other parties, who, while innocent, are also involved – her husband, and the child himself who believes this man to be his true father. Of course this can never come out, first because of the shame, but also because of the exorbitant fines for adultery. If you're still bent on pursuing this case, Herr Bailiff, remember you can't cite a child's features as evidence of adultery.

"Moving on, we have the claim about the herds of cows. Is it true that the weaves can bring about an unfair advantage, and that the girls can therefore be accused of *signeri*? Perhaps. But almost every farm in Butangen has secured itself a weave made by the sisters' hands. The designs that show ears of corn are said

The Will of the Yarn

to bring good harvests, those that show cows or horses are said to promote plenty of milk or strong draught animals. The truth is that they are all a homage to the well-kept farm. An inspiration to work. The weaves themselves cannot improve the crops, though many believe it. I can vouch that the crops here have *always* been good, in this God-blessed village, irrespective of whether a weave hangs in the living room or not. Butangen is south-facing and gets plenty of sun and rarely suffers ruinous floods. Which is also a cause of envy in these parts. But more importantly, Herr Bailiff, all of the cases that you have so dutifully and meticulously gathered have something in common. Not one of the supposed victims will stand in court against the sisters. It is others around them who keep these stories alive. I made enquiries and I found that these rumours are stoked by five or six people who frequent the taverns. I have made a list of their names. And they are all alike in one thing: *they are themselves weavers!* Some are skilled, but two are barely mediocre. It's not difficult to draw a conclusion, Herr Bailiff. It would be good for business if nobody dared to buy a weave from the two finest and fastest weavers in the valley."

The bailiff stared at him with cold eyes. He asked Krafft about the ram grazing upon unconsecrated graves, and received the reply that orphan lambs often lived their whole lives with those who had nursed them, that it was a common enough ram, and that unconsecrated graves were unconsecrated precisely so that animals and others could walk over them heedlessly.

"What we have before us, Herr Bailiff, are two of God's creatures that He now and then finds reason to create and join together inseparably. It is not ours to ask why. They are denied love during their earthly life, but shall receive it in death, for they shall be loosed from each other when they reach the Kingdom of Heaven. I don't doubt the despair of childless couples or farmers whose cows go missing from their pastures, for without

Stigma Diabolicum

explanations we grope in thin air, and life seems untenable. Nevertheless, I do believe, sir, that we cannot, nor should not, annihilate everything that seems strange to us. Let us keep to what God has made for our eyes."

The bailiff gazed at him in silence. It was impossible to tell whether these illuminations had made any impression on him.

"We shall see," he said. "Whatever the case, Pastor Krafft, you ought to have notified the bishop about this *monstrum*'s arrival on Earth. That fact cannot be ignored."

The battle was not over. The bishop was furious and tried to banish Krafft to a parish in Nordland, and disputes over his office followed him for the rest of his life. He never found out who in Butangen had cast suspicions on the Hekne sisters. In the surrounding villages the rumours continued to come and go, varying in magnitude and damage capacity, like the floods of the Laugen. The Fron girls had been burned alive for crimes far less serious than the Hekne twins stood accused of, and eventually Pastor Krafft decided to gather all the village's farm owners in the church. He wanted to ask them if they would give the Hekne sisters *skussmål*: a solemn testimony of their innocence and good character. This ancient tradition, designed to defend citizens from slander in their communities, was the only thing that might offer the sisters protection in any future trial. In those days a paragraph in *Gulatingslova*, a thirteenth-century code of law, still held sway: *One man's witness is like no witness. The witness of two men is as good as the witness of ten, unless a better witness is brought.* That day twenty-eight farmers stood up and vouched for the Hekne sisters' reputation, and their names were formally recorded.

The sisters lived for many more years. They had constant nightmares about the hearing, and it is said that they gathered all their views of the world's follies in the Hekne Weave.

The Will of the Yarn

When illness struck the sisters down, Eirik Hekne went to Pastor Krafft with a prayer that they be allowed to die upon the same day, so that neither twin would be forced to drag around the corpse of the other. Krafft felt sure that God would listen to such a humble wish, and followed Eirik back to Hekne. The sisters' legs were swollen, and they felt a weird pressure in their chests. He asked if they were bitter about their fate. As usual, it was Halfrid who spoke first.

"Nay," she said. "We have been graced to see so much and know so much."

Then Gunhild said: "In truth, we have both tasted all life can offer, bar that of having a lover wholly and completely. But she sits here within us, this Love. She has a place here in our bed, and Halfrid shall go and find him again, her true love, and I too shall find him a place."

And in unison they said: "For God, she told us that we shall return, each one for ourseln."

Then they said they were sorry, but they must turn back to their work now, for it was urgent they complete this weave.

"But," said Gunhild, her back turned, "what if he comes here again, the pastor from Fron, when we be dead? Happen he shallna' be content that we lie in consecrated ground."

Krafft thought about this. He had long seen that the only thing we can know for certain about mankind is that it always lets insanity repeat itself, but in new forms that make it unrecognisable. He not only feared the folly of the present, but that the people of the future would think themselves wiser and entitled to stand in judgement over his time.

"I will secure a good grave for you," he said. "One that may only be found if the earth is scraped down to bare rock."

The sisters stopped weaving. They turned on their stool, looked into Pastor Krafft's eyes and thanked him.

Gunhild: "If it please thee, Herr Pastor, ye may—"

Stigma Diabolicum

Halfrid: "—hang this great weave in the church."
In chorus: "*If it please thee, Herr Pastor.*"

Sickness abated a while. Death stood in the room but waited, as though even Death was curious about the weave and how it would look. The sisters had learned from their teachers to recite rhymes and verses in chorus to help them keep time as they worked, and while they sat before the loom the residents of Hekne could hear them quietly chant:
Under earth, under rock,
Under cross, under God,
We two shall rest our heads.
It had been whispered that the girls could see into the future. A talent they were said to have acquired when, seeking to be free of each other, they had tried to sever the flesh that bound them with a dwarf-forged knife, the kind of superstition to which Pastor Krafft gave an indulgent nod.

The end was dawning.

Halfrid, her skin pale and her lips blue, said: "Bring forth our head pillows, Father. Today our bed shall be made for the very last time."

Then they asked their father to fetch their travelling chest. They had had a vision on the previous night that they must place the pillows and knife within it to give someone guidance.

When the sun was at its brightest and fullest, Halfrid died.

Gunhild continued to weave as the weight of her sister's body tore at her. In life they had shared their senses, and now, through Halfrid, Gunhild could peer into the Kingdom of the Dead, where, so Krafft let himself believe, a circle of events encompassed all time and place. Gunhild now added something to the corner of the weave, a terrifying image that depicted the death of a priest. The work took her some hours, and she used the yarn from the blind ewe, who had known, but not seen. And when the Hekne Weave was done, she let the shuttle fall to the floor, took Halfrid's hands in hers and said: "*Ye shall shuttle wide, and I shall shuttle close, and when the weave be woven we two shall return.*"

Leaf Drifter disappeared from Hekne and never came back. Later it was said, based on a village goatherd's account, that the sheep in the mountains had lined up in a row that day and stopped bleating.

The sisters never got to see the Hekne Weave in its entirety. The weave on an upright loom is rolled up as it is made, and it was only after the girls were buried that Eirik Hekne cut the warp strings.

Then he and Pastor Krafft unravelled it.

Neither could find words worth saying.

Never had they seen anything so magnificent, so enigmatic, so strange. They had known that the sisters were mistresses of their craft, but this weave testified to their contact with something *greater*. The innermost section of the roll had been started many years earlier, but a single sensibility ran through the whole.

On a deep blue background, a myriad of motifs ran around a massive, glowing wreath. In a certain light the wreath might look like Christ's crown of thorns; in another it looked like a sunrise, or a ring of fire. Around it were depictions of births and deaths, joy and sorrow, floods and forest fires, pestilence and war, livestock and work. One motif showed a man in a checked skirt-like garment being threatened by soldiers, and Eirik felt sure that the reddish-brown was blood taken from a Scots tartan left behind after the Battle of Kringen in 1612.

Krafft studied the images within the wreath. They must show the Night of the Scourge, the villagers' idea of Judgement Day, when a fire would wipe everything out before the earth was scraped down to bare rock, and the living and dead were brought

Stigma Diabolicum

to judgement at sunrise. The fire was kindled by flying creatures who spat flames. Some half bird and half human, others birds ridden by humans. Beneath them, houses and people were burning.

For a long time he sat and stared at the image in the corner. The death of a pastor. His own death? Would he meet such a gruesome end?

Krafft had secretly hoped that the weave would be filled with biblical motifs, preferably on the naive side. What he was looking at here was made in the pre-Christian tradition. He wondered whether it was right to display it in his church, but concluded that the old and wise stave church did not only serve Christianity: with its carvings of mythical beasts and shape-shifters, it also conveyed insights from ancient times.

Eventually, still wrestling with doubt, he hung it near the pulpit.

The next day he wanted to take it down, but could not.

Why was it so hard to discriminate between these forces that pulled him this way and that? Had the sisters been a *monstrum* after all? Could all things run simultaneously? Conjoined twins were said to warn of doomsday, and now it was revealed that they had spent years making a weave that depicted exactly that: the End Times!

He had seen to them on the funeral bier. They were prettily dressed for the journey. They had, in accordance with tradition, made their own long linen burial shirts, and wore red mittens drawn over their hands and sewn onto their sleeves. Each held a large bouquet of dried flowers with ripe seeds. Gunhild's was of rose madder, while Halfrid held thistles.

They had asked to be wrapped in a blanket of wool. It was deep red, edged with eight-petalled roses in autumn yellow. Large black crosses ran across the back and breast to protect the sisters against evil forces from all sides.

Thus were they laid in the earth's cool darkness.

But, as the girls had foreseen, they were in danger even in death.

Stories about their lives abounded after their death, many wildly inaccurate. But it was the dreadful misinterpretation of the verse that the sisters had chanted on the day of their death – *Under earth, under rock, under cross* – which posed such a danger. It was a young Hekne lad who was less than wise and told of their death and the verse in a tavern in a neighbouring village. Soon it was relayed further north in the valley, but with one very small but significant change. Where the Midtdal dialect said "under" – *onne* – the Nordal dialect changed its meaning, purposely or otherwise, to "evil" – *onde*. Soon a copy of this verse, which now read *Evil earth, evil rock, evil cross*, reached Pastor Mortensen in Fron.

Days later the bailiff's and bishop's men were back in Butangen. They dismissed the *skussmål*, since this verse was the ultimate proof that the Hekne sisters had practised diabolism. Their grave should be opened and their bodies burned at the stake.

Events reached such a pitch they had to be omitted from the bishop's annals.

By that time Eirik Hekne had already had the Sister Bells cast in his daughters' memory, with the remaining lengths of their mother's hair entwined in the bell ropes. He had taken all the silver that his daughters had earned from their weaves and thrown it into the smelting pot. The casting was done on a Thursday by the new moon as ancient custom demanded, and the bells would prove as inseparable as the sisters.

The villagers demanded that the weave and the bells remain in the stave church, and it was soon firmly believed that the bells could ring of their own accord to warn of danger, danger that a wise man or woman could deduce by studying the images in the Hekne Weave.

Stigma Diabolicum

A new era dawned, and fear of witchcraft waned. In tar-coated silence, the stave church brooded over its secrets, as it had done for centuries. The story of the sisters' fate in death was forgotten, but it would be impossible to forget the Hekne Weave that told the story of the Night of the Scourge, the last day of the known world, and equally impossible to forget the Sister Bells that would ring that fearful night in.

First Story

I Shallna' Be Content with Less

The Wedding Ring

SHE MUST CLIMB OVER THE DEAD. TOUCH THE FOOT OF the crucified one. Let herself into a pastor's study. Crawl out through a corpse hatch.

As usual it was a decision made in haste, with little thought, impossible to go back on. Astrid would see Gunhild, the Sister Bell that had been cast in the Heknes' heirloom silver. She *would*! Her mother had no right to deny her this. Nor did her father, nor the pastor.

The idea had come to her on the previous evening, and only grown in strength during the night, and when her feet touched the chill floorboards that morning, it was decided. It would happen this very Sunday. Today. During the service. When nobody would be around to see. Pastor Schweigaard and Churchwarden Røhme would naturally be in church, and although few villagers went to church, even fewer walked outside during Mass, for fear it might trigger gossip – even if anyone who spread such gossip could not, logically, have been in church themselves.

She scraped her fingernail in the rime on her window. Looked out over the farm that was Hekne. Just as she was Astrid Hekne. It had been snowing for days now, snowing and snowing with the odd pause, like the gap between the verses of an endless song. Everything was white and dark brown outside. Old log buildings with snow up to the windows, not a sound other than the spasmodic bellow of cows and the scrunch of a shovel through snow, as Isum, the farmhand, cleared the path.

The odour she caught was that of the barn cat. What moved was the milkmaid on her way to the barn. What stood still was Butangen.

She felt it in her gut. This compulsion. That told her that her life would be unbearable without seeing the church bell. A notion fostered perhaps by Adolf and Ingeborg. They had been like grandparents to her, and had often told her stories from Butangen's past, including the events of 1880 and 1881, the Silver Winter they called it, which had ended with the old stave church being carried far away, and with one of the two Sister Bells being left behind, to hang alone in the mysterious, sun-scorched bell tower below the church.

As a child Astrid had been enraptured by the stories of the Sister Bells and the Hekne Weave. They chimed with a restlessness she had felt ever since she could walk. A wild impatience that meant she could never resist scratching a gnat bite, that she played with kittens as though she was a cat herself, and always had grazed knees and scratched arms when she was small.

Now and then she thought she saw traces of the sisters. In an outbuilding there was an old upright loom, though its weights had gone, used now as fishing net sinkers, she assumed. Then, clearing the kitchen garden of weeds, she found some plants that she thought the sisters had used to dye yarn.

The hatch at the end of the hallway downstairs also seemed to hold the memory of their presence.

The *corpse hatch* her parents called it. Wide enough for two.

The farmhouse had been built centuries ago when the dead must not be carried through the front door, for fear they might recognise the path along which they were carried and return as ghosts. Coffins were therefore brought out through a hatch in the wall on the shady side of the house, where the nettles grew tall and folk rarely ventured, so that souls would get lost and choose to go up to heaven. Astrid wondered if this belief should

The Wedding Ring

have been maintained, for she remembered what Ingeborg had said: "Naybody has ever disproved it, my child, that when a person be dead their will lives on."

Old Ingeborg had been horrified one winter when Astrid and her younger sister Esther had, in a wild game, managed to open the hatch so the snow spilled in on the floor. She was still more horrified when their brother Tarald got a shovel and dug a tunnel out into the snow, and scared Esther, saying it led to the Kingdom of the Dead.

But from then on they dug tunnels in the snow every year for Esther to play in. She had quickly lost her fear. Nobody could find their way in the dark like Esther, for darkness is invisible to a person who inhabits it. Her snow tunnels never collapsed. She always stopped at the right place because she could sense the slightest shift in temperature, and thereby determine how close she was to the surface.

They were dead now, Adolf and Ingeborg, the two crofters who had raised her father on the Halvfarelia croft. Neither her siblings nor her parents ever showed much interest in the couple's stories of Butangen's past. But Astrid had never tired of hearing them, and now she was the only person who could recount them with any accuracy, so felt she had sole responsibility for them.

Sometimes she would go to her grandmother's grave and stare at her own name carved into the stone. This Astrid had scarce reached the age of twenty-one. Death in childbirth after giving birth to two sons and sending one to a foreign land. Astrid had often wondered about her grandmother's choice all those years ago. She wished she was here to explain. She had found a suitcase in the loft filled with her grandmother's clothes, and some letters and sketchbooks belonging to Gerhard Schönauer, the German architecture student who would be Astrid's grandfather. So vivid were Ingeborg's stories about them both that when little Astrid read their letters it was as if she already knew their contents.

Vivid in her memory, too, were their stories about the old church bells, and how her grandmother had fought to keep them in Butangen. And the myth that only an unmarried woman from the Hekne family could lay eyes upon the Sister Bells; anyone else would be struck down and die of a sudden illness. She had sometimes wondered if this curse had been invented by her grandmother to protect them.

Astrid would soon turn seventeen. An adult by village standards. Yet her questions about the church bell were always met by her parents with dismissive mumbles. Kristine and Jehans were busy, always busy, sitting bent over their paperwork every weekend, her mother checking the dairy's accounts, her father perusing a plan for a new road up to the seters.

Accounts and roads. So uninteresting compared to Gunhild, who had rung throughout prehistory, when her parents were not this overworked couple who were always late for supper, but Titans in battle. And Kai Schweigaard was not the wrinkly old pastor who had confirmed her, but a messenger of God.

But Gunhild had a unique protection, guarded as she was by the dead in the bell tower – the quadrangular log building below the church that lied about its contents and denied its purpose. Within its walls frozen corpses lay in coffins, stacked high, she had heard, because Butangen still held to the tradition of burying its winter-dead in the spring, when the frosts had left the ground. They were no longer kept on the farms through the winter, but gathered here, in this consecrated tower, with a silent church bell hanging above them, overseeing their extended wake.

Equally creepy was the idea of getting the key to the bell tower. It was kept in Schweigaard's study, but did not dangle from a hook by the light switch. No, it hung from the big toe of Christ himself. It was a wooden statue, but so lifelike that it had made her tremble throughout her childhood. Christ the Saviour hung on the cross with his head slumped but his eyes ever wakeful. Blood ran from a deep cut down his thigh and out towards the toe from which said key hung. So lifelike was the paintwork, she thought her hand would be wet with blood if she touched it.

At a quarter to eleven Astrid sneaked out of the corpse hatch. She walked round the farmhouse, sticking close to the wall to avoid Tarald seeing her from the first floor. All around her lay a glittering winter. Thick snow curled around the eaves of the farm buildings. The fences along the fields looked as though they were wearing white woolly hats. Below her she could hear the church bells ringing. The bells that sounded so tame compared to Gunhild, which Herr Røhme only let chime on big occasions.

Astrid hurried down to the gate. The parsonage was not far from Hekne, but was impossible to see from here, for Butangen was so steep and hilly that each farm lay alone, as if at the mercies of the Breia, the river that had carved out this landscape. The village had only one real crossroad, which she was walking towards now. Above it stood her mother's dairy factory and shop, and still further up the school building.

She slipped into the copse. Changed direction and struggled through the snow towards a tall scree slope. From here she could see the road again. The churchgoers were on their way down. Wealthy folk in their horse-drawn sleighs, humbler folk on foot.

The view of the village opened up more and more, and soon she could see the church, and the fields that led to the parsonage and Gildevollen Farm. They were covered with ski tracks going down to and across Lake Løsnes, which stretched out like a large floor to the village. The road to Fåvang formed a snow-cleared ribbon around the north end of the lake, but since during winter

I Shallna' Be Content with Less

it was possible to go across the ice, folk could see from afar who was coming and going.

Astrid crouched down and watched the church. At last, she saw Pastor Schweigaard hurry down the footpath from the parsonage. A black, slightly bent figure in the snow. Old, yet ageless, seen from up here.

Astrid alternated between calling him Herr Pastor and Kai. He visited Hekne so often that Esther even called him Grandpa, although something in Astrid flinched at that word.

The bells rang their last round for Mass, and with that there would be no more comers. Never was the village quieter or emptier than at this hour on a Sunday.

A lone straggler in a green and yellow bobble hat was trundling down the slippery road.

It was Hekne's farmhand, Isum, whom the villagers called Giant Isum because of his enormous stature. His appetite was so huge he had to eat from an old serving platter. He must have been drunk last night, since Astrid had been woken in the night by Pelle barking, before the farm's faithful Buhund had realised who it was and calmed down.

It was the same every Saturday. Isum drank, danced, horsed about, then staggered home to his tiny room in the workers' cottage at Hekne, with only a wash basin, a peg for his distinctly old-fashioned clothes and a shelf stacked with brightly coloured woollen hats. Once, at a dance up at Høgvang village hall, egged on by his fellow revellers, Giant Isum tore the hall's huge iron wood burner from its chimney and dragged it outside, still burning. Most Sundays he woke up full of regret, unable to remember what he had said or done, and when his drinkers' remorse got too much, he took himself off to church. Today must be one of those Sundays, Astrid thought, as she watched him stumble along, still doing up the buttons on his only good jacket, this two-metre-tall man who was the gentlest soul she knew. She

The Wedding Ring

hoped, at least, he would not be tempted to join in the hymn-singing, for when Isum had been on a binge his breath reeked from miles away.

Nearly there now, he almost fell on the church steps; the soles of his boots were doubtless slippery.

Astrid ran down to the parsonage. She regretted not having told Mari Slåen her plan. It would have been good to have someone to keep a lookout. But she had seen her friend change lately, parting ways with her, giddier perhaps.

That's the way it was for those without church bells in their lives.

Again, Astrid walked close to the wall so that Fru Røhme would not see her from the parsonage window. She opened the front door and went soundlessly into the hall. His overcoat was gone. His summer hat hung from a hook. The house smelled of Sunday roast and freshly scrubbed floors.

Astrid crept up the stairs. The door was unlocked. As usual.

So, this was how it felt. The study without him. Mahogany brown and bare. Smelling of papers and tobacco. A cast-iron stove with a half-full log basket. Two cupboards. An untidy table, and a desk with peeling varnish. A worn-out swivel chair with a brown, leather seat. Buckled windowpanes, one looking out onto the church and Lake Løsnes. A welcoming room, in truth, with a couple of chairs for visitors. The only sound was the pendulum of the grandfather clock.

She forced herself to look up at the Saviour. The crown of thorns. The wound. The tormented, yet attentive face. The large, wrought-iron key hanging from His big toe high above. She fetched a stool, but as she climbed closer, she felt His eyes upon her.

"Sorry," she whispered. "Needs must."

Bolt down the stairs. Key in hand. Into the light, the snow and fresh air. In a sweat she ploughed through the deep snow

I Shallna' Be Content with Less

outside the cemetery wall, where she was out of sight. From the church she heard hymn-singing. At last, she was standing on the stone steps to the bell tower. Before she even knew it, the key had turned in the lock, and she found herself in the dark.

Astrid had been waiting for this moment. She thought she would be safe once she got inside the bell tower.

But she was only safe from the world outside.

She sensed she was not alone in here. Nor was she welcome.

A reddish light crept in through the narrow leaded windows high above her head. Then, as her eyes adjusted, sharp, rectangular contours emerged from the gloom.

Coffins.

Six corpses. Six coffins. Artefacts unseen and unwelcome in any place but here or at a graveside. On the side of each, the name of the departed written in chalk.

Jørgine Aasen, the old woman from Gardbogen. The young boy from Moen, whom she had known vaguely, who had recently died before his twelfth birthday.

They were here now, surrounded by this stale, fetid odour.

She regretted coming and wanted to get out.

But no. Not you, Astrid Hekne.

The coffins were stacked in pairs in front of the staircase that led up to the belfry, as though to block access. She gripped the lid of a coffin, and setting her foot on a handlebar pulled herself up and sat on top of it. She shivered when she realised that there was just a thin plank of wood between herself and a corpse, and swung herself swiftly over. Dust rose in the stairwell, a sure sign that nobody had been up to the bell for years. Perhaps due to the curse?

The staircase ended in a narrow opening. A wintery light glinted through the louvres that were meant to release the ringing of bells across the heavens.

In the semi-darkness a grey-brown presence.

Gunhild.

Larger than she had imagined. So solemn. So aloof.

Astrid took a step forward.

This was not silence. This was chosen silence. A vigilance. Gunhild was made to give warnings.

Where there were gaps in the timber walls, the snow had blown in, making little pyramids here and there. On the floor lay coils of rope, short link chains and a hoist. Presumably used when her father and uncle had brought Gunhild up here from Lake Løsnes after she had lain there for more than thirty years.

How extraordinary the bell was. Beautiful and alert, like the reindeer in the mountains. Gunhild. So complete in form. All darkness and verdigris, unembellished but for an inscription that ran around her in a band.

The clapper hung in the darkened sound bow, ready to report to God on high if anything happened down here in little Butangen.

Astrid ventured forward. Circled the bell to read the inscription.

"IN LOVING MEMORIE OF GUNHILD AND HER MOTHER ASTRID."

There was an empty space on the beam from which Gunhild hung. Her sister, Halfrid, would have been there had she not disappeared to Dresden.

Adolf had said once that only *chain-brothers*, brothers born with no sister between, would be able to reunite the Sister Bells. Astrid had asked why, and Ingeborg had answered that it took brothers to reunite sisters. Such were the laws.

Astrid was calmer now. She looked around her. Everything in here seemed so rough. Rusty suspensions, worn bell rope, dull bronze.

A gust of wind disturbed a pyramid of snow and caught her

attention. On the other side of the belfry, on a crossbeam, something glinted at her.

She went over to it and blew the dust off it.

A ring. It must be gold. Heavy and wide. So that an observer should really notice it. Smooth. Without a single scratch, as though it had been crafted that morning.

She lifted it up to the shafts of light and saw an inscription inside.

1881. Eternally yours. Kai.

Had Kai been married? No, the ring looked unused. Had he come up here? Stood here alone and set it carefully aside?

She held it tentatively over her finger. Let it slide over her nail, past her knuckle.

It was then that the church bell began to ring. It was just a hum at first, barely audible, before it shifted form and gained strength. The sound flooded out over the floor, ran down from the ceiling, radiated from the walls and gripped her body, forcing her to tremble to its beat.

She hurtled down the stairs, flung herself over the coffins, sick with regret, regret, such regret! This was the will of the dead! They had told the bell to ring! She sprang towards the door with the bell ringing in her ears, then, blinded by the sharp winter light, she got another shock.

Mass was already over. The congregation was coming out of the church. Schweigaard was already standing on the steps shaking everyone's hands.

She slipped back inside and tried to gather herself. How was it possible? She had got here as the service was beginning. Surely she couldn't have been here for more than ten minutes? What had happened to the time?

She realised now that it was the new church bells that were ringing. Not Gunhild. That had been a figment of her imagination. And if she came out now, she would be surrounded by gawping villagers. It was impossible to reach the parsonage in time to replace the key.

Astrid sat on the floor.

There was nothing for it but to wait here in the company of the dead, who had all the time in the world.

She fiddled with the ring. That at least was real.

His coat hung in the hallway. There was melted snow around his boots.

She walked quietly up the stairs, took a deep breath and knocked.

"'Tis me. Astrid."

A pause.

"One minute. Your pastor is getting changed."

The rustle of cotton clothes which she knew were black. Slow steps. A cough to clear his throat.

"Come in."

Astrid reached for the doorknob. The ring! Good Lord! She twisted it off and hid it in her mitten.

He was standing before the wood stove in a creased flannel shirt, sleeves rolled up, a matchbox in his hand.

Astrid stared at the floor as she walked over to his desk and put down the key.

"I'm so sorry, Herr Pastor. It was just – I *had* to go in."

Kai Schweigaard grunted. He crouched down, straightened the kindling and lit it with some crumpled newspaper. He crossed the room and looked up at the figure on the cross.

"We have a young lady here," he said. "She wants to return a key. You saw her earlier today perhaps. If you were watching. Which, of course, you always are."

Astrid felt her cheeks burn as she climbed onto the stool before the crucified figure. Then she grew calm. There was comfort in the gazes of both these men.

I Shallna' Be Content with Less

Schweigaard drew two chairs up to the stove and said it was best she get warm. And they sat in silence together.

Kai Schweigaard cleared his throat.

"I think the time has come," he said.

He went out through a small back door, leaving it open behind him, returned with an old wooden chest, and said that this was probably the Heknes' most precious heirloom, but that he had not told Jehans of its existence. Nor anyone else.

"Help me to clear these documents and newspapers," he said, nodding towards the messy table. "Just put it all on the floor. No, try to keep the piles in order."

It was a large table and Astrid wondered why its entire surface had to be cleared. Kai Schweigaard put the chest on the table and stepped back.

It would look out of place in any room. So weather-beaten it looked like the derelict rowing boats along the shores of Lake Løsnes. The wood was grey with age, the lock fittings pitted with rust. A carved letter H was just about visible on the lid as he stepped forward and opened it with a creak.

Schweigaard lifted out a very worn, sunken pillow made of rough material in a checked pattern. He turned it over and held it up to the window. The glistening yarn showed a fairy-tale landscape with animal figures. A second pillow was similar, though the checked pattern on the front was not so worn.

"These two pillows belonged to the Hekne sisters," he said.

Astrid studied the animal figures. A one-horned bull that resembled the emblem of Hekne. Two reindeer standing beside another dead reindeer. A pale yellow bird swooping through the air. Another bird lifting a bull into the air.

"This is some sort of cutting tool they must have used," Schweigaard said.

In his hand he held a blade. Its edge was shiny and looked sharp; the rest was dull with rust.

"But," he said, turning back to the chest, "this is our great mystery object."

Gingerly he lifted out a dark, pliant scroll. A weave which, as he unrolled it, exceeded the edges of the tabletop and all comprehension. It was so finely woven it looked as though it had been embroidered with the thinnest of needles. Endless hours of work must have gone into it. In places the yarn shone like silver, elsewhere it was dyed in a multitude of colours. Her eyes were drawn to the large, orange-red wreath in the centre. Within its bounds, fire-breathing creatures flew over a sea of flames. Beyond it were figures of all kinds, human and non-human. Men and women carrying out indefinable tasks. Jet-black cows and snow-white sheep. The Cross of Christendom. So difficult to take in that her eyes needed to slow down.

She noticed she had held her breath too long.

"Is – is this – *it*?" she said.

Schweigaard nodded.

"The Hekne Weave?"

He nodded.

Silence fell. The clock ticked.

She studied the wreath again. Kai Schweigaard knew what she was looking at.

"I think it depicts the night, a fire and a sunrise all in one. The Night of the Scourge."

Astrid could feel that her life had taken a new course. Right here. Now. On Sunday. February 18, 1936.

"Ingeborg," Astrid said, "believed this had vanished more than a hundred years ago."

Kai nodded.

"It was hidden from an ignorant, foolish pastor. The villagers hid it in the church's old chasuble. I found it in 1914."

"And ye didna' tell anyone?"

"No."

"Why?"

He threw out his arms.

"There didn't seem to be anybody... worthy enough. No, that's not quite right. Your father *is* worthy. It's more that I always considered him a part of the story. I discovered the pillows back in 1903. Originally they were in a chest under the church floor. Then... well, I made a mistake. They lay in a grave for more than twenty years."

Astrid leaned against the edge of the table. The weave must be more than two metres long. According to what Ingeborg had said, the Hekne sisters had spent fifteen years weaving it. It was showing its age now. The edges were ragged. In places the patterns were so worn as to be unclear. In one corner, the yarn hung in loose strands.

"I've studied it for years without ever fully understanding it," he said. "And I've spent as many years wondering what happened to the sisters."

He pointed at an image of two girls standing tightly together, surrounded by an oval. "I think this is them."

Astrid studied the two faces. There was a play of shadows in the weave, so that when one seemed to look her in the eye, the other looked to the side. But when she shifted position, the other looked at her. As if they took turns watching, each from her own perspective.

"What strange skirts they are wearing," said Astrid. "So wide and round-shaped. If ye compare them to her, for example," she said, pointing to the skirt of someone surrounded by warriors.

"I'm not sure that's a woman," Kai said. "In fact, I wondered if it might be a Scotsman in a belted plaid. One of the soldiers perhaps who fought here in the Battle of Kringen in 1612. There's evidence to suggest that one of the Hekne sisters was in love with a lad from the Scottish army."

The Wedding Ring

"But Ingeborg told me that the Hekne Weave shows what *will* happen. Not what happened before it was woven."

"I'd say it does both. You see that figure? It helped me when the Spanish flu struck," Schweigaard said, leading Astrid's gaze towards a skeleton riding on the back of a wagon which had no draught animals pulling it, yet clearly seemed to be moving forward.

Astrid looked back at the girls. Their skirts were dome-shaped and plain brown. "D'ye think they could be church bells? Two church bells with human heads?"

Kai Schweigaard frowned. But did not disagree.

The sun was fading outside. The greying light came in through the window, altering the colours in the weave. She thought now that she saw a pair of eyes in the oval that encircled the girls. "Is that a face?" she said. "And that yarn – is't made of hair?"

Schweigaard tilted his head.

"Your eyes are sharper than mine. It was said that hair from the sisters' mother was twisted into the bell rope. More than that, I don't know."

Astrid took a step back. "I canna' make any sense of this."

"You have your whole life ahead," said Kai Schweigaard.

"What d'ye mean by that?"

"I've often asked myself what I should do with this. I won't live forever, even if I heard you and the others say in confirmation class that I was over three hundred years old. No, don't blush. I took it as a compliment. The only right thing is that *you* take this over now, Astrid. Your father and your uncle Victor – they have trouble seeing beyond what's in front of them. I'm concerned they'll just see these things as *objects*. Whereas you can see the will of an object. Just as your grandmother did."

"Not now," she said. "I canna' take it with me now. Not today, not . . . yet."

"It's yours when the time comes," Kai Schweigaard said.

The clock struck.

She tried to smooth a patch in the corner where the threads were loose, but he placed his hand on hers. "Leave it now," he said. "Let it be."

Kai began to roll up the weave, but rather too hastily perhaps, since a few threads came away, and he seemed suddenly strange. "It's started to fall apart," he said.

"'Tis very old. We need to be careful."

"That's not what I meant. It was said that some of the Hekne sisters' weaves fell asunder when they had done what they should do."

"Done what they should do? Meaning what?"

"That the end is perhaps close. That the end has already begun."

She felt her head go into a spin. She had no wish to hear this. That the end was close. It was as if the Hekne Weave blurred all division between past and present. Her gaze fell on a greenish-black ink stain on his desk, and she pointed to it and heard herself say: "Ye were so angry that day, Kai."

A Map of a Seter Road

The wood stove went out.

Schweigaard sat drifting in thoughts long after she had left, so long that when he surfaced from them the room was cold.

The one. The one Astrid Hekne. Again.

For twenty-two years he had lived alone with the secret of the Hekne Weave. And with each year his age had weighed more heavily on him, while the weave called out to him ever louder. It coaxed and cajoled, and nagged to be taken out of the chest in the night, saying: *This time ye shall understand me, Kai Schweigaard.* He was never the wiser. Until now, when he saw it through Astrid's eyes.

Kai unravelled the weave again and fetched his magnifying glass. She was right, these must be the church bells. The weave featured many female figures, but they all wore recognisable skirts; only these two had these wide, bell-shaped skirts. And the oval that framed them – yes – it only needed a certain light and a little imagination, and he saw it as a woman's face.

He stood where Astrid had stood. Followed the play of the evening shadows on the wool threads. Turned to the desk as she had done.

Ye were so angry that day.

Had she really said that? Or had he imagined it?

A terrifying spectre lurked in the corners. Old age. Was he starting to get confused? To mix up old times and new? Only one person knew the circumstances of that ink stain, and she had been dead for over fifty years. They had quarrelled and he had thumped the desk so hard that his inkwell spilled over. Any other ink could have been washed off, but this was the registrar's ink that he used for the church register because it was permanent and never faded.

Please God, he wasn't going senile! The body could age with dignity. Not the brain.

He was eighty years old now. It was the shortage of pastors in the 1920s that he had to thank for staying in office, despite his being well past retirement age. Elderly pastors had been asked to continue in the Church's service indefinitely. There had been a push to ordain more pastors in the thirties, but vacancies in the backwaters were rarely even advertised, since the only likely applicants would be crazed missionaries and preachers returning from America, and the bishop knew he would face trickier

I Shallna' Be Content with Less

problems with them than if he just let Schweigaard potter on in Butangen.

Still, Schweigaard lived in constant terror that he might say something silly in the pulpit. Reveal his frailty. Lose his power over words. His firmness of delivery. It would mean having to leave the parsonage. Presumably Jehans and Kristine would take him in, give him a room next door to Isum perhaps, where he would wander in an ever-tighter labyrinth of diminishing sanity.

But no.

No.

He carefully smoothed the threadbare corner where his own battle with death was presented. The fulfilment of the ancient prophecy of how the last pastor in Butangen would meet his end. It was certainly gruesome, but it showed that he would be of sound mind and body when the time came.

For years he had wondered what this event might actually *mean*. He had concluded that he would – in the very moment he understood – die.

Again and again the question had come to him: what had the Hekne sisters been able to see? With what gifts had they been bestowed? And, closely related, another question that haunted him: when did they die, and where were they buried?

Their coffin had not been under the church floor, as village legend had it. Although, it was there that the travel chest with their pillows had been found. For decades he had collected information about the sisters, but nothing new had surfaced since February 1921. It was then that Fron's pastor had moved office and had come across some centuries-old transcripts of witness statements. One of them indicated that the Hekne sisters had been accused of witchcraft, because someone had overheard them engaging in the use of spells and diabolism. The witness, a Dovre man, alleged that the sisters had chanted, over and over

again as they wove, a spell that imbued their weaving with the Devil's power:
Evil earth!
Evil rock!
Evil cross!

What could this mean? For all these years Schweigaard had imagined the sisters to be good Christians, and now this? And whether the accusation was true or not, if they were found guilty of possessing magical powers, they would have been burned at the stake.

A very different finale from any he had considered before.

The only person who might offer any answer as to what had really happened was Pastor Sigvard C. Krafft, Butangen's pastor in the sisters' lifetime. Kai had visited archive after archive, to wade through one mouldy cardboard box after another, and any documents not eaten up by bugs were water damaged. But he could find no trace of Krafft. Even his old *kirkebok* – his church register – had gone missing.

Kai sat behind his desk now, and let his fingers run over the keys of his typewriter, a splendid machine made in the United States by Underwood. He had splashed out on it in 1916, when his handwriting was showing signs of a disconcerting tremble. It was so modern that the letter "å" had its own key, even though a debate over this letter's place in the Norwegian alphabet was still raging after six decades. It was on this machine that he had authored his enquiries about Krafft to every conceivable church archive, letters he supplemented with long, costly telephone calls.

He had had to give up looking.

But to the present. A letter had arrived that required an answer.

It was postmarked from the German Reich.

Back in 1880, when the Germans had bought the stave

I Shallna' Be Content with Less

church and moved it to Dresden, their correspondence had been beautifully handwritten and courteously phrased. This time their letter was typewritten, rubberstamped and filled with accusations of breaches of contract. The sender was a certain Jankuhn, who, on behalf of some foundation with "interests in the stave church", demanded to be allowed to undertake another search for the church bell in Lake Løsnes.

The Germans were clearly unaware that Gunhild had been pulled from the lake in 1918 and was now hanging in the bell tower. Well, who would have told them?

The tone of this letter troubled him. It was as austere and menacing as the eagle emblem that the regime over there had adopted, whose wingspan had grown since Hitler's rise to power. The letter ended with a postscript: "We are additionally interested in expanding our knowledge about the 'magic' tapestry which hung in the stave church, but which appears to have gone missing."

Schweigaard fed his headed paper into the Underwood and turned the platen knob. But instead of typing his letter to Jankuhn, he got up.

So many thoughts and memories today.

Astrid.

When she and her twin brother had been confirmed, she had the most challenging mind in the class. Tarald was an eager pupil, but he was the type to raise his hand without knowing the answer. He had struggled as a youngster. Always wanting to be liked. Impulsive, like all the Heknes. As the firstborn son – the *odelsgutt* – he was expected to inherit Hekne. But with no bent for farming, this was as much a curse as a privilege. Tarald only understood things you can point to, see, explain. Astrid, by contrast, was interested in the things one cannot see. He recalled one question in particular. Although it was in fact two.

"Tell me, Herr Pastor, does the soul age with time? And might it be that the soul doesna' die with us?"

Her classmates sat in absolute silence. You could hear a pin drop during these classes. It had been drummed into them by their schoolteacher that when they visited the pastor, they *must* be quiet!

"Well now," Kai Schweigaard had said, "that's a difficult one. The real question is whether the soul has any age at all. Jews, for example, make no division between your soul and your body. When you're dead, you're dead."

"But for the rest of us when we die – do our souls knock about someplace else afterwards?"

Schweigaard rubbed the bridge of his nose, giving himself time to think.

"When we talk of *eternal life*," he said, "we must think along other lines. There are perhaps things we can't understand in the same way we do the world around us. Perhaps there's a place, a state of being, where time doesn't exist."

"But this soul," Astrid continued. "If she in't a particular age, then she canna' have much bearing upon us, for then we would act the same whether we were bairns or full-grown or old."

The other confirmands exchanged glances.

"So where, Herr Pastor, is this soul? If 'tis the soul flies up to heaven, then she must surely be alive? How else might she be punished on the Day of Judgement? She must be down there in t' grave, or up here with folk, or in t' mountains, or someplace."

"I really have no idea where the soul goes," said Kai Schweigaard. "Something begins on death that normal rules can't explain. I believe that in heaven everything takes a different form: a state we know nothing about. I heard someone say once that when a person dies they *step out of time*. They are freed from time, they stand outside time."

"And they thought about all this, the folk who wrote t' Bible?"

"Of course. So no, I don't believe the soul grows old. It just *is*.

I Shallna' Be Content with Less

It is us, the whole of us, from when we're little and up until we die. The soul just *is*. Outside time."

"Aye," said the young confirmand. "That is my way o' thinking too."

From anyone else it might have come across as insolent, or at least cheeky. And were it not for the fact that her Butangen dialect was milder, she sounded just like her namesake, her grandmother, with whom he had once argued over equally deep questions. As with so many things, he almost regretted its gradual disappearance from the village.

But to business. His letter to Herr Jankuhn would have to wait. There was a meeting coming up tomorrow that would decide the village's future. From a drawer, Kai took out the map that outlined the plan for a new road.

A bold pencil line ran across the map. It wound from the village's topmost farms, followed a steep valley, then crossed sharply over the Breia, before continuing along the opposite bank.

It was Jehans who had put his mark here. It shone with all his skill and daring. And Kai imagined Kristine standing behind him with her hands on her hips. It was a proposal for a road up to the seters, a risky but visionary project. One that could bring an end to something that had dogged the locals forever: the lack of proper transport links to the abundant upland pastures with their attendant potential for food production.

At the heart of all this again – with no specific plans yet in place – was Kristine's dairy. The factory that she had founded in 1910 with nothing but stubborn determination, a rickety machine with ragged drive belts in a leaky barn, had now been extended several times over. In 1926 the village had got a proper road down to Fåvang, and that same year its first motor vehicle, a red Reo Speedwagon with a home-carpentered cargo bed. It belonged to the dairy and was used to collect the milk churns from the farms, and to drive Kristine's butter and cheese down to Fåvang and bring other goods back up.

What Kristine had not foreseen was that when the villagers saw a truck coming down the road, they might want a lift. And if the Reo was driving to the railway station, a trip that might take them all day, then even more folk would want a ride, and be willing to pay a few coppers for it too. They might even ask when the truck was going back, so as to catch a ride home. Jon Mossen, a morose but punctilious boy from further up in the village, was hired as a driver. Butangen had not only gained links with the outside world now, but a daily routine. It was no longer just the schoolchildren who had to live by the clock, but the dairymaids, because the truck only passed the milk churn stands at fixed times.

Something else Kristine had not predicted was that the Reo would require so much upkeep. Jehans had to stand with his head under the bonnet every other night, with a light bulb suspended over the engine. Truth was, one of their main reasons for choosing the Reo was that it came with a repair manual. Only after the purchase did Jehans discover that this was blotted with black fingermarks, and pretty soon he realised it can be a good *and* a bad sign when a car manual is dog-eared and covered with smudges.

For the Reo *must* run. It was the milk truck. Without it the milk went sour. Without it everything stopped.

And by the way, it's snowing, how's about we fix a plough on the front?

Wagers were made on who would buy the first car, and those who staked their money on Ole Asmund Gildevollen won. In his desire to be first, he ended up with a clapped-out Chevrolet that left behind it a trail of thick, blue smoke which smelled so good to Gildevollen – blue smoke being a signifier of modern times, like telephone poles and power lines – that he was convinced

I Shallna' Be Content with Less

that all was well, until one day the engine seized, giving Jehans more to do. He erected a roof so as to do the repairs in the dry, and on a wall he hung his tools and tyres. Motorcars need fuel, and more and more often the Reo drove up from Fåvang with barrels of petrol on its cargo bed, like some draught beast fetching drink for itself and others. The barrels were red and white, and decorated with a beautiful winged horse, and Jehans and Kristine bought a handpump with a gauge, hammered up some walls around the roof, and realised that the village now had a petrol station, a motor repair shop, a snowplough and a regular bus route.

Schweigaard had always thought that the dairy's outlet shop was a bit cramped and messy. Dairy products, sugar and tobacco were sold alongside hemp rope, mousetraps and bullets. Kristine decided to take things in hand. The following year, Widow Fløter – so-called because she had been the wife of a logger who got swept away by the river – was made the proud manager of a new general store with a large window, advertising boards and a bell over the door. Astrid had been a Saturday girl here from the age of eight, and stood alongside her behind the counter, with a coffee grinder and white scales. When Widow Fløter managed to order in a half-crate of bananas that summer, it was such a sensation that Butangen's name-smiths immediately baptised the shop the Colonial.

Business had been reasonable, but increasingly during the thirties folk came to the Colonial just for a chat, with no money to buy anything. Kai Schweigaard, who had always kept a close eye on the village's poor, had to admit that, bad as things had been in the past, the foundations of life here had never been so threatened. Even a backwater like Butangen felt the effects of the bank crashes in America and Germany. Six good farms had been sold in forced auctions in the last three years, and penury hit family after family. Farms were no longer self-sufficient.

A Map of a Seter Road

Everything had to be paid for with money. Soon Butangen's folk felt that the road down to Fåvang only went *there* and not *back*, since they had so few goods that anyone down there wanted.

A seter road would offer the village new hope. Enough fodder could be carried down from the upland pastures to sustain the cows properly all winter, so they would no longer have to be dragged from their sheds half dead in the early spring. Problem was that the idea of building a road to the seters, across such difficult terrain, seemed impossible. Which was why some farmers were eager to turn the clock back. During Butangen's annual farmers' meeting in the village hall earlier that year, at which they had planned to discuss the May 17 Independence Day celebrations, a farm owner took to the floor to suggest they go back to the old tradition of using winter seters. Kristine got up.

"Winter seters? They belongs to another time. We need a new seter road now! More cows, more milk, more trade! All of us present knows that the upland pastures be our only way out of these wretched times. 'Tis time to build! Time t' stop yer whining and snivlin'. To put on yer big men's boots and build! Ye needs t' found a Land Association!"

The moaning ceased, although not the furtive head-shaking.

It was then that Jehans stood up and cleared his throat, slightly uncomfortable that it had fallen to him again to spearhead a new enterprise.

"Nitro-glycerine. That be the answer to the problem here," he said. "'Tis costly, but a hundred times more powerful than gunpowder. We always believed a new road mun take the same path as the old. But 'tis clear now that it mun run along the mountainside next to the Breia. We mun build a bridge down there."

There was uproar. The terrain was so steep that not even a stoat would try climbing up there. Still, the meeting ended with

Jehans and Fugleslåa's farm owner being given the go-ahead to stake out the route, clear any land that must be cleared, measure what could be measured, and from that calculate the requirement for explosives, cement and man-hours – at their own financial risk, naturally.

It was these calculations that Schweigaard had before him now. All logically set out, with a fifteen per cent margin, in a handwriting he had watched develop from childhood into youth and manhood. Jehans was a master of the grid sheet. After working for years on every hydroelectric plant in the valley, he had all the corresponding certificates and was conversant with dynamite sticks and gunpowder. But, as you might find in all Norway, Butangen's farmers were as stubborn as the terrain they issued from. Tomorrow, twenty-five men would gather here to decide whether to proceed with the seter road. Schweigaard had the right to vote since the parsonage had a seter. And since he was hosting the meeting and providing the refreshments – coffee and Fru Røhme's platters of fresh rolls with cheese and meats – he would act as chairperson.

It was a welcome appointment.

He liked – more than he would admit, and more obviously to others than he perhaps realised – taking the role of the village's protector, a beneficent patriarch to this little kingdom between the Løsnes Marshes. He missed the days when he was civilisation's sole representative in Butangen, asserting influence on all things great and small, making on-the-spot decisions – emperor in a spruce-clad autocracy. It had been his lot to bring the village into the modern age. So, he mustn't lose his grip tomorrow. No slip-ups, no lapses of memory, no reverting to 1880.

Over This Smell, the Smell of the Pastor's Pipe

Images of the past flickered through her mind. So, it hadn't disappeared after all, the weave that had been made in this house three centuries ago.

She looked out of her bedroom window. Imagined the sisters down there in the forecourt, walking past the old *stabbur*, eternally bound together. She pictured them entering the house. Wondered how their footsteps would sound in the hallway below. A specific beat, a distinct rhythm and weight on the floorboards.

Astrid had always felt different as a child. Now she felt chosen. Adolf and Ingeborg had told her that the pastor had looked for the weave, but that they believed he had given up. But she still couldn't understand why he hadn't mentioned it to her father. Was it really because Jehans was so much *a part of the story*, as he said?

And again. This gold ring.

Astrid turned from the window and sat on the bed. Twirled the ring between her fingers. Was this how love was? With no beginning or end? With every passing day it would be more difficult to return the ring. She could not sneak into the bell tower again, and it was equally impossible just to leave it on his desk.

She looked around.

She had this little room to herself: a small bedchamber with a wood stove, a washbasin, books on a shelf, a map of the world and cuttings from weekly illustrated magazines on the walls. Under the bed was an old sewing box that she rarely opened because she hated sewing. She put the ring in it and went out into the hallway.

I Shallna' Be Content with Less

How often had she gazed down this hallway? It felt now as though she must look at everything anew and ask herself what the house had looked like in the time of the Hekne sisters.

The floor was grey, most of the doors were painted a traditional pale blue and rust red, but the door to Tarald's room was orange and umber, with sage borders to separate the blocks of colour. He had painted it like this last year.

She paused outside Tarald's door. Heard the voice of Sigmund, a boy in their class. The two friends had been down to Fåvang the day before for some sort of public lecture, which, from their voices, seemed to have fired debate.

She went down the stairs and passed Esther's door. Her room had previously been the pantry, and Astrid remembered the day her father took down the shelves and painted it blue, explaining that Esther must have it to avoid climbing the stairs.

The kitchen stood empty. Their parents were out working as usual, despite it being a Sunday. Back when the siblings were small, Ingeborg had always been there making food while Adolf saw to the fire. It was a very different house now. Still a good house, but hectic in the mornings and always messy. Other farms had women who came in to clean and help out, but her mother loathed the idea of having staff in the house, cleaning up after her, primping her cushions and nosing in her privy.

Some years ago the three children had moaned at their parents for being away too much. Kristine fumed and said they should take a look around them and note the difference between them and the other bairns in the village.

"Ye have sommat yer father and I never had. Time to yerseln. Time to read and draw. Time to do yer lessons. Take a look around. Folks have it hard, and their bairns mun pitch in from when they be knee-high. Ye have been allowed to play! And there ye sit, whining cos we be away from home? Workin' for the three o' thee!"

Astrid went into the living room. It too was empty. Rooms like this needed people in them; when they were empty they screamed loneliness to anyone who walked in. The homebuilt radio was playing quietly under the window. She assumed Esther had been here and left when the classical music programme started.

Astrid turned it off.

There was a door at the far end of the room. She tried it and, finding it swollen in its frame, gave it a shove with her knee. It opened onto a cold, low-ceilinged room. A smell of dust. Old newspapers and junk. An abandoned cradle. A backpack on a peg.

The farmhouse had been extended multiple times. This room belonged to the oldest section of the building.

She closed the door behind her.

She had never asked herself before why it was so wide.

It was in here that the Hekne Weave had come into being. Over many years.

The room was dingy, its timber walls brown with age. It lay in the corner of the house, and had more windows than usual. Perhaps to ensure that the sisters had light to work by all through the day?

There was glass in these windows now, unlike in the 1600s when this extension had been made. But the sisters would have leaned on these same sills, to look out, as she did now, over Lake Løsnes. Her mind drifted back to the image in the weave. Might its meaning be that they lived on as two church bells?

Astrid walked into the middle of the room. There, on the spot where the morning light was likely to fall, was a long indentation in the floor, and the wear marks from two pairs of feet.

She went down to the cellar for potatoes. A light bulb shone through the cold, damp air. Another upshot of her father's passion for all things modern.

I Shallna' Be Content with Less

Up in the kitchen Astrid turned on the electric stove. Ingeborg had been beside herself with excitement about this appliance, and even more so when Jehans laid a pipe from the stream into the farmhouse and connected it to a water heater. The old lady had been overjoyed every time women's work was lightened. No more fetching of water. No more lighting the wood stove to heat water – even in summer.

Astrid put the potatoes on to boil, then a lump of butter in the pan. But it was too soon to start frying the blood sausage. She tapped a saucepan idly with a wooden spoon. There was no musical ding, just the clank of women's domestic bondage.

Huff!

She went off to see Esther. As usual she did not have time to knock before a voice called out: "Come in, Astrid."

Esther was sitting on the bed with Mopsi in her lap. Mopsi was a rather sulky, long-haired cat that glared at visitors. Some people found it unsettling that Esther could sit with her head turned away but know exactly what was happening. As though the cat were her eyes. Esther wore her hair loose, brown as pine bark, shiny as still water. Two years younger than Astrid, she was annoyingly mature for her age. She had gone to the blind school in Trondheim from the age of eight, but last year she had started to get bored and to rebel against the school rules.

"Come over here, Sister."

Astrid held out her hands. Esther sniffed the air.

"Carrots," she said. "Grated carrots. And sliced blood sausage. Cabbage, I can smell that from afar. And ye have been down to the cellar, so the tatties'll be fresh boiled. Not reheated."

"Wrong!" Astrid said. "There are peas too."

"Pfff," said Esther. "Ye just made that up."

"Aye. I made it up."

Astrid rolled Mopsi onto her back and scratched her chin

hard. The cat went into a trance and lay there with her mouth half open.

"What were ye up to earlier?" Esther asked.

"What do ye mean?"

"Ye couldna' have gone to Mass, like ye told Ma. There's a peculiar smell about thee. Sommat I have never smelled before. Sommat old and cold. And over that another smell, the smell of Grandpa Kai's tobacco. And I can sense ye were scared."

"Sister, dear," began Astrid, "I have seen sommat t'day."

"Oh?"

Astrid was suddenly filled with misgivings. What she was about to tell her sister defied all rational explanation. And what was said could never be unsaid.

She got to her feet. Mopsi pushed off and landed on the floor.

"Dinner's ready in half an hour," Astrid said.

"Are ye peeved wi' me?"

"Nay. Not a bit. I just have to take the potatoes off."

Astrid returned to her cooking, but her thoughts kept drifting to the moment when she had touched the weave, and the weird feeling it had prompted in her. That all time was gathered there, condensed into one, like the pages of a book. But that she could only see, and later remember, the page that was being written there and then. Everything beyond it was as dust, invisible, as though the words were a disappeared telegraph signal.

It reminded her of the Morse code machine their father had given them as children. Jehans had built it in the summer she turned eight, the dynamos in the power station had been playing up, and he kept having to go up to Hellorn to repair them. "If the lights be flickerin' here in Hekne, they be flickerin' everywhere in t' village," he said, before abandoning his half-finished supper. He regularly had to stay up at Hellorn until late, working to secure a steady current. It was then the messages in Morse code went back and forth between him and the children.

I Shallna' Be Content with Less

Brief conversations with a busy father, conversations that emerged letter by letter and then vanished. Their father often said more in code than when they were face to face. Esther learned the Morse alphabet straight off, just as she had learned braille, which meant that when her father was up at Hellorn, there was nothing to separate her from her siblings. Astrid remembered how they wished the messages could go on forever, but the longer they sat, the closer it loomed, the dreaded message that was doubtless as painful for him to send as for the children to receive:

-... . -.. - .. -- .

Bedtime!

"'Tis witchcraft," Ingeborg said of the beeps from the Morse code machine. By contrast, she never called all the strange things *she* believed in witchcraft. Her belief, for example, that seter cabins were inhabited by underground spirits over winter, so that when she returned to the seter for the first time each spring, she would pound on the door and shout: "We be comin' in now," and demand that Astrid and Tarald wait fifteen minutes before going in, to give the spirits time to pack up, and, in appreciation for their winter stay, not leave a mess behind them.

Astrid had thought it a silly custom. Now she wondered if Ingeborg's rituals weren't the remnants of a bond with something beyond the visible. Morse code without the Morse alphabet.

Astrid shook the memories off. She felt a rare need for company and went up to see Tarald. She knocked and peered round the door. His room was spic and span as always. Sigmund was lounging on the floor, reading the papers. He was the type who was always up for a debate, and he had begun smoking a pipe and wearing a hat. Tarald was at his drawing board. He pointed with satisfaction at a pastel sketch on the wall. A train rushing through the prairies of America. Smoke billowing from its chimney and buffaloes all around. "What d'ye think?"

A Map of a Seter Road

"Nay bad," said Astrid.

"Too many buffaloes? Ought the train to be green? Sigmund here had doubts."

"'Tis grand with plenty of buffaloes. How was yesterday's lecture?"

"Boring," Sigmund said.

Astrid looked at them. They were giving nothing away.

"'Tis dinner soon," said Astrid.

"'Tis always dinner at this time," Tarald said.

She was minded to call him a spoiled brat, but just snorted and shut the door. How would things turn out for him, she wondered. They had realised long ago that their parents had plans for all three of them, including Esther. Jehans had heard that abroad, in Germany no less, the blind were trained to be back doctors, since they could twist and press painful necks and spines to put them right, and if something was needed it was that, for there were always folk who had injured their backs in the forest, or in fields and kitchens everywhere.

Tarald's future was taken as read: he would inherit the farm. And Astrid would take over the Colonial and dairy factory.

Maybe that was why she and her brother were as they were. From their birth the world had been divided between them. Anything that interested Astrid left Tarald cold, and the reverse. Any dish from which Tarald helped himself was empty when she arrived. Any bonfire was burnt out if Tarald reached it later than Astrid.

For years they had shown compliance with their parents' plan. Tarald had tried to be the clever young *odelsgutt* who smiled and looked folk straight in the eye. With Jehans always busy at the power station or leaning over the Reo's engine, it fell to Isum to make a farmer of Tarald. Riding on his shoulders, Tarald pointed the way, shook his fist at the forest and newly broken land, and shouted his orders: "Chop down that pine! Break up that rock! Gee that Døla horse through the deep snow!"

Much later Astrid realised that Isum only feigned obedience. In reality he redirected Tarald's attention, and continued with his tasks as he had learned from the generations of farmworkers before him, at a slow, even pace, without fuss, *steady wins the day*, as he said.

Thus should Tarald have learned how to farm, through the seeds into his fist, through the soil into his being. But Astrid could see that none of this affected her brother. It was as though everything that happened was just a spectacle to him. A display of something while reality took place elsewhere. She remembered how terrified he was when, on their way home from school one day, they had bumped into three older boys from up in the village.

"Oi, Hekne!" they shouted.

Astrid and Tarald stopped. The boys only addressed Tarald.

"'Tis yer folks runs everything in t' village, in't so?"

"Well, Ma has the dairy," said Tarald. "And Pa started the electric station."

"In't right that yer folks own everything," the boys continued. "Come the next election there'll be an end t' private property rights. Everything shall be shared out justly. Yer kind shall be made t' live in hovels."

The boys laughed and strode on. Tarald was shaken. This had not been a show or theatrical performance.

"'Tis just talk," said Astrid. "D'ye think these mutts know their arse from their face in such matters? It mun be sommat their mas and pas have droned on about round the supper table."

They walked on down to the dairy factory, where they usually went after school. They were barred from the manufacturing hall, not that they ever wanted to go there, it being so cold in there, with its concrete floors and sour smell, and stern-looking women in white smocks, and straps that spun from wheels in the ceiling to appliances that went up and down and around, and along the wall open vats of warm curds, all of which must be *sanitary*!

Which was why they always sat in the packing room to wait. It was on such a day that Tarald's talent first came to light. He had picked up a sheet of the paper in which the hard cheese was to be wrapped – smooth and glossy on one side, and matt on the other – and taking some coloured pencils had begun to draw. Astrid sat reading and longed for her mother to be finished. Tarald continued, taking more sheets from the pile, sharpening his pencils, and drawing the Butangen he saw outside the window: the fields that sloped down towards Lake Løsnes, the forest and the marshes beyond. Then letting his imagination roam up to the seters, he drew some little cabins on steep slopes with mountains in the distance. A goat by a trickling stream. Like this perhaps? No. A fresh sheet of paper.

The delivery crates had BUTANGEN DAIRY burned into the wood, and now he wrote these words, but with new shapes.

Time passed. More attempts. More paper.

When Kristine finally came in, she had to walk straight back out again to calm herself. All her wrapping paper had been drawn on. After a word with Ada Borgen, her loyal co-worker in the dairy, she decided they would use the wrappers just as they were, and sell the cheese in the village, since an eraser would only make them look worse. It was best to fold them, so Tarald's scribbles were visible, and tell their customers what had happened.

As the two women wrapped the cheeses, they could not help but see that some of the drawings were rather fine. They were quick line sketches, which was probably how Tarald had drawn so many, but that was their strength. Most depicted a cow and a goat on a grass slope, with a cabin in the distance, and, in slanted lettering across a blue sky, the words BUTANGEN DAIRY.

I Shallna' Be Content with Less

There was no looking back.

Two city folk, who were busy stocking up for a long ski trip, asked for two with drawings. Yes, it was obvious they had been done by a child, but that was their charm!

Tarald made a fair copy of his best drawing, eliminating the more childish elements. Jehans asked what it would cost to print it in two colours, and soon the dairy had its very own packaging and trademark.

From then on, Tarald decided never to follow the expected path. He sat in the back room, watching the customers. Listening for praise. In there, Astrid believed, a struggle was taking place between the *odelsgutt* and someone else about whom nobody really knew anything, except that where he had failed in the field, he had been victorious with a pencil.

Dinner was finally ready. With the promise of liver cake at home, Sigmund left. Soon afterwards Jehans arrived. Taking off his jacket and boots, their father stood in the kitchen doorway, looked around at his three children, the cat, the kitchen counter and dinner table, as if he was surprised to have become part of this. He smelled of forest and wet wool and apologised for being late.

"Blood sausage. Looks great. But we mun wait for yer ma."

Kristine arrived fifteen minutes later. She had changed at the dairy and looked at herself in the mirror before coming to the table.

They were among the few farming families who ate supper in the kitchen. Others sat in dining rooms at long tables, in order of generation and station. But this was not a tradition Kristine would ever follow.

"Mmm, fine tatties," said Tarald. "Shall I peel one for thee, Esther?"

"D'ye think me a halfwit?" Esther retorted.

"Sorry for asking!"

"Hush, we shall have none o' that here," said Jehans. "Aye, they be fine potatoes. And a very good blood sausage."

"How is't with staking out the route?" said Tarald.

Jehans said it wasn't easy. He had to dig through the snow to get any idea of how porous the rock was.

"So, why not wait till spring?" Tarald said.

"Aye, well," Jehans began, "we needs to be well underway afore Easter, as ye well know. Or we'll not be able to pull the timbers there."

Wait until spring indeed, thought Astrid. The very idea showed Tarald's ignorance. When the snow thawed, it would be impossible to get the logs out there.

This play-acting. Tarald's attempt at adult engagement. Their father's all-too-polite answer, with his ineffectual *aye, well*. Their mother's pursed lips that said: *How will all this end?*

They continued to eat but Astrid was no longer listening to their talk. She was thinking about the weave. *Each shall see their own face in t' Hekne Weave*, Ingeborg had once said.

Astrid had a chill feeling that this was true.

There'll Always Be a Use for Dynamite

"They has begun to arrive," Fru Røhme called up.

"As always when there's food on offer," Kai Schweigaard said.

His watch showed eleven thirty. He could go down now to ensure that no clown sat at the head of the table, but if he was the first there, he would have to make small talk, something a village pastor should avoid. Then again, it would be useful to know what the locals were talking about. He went down the backstairs and into the workroom that shared a thin wall with the dining room.

It was here, more than fifty years ago, that he and Astrid Hekne had stretched a long tablecloth out between them, and their eyes had met across it. It was so desolate, this room, now. Just a sewing table and a linen cupboard.

He came in here for the thinness of this wall, which had once allowed the maids to hear when a top-up was required, and behind which he could now overhear the farm owners.

The mood was glum. No bullish excitement. It did not bode well.

He recognised the voice of Ola Mossen, father of the milk-truck driver. He owned an old cottar's farm and did some forestry work. His wife was a pleasant enough woman, and their two sons, Jon and Odd, had been polite and attentive in their confirmation classes. Mossen himself was a stout man with strong eyebrows, and a habit of not turning his head, just his eyes. He took it upon himself to be a voice for the smallholders, and while most folk thought he was a communist, he had launched the local branch of the recently established Nasjonal Samling Party. Having advertised their first meeting in the Høgvang village hall, they had set out coffee cups for forty, but only nine people had turned up. Of these, two had come by mistake and three were bachelors who were there for the free coffee. Broadly speaking, voters were unimpressed by the NS' first manifesto; they thought a lot of it made good sense, but that the party was too small to bother voting for, that it would never gain influence. The only people who voted for Mossen in the end were his sons, though not, it seemed, his wife. Despite this, he never gave up his fight against injustice.

Behind the wall Pastor Schweigaard heard Mossen talking about another forced auction in Brekkom. A farmer had defaulted on his bank loan.

"It were the sheriff oversaw the auction. Sold the livestock and tools first. Then the axes, scythes and rakes. The whetstone. Then the fixtures. Bed sheets. Sheepskin rugs." Mossen went on to describe, with fervent anger, how the bailiff had then sold the children's shoes. Followed by the pots and pans, and kitchen utensils. At which point the bailiff had brought down the hammer and announced that enough money was raised now to cover the bank's claim.

"There are nine of them in that house," said Mossen. "Ye know how they eats? They shares three knives and six forks. They kept the farm right enough. But what good be a farm wi'out scythes and a whetstone and cows? Bah. We live in a land now that takes the shoes from bairns."

Schweigaard had heard too many such stories. Several men had taken their own lives over the last few years. One had shot himself after a game of poker, another had jumped off a cliff because he had defaulted on a loan. The old order, in which every farmer was self-sufficient and lorded it over their crofters, might be unjust, but at least such disasters stayed within the fence of each farm, where each person could do a little of almost anything. Now everything was divided into specialisations, and where hand tools and utensils had been crafted at home, most things were now made in factories. Folk were increasingly dependent on a wage economy, and when their wages failed to cover their bills, their anger inevitably rose. Never had Norwegians been more divided, never had the country's politics been fuelled by such bitter resentment. Tables were thumped at the least dissent, and thus it was in Butangen too.

"Have ye heard the latest on Jehans Hekne?" a voice said from behind the wall. "He has already begun to clear the land where

I Shallna' Be Content with Less

he wants his seter road to go. Canna but wonder what he hopes to reap for himseln this time."

"It were agreed at the last meeting," another voice said.

"Oh, were it indeed?"

"Shh. Not here!" said another.

Schweigaard shook his head. This was typical of how the villagers talked about Jehans and Kristine. They had grown fairly wealthy over time, making money they hardly had time to spend, treating themselves to little more than the odd hunting expedition or cloudberry-picking trip.

Schweigaard padded back up to his study. He could only hope that the mood would improve when some of the other more genial farmers arrived, from Dokken perhaps or Hjelle.

"Let's get to business," said Schweigaard. "First, we should seek agreement on exactly how much labour each farm should contribute to the construction of this road. The proposal stands as follows: thirty metres of land clearance for each cow a farm kept up on the seters last year."

There was instant uproar.

What about the farmers who mainly herded sheep? Or the farms that kept goats? They'd be getting off too lightly. The goat farmers retorted that their herds could get along fine enough without a seter road, they coped with any terrain. The mood had gone sour even before the third speaker stood up to say that one thirty metres was not the same as the next thirty metres, with this side of the river being harder to clear than the other! Each objection brought another two, and even the most reasonable suggestions became impossible to consider, because the farmers saw hidden insults in them. It was not until ten past three that the Butangen Land Association voted, with a slim majority, to adopt a contribution of twenty-six metres' clearance for each cow, three metres for each ewe, and one and a half for each goat. A nine-point addendum laid down tariffs for those who wished to take their pigs up there or who went up to fell trees, and finally toll charges were set for non-villagers, with and without handcarts.

Schweigaard gave a sigh of relief when Jehans finally began on his plan for the blasting work. He was allowed to talk almost without uninterruption, with his usual understated competence. Nobody crowed, for the moment at least, that his only motivation was to line his own pockets. Despite everything, he was still the village's dynamo master and blasting expert, a true Butangen man who knew every metre of the terrain and could even name every single rock type, including the strange, blue-black crags that hung above the Breia.

"'Tis hard to say precisely how much dynamite we needs," Jehans said. "The rocks vary in density and formation. Even with detailed calculations we canna' say surer than we need 'twixt 370 and 550 kilos of dynamite."

And here lay the problem. The *Norsk Sprængstofindustri* price list for dynamite indicated a discount on any quantity in excess of 500 kilos, and Schweigaard immediately spoke in favour of their buying 550 kilos straight off. Ola Mossen stood up and said this was a nonsense. It was better to buy 370 kilos now, blast the road as far as they could go, and order the rest when they had an overview. The most expensive thing was to buy too much! Who would be left with the surplus? And were the Land Association being completely honest about this deal? Was a percentage going straight into the pockets of certain folk present?

Schweigaard recognised it only too well. Poverty dressed up as prudence. The construction of the seter road would make big financial inroads on all of their pockets. The plan was to make the road four metres wide, and Jehans' map indicated passing places every two hundred metres, in the eventuality of cars driving from opposite directions. Several farmers were against this, it would be too costly, besides, cars would never be that common. Soon the conversation was no longer about dynamite, but had degenerated into a word-slinging contest, a well-established ritual among all Gudbrandsdal folk, in which accusations of the most heinous kind were flicked down the table, the art being to send double-edged comments back again. Others were just biding their time to get an extra helping of Fru Røhme's fresh rolls. When the clock struck five, Schweigaard had no choice but to ask her to make another round of refreshments, and soon six beautiful platters were set out on the table. More coffee was poured into porcelain cups so dainty they looked like egg cups in these working men's hands, and still the arguments flew for and against 370 or 550 kilos of explosives.

Schweigaard lost his patience.

He stood up and cleared his throat, but nobody took notice.

His old temper flared. He thumped his fist into the table so hard that the walls shook and the coffee cups spilled, and he followed each word with another blow of his fist.

"Your pastor – is – speaking!"

The farmers went as quiet as confirmands. A slice of goat's cheese fell from a roll. Lars Romsås, who had reached for it, put it gingerly back.

"We'll order 550 kilos of explosives," Kai Schweigaard said. "Then we'll get the quantity discount. I myself shall advance the difference for the 180 kilos. If we have any dynamite left, it will be stored in the stone barn here, which is dry and safe. Anyone here with a share in the road may buy it later when needed. No, don't interrupt, Herr Mossen! I know what you're about to say. The remaining stock will be sold at the purchase price, that goes without saying! The discount belongs to us all. There'll always be a use for dynamite."

*

The meeting had been so stressful that Tuesday, and then Wednesday, passed without Kai Schweigaard surfacing. Fru Røhme put food next to his bed, but he pretended to be asleep. She had pleaded with him to go to the doctor several times in the past year, but nothing had ever come of it.

It was on such days that longing, in its many forms, made its appearance in his narrow bed. He missed the suppleness and industry of youth, he missed the old times, he missed being touched.

And he missed Widow Stueflaaten.

Not with a desire like the deep, lifelong draw he felt towards Astrid Hekne, but something livelier. Not without commitment, but not for eternity either. Two years had passed since they had seen each other last, although they still corresponded. Occasionally a certain frisson could be read between the lines, for old age's only daring was to relive the daring that once was.

When the Dovre railway had opened in 1921, they had done the unspeakable and travelled to Trondheim together. She waited for him at the new station at Dombås, which, like so many train stations, lay in the middle of nowhere, with not a house or building around. There she stood, in a newly tailored, burgundy travel dress, and her hair elegantly set up.

On the train, particularly on the terrifyingly precipitous stretch of line through the Rosten Gorge, he could feel his heart beat in time with the clunk of the train on the tracks. Not just because of the churning river below, but because the train was taking him on a corresponding journey to the edge of a potential spiritual abyss.

She was a formidable woman. Sparklingly intelligent, quick on the draw, well travelled, and vociferous about the women's cause. With her he let go of being a priest, of the battle to be the wisest, and felt drawn to touch her, to partake of everything he had let pass, but of which he might now taste the remaining morsels.

I Shallna' Be Content with Less

He had often debated it with himself. An affair would be scandalous for a pastor like himself. What the bishop said mattered little to him. What God thought, he had grown more regardful of. But it was what Astrid Hekne might think that troubled him, even though she lay in the graveyard.

Nonetheless, having arrived in Trondheim, he was liberated by a remark Astrid had made once about wedding rings: *That a woman's ring finger be created with room enough for two.*

Besides, he thought, it couldn't possibly be a cardinal sin at his age.

Arriving in Trondheim they wandered about for a good while. Dined on Seaman's Beef and prune compote, then took another stroll for digestion's sake. They paused at a pool by the river, and looked at themselves in the water's reflection. He found pleasure in the fine wrinkles around her eyes, like the year rings in a beautiful piece of wood, but what pleasure she found in him, he did not comprehend.

Perhaps all she saw in the waters below was that the time had come.

Kai Schweigaard's bed did not need making next morning. In her hotel room his desire had revealed itself as more dammed up than extinguished. Afterwards she had propped herself up on one elbow, put a forefinger on the tip of his nose and said: "Relax now, Herr Schweigaard. You needn't make up for forty years' celibacy in one night. We have all the time in the world."

Flattery on her part, of course. He was old and utterly inexperienced. Nor did they have all the time in the world. Marriage was never discussed, but their contract was honest. They could never have each other entirely, for she too had a gravestone to visit.

"We do each other good," she said. "We're feeding the animals. The soul, the brain and the body."

They were good years, though age eventually caught up with him and desire sank into contentment. She had told him in her last letter that she had arthritis in her fingers, and that sadly he could not count on a new sweater that Christmas.

But, thought Kai Schweigaard. They'd had *something*. And, as the Icelanders say, now and then a little *something* is quite marvellous.

Von der Maas bis an die Memel

Esther turned the radio dial to 1040 KHz. Mystery's frequency. They had dropped in on a sports broadcast from Stockholm, heard trumpet music from Madrid, swept past the incomprehensible Radio Odessa, and listened to London, where the sonorous voices spoke in Uncle Victor's language. Now, after passing through the crackling no man's land between Paris and Linz, the cat's eye – the luminous but illusive tuner – narrowed at last, and they heard German voices.

They seemed to have come in at the middle of a public speech by an angry man. They had, thanks to Kai Schweigaard's belief in youngsters' capacity to learn, some German, but it was hard to understand what the man on the radio was talking about.

"Did he just say Memelland?" Tarald whispered.

"Aye, he did so," said Esther.

The radio had arrived one Christmas, when the twins were eight. It had come as a kit, which their father soldered together in secret. The first thing the young Astrid had done was to set the dial to 1040. There, between Tallinn and Kalundborg, was

I Shallna' Be Content with Less

Radio Dresden, the frequency on which she had hoped she might hear a certain church bell.

But all they had heard on that first Christmas night was a loud hissing and crackling. Jehans sat at the supper table that evening oblivious to the festive roast pork and vegetables that were being passed round, and sat late into the night with a pencil and squared paper. On the second day of Christmas Kristine said: "Stop that! Pull yerseln together now. 'Tis Christmas!" Jehans said he was nearly done. "Oh aye! Ye were nearly done yesterday too!"

On the third day of Christmas, he switched on a home-made signal booster and connected an antenna all the way from the barn roof to the farmhouse. And then it came to Hekne, the great outside world. With a little turn of the dial, hissing from all the named cities on the scale, and from the medium wave, came the sound of music and unintelligible languages, and from then on, loud and clear, Radio Dresden.

The siblings went on listening. Yes, the speech was about Memel.

Their connection to Germany, as distant and fragile as the radio transmission across the Baltic, was unshakeable. Gerhard Schönauer, their grandfather, had come from there. Among the letters in the travel chest, they had found some postmarked Memel. They were from Gerhard's mother, their great-grandmother. Tarald had sent a letter to the Schönauer family at the sender's address on the envelope, but no reply ever came, despite his rushing down to the mailbox all that summer and autumn.

Later, after listening to various radio broadcasts, Tarald was convinced he knew why there had been no answer: "I reckons they must have been deported."

He had been reading up on the history of the city and found it almost unbelievable. Memelland lay on the outer edge of East

Prussia, the once powerful country that had disappeared after the Great War. Memelland had been under French military control, before being taken over by Lithuania.

Tarald had followed the news from Germany ever since, and this year the Hekne siblings had pricked up their ears once more, because the remaining Germans in Memelland had planned a rebellion. Hundreds of insurgents had been arrested, and their execution seemed likely.

Perhaps it was these executions that had prompted the fury of the man on the radio.

"What did he say?" Esther asked.

"That Germany should take Memelland back," Tarald said. "And some other German territories too."

"Imagine," said Esther. "If Grandfather hadna' died of pneumonia down in Dresden, he would likely have come back to Butangen and taken Grandmother with him to Memel. And been an architect there. And then Pa and Uncle Victor would have been born there. And we'd have been German."

"Aye, if Grandmother had survived their birth," Tarald said.

"They'd still have lived there. Father and Uncle Victor." Esther continued. "And then, so would we."

"Nay, cos then Father would never have met Mother at Orm seter," Astrid said. "So we wouldna' have been *us*."

The speech was over, and a choir began. Tarald recognised the song instantly. The German national anthem. "Von der Maas bis an die Memel" – from the Meuse to the Memel, Germany's true borders.

We All Turned Crazy

A four-day journey away a man was listening to the same broadcast. He was of course just one of thousands, but he was probably the only one who, like the young Heknes, fell to thinking of Gerhard Schönauer.

Churchwarden Karl Gustav Emmerich was sitting in the old Butangen stave church in Großer Garten, Dresden. His battery radio was on low, and he was eating rye bread with black sausage and drinking broth from a thermos. As always, he had folded his work smock in four, placed it on a pew, and sat on it. Each of the little doors you had to open to get into these box pews was painted with the name of a farmstead in a faraway valley he had never visited but felt he knew. His two favourites to sit on were the one marked Kinn and another marked Romsås.

It was a Monday. The church would open at nine, when he expected the regulars to come and pray. The wounded war veteran and his mother, the bald man who taught some obscure handcraft, the young woman in a blue coat who was so exceptionally ordinary.

Emmerich was getting old, but he continued to serve the stave church as dutifully as ever, and every year he marked the anniversary of the death of his old friend Gerhard Schönauer by laying flowers on his grave. He had worked here for fifty years, but still experienced the stave church as a breath of something barely knowable, in which mythical animals and twisting patterns cavorted, carved in a time when human beings believed that the visible influenced the invisible. The portal still held him under its spell. A magnificent play of gaping lizards with fangs and curling tongues, intertwined reptiles and lions with long tails, made to keep evil spirits out of the church. Most powerful of all was the writhing serpent that wound its way around the entrance that had been built purposely low, to prevent the largest and most dangerous spirits from squeezing in over the threshold.

Perhaps there was some sense to it.

The church had aroused curiosity and enthusiasm and attracted sightseers and its own rather quirky congregation for decades. But increasingly Emmerich got the feeling that it was being besieged by something twisted and warped.

This evil power – for that was how he perceived it – had never managed to get inside the church. It was never proclaimed from the pulpit. But it cavorted outside. Clawed at the walls. Wanted to get inside. What would *he* have said, young Gerhard, if he had known what the stave church was to become a symbol of? The present-day Germany was certainly not the Germany that had brought it here.

In the beginning the visitors had been a pleasant enough crowd. Ordinary churchgoers, architecture connoisseurs, friends of Norway who wished to get married here and baptised their children Sigurd or Ingrid. And, unsurprisingly, a multitude of opera buffs who were impressed by Wagner's *Der Ring des Nibelungen* and wanted to know more about the Norse mythology upon which it was based, and which shared so much with Germanic mythology. One or two of the carvings depicted creatures recognisable from *Der Ring*, leading some Wagnerians to infer a direct link to ancient Germanic times. But they had never read more into it. The stave church was seen simply for what it was: one of thirty remaining examples of an architectural style without equal in the world.

It was at the turn of the century that the first real cranks began to turn up. Men with haunted eyes who seemed to have a secret that was theirs alone to bear. They never spoke to anyone, and positioned themselves so that nobody could see the sketches they made. As the churchwarden, Emmerich was permitted to monitor visitors closely to make sure they didn't poke the carvings or leave fingermarks on the beautiful paintwork – the traditional *rosemaling*. And being familiar with the acoustics in the church, he knew where to stand to catch what was whispered behind pillars or mumbled in corners. He overheard increasingly outlandish ideas, and concluded that these visitors were occultists, Ariosophists, mystics who believed that the Germanic peoples were descended from a people in ancient India.

Emmerich thought it a noble task to look into the past. Since the Germans could never reach any agreement in politics, it was sensible to seek fellowship in culture, especially from the past when they were one people.

Emmerich soon realised what the Ariosophists were on the hunt for. Runes. Major studies about the history of runes had been made in Germany during recent years. There was no shortage of theories about these strange symbols, one being that before coming to the north, they had been given to the Aryans as a gift from the gods. Thus, the runic alphabet was not just a series of letters, but a medium through which man could communicate with the cosmos.

And there were indeed some runic symbols carved here and there in the church. Emmerich had never paid them much attention, but after six days of searching under the box pews with pocket torches, his new friends managed to find more. More Ariosophists arrived, mostly rather scruffy young men, who lived in tents and read too much, and who would eventually develop the "great stave church theory". They had studied the Norwegian legend of the church bells in the tower, which rang of their own accord to warn of danger. Nobody had been able to explain what kind of power gave the bells this ability. So they asked themselves: what if the power was not in the bells at all, but in the church? Could the runic symbols be the receptors? The ancient Norwegians had surrounded themselves with runic signs, on their houses, ships, swords and stones. Thus they had continuous contact with the gods, enabling them to safely navigate the most dangerous routes over sea and land. In a largely Christianised world, the stave church was among the very few places that still honoured the old Norse faith. Might it then still be in contact with those greater powers?

If so, why had the bell never rung of its own accord in Germany? Not even at the outbreak of *der Weltkrieg*?

"It must be because the bells were taken from each other," Emmerich would often overhear. A law had been broken, but if they were reunited, the runic signs and bells would act in partnership once more. The runes would receive the signals, and the bells would broadcast them.

Emmerich put a bigger padlock on the door that led up to the belfry. He did not tell them, but Halfrid had in fact rung a few times of her own accord. He left the Ariosophists to it down in the nave.

In the years that followed, the stave church was visited by sect after sect. The Edda Society, the Order of the New Templars, the Theozoologists, the Pilgrims of Odin. Year on year they came up with increasingly outlandish theories.

Emmerich understood what was driving them. Like millions of other Germans in the post-war era, he shared their longing for something more than the sad reality of this hungry, miserable life, in a country that was on its last legs and had proved such a terrible disappointment. He remembered the war years when everyone was constantly waiting for news from the front. School children dashed to the newsstands at lunchtime to check how the latest battles were unfolding, then went and played war. For four years they were fed stories of steady military progress, until one day in November 1918 it was suddenly announced that Germany had lost.

I Shallna' Be Content with Less

Lost? Us? Surrendered? To . . . *them*?

Through the 1920s he saw it clearly. Two generations of Germans were disillusioned and humiliated. They were attracted to order and structure, but wanted something to feed their souls too, and the young turned to spiritualism, hallucinogens, hypnosis and erotic adventure.

So Emmerich was unsurprised when the Thule Society turned up. In fact, he rather warmed to them, as they had a spirit of adventure and were not as glum as the Ariosophists. They had also taken the swastika as their emblem, saying it had been a symbol of good fortune in the ancestral lands of the Aryans. They waved aside Emmerich's tentative comment that the swastika had been used all over the world and at various times and had always been attributed different meanings. What interested them was that they had "absolute proof" that the Aryans, angered at the introduction of Christianity, had emigrated hundreds of years ago to the land of Ultima Thule, and still lived there in total isolation, possibly speaking in verse, and always keeping their race and traditions pure. Excitedly they showed Emmerich copies of Greek documents from AD 310 in which the geographer Pytheas described his journey to the land of Ultima Thule. The island lay six sailing days north of Britannia, placing Thule in northern Norway or Iceland, or possibly Greenland, depending on the ship's speed, and they had already collected money for an expedition to find the Aryans and bring them home.

"So how might *we* be of service?" said Emmerich, who had the habit of presenting himself and the church as one.

"Well," said the delegation's head, "the ancient Norsemen must, with their connection with the Aryans, have known where Thule was. And since they too were so reluctant to adopt Christianity, filling their churches with so many Norse symbols, it seems plausible to us that there is an important but hidden message in this stave church – one that can be deciphered by the right people."

The right people were, naturally, them. They hoped they would find within the very geometry of the stave church a map to Ultima Thule.

Three days later they had indeed discovered something. One of the big Andreas Crosses that connected the timber columns had an arm at the wrong angle. It pointed eighty-two degrees north, and with a little adjustment and if you enclosed it in a circle, it would form a sun cross, the sign of rebirth.

"I'm sorry to disappoint you," Emmerich said. "But this is a *Christian* detail, made in God's honour." He told them how every Norwegian stave church was built with *one* visible and clumsy mistake, to indicate that only God is infallible, and that it would be arrogant for man to build something perfect.

No, they dismissed his story as a smoke screen. Soon they set off on a ship going exactly eighty-two degrees north, visited Nordaustlandet in Svalbard, then headed for Greenland, and turned back home when the cans of food ran out.

Other groups were outright unpleasant. In particular the Armanenschaft – Armanists. Their leader – what was his name again? Von List or something similar – strode arrogantly into the church wearing a long robe and green velvet beret. His face was almost lost in a huge white beard, his chest weighed down by various amulets, the largest of which was a gilded swastika. He did not even deign to talk to Emmerich, but his lackeys claimed that he was an excellent researcher of race, a subject of major import for an association that sought to uncover the origins of the Germans. They took ever more liberties, until Emmerich had to get the police to throw them out.

The church was meant to get a new coating of tar in the 1920s, but inflation was so high that the money sent to him for this was worth nothing the next day. His wage packet was no less

I Shallna' Be Content with Less

affected, and he would join the queue outside City Hall to collect his cash, then dash to the shop, stand in another queue and buy food with *all* the money. Eight thousand marks had been granted for the retarring of the stave church, but by the time he had come to buy the tar, it cost three and a half billion marks.

Years passed, the sun shone, and the old tar blistered and cracked. To ensure the stave church looked its picture postcard best overlooking Lake Carola, the builders had rebuilt it at a different angle from its previous position in Butangen, so that the wall that had originally stood in shade, was now in the blazing Central European sun. Eventually the tar turned into a dry dust that gradually fell away. But what came into view, high on the wall? Yes: row upon row of runic symbols, all scratched over with a knife.

A professor and two assistants from the University of Marburg came to interpret them. Letter by letter they spelled out a lengthy inscription, until they realised it was a crude jibe against a named man with such bad backache he needed help to go to the toilet. The professor left for home before lunch, having concluded that the other inscriptions were also profane scribblings.

Just hours later, five smartly dressed and clearly irate men from the Deutscher Orden – the Teutonic Order – turned up at the church. They only admitted pure-bred Germans, and the Dresden branch had attracted a hundred members in just a short time. They protested against any plans to retar the church. The professor's interpretation had been rushed and priggish, and had no bearing on the meaning of the runes – didn't Emmerich appreciate what they had here? Germany's only physical example of the Aryans' own alphabet? The fact that the runic symbols had been scratched out and covered with tar merely proved that someone had tried to neutralise their power. It didn't matter *what* they said, because each individual symbol was a receptor for a cosmic frequency, and what made this so clever was that they had – with this odious text – used the *entire* runic alphabet. Every character from both the old and new runic alphabet! Which meant the church was in touch with the ancient gods. And the professor had failed to see it!

That was it. From that moment on, there was no limit to the interpretations that were made of the stave church's Norse heritage. It was not retarred. At the National Socialists next congress, the Deutscher Orden was allowed extra talk time, and a motion was passed that said all true German family trees stemmed from the Aryan ruling race, and that ancient runic signs must be protected.

Emmerich had often reflected on how weird the Thule Society seemed. Now the German flag had been altered and had a swastika in the middle.

Meaning the whole country was gathered under the Thule Society's emblem.

Perhaps everyone had gone a bit weird.

That Monday, Emmerich walked down the aisle and opened the doors. He had just put out the old wooden collection box when two cars and a lorry appeared along the gravel path above the church. What was this? It was forbidden to drive here, and none of these vehicles belonged to the Park Service.

The cars swung off the path, making tyre marks across the lawn.

Soon he was surrounded by six men – two in suits, four in the black uniforms of the Schutzstaffel.

"Close the church," one of the uniformed men said. "No visitors are to be allowed in here in the next few days. And absolutely no church services."

One of the men dressed in civilian clothes introduced himself as Jankuhn, and asked if Emmerich hadn't got the letter.

I Shallna' Be Content with Less

The churchwarden asked him what letter was that.

Jankuhn chuckled. "Quite. Then you don't perhaps know that you have a new boss? And that from now on this church is considered a museum? Which means, of course, you'll be free on Mondays?"

He put a hand on Emmerich's shoulder, and continued in a jocular tone: "Or that you'll get a ten per cent pay rise *and* a forty per cent bigger maintenance budget?"

Emmerich was speechless.

"Take it easy, old chap. You'll have a job here for as long you're in health. If anyone values age and wisdom, it's us."

Two uniformed men began unloading floodlights on tripods.

The stave church, he was told, had been taken over by the new research institute, the Deutsches Ahnenerbe, whose purpose was to secure the country's cultural heritage. Jankuhn showed him the emblem: a sword in a runic symbol.

Emmerich was told that he would be issued new work clothes with this emblem on the chest, and that some archaeologists would come the next day to make new drawings of the church. The truck was carrying four barrels of tar imported from Sweden. When the archaeologists were done, the church would get its much-needed coating of tar, but the runic signs must not be spoiled – they would be protected behind glass.

Jankuhn was barely thirty, and Emmerich had rarely come across such an optimistic man. It was infectious. "This matter with the tar has gone back and forth for years now," Emmerich said.

"That's how it is with so much here in this country, eh? But between us – the Ahnenerbe works directly under Himmler and the Allgemeine Schutzstaffel. We can talk sense and get things sorted. *Schutz* and tar. One and the same."

A Hungover Scientist

It was Easter.

The freest and best of time of year, according to Astrid. When pine needles lay on sunken snow and water dripped from the roofs and winter stood in the hallway waiting to depart, while the spring kicked the slush from her shoes and announced her arrival: I'm here to keep my promise this year too.

Best also, because it was her job to make the dairy deliveries to Annor Seter in the next village, the hotel where Mari Slåen had a winter job and the guests were all city folk and eccentric foreigners.

Astrid and her father stood waiting for her at the turning point on the forest's edge, behind them the Reo, its engine idling. There was a strong sun today, snow slid from the branches of the trees, and she took off her mittens. They had driven the truck up to where the snow-cleared road met the rolling, white landscape. Before them a tangle of ski tracks ran across the slopes and snow-covered fields, before they converged and disappeared into the forest.

She shoved her heavy leather boots in the ski bindings and fastened the straps at the heels. Then she put the leather harness over her shoulders, and her father hitched it onto the travois. Secured with rope on the sledge were five large crates containing milk, butter, cheese and sour cream.

"They puts in big orders up there," Jehans said, giving the sledge a push from behind as Astrid tramped herringbone style up a mound of ploughed snow. The sledge was so heavy it risked slipping back if she slowed down, so she dug her ski poles in deep, turned her head and shouted back: "Aye, they buys a lot. Ma were pleased."

"Aye, that she were," Jehans said with a laugh.

I Shallna' Be Content with Less

"See thee tonight, Father," Astrid called over the swish of her skis.

"See thee tonight," said Jehans, his voice raised so she could hear him over the distance she had already covered, and added, more quietly, but so she could still hear: "My Astrid."

Going up the heavy slopes her back dripped with sweat. Where the track went under the trees there was no sun. She grew cold and her skis rapidly lost their grip, and the sledge felt increasingly heavy behind her. But as she came out onto the plateau and back into the sun, the ski wax took hold again, and as the sledge slipped more smoothly over the snow-covered fields, other skiers came into view. Their baggy trousers and short anoraks told her they were city folk. They all had a strong, rhythmic diagonal stride, and sped towards her. She looked straight at them, refusing to depart from the track, since the skier with the biggest load always had right of way, even daft city folk must be able to grasp that much.

Here and there she spied new holiday cabins. Adolf and Ingeborg could never grasp the notion of either a holiday or a cabin, and to Ingeborg they looked oddly aimless in the landscape, without any surrounding barns or byres or cheese-making huts, with the sole purpose of housing city folk who wanted to "relax".

"Surely no right-minded folks would traipse up in t' mountains to take a rest?" she had said, always dismissing Jehans' explanation that the great explorers, Nansen and Amundsen, had made it fashionable to ski for skiing's sake.

Adolf shook his head. In the old days, he said, snow and ice were the enemy. It was unthinkable to go up to the seters in the winter for anything other than to hunt. The cabins lay snow-locked and silent. Here and there the tracks of hare or elk cut across the fields, and on rare occasions ski tracks, left by a free spirit out hunting capercaillie. He believed these new ski lodges and mountain hotels were a flight of fancy. He was even more sceptical of the stories about bottles of fizzy pop and stands of chocolate bars.

Astrid looked at her wristwatch. She was hoping she might hear the hum of the plane that flew over the mountain hotels every Easter, coming in low over the nearest plateau to drop a bundle of the day's national newspapers as the local children raced through the snow to be the first to reach it.

Oh, that plane! Every time she saw it, she thought of Uncle Victor in England. The partially deaf war pilot, who now ran an airline and had two sons. For years she had lived in the childish hope that Victor would visit them one day, preferably landing in a seaplane on Lake Løsnes. But, like her father, he was doubtless too busy.

The guesthouse was drawing near. A dark and imposing building on the slope where the fields ended further down. The travois jolted into her back, and she ploughed downwards, yelling at some kids who luckily hopped out of the way; it wasn't done to come crashing down amid a gawping crowd with a sixty-kilo load. She turned into the large forecourt, where about thirty pairs of skis stood against the log wall. The sun had dried out the benches, and the city folk sat in their knickerbockers and sporty new anoraks, chatting in their city accents. The smell of menthol cigarettes and oranges hung on the air around them.

"Ah, there ye are!" said Mari.

Astrid turned to her. She had been leaning on her ski poles and had not heard her come.

Mari stood there with her hair in a bun and wearing a grey apron. She helped Astrid out of the harness. Then, while her friend unfastened and took off her skis, Mari fetched a brush to sweep the snow from the wooden crates. But as she worked, Mari's eyes darted back and forth.

"Is sommat up?" said Astrid.

"Huh?"

"What is't? Ye look so queer."

"'Tis those two," Mari whispered, nodding quickly towards the nearest bench. Astrid took a discreet glance at a couple in their forties.

Together the two girls dragged the sledge over to the entrance. Mari disappeared inside without giving Astrid any idea what she was doing. Astrid leaned her skis against the wall. The sun was beating down, and the densely packed snow on her ski bindings had already started to melt. The balding man stared at her. He was wearing knickerbockers, but shoes rather than boots. The lady was pretty, with blond curls. She was wearing ski boots, trousers with a very high waist, and braces on top of a red and green woollen sweater.

Astrid started to untie the crates. Mari reappeared, and, beckoning her inside, closed the door halfway.

"They are foreigners," she whispered. "The couple on t'bench. They lives in Germany, but the lady's from Norway. The man speaks good Norwegian. That be why I couldna' talk out loud."

"And so?"

Mari peered out through the gap in the doorway and whispered: "They're asking about the Sister Bells."

Astrid jumped.

"The man," said Mari. "He were in t' fireplace room yesterday, actin' like the big man. Handing out cigarettes and schnapps. Saying he were *a man of science*. Asking around about the old legend and the church bells."

"But this lot all comes from the city. They know nowt about the bells, surely?"

"He must have twigged that soon enough. Later in t'evening,

he went out on his sticky skis t' the cabins opposite, where a gang of journeymen from Brekkom are on an Easter bender. He came back last night. Drunk as a skunk, wi'out mittens and with one broken ski pole. He's had a sore head all day and didna' go out t' ski. I heard him talking to his wife in German. I reckons he said *Schwesterglocken*. That means Sister Bells, right?"

Astrid nodded.

"Then a bit later," Mari Slåen continued, "I heard him say sommat about brothers. I reckon he knows that your father and uncle pulled the bell out of Lake Løsnes. For I'd swear he said the word *Hekne*."

Metron, Temperantia

Kai Schweigaard was debating with himself. In two hours' time he would hold Easter Mass, which had always been his star turn. The nave was already decorated in white, but this year his sermon refused to take shape. It lacked the wonderment and zeal commensurate with the resurrection.

"*I know that ye seek Jesus, which was crucified; He is not here: for He is risen!* Yes, thus spoke . . ."

Oh dear!

Schweigaard reached for his tin of tobacco. He was unable to give Matthew any oomph this year! The apostle sounded like a bank clerk!

Old age again. Next year Mark would probably be equally stubborn.

Should he steal a couple of lines from John Donne? Borrow a few dazzling phrases with double meanings, a gentleman's theft

I Shallna' Be Content with Less

between intellectuals? He pondered some quotes from Donne's *Paradoxes* and took a stroll in the clear winter air.

Down towards Lake Løsnes children were out playing on their sledges. It had snowed in the night, sticky and wet in the mild weather. The milk truck passed him with the snowplough on its bumper. Jon Mossen waved. He had ballasted the cargo bed, indicating that he planned to clear the snow all the way to Fåvang. The truck left a trail of exhaust. The sweet smell of progress.

Oh yes, they had control over nature now. For two weeks the explosions had thundered above the village. Work had been put on hold for Easter, but was due to start again on Tuesday.

Schweigaard looked out over the churchyard. The new times were coming here, too. Next year they would begin to hold funerals in the winter, so that the village's dead would no longer have to wait in the bell tower. The contraption that would end this ancient burial rite was an electric heater shaped like an iron bedstead. It even had to be covered with a quilt. In just forty-eight hours it could thaw the hard, frozen earth to a half-metre's depth.

At least, Schweigaard mused, the graveyard still harboured its old sense of eternity for now. The sight of Herr Røhme, for example, brushing the snow off his son's grave. He was wearing the same kind of clothes he had worn for decades, with perfectly polished boots that had been resoled many times over, an old but well-brushed coat, and the grey, narrow-brimmed hat they had found on the church steps in the summer of 1930, but whose owner they never discovered. He was loyal to a fault, this man who had stuttered so badly in his youth that he was taken by some for a fool. Once, Kai had stumbled across an old love letter to the young Fru Røhme, who could barely read back then. *If I had to choose a fault other than my stammer, I would pray for blindness, so I should never see thee wed to another.*

Like the pastor, Herr Røhme was no longer young. His hair had gone grey, just a year after Simen's death, and he had started coming here to stand at his son's grave and gaze out over Lake Løsnes.

Schweigaard felt he knew what Røhme was thinking as he stood looking quietly out. *If only Simen could see what I be seeing. If only Simen were walking down there now, near the boatyard, and could come home and tell us what he were doing.*

The other children had long since grown up. Herr and Fru Røhme were grandparents now. But Simen had been with them for fourteen years, and sometimes there was a void at the family dinner table, a void that said: *If only . . .*

If only Simen could . . .

We canna' afford to lose even one.

Back then in 1918, Herr Røhme had dug his own son's grave, and instead of the usual wooden cross he had taken a chisel and carved his name in granite. Later he had set up a small workshop and started a business making tombstones. Electricity made it possible to grind and polish rocks, so that it became commonplace, even in Butangen, to have memorials of stone. Schweigaard often noticed that Røhme got a particular satisfaction from this work, a hint of revenge, perhaps, for the torment he had once endured for his stammer, knowing that the letters he carved would remain forever. As he once said:

"'Tis the stonemason has the last word."

Schweigaard could see Røhme wasn't himself today. When he was troubled he became indecisive, walking a few metres in one direction, before his thoughts made him turn, and then turn again.

And so it was today. He was craning to see something down by the graveyard wall, not far from the bell tower. Catching sight of Schweigaard, he hastened towards him.

I Shallna' Be Content with Less

"There be strangers down yonder, Herr Pastor. A man and a lady in *trousers*. She be takin' photographs of the new church."

Røhme had never got used to the new phenomenon of tourists. He was not inhospitable, but preferred it when things were predictable. Schweigaard leaned forward and peered at the village's visitors.

He presumed they were the couple from the ski lodge whom Astrid had told him about. They were dressed in formal clothes now. With dark green, felt coats. And shoes, not boots. Which meant they must have come here by car.

This did not bode well.

Schweigaard moved back to avoid acknowledging them. He saw the woman take out a grey-blue sketchbook. Noticeably old and worn out. With long laces on the edge of its covers.

Sketchbooks like that. With those laces. He had seen them before.

Gerhard Schönauer had owned some like that. In that blue-grey colour.

He spotted the two visitors again from up in the pulpit. They were sitting at the back, their heads inclined and whispering to each other whenever the church bells rang.

He struggled through High Mass and had barely managed to change before Herr Røhme knocked on his study door.

"Ye has visitors, Herr Pastor. I told them to wait downstairs."

Schweigaard let five minutes pass before making his way to the living room. As he expected, it was the couple from the church. They were standing, hands behind backs, perusing his bookshelves. He noted the woman's close-fitting suit and modern hairstyle.

She nodded politely. "Maggen. Maiden name Blom. Originally from Skien."

The man held out his right hand. In his left was a book wrapped in blue tissue paper. "Hans Friedrich Günther."

A fine voice. He might have been put to good use in the hymn-singing.

"We apologise for disturbing you during Holy Week," Günther said. "We were wondering if we might arrange a visit later this week. It's about—"

"I think I know what it's about," Schweigaard said. "And *now* would suit me fine."

He asked Fru Røhme to arrange coffee. The book in blue gift paper lay on the table while Maggen talked about her years as a student in Germany. After their marriage, they had lived in Norway for a few years, where Hans had continued with his academic research. She presented the book to Schweigaard, which, when the tissue paper was removed, proved to have the title *Der Nordische Gedanke unter den Deutschen*. She pointed out that it was a signed copy, and suggested rather clumsily that Schweigaard should feel honoured to meet the author himself.

"Race and culture are my main field of research," said Günther. "I've always had tremendous respect for Professor Mjøen's work and have carried out a number of studies of both the Norwegian and the German populations. Looking at the greater picture, if I may be so bold."

Maggen said this was elucidated in the book, which she was keen to point out had proved very popular and enjoyed several print runs. "Although Hans is *far* too shy to say so himself!"

Schweigaard nodded. He had followed current trends in Germany and suspected that the book, whose title meant something like *Nordic Thought and the German People*, reflected the culturally pessimistic and racist ideas that were fermenting among the National Socialists. They wallowed in historical distortion and theft, even managing to make a brutal pre-Christian Norway look like an ideal society. Nor were they without supporters in

Norway. Many high school students were enthused over what the National Socialists were achieving in Germany.

The couple had still not mentioned the church bell. Clearly there was something else they wanted to bring up before moving on to that subject.

So, what now? Schweigaard had to avoid a situation where he must either lie or admit that Gunhild was in the bell tower. An old adage popped into his head: *Know thine enemy*. Luckily Fru Røhme came in with coffee and biscuits. He said he would love to hear more about Günther's research in Norway.

That afternoon was to be one of the strangest in Pastor Schweigaard's life, and there were a few from which he could choose. A doctrine known as Hylozoism – postulating that *all* matter was alive or animated – was offered up as blithely as Maggen's praise for Fru Røhme's ginger snaps and wafers. Günther discussed his studies of the Norse legends, and Maggen described the trips they had made to Norwegian villages to collect evidence of similarities between the Nordic and old Germanic races.

"The Nordic race is not absolutely pure anywhere, but both here in Gudbrandsdal and in Setesdal we have observed many people whose features resemble early Germanic nobility," said Maggen. "This is due, of course, to the isolation of these villages, which means that their hereditary material remains undiluted."

Schweigaard ventured that this might be more flattering than factual.

"Ah, I recognise that! And I *admire* it!" Günther said. "You Norwegians don't like to get all stirred up or dig about in other people's inner lives. *Metron, temperantia* – temperance and moderation – these are the traits of the Nordic spirit! As I explain in my book, you hold the seeds of racial nobility, those of you who dwell in these remote areas. The further from cities the better. Rural Norwegians are the stuff from which the *herresjikt* – the hero class – emerges in every productive period in Western history."

Schweigaard's biscuit crumbled. *Herresjikt*? As a pastor, living in Butangen through the most wretched of times, he had seen many an example among the locals who ought not be entrusted with any greater task than to fetch water or haul timber. He recalled a villager who had delayed burying his wife, because the smell of her rotting corpse lured the foxes, which he shot for their pelts.

Such details would not, he assumed, fit into his guests' theories.

"Even more significant," Günther continued, "is the Norwegian principle of the *odel*! The German word *adel* – meaning noble – stems of course from *odel*. The very life source of the Nordic race! For centuries, fathers have chosen their strongest and most capable son to take over the farm! Good breeding! Positive selection!"

Schweigaard tried to interject that it was the *oldest* son who took over, no matter how daft or inept he was, but Günther was on a roll now, and was busy leafing through his book, showing Schweigaard tables with the measurements of the skulls of people who lived in the remotest areas of Norway.

The conversation came to a natural halt when Maggen asked where she might find the lavatory. Schweigaard felt somewhat embarrassed at having to admit that they had no such thing indoors, and had to fetch Fru Røhme to take her to the guest privy next to the *stabbur* outside.

When Schweigaard returned, Günther had taken off his spectacles. He rubbed his bald pate with an expression that said the time had come to get to the point.

"Thank you for your marvellous hospitality, Pastor. You presumably know that we're here on a specific errand."

"I guessed as much."

Günther said he had been sent by the Ahnenerbe Institute to negotiate a deal. In respect of the church bell that was sunk in 1880. Which was now housed in the timber building below the church, was it not?

Schweigaard coughed and nodded ambiguously.

"You're probably wondering why I talk in such detail about racial hygiene. I'll say this: it means everything! The stave church is the strongest physical link between old Germania and the Nordic lands. Its previous owners saw the church purely in architectural terms. We see it as something far more powerful. Our purpose is the study of ancient Germanic culture, and very soon we'll have sixty archaeologists at work."

"Sixty?" Schweigaard said. "I'm hardly an expert, Herr Günther, but so many – surely even the biggest university couldn't pay for that many?"

Günther lit up with excitement.

"We're state funded. Our government agrees wholeheartedly that research into the history of the German people has been sorely neglected. We have plans for excavations from Spain to Tibet, but one of the first things we want to tackle is the re-interpretation of rock carvings in Norway and Sweden. Our organisation is not the least secretive. We're opening an office in Oslo, and our work will benefit Norway too. So, here's the thing: the reward that was promised in 1880 for the reunification of the church bells has accumulated substantial interest in the bank. We're very keen for the stave church to be complete, and we wish, quite simply, to *buy* Gunhild for two thousand kroner, despite her already being contractually ours. What good does it do for the two bells to hang separately, when our people are one?"

Schweigaard took a sip of coffee and carefully set down his cup.

A farm labourer's daily wage was ten kroner. Two thousand was more than enough to inspire treachery.

Metron, Temperantia

"One more thing," Günther said, sitting on the edge of his chair, eyes lighting up. "We wondered if there might be any drawings or other traces of the lost weave. Looking in the stave church's archive, I found an unpublished manuscript by a Norwegian by the name of Kveilen. It states that the Hekne Weave was woven in the Norse tradition. Drawings would allow it to be reinterpreted by specialist archaeologists."

"There are no such drawings that I know of," Schweigaard said.

Günther seemed a little deflated. "A pity. Posterity is plagued by too many tragic losses."

Schweigaard observed him, and pondered. He seemed like an intelligent man with an excellent memory. It was as though he had an internal archive in which he was constantly filing information under the correct categories.

"Ah well," Günther said, straightening up in his chair. "We still have the church bells. What do you say?"

Schweigaard turned his plate so the pattern was at right angles to him. "I can see some value in their being brought together. Quite so. I'm not familiar with the German legal system, but here in Norway there are limitation periods for breach of contract. The Sister Bells sank in December 1880. Many years have passed since then, and this artefact has become rather important to us here in Butangen. It's a last remnant of ancient times and beliefs, and a tangible object which is a reminder of great events. So, I'm sorry, Herr Günther. The church bell must remain here. Nor, I'm afraid, can I give you permission to see or photograph it. You see, I too have a legend to protect. A legend which may in turn protect *you*. It says that anyone who looks upon the bell who is not a descendant of the Hekne family – who bequeathed the bells to this village – will be struck down and taken by a sudden illness. I think, therefore, that it would be best we both appreciate the value of *yearning*, Herr Günther."

107

A Sketchbook Comes Home

"We mun go up there and take a look," Kristine said.

"Why?" said Astrid.

"Menfolk needs t' be seen when they works. Unlike us womenfolk."

Astrid flung on her coat and boots and went out to the stable. She put a harness on Raumann, attached the sledge to him, and she and her mother set off on the slope to the seters. It was the first working day after Easter and the blasting had been underway since midday. They had picked up speed now, and the spring wind rushed against their faces. Jon Mossen had been out with the snowplough that morning, and the whistling of the sledge's runners against the smooth-cut surface sounded like a violin.

They came up behind a couple on skis, pulling a sledge of firewood. It was barely half full, and Kristine told Astrid to bring down the pace.

"Slow down now," her mother said. "Past humbler folk in particular. Naybody shall say the Heknes ha' gotten too haughty."

"Nor have we," said Astrid.

"It doesna' take much for folks t' say it."

Fifteen minutes later they had passed the topmost farms in the village and were surrounded by more forest than fields. The Reo stood where the road ended. All along the riverbank there were huge piles of branches, from the gigantic conifers that had recently been felled. The smell of fresh resin mixed with the warm smell of horse manure.

They hitched Raumann to a post and continued on foot. Far down the cleared passage they could see that the men were in full swing, even though the evening was closing in. Farmworkers from Hilstad and Nordrum were throwing a chain around a tree trunk thicker than you could put your arms around. Further along, the two women came to a place where the snow was strewn with sharp-edged rocks the size of a fist and powdery grey gravel. A burnt, almost dusty smell hung on the air.

"Yer father blasted it through down here," a man told Astrid. "And up there too look."

He pointed up at the mountainside, to a pale gash in the rockface.

"Were a giant rock up there came loose. Fell right past where ye be now. Wonderous t' behold. Tall as a man. With pretty blue stripes. Ne'er seen the like. The ground shook, and the rock seemed t' teeter a moment before it tipped over and fell, almost bouncing as it went. It seemed like it stopped to glower at us, afore we heard it thunder on and smash through the ice," he said, pointing towards the valley floor.

Astrid looked over the edge. A trail of torn saplings marked the rock's journey, but it was impossible to see all the way down to the Breia.

They walked on. The ground got so steep they were forced to lean forward into the slope and grasp twigs so as not to slip back down. Giant Isum was up there with Svarten, his Døla horse. He was lifting the trunk of a massive spruce, and was about to load it onto his sledge when he spotted them. Shifting the timber to the crook of his arm, Isum touched his hat.

"Jehans be working further in."

He stood aside politely and let them pass, as though he'd forgotten he had a tree trunk in his arms. Astrid and Kristine gathered their skirts in their fists and trudged on. They reached the area yet to be cleared, and Kristine tripped and scraped her knee.

"Nay, I mun call it a day," she said. "Go on now, Astrid. I shall wander back and talk with the menfolk."

Astrid had to grab more branches and dig her feet firmly into the snow, so as not to slip. Further down she heard the Breia rumbling beneath the ice.

There, leaning on a crowbar just as Pastor Schweigaard leaned on his walking stick, stood her father. He was looking down at a very battered map, then lifted his head to assess the rough terrain before him. Astrid allowed herself a moment of pride. While others were loath to spoil their maps, her father challenged the contour lines and the mountains, sketching things in and erasing others. And she knew that the next time a map of Butangen was printed, it would bear his mark, and she managed, in some small way, to convey this to him.

"We just wanted to see how things be going," Astrid said.

"I guessed as much," Jehans said. "I shall be down after dark."

Back at Hekne they sensed trouble. Near the *stabbur* there were tyre marks from a car with snow chains, and the hallway smelled of coffee, even though Tarald never usually bothered to put the kettle on.

"There were folk here," Esther said. "A German man and Norwegian lady. They wanted to know about the Sister Bells and the weave."

"*They were here?*" Astrid said.

"In the house?" Kristine said. "When 'tis such an awful muddle!"

"A bald man and a lady with fair hair?" Astrid asked.

Esther laughed. "You'd better ask him about that," she said, pointing behind her, where Tarald was loafing towards them. "Although," Esther added, "whatever she looked like, she sounded pretty."

Tarald looked pleased with himself and worldly-wise.

"Aye," he said. "We had visitors. They brought us a gift."

He held out a grey sketchbook.

"Grandfather's!" Tarald said. "They found it in the archives of the Dresden Art Academy. Student works are usually the property of the school. But they reckoned it belonged with us here. With the family, as they said."

Tarald handed it to Astrid.

This must be his juvenile work. Random motifs, rather tentatively drawn. Streets and apartment buildings in Memel. Ships in dock. The house that had been his childhood home. A Labrador. And sandwiched in the middle of the sketchbook, a bunch of loose drawings. Here the line was firmer and more daring. Doubtless from his time in Dresden.

"And look at this," said Tarald, unfolding a sheet of paper.

Astrid had seen a few of her grandfather's drawings before, but none that showed how the stave church had actually looked in Butangen. He must have spent hours on it.

"It was fun hearing them talk," Esther said. "Did you know that more than twenty streets in Berlin and Kiel are named after Norwegian places or Norwegians? Lofotenweg, Nansenpfad, Björnsonstraße, and more?"

"But they got a surprise!" Tarald added, "when I could match that with a Keiser Wilhelm Gate in Bergen, a Kirkenes, Ålesund, Bodø and—"

"So what did they want? Really want?" interrupted Astrid. "They didna' come here without wanting sommat."

"It was so interesting," said Tarald. "He told me he's going to write a new visitors' guide about the church and the Sister Bells that gives Grandfather greater acknowledgement. And he's found a pile of drawings from the time when Grandfather toured Norway and drew all the stave churches. His plan was to make them into a folio book wi' fold-out plates, but it was never published. Now he wants to turn them into a beautiful big book. Together with some working sketches Grandfather made of a modern stave church!"

"Aye, very interesting," Kristine said. "But 'tis as Astrid says. What did they want *really*?"

"Ye have surely realised by now?" said Tarald. "They came to find out more about Grandfather and Grandmother."

"And?" Astrid said.

"Well, I showed them what we has," said Tarald.

Astrid tore open the door and sprang into the living room. In the middle of the floor was the wooden chest that held some of the objects that were most precious to her. The lid was open and everything was spilling out. Her grandmother's blue shawl was draped over the edge of the chest. Scattered over the floor were all her grandfather's maps and train tickets, rolled-up drawings and a small book with a brown cover. Meyer's *Sprachführer für Reise und Haus*. Astrid Hekne's tattered apron. Her heavy, woollen skirt.

"Did ye give them owt?" said Astrid. "Did they take owt?"

Tarald looked at her in astonishment. "Of course not."

"Why are ye so angry?" Esther said. "We only told them what Grandma Ingeborg and Grandpa Adolf told us."

"This was ours and ours alone," said Astrid.

"But Astrid," Tarald said, "it were just so the German might get a better insight."

"Strangers shouldna' go poking their noses into these things. Esther, couldn't ye have talked sense into him?"

"He didna' ask me."

"Aye, naturally. When have ye ever asked anyone for anything, Tarald? When have ye ever done anything but follow yer own fancies?"

"Pah. As if I'm the only one."

"Ye are nowt but a dolt, Tarald."

"Calm yerseln, Astrid," Kristine said. "'Tis enough now. They gave us the sketchbook at least."

The clock struck seven, and they heard Kai Schweigaard out

in the hallway. On his daily visit to lend them the national newspapers and take yesterday's back.

"Have they been here?" he muttered. "Here? They said – said they were planning to go home yesterday."

He went through to the living room, to find Astrid on her knees picking up clothes.

He was clearly shocked. Blindly he put the newspapers on the linen cupboard by the door. They knocked into a candlestick that fell to the floor without his noticing. He staggered further into the room, but seemed to lose the ability to walk. As though he was in one of those dreams where our steps grow impossibly leaden.

He came towards Astrid, but did not look at her, and she got up and backed away.

And now it was as though a stranger had entered the room. Or that somebody had been standing there in the shadows, all along, watching.

Her own grandmother.

Astrid wanted to get out, out into the fresh air, but she couldn't free herself, it was as though she heard the echo of a conversation in which her own name was spoken. The words *Schwesterglocken* and *Liebe* had been said here. Personal questions about Gerhard and Astrid, and about what had happened when she gave birth to her sons and sacrificed her own life, but Astrid sensed that the story that had been told was incomplete.

Kai Schweigaard stepped forward. He picked up Astrid's blue shawl. Clutching it close he turned his back on them.

For a long time, he stood like that.

When he finally turned round, he had folded the shawl neatly. He laid it carefully back in the chest. He didn't ask what the Germans had wanted. Just stood there bent-backed and said he was tired, no, nobody need accompany him, and seconds later he had left the house, faster than was polite, and

I Shallna' Be Content with Less

Astrid caught sight of him from the kitchen window as he walked past the heaped snow, a black winter bird, alone in the dark.

She understood now who the wedding ring in the bell tower was meant for.

The one, Astrid Hekne. Forever and always.

Adolf and Ingeborg had once told her that the pastor had been in love with her grandmother, but that had been when he was young, and she had assumed those feelings were long extinguished.

But the words *Eternally Yours* actually meant eternal faithfulness to Astrid Hekne.

She forgot the Germans. Overlooked Tarald's foolishness. Felt nothing but a wonderful tenderness for the old man. All his life, she thought, he has been in love with her, and he still is, more than fifty years after her death.

When I find a man myself, this is what I shall look for. This kind of devotion.

I shan't be satisfied with anything less.

The Law of Nature's Many Paragraphs

The shawl. That shawl.

She had worn it that day, here, at this time of year, when they had finally taken a *stroll*, and come down to this spot, where he stood now, in front of the new church. A shawl he brought home from the Birthing Institute in Kristiania with her coffin. When he was up at Hekne yesterday and held it to him, it felt as though he was drinking a truth serum from a chalice that would never empty, and afterwards he felt both aggrieved and deserving of punishment.

No. Life was never meant to be free of pain. But certain sorrows were strong enough to derail a person's life. He had gone all these years like a bird with torn wings, torturing himself for his failings, crippled as only those who grieve can be when they nurse the misapprehension that a person's death is made less painful the more one torments oneself. An old sorrow crowded in on him now, namely that he would die childless. Nobody would visit Butangen to enquire: "Who was Kai Schweigaard? Who was he *really*?"

He had bought a wedding ring. He had had it engraved. It had vanished that same winter, he had never known how. Flown away perhaps as chances flew away, like a wood pigeon winging through bare winter trees.

These old man thoughts!

This melancholy!

These intruders!

In the beginning he had thought Günther was just another Nordic dreamer of no real consequence. Earlier today he had finally remembered where he had seen his name. In his newspaper archive he found an article about the National Socialists in Germany. They had published a list of ideologically significant books. Hitler's *Mein Kampf* was top of the list. Günther's book about Norway was at number four.

Not only had Günther brought the winter of 1880 sharply to mind, but he had reminded him that his own time was running out. Death sat on the *stabbur* steps chewing tobacco, impossible to chivvy on, and he could picture Hans Friedrich Günther walking up to shake hands, sitting amicably down and giving Death a slap on the back. Yes, when this Schweigaard chap is out of the way, we'll overturn everything! The bell will come to Germany. And we'll find the Hekne Weave.

I Shallna' Be Content with Less

Schweigaard shook off these thoughts. Looking up at the new church, it struck him again how much he disliked it.

As unimpressive as a prairie church, this white timber building had been here in Butangen for fifty-five years now. The stave church had stood here for seven hundred. The new church was already showing the first signs of decay. The paint was flaking, the stains under the window frames were visible from afar, and lines of mould on its walls were unworthy of a House of God.

Again, he remembered their stroll in the spring of 1881. When the church had just been completed and she remarked how new everything smelled.

He let himself in.

Nobody could say it smelled *new* in here anymore. When it came to the church's furnishings, he was as frugal as a vulture was greedy, but now that he looked closely, he saw that the entire building was in a woeful state. Money had been allotted for repairs, and he and Røhme were meeting today to decide on the necessary improvements.

The church's decline had passed him by because he had never really rested his gaze on it, or anything in it. He had shut his eyes to the wear and tear, perhaps even welcomed it, for in moments of painful self-accusation, he saw that his distaste for the new church stemmed from his distaste at his own wrongdoing in 1880. The church was a memorial to his own failings. A white scream among the log buildings of Butangen. An edifice he had to enter at least once a week to fulfil his pastoral duties, and which the entire village connected with him.

No, these thoughts must let him go now! Each generation was blind to its own time. He had not been the only one to have a stave church demolished. It had happened throughout the country. This was the curse of Norway. A nation that built its masterpieces in wood, not stone, was doomed to lose its connection to the past. About thirty stave churches had been rescued, but he wondered what Norway would look like with a hundred.

But no good would come of brooding! Røhme would be here soon! It was agonising to go around thinking about his younger days, when one or other woman, all good women, showed an interest in him, women he never allowed to come close, over whose marriages to other men he officiated, before baptising their children a year later.

His footsteps echoed. How utterly bare the church was, how cold despite its comfortable temperature. It was built according to the ruling that a church must have enough space for a third of its parish, but this only led to services feeling poorly attended.

Yet, on reflection, the new church was not altogether powerless. Now and then he had a sense that there was something here. *Something*. Perhaps this was due to the feeling that the old stave church was not quite gone. Its foundation walls were under the floorboards. And they were made of rock, the material of eternity. He had no idea how the walls looked down there in the dark, reminiscent of an old crypt no doubt, he remembered the rocks had been beautifully hewn. When the new church was erected, the work team had left the foundation walls of the stave church in place and built the new concrete wall outside it, simply because it saved time and money, an argument Schweigaard always favoured.

He stopped in the aisle and rocked up and down on the floorboards. The underfloor beams spanned a fair distance and some might be rotten, something that often worried him at the funerals of his more obese parishioners.

But the floor was firm in certain places, marking out where the beams rested secure on the ancient foundation walls, and, as he walked around the church, he felt the presence of the solid cross-shaped structure of the old stave church itself, as though the old church was buried under the church floor.

There was an area near the altar where he had on occasion felt a peculiar power. Something under the floorboard there seemed to exude a vitality. It reminded him of the feeling he had experienced when he put on the chasuble with the Hekne Weave concealed in its lining. Now, as his own end drew closer with each day, he felt the connection between himself and the Hekne sisters grow stronger.

Was it really important how they had died?

Yes. It was pivotal. If the girls had in fact been arrested and burned, it was untrue, the legend that Gunhild had seen into the underworld after her sister's death. Nor could they have woven the prediction of how the last priest in Butangen would depart from this life.

The sun shone in on a slant from the high windows, forming channels of restless dust particles. Visible in the light, invisible in the shadow. But impossible to catch in your hands in either place. Just as the knowledge he now sought.

It was here, before the altar, that Pastor Krafft had stood. Right here. In the old church, but *here*.

Schweigaard went down on his knees. Sought connection with the ancient walls of the stave church beneath him. Looked up at the crucifix by the pulpit. It was here that he occasionally felt as though someone summoned him. Filled him with strength. Called out a wish to him.

"Herr Pastor?"

Schweigaard jumped. It was Røhme.

He was standing by the hymn books. He waited for the pastor to calm himself, and then went over to him.

He held out an open notepad. "'T-tis all here, Herr P-pastor."

Hmm, thought Schweigaard. Surely Røhme didn't stutter these days?

The Law of Nature's Many Paragraphs

Ah! The list of *urgent repairs* covered a whole page. The nails that held the roof slates in place had rusted away. The sacristy windows were about to fall out. The south-west wall was sagging, presumably because it had been built on top of excavated graves.

"We needs skilled carpenters, and for a while," said Røhme. "Borgedal the Younger's son runs a good team."

This was going to be costly. Then Herr Røhme pointed out that the next page in his notebook was equally full. Documentary evidence of Kai Schweigaard's violations of the law of nature's numerous paragraphs. The punishment for decades of sins of omission.

Schweigaard could only nod. He did not have the will to check whether the sacristy windows could be reputtied, or whether they should replace only the worst gutters or all of them. And he had no wish to know the difference in cost between two or three coats of floor paint.

"Will it take long?" he said.

"I reckons on at least three weeks, Herr Pastor."

"So are we saying, Herr Røhme, that we'll have to close the church for three whole weeks?"

"Aye. Happen Herr Pastor may take a holiday with so much fettlin' adoing."

Schweigaard hesitated. Time, he realised, was running out for a final *fettling* of his own life's path. One last attempt to find out the truth about the Hekne sisters. One last attempt before it was too late. Because the day it was too late would also be the day he would find out if the sisters' prediction was true.

Evil Earth, Evil Rock, Evil Cross

Schweigaard arrived at the state archives in Hamar on a Monday morning, cutting a slightly stiff but imposing and elegant figure, equipped with a new notebook and magnifying glass. Standing at the front desk, he banged his walking stick into the floor and announced his purpose, namely to study any papers pertaining to life in Gudbrandsdal in the first half of the 1600s.

"In particular," Schweigaard said, "I'm looking for records relating to a certain Pastor Sigvard C. Krafft."

The archivist returned full of apologies. The problem was, he said, that Hamar, of which Butangen was a part, had not been a separate diocese for some while after the Reformation. But the archive had, over the years, received the occasional item connected to church life in the district. In fact, some letters and other loose papers had recently been found during the demolition of a parsonage in Vang. They had been used as loft insulation. They were still in the shoeboxes in which the demolition crew had put them, and not yet accessible to the public. It would be some time before they were sorted. Fru Martinsen was the archivist responsible, but she was expecting and would be off duty until after the birth.

Low on the ladder of importance, thought Schweigaard. Letters used as insulation, his errand, Fru Martinsen.

Well, he had three weeks free now and said he wanted to see whatever they had. Perhaps Pastor Krafft was mentioned in another source?

One moth-eaten document after another was placed on his desk. County accounts. Court judgements. A visitors' book from Fron.

The curiosity of his student days was reawakened. Were it

Evil Earth, Evil Rock, Evil Cross

not for his arthritis and occasional double vision, he might have been sitting in the reading room of his youth. He was adept at navigating index files and bookshelves, and for the next few days he tested the archivists to their limits, while he was driven mad by the coughs and whispers of other visitors, many of whom were clearly seeking an outlet for their obsessions. Among them a man from Trondheim, who believed he was descended from King Sverre. A lonely soul, he had an insatiable need to talk. One morning, when Schweigaard failed to avoid him on the stairs, he thrashed about with jokes about how a sex drive was nothing when you encountered the wonders of tracing your family tree.

Schweigaard did let him in on what he was doing. Through stiff, yellowed pages of Gothic script he looked into a time of frosts and drudgery, of bands of child beggars, of disease and hunger, hard liquor and fornication, cruel taxes and a chasm between rich and poor. Not to mention the bestial, untrammelled use of power, in which priests were used as experts by the judiciary system, comprising bailiffs, magistrates and "mastermen". A startling word for an executioner, whose wages he found listed.

For one hanging: 10 riksdaler.
For removal from the gallows: 4 riksdaler.
For each hand or finger to be cut off: 4 riksdaler.
To break limbs on the wheel: 14 riksdaler.
To burn a criminal or witch at the stake: 10 riksdaler.

At first this period in history seemed hazy and unclear. But then it was as though somebody lit a match and gave him a better view into the Hekne sisters' world. At the start of the seventeenth century, forty to fifty Norwegians were executed each year. Adjusted for present population figures, this would mean one person being executed per day, including Saturdays

I Shallna' Be Content with Less

and Sundays. Schweigaard could almost hear the screams rise from the pages. Criminals were tied to cartwheels and the executioner would, in full view of the crowd, spend many hours breaking every bone in the prisoner's body while ensuring they stayed alive. A mild death sentence consisted of being permitted to die quickly. Severed heads were rolled downhill, and families had to run and retrieve them, before handing them over to be raised on stakes. Horse theft was punishable by death, because a horse was a farm's most important asset. But the worst crime of all was *witchcraft*.

In one court ledger for 1619 he read that the executioner had returned home from Fron, a village near Butangen, with forty-five riksdaler in his pocket. He had burned three girls alive and was paid fifteen daler per head, because his journey had been so long. In just a few hours, Schweigaard totted up forty women who had been burned at the stake in the county of Oppland during the seventeenth century.

Most around 1620.

Within the Hekne sisters' lifetime. How were *they* seen in a time when anything that deviated from the norm was suspect? These girls, with a weave that was said to show the future?

He forced himself to sit still and allow it to rise in his imagination.

To die in flames.

To be burned alive. To have the body's largest sensory organ – the skin – burn, until death came as a release.

An accounts book showed that the pyre had been colossal. Twelve cords of wood in all. The purpose of the flames was to purify the soul, which the accused had sold to the Devil, so that they would avoid ending up in hell.

There it was again.

Astrid's question in her confirmation class: "Does the soul grow old?"

Could it really be cleansed, the soul? He remembered Oldfrue Bressum, his former housekeeper, who had asked him, just before she died, to open the window to allow her soul to escape. And he recalled those freakish moments when she seemed to wake up again and said she had seen into the hereafter.

Had he failed to find the Hekne sisters' grave because they didn't have one? Because they were burned at the stake?

He imagined the smell. Started to hear crackling flames. The screams from a drawn-out execution that tortured the body in front of a jeering crowd. He saw the Hekne sisters. More and more clearly.

And.

He was in the crowd now.

He watched them being brought forward. Hair cut short. Forcibly tied to a ladder that lay on the ground. Left to lie there so they could feel the heat from the pyre as it burned bigger and bigger, and, when it was big enough, the executioner's men stepped forward and took hold of the ladder. Using ropes and wooden posts they stood it upright. A wild commotion in the crowd as the sisters screamed and tore at the ropes, before the men pushed the ladder off balance. Slowly the sisters sank face down into the raging fire, and for a moment their bodies dampened the flames and the air filled with smoke. Still the girls managed to scream, until finally the fire flared back up and began to crackle and hiss. The odour of scorched skin was borne on the air to the spectators before it changed to the stench of burnt flesh. Still momentarily recognisable as human beings, the girls' bodies twitched, before vanishing in a sudden blast of heat. The crowd moved back. The screams in the fire had been silenced, but not those of the crowd, whose cries were soon drowned out by the crackling of flames. And the smoke was followed by steam as the sisters' entrails boiled, and what was now taking place behind the curtain of heat was broadcast by smell rather than sight, until the pyre was just a fire, and the evil spirits were gone, if the Devil himself did not step forward to—

Schweigaard? Herr Schweigaard?

A woman's voice.

Get help!

What's the matter with him?

I don't know. *Herr Schweigaard!*

His vision cleared. The walls looked so strange. The lamps. Surely they couldn't hang right out from the cables? Was he lying on the floor?

Three faces over him.

"I – my head. My head hurts."

"You must have had some sort of attack. We tried to bring you round."

"Oh."

"Maybe that's enough studying for today?"

"Possibly."

A woman followed him out. There was talk of hailing a taxi-cab. He felt nauseous and faint, his vision flickered, and only when he was out in the fresh air did he realise she was there.

"Is that – are you Fru Martinsen?"

Hesitantly, she confirmed that she was.

"The letters from Hamar," he murmured. "I've been looking for thirty years – his name is Krafft. Sigvard Krafft. A pastor like me. Vang parsonage. The letters in the loft. God bless you, Fru Martinsen."

He stayed in the guesthouse all that weekend. From the street he heard the honk of modern motorcars. But then again, what was *modern*? Were motorcars not merely proof of the diversity of the realm of human ideas? Ideas on the shoulders of ideas, which ultimately produced such a powerful device as the internal combustion engine, which was dependent on the refining of oil from the depths of the earth, which was in turn formed by fossilised organisms, dead hundreds of thousands of years ago? If anyone had claimed this possible in the year 1600, they would have been denounced as heretics. So, it was no wonder that ideas might run the other way, into the maelstrom of the human mind, where they were transformed into fear.

He went over to the window and looked out. You should have been here, Krafft, my brother in arms. I'd have liked to give you a tour. After which you could have taken me back to *your* time. Doubtless I'd have been the more surprised.

Sitting in the State Archives and reading the court records, he had been repeatedly amazed to see that enlightened citizens believed in bewitched cats and magic potions. He had seen judges, just weeks after sending someone to the stake, deliver wise and sympathetic judgements. How had they managed to negotiate a world where such obvious falsehoods were allowed to exist side by side with the truth?

Well, that reawakened the big question of his student days. What is truth?

Kai Schweigaard went to Kafé Ramseth. He ordered the roast veal. It was reasonably tender, but nowhere near as good as Fru Røhme's, and outrageously expensive. He had chosen this eatery primarily to avoid being seen by Bishop Hille. Outside the misted windows, the people of Hamar passed by, busy with their lives. They were all probably thinking, just as he did, what *modern* times we live in. Goodness, how avant-garde we are, look how bravely we lead the way.

But the only thing they could be sure of was, of course, that not everything had been discovered yet. In which case he too was probably lost in delusion without knowing it. Three hundred years from now, somebody could sit right here, gazing out over the city of Hamar, imagining his era, and say: "How on earth could you believe *that*?" Just as beliefs and superstitions, truth and falsehood, existed side by side and constituted reality back then, so truth and falsehood must exist side by side today.

Except that from here he could not see which was the falsehood and which the truth.

He ordered a coffee. He drank it in the old-man method he had adopted to avoid burning his lips: pour a little coffee into the saucer, let it cool, then slurp it through a sugar cube.

Lunch guests came and went without his even noticing.

What if there was a super truth, a greater logic, that was real but undiscovered? That was invisible to the eyes of the present, but that the people of earlier times had been able to understand? Perhaps there were forces that could destroy logic and disturb natural laws. Newton's Third Law said that every event had a cause, and every force had a counterforce. Which meant there must also be counterforces to causes. So that every cause had an *anti-cause*. A force that acted at random, with the intention of creating a disorder that gave impetus to the development of . . . well, everything. The origin of the planets, for example. If everything had been in law-abiding harmony, the earth would surely never have come into being, much less develop. Everything would stand still without an anti-cause, a logical-mathematical demon whose purpose was to create the coincidences of which human life was a result.

For if everything followed a plan, what plan preceded the plan?

On Monday he was back in the State Archives, and again he may have made a little too much of his arrival. He strode through the corridor like an old bronze monument, a little hard of hearing and slow, and a clerk who had, on his first visit, been so generous in explaining the principles of modern cataloguing, let him know that his generosity was wearing thin, since no principle of cataloguing was of use when there was nothing to catalogue.

"But what about Fru Martinsen?" Schweigaard asked. "Is she here?"

The clerk shook his head. Fru Martinsen had only been in by chance on Friday to pick up a forgotten umbrella.

Schweigaard stood, leaning on his walking stick. Was this it? Was this where it ended?

He was about to put on his hat, when he felt a *no* some place. Something told him that this was not it.

He heard a voice from within the building say "Martinsen?" and a young man in a black waistcoat and modern trousers came out from behind a screen.

"Fru Martinsen came back," he said, "after helping you to your cab. She spent the whole evening in the archives. Last night she gave birth to a healthy girl."

Then he placed a water-damaged folder on the counter, sewn together down the spine with coarse thread. On the cover was written: *Loose Addenda: Butangen 1613–1658*. Alongside it, a small box that contained envelopes speckled with black mould, and a Latin pamphlet entitled *Monstrificus Puer*: The Monstrous Child.

"Pastor Schweigaard," said the archivist, "in light of Friday's bad turn you can sit by the window. I'll set it ajar."

But Schweigaard had already started reading.

Eighteenth Day of March, Anno Domini 1620. Rebuke of Pastor Krafft

Pastor Krafft is hereby Punished and Admonished, after a Scholar was called to investigate the Warning of the Apocalypse, at the terrible Event when a Monstrum was born in the Village of Butangen. I offered him a Call in Nordland.

I Shallna' Be Content with Less

Third Day of September, Anno Christi 1626. Dismissal of Pastor Krafft

I have sought Krafft's dismissal. He sais he hath buried in the Church's Ground the two Shameful Women, whom he had previously helped, against the Bailiff's Request. By this melded-together Creature, God and Church are gravely insulted, and I am afeared whether I can enumerate their Transgressions and Gross Sins. The two women are sayd to have chanted incantations to the Devil before they died, and with their known Signeri and Maleficium they bespoiled the Churchyard Soil and the Cross itself. They had a vile and terrible Verse, with which they dishonoured our Omnipotent God, which Verse reads Evil Earth, Evil Rock, Evil Cross. It was ordered by myselfe that the women's corpses be taken and Burned till nought be left. Pastor Krafft was afterwards founde to be a Liar, for he pointed to a Grave, and it was Opened, but there was Nought within but the Bones of a Cow. When the Bishop soon afterwards examined Pastor Krafft, he confessed that he had taken a weave out of and into the church.

Twenty-Seventh Day of March, Anno Domini 1627. New Search for Pastor Krafft

For two days the Bailiff and other men were out searching for Pastor Krafft and his Wiffe, but they were no where to be found. Krafft's Farm is in sound Condition. It is believed that he has a secret Hiding Place in the Mountains or in some Seter. Some believe that he received warning of our coming, for on the same day that we came to the Village, the new Church Bells rang loudly, having begun long before we arrived. The good people of the village seemed most distraught. Some weeks *later, Pastor Krafft was searched for once again. This time we hoped to come upon him unexpectedly in the Mountains, but again he was no where to be found. The same Bells began to ring as we descended. It is of the utmost importance now that we find a new Pastor for this Holy Diocese.*

Twenty-Third Day of October, Anno Christi 1628

The new Pastor, Herr Fridthun, was despondent and left after a few weeks in Butangen, in which Village he was greatly abused by the Populace. A Tax Collector from the village of Fodevang advised we undertake a Search beneathe the Church Floor, where the highest borne Folk are buried. This was done, but the Monstrums, that is the Sisters, were not found in any of the Coffins that were there. The foule Verse Evil Earth, Evil Rock, Evil Cross was sung by a Possessed Woman who threw Stones at the Bailiff.

Another sleepless night in the guesthouse.

So Krafft had not been sent north in 1620, as Schweigaard had previously read. He had, much like himself, clung on in Butangen.

All of this had taken place at a time when Martin Luther's influence was at its height. Schweigaard remembered how he and his fellow students had been particularly shocked by what Luther had written about these so-called *monstra*. Two creatures had, he said, been sent to Earth to warn against the wrongdoings of the Catholic Church. One was a child with the head of a calf and its body covered in lizard scales. The other was a donkey that looked like a human being. Both were clearly born with deformities, but Luther claimed that any birth of a *monstrum* was a sign from God. When the students reached *Tischreden* 5207 they discovered Luther's proclamation that all crippled children were *massa carnis* – flesh without soul – and should be drowned.

The teacher brushed it off, noting that Luther had a fondness for impossible paradoxes, that much beer was served at table back then, and that Luther's *Table Talks* were transcribed by other men. But Schweigaard recalled how a fellow student, until then deeply religious, grew terribly angry on reading the *Tischreden*. His own brother was a hunchback, and he was increasingly convinced that Luther's teachings had caused a shift in how deformed people were viewed. Before the Reformation they had been met with curiosity, afterwards with suspicion and hate. Furthermore, this young theology student discovered that anomalies in intellect were also met with mistrust, for in the 1500s church scholars called a gifted child a *prodigium* – an omen of disaster.

In the State Archives Schweigaard read the pamphlet in the shoebox closely. It showed that the bishop had sought advice about the twin sisters in Butangen. It listed examples of the births and the fates of abnormal children from all over Europe. Between accounts of women who gave birth to fish, children who walked on all fours or had cloven hooves, Schweigaard discovered which *monstrum* was the most feared: conjoined twins. A double *monstrum*.

A warning of the Apocalypse. A clear sign that doomsday was approaching. For this was the greatest paradox of all. Two souls or one? A bridge between the human and the divine?

Was it *here* that the link with the Night of the Scourge lay? Had the sisters created a depiction of the End Times, in the form of the Hekne Weave, as a kind of response to these suspicions? Or did they actually know how the Day of Judgement would unfold because they themselves were its harbingers?

The archive was taking him ever deeper.

Not until 1628 was a new pastor installed in Butangen. So it was Krafft who must have determined that the Hekne Weave should continue to hang in the church. Whatever the case, the girls had not been burned at the stake. Krafft had protected them. But then, soon after their deaths, the bishop's and bailiff's men had returned to Butangen, intent upon opening their graves and burning their bodies. But why had they not found them when they looked under the church floor?

And why this terrible spell? *Evil earth, evil rock, evil cross?*

It made no sense that they were evil. A pair of church bells had been cast in their name!

Sitting up in his bed, he thought of the story of the Night of the Scourge. In it, Christian beliefs and folklore came together, to create something amazingly congruent with the Book of Revelations. *And I saw a new Heaven and a new Earth: for the first Heaven and the first Earth were passed away; and the Sea was no more.* Not before the final judgement would the world be created anew, and nor would the dead go immediately to heaven. Their fate would not be decided before the very last day. Until then, they would lie in their graves, facing the dawn in the east, while they awaited Judgement Day. And, on the Night of the Scourge, according to Butangen belief, the earth would be scoured to bare rock and the dead go to their judgement at sunrise.

He fell back onto his pillow and slept.

In the middle of the night he woke in a sweat, still fully clothed, and with the ceiling light on. He padded over to the chamber pot, brushed his teeth, got undressed and went back to bed.

It happened now and then, as he lay like this, that he thought of Widow Stueflaaten. Her touch, her mild voice, her wisdom. He drifted on the cusp of sleep, in the no man's land where sight and hearing were inactive, but other senses became receptive, senses without name that filled him with thoughts and visions, visions that were absolutely sovereign and real, with which neither dreams nor the conscious mind could ever compete.

I Shallna' Be Content with Less

Evil earth. Evil rock.

Memories of the Stueflaaten farm in Dovre floated before him. A voice from the past seemed to move outside in the night, shouting: *You're mistaken! Listen more closely!*

Ond. Onde. Onder. Under.

Kai Schweigaard sat up. The dialect! It was different in North Gudbrandsdal, where the sisters had completed their apprenticeship. There, the word *under* – or beneath – was pronounced *onde* – meaning evil.

Was the sisters' verse actually a song of praise? A prayer of thanksgiving for God's protection? In which they looked forward to the day they would rest peacefully *Under earth. Under rock. Under cross.*

His mind rushed back to when the stave church was demolished. They had only cleared the ground under the old church floor with a rake.

They had never scraped the earth down to bare rock.

A Stave Church of Stone

Borgedal's team had left for the day. Their materials lay in tarpaulin-covered heaps outside the church. Five windows had been taken out, and the rotten frames had been spliced with fresh timber. Spring had set in, but in many places the snow was prevented from melting by heaps of dark yellow sawdust. The carpenters had acquired a new invention, a gigantic electric saw. Its loud whining could be heard over the whole village, but it could cut at any angle without splintering the wood.

Astrid wondered why Schweigaard had asked her to meet

him here. Close into the church wall, she saw the gravestone. The one she had found it increasingly hard to look at, because it told her she was dead. Now, while waiting for Schweigaard to meet her, it was as though she could no longer excuse herself.

She stepped towards it. A black, neatly chiselled rock, surrounded by grey grass and sunken snow. In gold leaf her name:

ASTRID HEKNE
1860–1881

She felt an expectant silence between herself and the stone, something unsaid that should be nonetheless challenged, something that seemed to harden if she stepped too close.

A mass of snow slid from the church roof.

She heard hurried footsteps behind her.

"Why are ye wearing yer cassock?" Astrid said.

"Because we must break a . . . sacred peace."

Schweigaard rushed past her, already holding the key in his hand, and then they were inside the church. The wind blew in through the empty window frames, the pews stood stacked against the wall, the skirting boards were unattached. Tools and materials lay in small groups, revealing each carpenter's task.

In the midst of all this. Bursting with energy. *Him*. Kai. Pacing about and staring at the floorboards.

"Thank goodness!" he said. "Borgedal's crew haven't been down there!"

"I think it's time to explain why ye sent for me!"

He told her what he had discovered in Hamar. Told her about the verse *Under earth, under rock, under cross*.

"It must mean that it's *here* somewhere," he said, banging the floor with his walking stick so that sawdust danced about their shoes. "Down in the old stave church. I mean, within its foundation walls. The stone walls are still there."

I Shallna' Be Content with Less

"I reckons Herr Pastor has bumped his head. He mun go straight home to bed."

Schweigaard stretched out his arms so that his robes flapped about him.

"I'm assuming that the churchwarden, or even the pastor himself, crouched down and dug a grave for them. Right down to the bare rock, and that they lowered the Hekne sisters' coffin there. All the other coffins were arranged on *top* of the dirt floor, and so the bishop's men couldn't find it. And neither did I. When the old stave church was taken down we examined the postholes, and walked about carefully, collecting coins and amulets. But we only ever examined the top layer of the earth."

"Tell me, what are ye after? What d'ye want?"

"To find out if their coffin is down there."

"Aye, and what difference will that make?"

"Certainty," said Kai Schweigaard. "We'll finally know what's true and what's untrue in the legend. If their bodies were burned, it can't be them with whom I feel . . . this strange connection when I'm in the church. And you, Astrid, are the only one left to pass the story on. You need to *know*."

Schweigaard hurried back down the aisle and locked the doors.

Astrid wandered further in. A few lengths of timber were propped against the pulpit. There were wood shavings in the font.

"I'm not sure I can do this," she said. "Happen ye should ask Røhme?"

"It was *you* who asked about the soul, Astrid. About whether it ages. You're the only one who understands. Besides, my knees aren't what they used to be."

She looked down at the scuffed church floor.

"It canna' be more than crawling height down there. Heck if I'm going to start digging up dead folks!"

"We just need to find the coffin."

"It's been three hundred years, Kai! They must have rotted away, even if it's dry down there! I'm just an ordinary girl who serves folk up at the Colonial."

"You went up into the bell tower, Astrid. You're not like everyone else. You've never been like anyone else."

In the sacristy they eased a heavy cupboard aside and a trapdoor came into view.

"What you will see down there are the remains of a cross-shaped wall. Built sometime before 1170."

Astrid tugged at the iron ring on the trapdoor. She was hit by a blast of cold air. And the smell of earth. A rotten ladder led down into the darkness.

Kai handed her an old barn lamp with broken glass, and she leaned over the opening to look. The lamp swung back and forth so that things came and went from view. Long, hanging spiderwebs encased with hoarfrost. Beams overgrown with mould. A flat, dirt floor, the tracks of a rake. And further in, dry walls of large, rough-hewn rocks.

Astrid remembered that moment in the belfry. And the same sense of expectation entered her now. She lay down on her stomach, swung the lamp wider to get a better view, weighed up the fors and againsts, felt the Hekne Way shout its usual *for*!

She caught sight of something moving in one corner. A mouse darted away.

Then she climbed down into the cold.

Crouching low, she guided the light beam around her. The ground had thawed and it was like standing on a newly sown, parched field, fenced in by huge, frosty rocks, neatly hewn and tightly fitted.

She noticed a disturbance in the opening above. Kai Schweigaard was coming down the ladder. She saw his cassock; it risked getting torn.

"Careful not to get yer robe caught," she said. "I shan't be able to pull thee out of here if ye pass out on me."

"I'm not going to die here," Kai said. "That much I know."

Their voices sounded strange between the granite walls and dirt floor, as though hushed by the stave church darkness. Hunched over, they stumbled on, the pastor first, Astrid following after. He was visible and invisible by turns, in accordance with the fall of light.

He led the way with stories from a half-century ago, when they had dismantled the old stave church. The deep holes in the floor, he told her, were the remains of the old postholes. In them, under the old church pillars, they had found golden amulets with pictures of Norse gods. She lifted the lantern and was surprised at how easily she could imagine the rows of pillars.

"The font stood here," he said. "The altar there, where you see the cross in the old foundation wall. I think the pulpit was there. Yes. That was it. That's where I used to stand in those days."

He continued pointing out invisible fixtures, as though the stave church had been down here in the cellar. His voice shifted intermittently, as though he was moving back and forth between the old and new church. For her this was just a spooky crypt where old sins had eternal life. He pointed out the place where Klara Mytting had frozen to death in 1880 during the New Year Mass. The place in which Astrid's grandmother had sat when he announced that the old church was to be pulled down.

This wretched man really must find peace soon, Astrid thought. If he were flogged and then burned at the stake, the remains of his devotion would be left scrabbling in the ashes. A devotion that whispered the name *Astrid*.

He took the barn lamp and directed it towards the foot of the ladder. A trowel.

She said they couldn't just dig around aimlessly. Not down here. It was impossible and would take weeks.

He must have felt it too. That it was an impossible task.

He brushed the dirt from his cassock and sat on a spindle chair, feeling old and defeated. The trapdoor was still open. Never had a black square looked blacker.

She blew out the barn lamp, releasing the odour of paraffin and scorched wick. Neither of them made a move to leave.

"The coffins that ye found down there," Astrid said, nodding towards the trapdoor. "Were they just spotted around in no clear order?"

"A few, yes. But most seemed purposely placed. Along the foundation wall. And there were commemorative plaques on the walls of the nave above. A kind of headstone if you will. Placed directly over their respective coffins under the floor."

Astrid stood up. Wandered out of the sacristy and into the nave. She tried to picture the stave church in her mind's eye.

It would take chain-brothers to reunite the Sister Bells. So, what would it take to find a sister-grave?

When she returned, Kai had taken out his pipe. The draught from the open trapdoor drew the grey, aromatic smoke to it, where it folded itself in nature defying curls that were swallowed in the cavernous darkness below. As if the smoke sought the mystery there in the stave church's cellar, or the mystery itself tried to tell her it was smoke-like in form.

"So, where did it hang?" Astrid said. "The Hekne Weave?"

"On the wall to the left," said Kai Schweigaard. "They could see it from the pews, so it must have been at an angle to the cross. Let me think now – is that where we found the chest with the pillows? It was certainly in a corner."

They sat in silence. He took a match and relit his pipe, but said nothing.

I Shallna' Be Content with Less

She reached for the lantern to light it, but changed her mind. "Matches. Pass the matches. And close the trapdoor after me."

She was in Esther's world. A darkness of vision but not the senses. A darkness that was not an absence of light. A darkness filled with intuition. Intuition about what was around her.

She sat and listened. Thought she heard little creaks from the past. Crawled forward and searched with her hands until they touched some cold, sharp-edged rocks. It was eight hundred years since they had been laid here, but eight hundred years is nothing to a rock.

Astrid searched on. She stood on her knees and touched the wall with both palms. As though praying to a deity or trying to feel its shape. The rocks seemed now to give off a more intense cold.

A nameless sense came to her. A sense that fluttered and whispered, a sense that vanished in light, but was present here and now. In a stone church with an earth floor. A sense without name made itself known.

The absence of light dissolved all notion of height and depth. Schweigaard had told her there had been a pagan altar here before the stave church. She felt as though prayers from ancient times were floating around her.

Astrid groped onwards, following the wall that outlined the cruciform shape of the old stave church, until she eventually reached the place in the cross where a nail would have been driven into Christ's right hand, had she been crawling on an actual crucifix.

Feeling her way forward again she reached the point in the foundation wall that marked the centre of the cruciform. The nave. She lit a match and looked around. In the moment before the flame singed her fingers, she realised she had come to the right place.

This was the spot where the Hekne Weave must have hung

near the altar above her head. The sisters' memorial, which Schweigaard had likened to a headstone – such an inappropriate word for a thing made of wool.

She knelt down and lit the lantern. Then with the trowel she started to dig. The earth proved shallow, and she soon heard the clank of iron against stone. The perishable versus eternity.

Astrid moved the lantern closer.

She had uncovered a layer of stones, remarkably even in size. They looked like the smoothed rocks that appeared on the bed of the Breia when the water was low.

Astrid began lifting them aside, one at a time. There was barely any paraffin left in the lamp and the flame began to flicker and fade. The weight of the stones in her hands and their clinking sound guided her work. The lantern went out. Carefully she went on moving more stones to the side. Then came a strange, creaking sound, warning Astrid to be careful.

She reached down.

And felt – some kind of cloth? Lightly she ran her fingers across it and suddenly pricked herself.

A thorn?

Now she touched something thin and hard.

Bones. The bones of a hand. Of two hands.

Three hands.

Four.

No Electric Light at Such Time

Kai Schweigaard was unable to sleep again that night. His cassock hung to air by an open window, but the wind was blowing

I Shallna' Be Content with Less

from the wrong direction and the smell of earth and the church swept over him in uneven blasts that kept waking him.

Pastor Krafft had buried the Hekne sisters following the most ancient of customs. Not in a coffin, but in among rocks. Stones from the bed of the Breia, which flowed tirelessly down from the mountain and smoothed everything in its path. The river from which he could now hear the roar of the spring flood.

Had there been a purpose in burying the sisters in this way? Did Krafft know that corpses are preserved when they lie cool and dry, with air flowing around them? Or had he been struck by doubt, making him leave the dead recognisable, even to the bailiff and magistrate?

Schweigaard got up and looked out the window. Far below, Lake Løsnes stretched itself out in the moonlight, and the mountains stood just as they had stood in the Hekne sisters' lifetime. And now, patient and all-wise, their dead bodies rested beneath him whenever he stood in the pulpit and defended God's teachings despite his doubts.

He lit an oil lamp. The flame flickered with his movements as he crossed the landing to his study and took out the wooden chest.

Then he rolled out the Hekne Weave.

It glimmered in the lamplight now. As if gossamer-thin silver threads had been spun into the yarn.

Astrid had appeared through the trapdoor, grey-faced, wild-eyed, hair matted with earth, barely recognisable, like a creature that the old believers in folklore would expect to find hiding in a crypt.

They had both clambered down and everything was done by the light of matches. Just one box. Purposely so. In a stone crib he saw them. The skin on their fingers like yellowed paper. One sister had a bouquet of thistles in her hands. The other another

No Electric Light at Such Time

plant. They appeared to have had mittens on their hands, mittens that had almost crumbled away.

The rest of them was covered. With a threadbare woollen cloth embroidered with large crosses.

The match went out.

Astrid said nothing. Did nothing.

He felt his way over and lifted aside the cloth.

A rasping against a matchbox. A flash of phosphorus.

In the glow of the lighted aspen stick he saw that their skin, hair, teeth and nails were preserved. Two tarnished silver rings lay loosely on the papery skin around their knuckles.

Unable to help himself, he moved the match upwards. In the sheerest of eternities, they looked at each other, he and the Hekne sisters, until the flame burned him and told him he had *nay more time given thee*.

Seeds from the bouquets were strewn around. They tried not to disturb the grave further. They folded the blanket back over, gently replaced the stones and smoothed out the grave, and when they emerged from the church it was as dark outside as inside the crypt. Unable to speak, Astrid ran straight home to Hekne.

And here he stood before the Hekne Weave, searching for the key to this event. Some meaning that was to be found out there in the Butangen dark, the same darkness as in the Hekne sisters' lifetime, in this place where he now lived.

In his younger years Schweigaard had dismissed the idea that the Hekne Weave could predict the future. With age he had opened up to the possibility that it was able to warn of things, but only because it was so old that the events it depicted were bound to repeat themselves sooner or later.

He smoothed the threadbare corner that showed how he would die. It was impossible that this was a recurring event. So how had the sisters been able to see *him*? What might he have sent ahead of him through the weaves of time, before his birth?

A gust of wind blew in from the night and made the lamp flicker and his cassock flap.

Was he in touch with that sheerest of all weaves? The weave that is finer than spiderwebs visible in rain-wet sunrises, woven from the threads of fate?

He recalled what the old midwife had told him. That the sisters' weaves fell apart once they had done what they were meant to do.

Not foreseen, but *done*. This was markedly different.

Perhaps he had been mistaken for more than fifty years. In imagining that the weave predicted events, he had been thinking like a man of his time. From what he had read about the witches' trials in Hamar, he realised now that the world of sixteenth-century thought was different.

They had believed the weave *created* events.

He took a step back.

Which opened up another possibility.

That the Hekne Weave had created Kai Schweigaard.

Time Is Running Out

That morning she walked along the edge of Hekne's topmost field and to the first of the leafy forests, where she leaned against a silver birch, and stood for a long while tearing off little pieces of the bark and shredding them between her fingers.

Four eyes without eyes. Tiny, dry hands. Mouths without lips.

At peace as though they were sleeping. As though she could have woken them had she wanted.

Astrid walked on. The hillside flattened out, and soon she could see Daukulpen, where the fish were impossible to catch. There was rarely anybody here. So green and so flat with the willow thicket around the stream, and the secret black forest pool that mirrored the mountains. A large flat rock lay in the middle of the clearing. As though put there with purpose. On a hot summer's day, this rock would retain the sun's warmth until dark, but she was here early now, and it would retain the night's chill for as long as it would remain warm later.

She sat down upon it.

Let me escape them. These memories. Those from yesterday, and those that are older. Those that are mine, and those that I cannot be certain are mine.

An anxiety had wormed its way into her. Something that invaded everything she thought. A difficulty in accepting the coincidental. That the visible was the only reality. To say that a thing was thus and only thus.

Everything just slipped away in the attempt.

The woollen blanket with crosses. Thistles between fingers of bone. The feeling that they woke as the match went out. The question of what they were thinking as she spread the blanket back over them.

She had got up in the night and gone downstairs. In the darkness it had felt as though four dry hands tugged at her nightdress. She had stood before the wide door to the corner room and heard, or sensed, the sound of chatter and a loom at work. When she opened the door, the room was lifeless. When she closed it, the sounds or the feeling of sounds returned.

Astrid got up from the rock now and took the path down to the village. Entering the parsonage, she climbed the stairs, and even before she opened the door, she knew he would be standing before the Hekne Weave.

I Shallna' Be Content with Less

"I havena' slept a wink," she said. "My mind has been in such turmoil."

"If it's any consolation, I've been in turmoil my whole life," Kai said.

It was harder for her to look at the weave now. As in those stories where those who stare into the sun too long go blind. Or where those who look in the mirror too long go mad.

Kristine had noticed that something was wrong. Taking Astrid aside, she had asked straight out if she had been with a man and found herself with child. Astrid said no. It was impossible to share what was happening.

"I went to the bell tower this winter in the hope of finding answers," Astrid said to Kai. "Just one little look, and that would be it. Then, on that very day, ye told me the Hekne Weave wasna' missing after all, and that it had some sort of influence over things. Then that university man turned up, wanting to take both the weave and the bell. And then yesterday we found two dead women. Well – it just goes *on* and *on* wi'out stop."

Astrid gave the weave a glance. Was no wiser about the oval-shaped face that encircled the sisters. And turned away.

Schweigaard rolled it up and put it aside.

Still, it refused to let her go.

"How are things up at Hekne?" Schweigaard asked.

She shrugged.

"Let's go to the living room downstairs," he said. "We'll ask for some hot chocolate."

They sat down and soon Fru Røhme came in with two steaming cups.

"Hekne?" Astrid said. "Aye, where do I start?"

Schweigaard said that he had seen Kristine recently, when she had asked his advice about some idea Tarald had come up with. "I take it your brother's still hell-bent on going to Germany?"

"On a cycling trip, aye. He has persuaded Sigmund to join

him. Found out about sommat called the 'tourist mark'. Costs just half a mark, but 'tis worth one whole mark. Cos Germany wants more tourists."

"Do you think Günther has invited Tarald to visit him?"

"Not that I know. They say the Olympic Games shall be held in Berlin, but 'tis Dresden that Tarald has in mind. To visit the stave church, the Art Academy and our grandfather's grave. He planned to go to Memel, but they say 'tis unwise now with the communists. He's been lying on the floor, tracing all the drawings in the sketchbook with baking paper. He says it's to get Grandfather's technique in his fingers. Then, at supper, I said, 'I want to come too. To see Dresden.' It went dead quiet round the table. The kind of quiet that said, 'How could thee, Astrid? What about the cows up at the seter this summer? What about the Colonial?' They all thinks I was put on this earth to patch up whatever other folks leave undone, especially Tarald."

Kai Schweigaard nodded and said he understood, and that life offered her greater possibilities than to walk in Tarald's shadow.

"Mother and Father – they just sit tight and hope the question doesna' come up. The question of what I really want to do. Truth is they're old-fashioned. Reckons I want to take over the dairy. But I likes the smell o' whey as little as Tarald likes the smell o' old barns. Though the Colonial – I could work there."

"I can see the pleasure of running a shop," Kai said. "But we need someone in Butangen who doesn't just give people what they want but what they need. A little soul."

"I got more than my fill o' *soul* yesterday," Astrid said.

"Explore all those questions you have in you, Astrid. As when you asked as a girl if the soul could grow old."

"How exactly?"

"I've been thinking about something," he said. "For a long time."

I Shallna' Be Content with Less

"Which is?"

"That you should maybe take your middle-school exams and then the *artium*. That you might consider going to teacher training college. Getting good at something lets you become someone. You get a voice. Our village teacher is getting on in years, and to be honest I've always thought he was rather mediocre. Good at arithmetic and singing, but lacking any vision. When I'm gone, there'll be nobody here to offer that. The government are investing money in education now, and soon I think every child will go to school every day."

He reached for a biscuit but dropped it, and she noted his annoyance at himself.

"Time's running out," he admitted. "For me, at least."

"But I canna' really leave Hekne," she said. "If only we had a regular *odelsgutt*! Big, strong and stupid!"

He laughed.

"Hekne is nothing if ignorance prevails in Butangen. I regularly see clever youngsters who go to school but have no encouragement from home. Most only ever hear that they're destined for the cowshed, the scythe, the harvester or birthing bed."

Astrid crossed over to the window. The last ice floes had melted on Lake Løsnes, and down by the boatyard somebody had already turned over a couple of rowing boats.

"A good teacher enriches the soul of a village," said Kai. "Education can be used anywhere, and it's needed everywhere. Jehans came round to it late, but has used it to great effect. As indeed has your mother. If anyone broke with expectations, it was your parents. They won't hold you back. It's a matter of life itself. What was it you Heknes say? If we mun, then we mun."

She sat back down.

"I could get Mari Slåen to come with me."

"That would be good. But think about yourself first. You could be a qualified teacher as early as the spring of 1942."

"Happen. But . . ."

Her mind was drifting. The memory of the dry, papery skin on those four hands drove out her thoughts.

"But what?" Schweigaard asked.

She shook it off.

"Imagine if it makes no odds what I do, Kai. Imagine if everything is laid out beforehand. If nowt can be avoided. 'Tis as though I am driven by the will of others. Your will. My grandmother's. The will o' the legend. All calling on me to do sommat, wi'out even telling me what it is."

"I recognise myself in that," Kai Schweigaard said.

"'Tis possible I could take on sommat new," said Astrid. "But before that – I mun free myself somehow. Free myself from all this. Find out what they want of me. The sisters under the floor."

"It may be that we'll never find out," said Kai Schweigaard. "Meanwhile, you can't wait for answers, you must seize what belongs to you and to you alone."

She rotated her porcelain cup in its saucer.

"When Father and Victor discovered that Gunhild was in Lake Løsnes," she said, "how on earth did they find her? After all those others had tried?"

Kai Schweigaard shook his head. "I think the bell let herself be found. There's no other explanation except that they were the right people. That the chain-brothers had finally come."

"I should like to meet Victor again," Astrid said. "To see the difference between him and Father. I have begun t'wonder lately if he ever felt as I do about the Sister Bells."

A Pale Yellow Fokker Universal

Two letters arrived that day. One had *Westley Richards, Birmingham* marked on the back. The other was from Norway. Addressed to him in a stranger's hand.

Norway?

Norway.

Victor Harrison had adopted his stepfather's principle of hearing the good news first. The two guns he had test-shot six months ago *in the white* – that is, before engraving, bluing and the application of alkanet oil – would be ready in two weeks.

Slowly he slit open the envelope with the Norwegian airmail stamp, worried it might contain the news that must come sooner or later. The news that Kai Schweigaard had died. Although surely such a letter would be in Jehans' handwriting?

Oh?

It was from the daughter at Hekne. Astrid. She was five years old when he last saw her.

He could hear Edgar and Alastair out in the hall. They had set out their pilot helmets and equipment yesterday. Pidge wagged her tail so it slammed against the wall.

Astrid introduced herself. Her English impressed her uncle, even if her grammar was uncertain and word choice rather archaic at times – no doubt the influence of the old pastor and from reading old books. She was, she wrote, working every other day in the shop now, but wondered if she might one day be a teacher. Late this winter in Butangen, Germans had tried to get hold of the church bell in the bell tower. She had gone up and seen the bell herself. Something she wrote about the Hekne Weave indicated that it had been found and that she had seen that too. What did he think about the problem? *Methinks you would fetch home the Sister Bell from Dresden?*

Victor Harrison got up. The letter prompted unexpected feelings of guilt in him. He suddenly found himself transported back to the autumn of 1903, when Jehans had demanded something that had seemed equally impossible: that together they should raise a church bell from Lake Løsnes.

Victor looked at his watch. They should have taken off by now. This was his sons' big day.

"Isn't the wind a bit strong today?" Edgar said.

"Not a bit of it," said Victor.

Victor's son sat on his lap and took the controls of the Fokker Universal, just as he had taken the wheel of the Morris when he was ten. Edgar was now twelve, and they were in Alnmouth Bay.

"But look at the sea," Edgar said.

"The waves can get a lot bigger before you need worry. If it gets bad, you set the side of the plane to the wind and take her parallel to the waves. And you'll land her that way too. But it's not that rough today. So, you'll lift off as planned."

Five minutes later the seaplane was still bobbing on the waves. Victor straightened it for his son and urged him to try again. The plane was in fact a bit big for a beginner, but it was easy to fly. Victor had always admired Anthony Fokker's designs, even throughout the Great War when he was making aircraft for the enemy. He saw the fact that he now owned one himself – pale yellow with burgundy red stripes – as a testament to peacetime. Fokker had built his first plane by the age of eighteen, and the Fokker Universal was the summation of all his experience. It was originally intended for use in the North American wilderness; it had a huge cargo capacity and a flying range of almost a thousand kilometres.

The star-engine hummed and there was a smell of exhaust and machinery as the coast and the propeller spun in a grey circle before them, but still the plane remained motionless and they bobbed about aimlessly in the grip of the waves and wind while the whirr of the engine took on an impatient tone as if asking what kept them.

"Remember what we talked about yesterday," Victor said. "There's lots can go wrong on a runway. But not here. Do you see any trees? Any buildings to crash into? No. This is the sea, as the sea was yesterday and the day before. The only thing you need to look out for is driftwood or timber. And there's none today. So all you have to think about is not to pull on the joystick so hard that our tail goes in the water. I can keep my hands on yours if you like."

"But still," said Edgar. "I can't help thinking about all the things that could go wrong."

"Look, you're right to consider the things that can go wrong. But you ought to have gone through all of that yesterday. You've got to make friends with danger."

"Yes, so you say, Papa. That's easier said than done."

"Well, it's easier to remember when it's been said. Now then, we'll take one round as we agreed. Let's aggravate those prigs in their white sailing boats over there. Then it'll be Alastair's turn."

Half an hour later the boy had flown, landed and walked proudly into Elsa's arms, his father close behind with his flying helmet in his hand. The floating dock rocked gently, speaking to Victor of his love for the water and seaplanes, and for her and the two who had sat waiting, even though the plane was big enough for four.

War widows had learned this long ago. To keep one son back. So that not everyone's lives were endangered simultaneously.

The extraordinary feeling that Astrid's letter had prompted in him had not shifted. He felt he had been issued some sort of duty to report. To give account for his life over the years.

To him the war years seemed like an unremitting stream

of red fog. The plane crash. The months in the prison camp. Then the startling moment in 1919 when Elsa, the daughter of the ruined art dealer of the Galerie Apfelbaum, said *I do* in the stave church in Dresden. They had made it to border control with Gisela, Elsa's five-year-old daughter, expecting to take the train to peace and happiness, only to discover that Germans were not wanted in Great Britain. When her application was finally approved, it was on condition she report to the police every week.

Victor had a constant feeling he had deceived them. Both with the promise of a good life and his ability to offer it to them. The next few years had tested them to the limit. Neither he nor Elsa had any skills that were in demand. She knew about art and the piano. He knew how to hunt and fly airplanes. Servants' wages went up after the war, and they could not afford to staff the estate properly, even though Finlaggan was of modest size. Gisela was bored out in the rugged Northumberland landscape, and as consolation she got a Welsh spaniel that she talked to in German.

Peace felt temporary. Almost invalid. He was constantly searching for something. He failed to find any solace in his homeplace as Jehans did, and when he woke up long before he felt rested, there was nothing outside the grimy windows of Finlaggan to demand anything of him. Each dawn was a flaccid repetition of the one before it. Nothing was ever big enough to surpass the thrill of sitting behind the controls of a warplane.

A new kind of transport had come in recent years. Scheduled passenger flights between Europe's major cities. But to establish such a thing would cost a small fortune. And, like Jehans, Victor was bad at seeking help. He hated to be indebted to anyone and liked to be alone in plan-making.

In 1924 Elsa gave birth to Edgar. The following year, Alastair came along.

He often went into the boys' room when they were asleep. He wondered when he should tell them. That he was adopted. That their real name was Hekne. Not Harrison.

One question had haunted him over the years. Who would he be now if Astrid Hekne had sent Jehans away instead of him? He regularly tortured himself about this, as he stood on the grand staircase, studying the portraits of the many Harrisons. The family had such a long history, while he felt like an arrow that had landed by chance on Finlaggan soil.

One day he reached a decision. To this ancestral gallery he added Gerhard Schönauer's self-portrait, which might so easily be confused with him. Next to it he hung the large picture his father had painted in Norway, a rather troubling portrayal of a woman draped in scarlet robes.

He felt better afterwards.

The very next day he discovered that there were skeletons in the Harrisons' closet too.

The oldest property deeds for Finlaggan were from 1616. Registered in the name of a certain Archibald Harrison. There was no portrait of him, only a framed fragment of an old Scottish plaid. Was that why he had named this place on English soil after a remote loch in the Hebrides?

In search of the answer, Victor changed the oil in his Morris Eight, and the family headed for the west coast of Scotland, enduring torrential rain, a rusty ferry on stormy seas, and punctures on deserted roads. A wild and barren place, Islay was famed mainly for its whisky that tasted like the weather itself. Arriving as the skies cleared and the grass steamed, they parked the car and walked the final stretch towards Loch Finlaggan.

The instant they set eyes on the lake, his wife sensed that this was one of those moments when Victor needed to be alone.

He walked down to the shoreline carrying Gerhard Schönauer's Hardy Smuggler. It would be difficult to catch fish on a fly rod in such a large body of water, and he cast it mainly for the pleasure of watching the line of his blood-father's fishing rod touch the loch's surface.

Nobody around. Nothing but water, grass and sky. Just as it was before the advent of humans and probably would be when they were gone.

This loch must have meant a great deal to this man who had died centuries ago. The man whom Victor now accepted he would never know anything about. Except that he too must once have stood where he now stood, and have seen what he now saw.

Victor felt an unexpected sense of peace. The years had erased all explanation. But in the unexplained, in the impenetrable, lay a tranquillity.

He meandered further along the shore, cast a few lines, turned from the evening sun and looked up at the others. They had settled high on the slope above.

Four people who, each in their own way, loved him.

He crouched down to change the fly. Wearing his usual earth-coloured tweeds, Victor must have blended in with the shoreline, because six mallards came in low and landed close by him. It was so beautiful to watch them lean their bodyweight back before braking so elegantly on the water's surface.

The ducks disappeared into the reeds. Not wanting to disturb them, he walked up and joined the others.

There he turned to look back over the lake, thoughts and memories floating through his mind.

Schweigaard's parting words at Lake Løsnes returned to him now. The words he had spoken that dreadful morning after Jehans and he had come to blows. *When a bull loses its footing, it stumbles and gets back up. But when a bird loses its footing, it takes off and flies.*

"What is it?" Elsa asked. "Is your arm hurting again?"

I Shallna' Be Content with Less

He passed his fishing rod to Gisela.

"No. I'm not in pain. On the contrary. I just saw something peculiar."

He remained lost in thought. Was it that in such moments of melancholy or doubt he entered a heightened awareness that allowed him to see a hidden pattern? To see his whole life as a map? Or was it that vulnerability made him more susceptible to his own imagination, so that he interpreted everything as a sign?

"Peculiar as in an explanation?" Elsa said.

"Rather the reverse," Victor said.

In that moment he gave up hope of finding out more about Archibald Harrison. For now he saw something remarkable.

Loch Finlaggan was the same shape as Lake Løsnes.

Larger, but with the same curves, the same narrowing at the inlets. As though Lake Løsnes had been transported here, just as the stave church and bell had been transported to Dresden, and he had been transported from Norway.

An idea came to him, and he had the urge to bring it to instant fruition.

The journey here had been complicated, time-consuming, expensive. The aviator in him had been profoundly irritated by this, a feeling common to most pilots, who got grouchy in taxicabs and crabby on trains, and were rarely to be seen on a bus, because they wanted to travel in a straight line. His friend Arthur Harris, whose life he had saved in 1917 and who was still in the Air Force, was such a man. And during the war he had asked Victor: "What is a line really? I mean *really*?"

He was asking, of course, because he had read Euclid's definition: "A line is the shortest distance between two points."

Two points now glowed in Victor's mind. One here by Loch Finlaggan and one by Lake Løsnes. Both, in their own way, his nemesis. He was weighing the practicalities of a business idea. It was an idea others had had before him, but there was doubtless room for his too. Postal services were increasingly using planes rather than ships, but many important places were still unreachable. The reason being they were in such uneven terrain that it was impossible to build a runway.

But in most territories you could find the surface that he and his brother had broken through when they brought a church bell up from Lake Løsnes in November 1918.

Seaplanes could land on it, just like the ducks.

A surface that renewed itself after each landing.

A surface that could be found everywhere.

The water's surface. The earth's mirror to heaven.

This had been back in 1927. Harrison's Air Lift now comprised eleven seaplanes and three reserve planes, one being the Fokker out in Alnmouth Bay. The company had offices in Edinburgh and Aberdeen. Gisela was twenty-two now, the best trilingual office manager in the business, rivalled only by her mother, and Victor was hoping to win the bid for the Royal Mail's delivery service to Orkney and Shetland.

Life had been smooth and comfortable over the last few years. Like a trip in fair weather with a full fuel tank. Interrupted now by this letter of demand.

As the family drove back home from Alnmouth later that day, he seemed increasingly distracted, and as they parked, Elsa turned the same gaze upon him as she had by Loch Finlaggan.

Leaving his flying gear in the hallway, he dashed upstairs to reread the letter from Norway.

Methinks. She presumably had no idea of the effect of this antiquated word that could be read as either a question or a command.

The question of whether a bell might be brought home from Dresden, or a demand to bring it back.

As Victor put down the letter, he could not take his eyes from her signature.

It was as though his own mother was reminding him of his duty.

Winter Seters

Astrid sat on the back of the truck savouring every metre. The road so even and straight. The deep gouges in the mountain walls that towered on her left. Scars from the battles between her father and the terrain.

Jehans was driving the Reo today. The engine had to work hard, because so many villagers sat on the back. On they rolled, along each hard-fought metre through the stubborn terrain the villagers had battled with century after century.

There were no such battles now, just a red Reo Speedwagon and the road ahead. The engine's exhaust fumes took on a different smell with each change of view: sweet as they rolled downhill; greasier as the truck had to burn more engine oil to go uphill; then laced with the scent of fresh spruce as they passed the felled trees at the roadside, and a cool, damp smell from the Breia as they descended into the valley.

On the long, downhill stretch before the bridge, Jehans accelerated so fast his passengers screamed. Esther sat on a milk churn with her hair blowing out behind her. Pelle stood beside her, with his front paws on the edge of the cargo bed and his tongue lolling out. The Buhund had always had a special relationship with Esther, and in the last few weeks he had taken to following her about.

At the bottom of the valley they saw the Breia foaming, copper-brown and white. Then crossing the new-built bridge they could see far down the river. Astrid craned her neck to get a glimpse of the beautiful, blue-speckled rock that had crashed down the mountainside and into a pool, where, in the right light, as now, it glittered under the water. Her father put the Reo into low gear and they started on the steep slope up to the seters.

A young man sat opposite her. With his elbows resting on his knees, he followed the bumps and turns in the road. Rocked as she rocked. Their milk-truck driver, Jon Mossen.

"So, today ye are *our* passenger," Astrid said.

"Aye. Today. This'll be grand. In a year we mun build the dairy out more. To take all the extra milk."

We. Yes. Jon Mossen was a permanent fixture.

She looked back at the road. He was ten years older than her and dressed for the summer in a checked flannel shirt. His belt was a shiny brown.

The little ones squealed, whipping each other up before each turn, squabbling over who could sit closest to the cab to get shelter from the wind.

Mossen looked about him calmly. Unfazed by the road dust.

Was he always this way? So strong and unflappable. Or was he acting tough for her?

The others on the cargo bed faded a little. She and Jon Mossen sat there self-consciously calm and silent. Digging their feet in whenever the truck swerved, anticipating the bumps in the road, bodies yielding. A dance where the bends in the road set the beat, the engine's hum was the melody, and the blue exhaust was the perfume.

They reached flatter terrain, and her father paused to take the Reo out of low gear. Jon Mossen nodded to himself, as if to say that he would also do this when he drove along this stretch.

I Shallna' Be Content with Less

Astrid craned her neck and looked casually around, so she could throw him a quick glance.

But he must have had the same thought, and when their gazes crossed, they lowered their eyes.

The road wound on through thick spruce forest, until they finally saw a clearing, and still further up a slate roof and a field, and "Good Lord," folk said, "we be nearly there, the whole ride shall take us under an hour!"

And now she saw them. The seters. All the summer farms stretched out on the gentle slopes below Tromsnes and Flyen, and all the dairymaids standing outside the cabins. The mood was as vibrant as on National Independence Day. They had probably heard the roar of the Reo below in the valley, and now more villagers arrived, and the passengers on the cargo bed all clapped or banged on the driver's cab.

They drove on as the dust whirled in the wheel arches. How strange to see the seters from here, from this angle, and to drive so fast past the cowsheds and barns that she had always trudged past on foot before. The road followed along the fences now, and at regular intervals they spotted newly carpentered milk churn stands. The road ran in a figure of eight, and Jehans drove along both loops and into the middle. Someone had set out an old wood burner here and a steaming hot waffle iron. A huge copper kettle hung over a smoking fire. Arranged on a milk churn stand was a row of porcelain cups, and Astrid noticed that they all had different patterns, so each dairymaid could reclaim her own.

The truck stopped.

Mari Slåen took Astrid by the arm. "So," she said, "'tis truly happening."

"Aye, 'tis indeed," answered Astrid.

Everybody jumped off the cargo bed and headed for their friends and family. Mari ran towards her sister, with whom she was going to share a job as under-dairymaid this summer. Astrid got off last. She looked around and felt a tingle go up her spine.

These century-old seters, with their grey log cabins. These tranquil, chestnut-brown cows. All the goats that chewed on the juniper. The milk churns that lay cooling in the streams.

Yes.

She could have been in Dresden with her brother now if she had nagged enough.

But perhaps that was a victory rather than a defeat. It was rather a country-bumpkin thought, and embarrassing to admit. Yet it was fabulously true; dreams of Dresden paled to insignificance next to a seter road in Butangen.

Jehans turned off the engine, got out and put an arm around Astrid's shoulder. He was in his scruffy, cinnamon-coloured overalls with engine grease down the front and on the sleeves, and Kristine proclaimed that she was ashamed of him, for she had put on her fine *bunad* dress with its lacy apron and silver brooch.

Now Kai Schweigaard stepped out of the driver's cab too. When they had fetched him from the parsonage, he had been ready for fifteen minutes. Up here on the seters the pastor was clearly feeling the cold, since he stood in front of the Reo, warming his back against the radiator. Astrid realised that he had never been up here before. Maybe, for once, he too was lost for words.

A cow bellowed.

The pastor and her father began to discuss practicalities, always a solution when menfolk got emotional. The mountainside had proved somewhat easier to blast than Jehans had feared. There were three crates of dynamite left over, and they agreed to store them in the old stone barn at the parsonage.

Schweigaard gathered himself at last. Within Astrid's earshot, he took Kristine and Jehans aside, and said: "You two

I Shallna' Be Content with Less

mustn't forget to stop for a second and look at what you've accomplished."

And so they did. Her mother and father stopped and *looked*, and Astrid felt that they were taking stock of their lives.

"Aye, we has a seter road now," Kristine said.

"Aye, we has a seter road," repeated Jehans.

"And more, we has a road for motor vehicles," Kristine said, hoping her husband would hear the pride in her voice.

"Aye, we has a road for motor vehicles," he said, as though this were somehow unconnected to them both, and that the new road had just emerged in the spring melt.

Esther walked over, carrying a large tray of waffles. Folk turned to watch, fearful that she might trip. But she followed the voices and stopped right in front of Astrid.

The waffles were crisp and bursting with sour cream. Behind them the smoke from the fire and aroma of coffee wafted over the villagers' eager chatter.

"I recalls that first year, when I were an under-dairymaid," said Kristine. "I were trained by two wrinkled old womenfolk. They held to the old beliefs. When I cut my nails or my hair, I mun burn the clippings, for if I cast them outside, the magpie would fly down and peck them up, and then they would gets a headache. They quarrelled sommat awful about what day we should take the cows up t' seter.

"The weeks were like a plank that mun be kept in balance. They mun nay go on a Monday, for then the week were too front-heavy. Friday and Saturday, by that logic, left too little or nowt of the week. One of them were from Gudbrandsdal, where folks thought it a danger to go int' mountains on a Thursday. And in Østerdal they were dead agin travelling on a Tuesday, for the same reason as the others reckoned it were dangerous on a Thursday. And, of course, Sunday were unthinkable.

"So ye might conclude that Wednesday were good. But nay.

They both agreed it were unseemly to travel on the same weekday as the fourth day of Christmas in t' previous year, and that had been a Wednesday.

"So they bickered and fretted, and we ended up going on a Thursday, though it rained and the cows kept running off int' forest. It were a bad milk year that year. But I canna' but wonder what they would say today if they saw all this."

Esther bent down to give Pelle a waffle. Her brown hair swayed as she moved.

Kai Schweigaard compared it to the times when each farm was fenced off and self-sufficient. When all the food and hand tools were made on the farm. When everyone was always busy and could turn their hands to anything. And Jehans, in contrast to his normal self, dared to interrupt. "But those fences, Pastor, they was in our minds too. For what benefit would it be to folk if they wandered afar, when their lives would be just the same where'er they went?"

They stood there and were reminded that those fences were now torn down, and that Kristine Messelt's ideas had opened a view onto the outside world.

"'Tis nay me ye mun thank but her," said Kristine, pointing to a cow out in a field. "She and the sheep and the goats alike. They that canna' accept yer thanks."

Schweigaard said something that might have come straight out of the Bible, but had been said to him long ago by an old farmer's wife. That the livestock were at the end of a long, silver chain of well-being. These beasts that stood out in the wind and rain and ate what the humans couldn't eat. These beasts that turned moss and bark and leaves and grass into milk and wool and meat and leather. They were an infinite good to mankind just by their being and by giving what they gave. They always had been and always would be, so long as they got the chance.

Jehans agreed. Then went quiet.

"But in truth," he said, taking a step towards Kristine, "'tis thee we shall thank upon this day."

In full view of everyone, he reached his hand out to Kristine, and she took it and they stood hand in hand. They did not look at each other, but over the fields, at the cows and up at the mountains in the distance, but it was a long time before they let go, and for a moment they held their fingers outstretched to each other before returning to the milk churn stand.

"Have ye seen our Esther?" Jehans said a week later.

"She usually walks further up," said Astrid. "To that old, tumbledown cabin on the edge of the great marsh. She can sit there a good while. With our Pelle."

"I thought it were her up by the milk churn stand," said Jehans. "In the blue anorak."

"I swapped hers for mine. So she'd be easier to see from afar. Though my anorak's new."

"Did ye nay tell her?"

"That she's wearing the white one? Nay."

"'Tis perhaps for the best. With her being as she be."

"And is more with each day."

They walked up, Astrid following in her father's firm footsteps. The leaves had sprung on the mountain birches, and the grazing lines in the copse showed which plants the cows liked. Now and then they passed places where the clanking of cowbells from behind trees revealed the presence of a herd.

It was a warm day, and Astrid recalled the comedic scenario that had played out on the day Tarald had left for Germany. Sigmund had backed out at the last minute, but Tarald was still keen to go. He needed little more than his bicycle and a small book with a brown cover that had been among his grandfather's possessions, Meyer's *Sprachführer für Reise und Haus*. His plan was to follow Gerhard Schönauer's footsteps in reverse.

Kristine had been worrying for days. She had no idea what the weather was like in Germany in July, but like any Norwegian mother who sends their bairns travelling alone, her concern was not that he might get the wrong train, or be robbed or hospitalised with food poisoning or run over by a motorcar.

Of course not, thought Astrid.

What a Norwegian mother fears most, some might say the *only* thing she fears, is that her bairns might freeze. Kristine was no different, and forced Tarald to take a thick Setesdal cardigan, one of the few items of clothing she had ever taken the time to knit.

Two postcards had arrived since. He had drawn pictures on their blank sides. One was of the stave church. Surrounded by a crowd. The second, which had come some days later, showed the Art Academy. He wrote that he had run into two boys from Voss at the Dresden youth hostel. They were taking a train south.

Pelle barked. Among the silvery birch trees, they spotted something white. Esther was sitting on what had doubtless once been a slaughter stone. She straightened up when she felt their presence, said *hello* in a rather absent tone.

Jehans went up to the edge of the marsh and compared it with the remains of some old foundations further up. On his return, he confirmed that it was Hekne land. "It mun be the old winter seter. From the time when they had t' cross the old hanging bridge to get up here. It were easier then to chivvy a half-starved cow t' the winter seter than t' carry her fodder down t' the village."

Astrid searched the grass with the tips of her shoes. Her father found the old foundations of the cabin and a pile of what must have been slate from its roof. Being made of ore pine the walls themselves had not rotted, but the roof and floor were long gone, and there were nettles and crooked birches growing

I Shallna' Be Content with Less

everywhere. In the corner was a huge fireplace, almost hidden behind grey sallow and grass.

"I want to live here," said Esther.

"But 'tis impossible," said Astrid. "This cabin is more outdoors than indoors."

Esther never got upset when her siblings explained to her how the world looked. She had accepted that from childhood. What she did not accept was the word *no*.

"We can put it to rights," she said.

"This?" said Jehans.

"Just for once. Let me sleep alone and take care o' myself."

"But ye needs a fire," Astrid said. "'Tis cold here at night, even in the summer. This is just a fancy, Esther!"

Far down the slope, a stream could be heard. "And ye needs water too," Astrid said. "There's a steep hill behind thee, where water must be carried up from."

"Ye are making excuses, Astrid. Water, fine. But fire? How often does it get that cold here during summer grazing? And anyhows, I can light a fire myself."

Jehans walked over to the fireplace. "'Tis good soapstone. Block-cut. They mun ha' dragged the rock o'er the mountain on a sledge."

Astrid could see that he'd had an idea. Soapstone could retain its heat for hours. If someone came here and lit a fire for Esther in the evening, she could take care of herself. And with Pelle around, she need not be afraid of adders.

Astrid swatted a mosquito before it could bite.

It's just like you, Father, she thought. Only days ago, you drove up the new seter road for the first time. And no sooner is that done, but you want to resurrect a clapped-out winter seter. And now you want me to come and light Esther's fire.

"But that'll be perfect," Esther said. "I can get washed and dressed, have some bread or flatbread and milk for my breakfast, then go down to Astrid's for supper, and come back here to bed."

She was glowing, but as her body turned towards their voices, her eyes were fixed on a place further up. Up and over the mountains.

Was It Something You Bore?

At Hekne, when a thing was to be done, it should have been done yesterday. In the past it had always been a slow and arduous task to repair a seter cabin because materials had to be hauled up in the winter. But it dawned on them now, that *yes*: we have a truck. We have a road. We can bring everything up today.

Two weeks later, the cabin had a roof and a floor. Isum, who could never do enough for Esther, had lifted the heavy roof beams into place as though they weighed nothing, and the trees had been cleared from an old path so that Jehans could drive the Reo right up to the building site. On the back were forty sheets of corrugated iron, a new material that Kristine was very excited about, thin, light and everlasting.

They lit the soapstone hearth, and Esther and Pelle moved in.

It'll be good for her, Astrid thought. Spending the summer down in the village had always been hellishly boring for Esther. Seters were like little villages of their own, populated by young folk, and Astrid and the dairymaids would be up at the Hekne seter all summer with the cows.

But on the first night that Esther was going to sleep alone, Astrid left her cabin feeling somewhat wistful. She turned and watched the smoke rising from the chimney into the evening sky.

I Shallna' Be Content with Less

Esther had found what was hers. Asked for it, demanded it, and taken it. Just as Tarald had travelled without Sigmund because he wanted to and must.

Astrid had had a dream that night. She dreamed she was lying under rocks from the Breia while somebody rummaged above her, looking for something, incognisant of and deaf to her existence.

Where will I find what is mine, thought Astrid. Will I find it in being a teacher? How far must I travel to find it? Or will I realise that it is here, right here, and only here?

Two days later their mother stepped out of the Reo and Jon Mossen drove on to the next milk churn stand.

Kristine entered the low-ceilinged seter cabin, where Astrid was sitting at a table with a floral wax tablecloth. Her mother's hair had grown greyer this year, and she had started to wear a lightweight car jacket with a high collar against the draught from the truck windows. She held her hand against her jacket side pocket.

"Has sommat happened?" Astrid said.

"Post. There be post."

Kristine handed her a postcard with one of Tarald's drawings on the front. This time of an airship he had seen. A Zeppelin. They were in Regensburg now. He planned to stay there for a few days. Then he'd be off to Dresden and maybe Leipzig. They mustn't worry about him. He'd be back at the beginning of August.

"Thanks," Astrid said. "But wasna' that a long trail just to show me this?"

"There be more," Kristine said. From her jacket pocket she took out an envelope marked AIR MAIL with a red striped border. She watched Astrid's reaction as she handed it over.

"Who in t'world be that from?" Kristine said.

Astrid took the envelope. "Uncle Victor, I think."

"Victor?"

"Mm."

"But why would he address it to thee and not yer father?"

Astrid was annoyed. Why did she have to poke about in everything?

"I wrote him a letter."

"About what?"

"I was curious about how things were over there."

"Oh, were ye?"

"Aye."

"Well, open it, then! So we may hear!"

Astrid cut the envelope open with her belt knife. The letter was folded in four, and inside lay a small photograph. Her mother came to sit at her side, but Astrid turned away.

"He writes that the boys are grown up for their age and interested in stamps. That Gisela is a good big sister to them. That he has a painful knee. And that Elsa wants a new piano."

"Be that all?"

"More or less," Astrid said, giving her a peep at the letter that barely covered one side, knowing full well that her mother knew no English.

"Here they are," Astrid said, picking up the photograph. It had jagged edges and showed Victor, Elsa and their sons in front of a seaplane. The boys were dressed in flying suits, each holding a helmet.

"I see," Kristine said, looking from Astrid to the photograph and back.

"Ye still has time to get to Esther's before the milk round is done," Astrid said. "Take the picture and show it to Father."

The instant Kristine had gone, Astrid went over to the window and read the words slowly. Her uncle wrote that sadly he thought this letter was likely to be a disappointment. He did

I Shallna' Be Content with Less

not imagine that the Sister Bells would ever be reunited. Halfrid was now in the tower of a well-guarded cultural treasure in Germany. Gunhild was in Norway. He and his brother were now over sixty years old and lived far apart. He had come to the conclusion that if a legend had any power, it could not be controlled.

Astrid folded the letter along its creases and put it back in the envelope. She did not look at it again.

Later that summer Astrid witnessed that the milk truck could deliver something else. Love, or at least the promise of it.

Now that the milk was driven to the factory, the dairymaids no longer collapsed into bed with sore fingers and aching knuckles, only to get up again in the dark and sit half asleep on a milking stool in the barn. Nor did it take weeks to receive any supplies that were missing or forgotten, because the Reo could take shopping lists down to the Colonial.

It was even possible to have a good scrub and get prettied up.

One weekend, the Reo's cargo bed was loaded with boys. An enterprising young lad from Smidesang had invited them up to the seters for a party, no matter the weather, and a fiddler was coming to play.

"We have to go," Esther said. "Don't ye think, Astrid?"

"Happen," Astrid said. But in her head she was thinking what she could not say. Here I am, doing things for thee like I was yer mother. And I canna' say it to yer face, but it in't easy being yer sister.

In the last year the sixteen-year-old Esther had grown like spring shoots on a young, slender birch. Everywhere they went, the boys gawped at her. Sure in the knowledge, of course, that no blind person could know they were being looked at. So they ogled and stared as though she were some painting stuck up on a milk churn stand.

Saturday came, and about a hundred youngsters were already

there when Astrid, Esther and the over-dairymaid turned up. Some of the lads had bottles of beer in the stream, others were passing the homebrew round.

People were talking loudly. The fiddler tuned his fiddle. Those who knew each other formed groups.

Kristine had always been loath to spend money on clothes, but this year she had treated her daughters to new frocks, a blue one for Astrid and a deep red one for Esther that went with her brown hair. It was these they wore now.

At last Mari Slåen arrived. She had been held up by an obstinate cow, and had just managed to pull on her best green skirt. She had found some flowers at the roadside and put them in her red hair.

"What d'ye reckon?" Astrid said.

"I reckon," Mari said.

Fiddle music bounced off the barn wall and rang out over the meadow.

On the third dance, Mari was asked up to dance.

Meanwhile Astrid and Esther sat there. Nobody asked Astrid to dance, no matter how new or blue her dress. The boys were getting drunker, loafing around, or going to the stream for more beer. It was the fashion to put their little finger in the spout and dangle the bottle. The side glances at Esther were more and more prolonged.

It was then that Esther suddenly stood up, for no apparent reason, and turned her eyes upon them in a slow semicircle. All those who had gawped at her looked down and blushed, as though they had been cut down by a scythe called Esther Hekne.

Astrid stayed seated. It was as though she was watching things happen in another time to the one she lived in. So much hope was flying to and fro here, so much hope that never came to anything, and those who found each other found each other so easily somehow.

I Shallna' Be Content with Less

And now?

Now even Esther was asked to dance, by a young lad whom Astrid had never seen before. A handsome boy, of her age, in breeches and a linen shirt with folded-up sleeves, he did not seem to know she was blind, and he could most certainly dance, he led her beautifully, and Astrid was worried her sister might stumble, but she took a few steps and was off.

Esther could dance.

Typical Esther, she had probably learned to dance at the school for the blind. Without telling anyone.

"Well I never," said Mari Slåen, who had come alongside Astrid without her noticing.

"Well I never," Astrid said, in honest surprise.

The dance was over and the boy let Esther go, and for all Astrid could tell, he might still not know she was blind.

Mari Slåen got up and walked over to two girls sitting on a blanket against the barn wall. On her way, she was invited up to dance again. She vanished from view afterwards.

The fiddler launched into a melancholic tune that was impossible to dance to, and somebody shouted out for him to play something else. Taking no notice, he went on with his drawn-out notes, until finally he lowered his bow, rested his fiddle on his shoulder and sang of a lost friend so earnestly he seemed to melt into the verse he had penned.

> *Were it sommat ye carried*
> *Were it sommat that harried*
> *In ye, deep under yer skin*
> *Deep under yer skin*

Astrid huddled up.

This was a place for gathering, alright. But where folk gather, those who are alone are at their most alone.

Was It Something You Bore?

Where was he? The *one*? So far away that life passed by without their meeting? What was wrong with her? Had she promised herself to something too grand that day in the living room when she said she'd never settle for anything less?

Mari came back and sat down. Esther was nowhere to be seen.

"'Tis time ye stopped it," Mari said.

"Stopped what?"

"This weird thing ye do. When ye sit and look everywhere but where 'tis happening."

"Nobody asks me to dance, Mari."

"That's cos ye seem so far away that ye d'nay wish to be asked. All that's missing is for ye to shout out loud that there in't no point trying here."

"It's not like that."

"Aye, it is! Now stand up and show that ye are ready to dance."

The fiddler struck up a livelier tune. Amongst the dancing couples on the meadow, Astrid glimpsed Esther's hair flowing against the sunset and the boy's linen shirt, and felt a deep envy, then indignation, over the entire event.

She got up without looking at Mari, went across to the overdairymaid, and said: "Be so good as to help our Esther to her cabin when this is over."

She walked away, and the noise of the party faded behind her. At last, she was alone. She leaned on a fence and kicked at the willowherb so the petals whirled around her best shoes. Things had been fine, and then the serpent had crept up inside her and made everything ugly. When would it come, this love, and perform its miracle? This longing for someone, this longing was not big enough to justify such a reaction. To insult Mari Slåen!

But it was not just a longing for the "one".

It was a longing to be ordinary.

She stood for a while by the fence. Then headed off towards

I Shallna' Be Content with Less

the Hekne seter, but could not bear the thought of lying there unable to sleep, listening to the sounds of the party into the night. Soon she found herself on the ridge that led in towards the mountain. The marshes stretched before her, dotted with the occasional spindly birch.

The summer night grew no darker.

Astrid was at the end of the last steep hill and had a view of the mountain when she sensed something alive close by.

She stopped. Up ahead, almost blending into the willow thicket, stood a reindeer.

A lonely female.

Why didn't she run away? Did she have a calf?

But no calf came into view and neither did the reindeer move as Astrid drew closer. A strange animal, with bright, flaming streaks interspersed with the grey.

Soon they were standing a few metres apart, as steady as two rocks, each holding the other's gaze. Like two matriarchs without herds. Vigilant as church bells. Astrid could see every hair on her. The moisture around the nostrils. So close they could smell each other.

Then Astrid understood why the reindeer did not move away.

And they were equally startled by their mutual recognition.

A Swarm of Wasps He Could Not Be Stung By

Tarald stood on the doorstep. Sunburnt, contented, pockets empty and sketchbooks full. Kristine gave him a telling-off for coming six days later than promised. He hunkered down until the storm had passed, and Astrid could see he had factored in that he would get a good scolding.

He opened one of his sketchbooks and said he had found the way to a large park in Dresden. The sun had been baking hot and the smell of tar had grown stronger and stronger as he approached. "And there she was. Down by an artificial lake. In the best spot in the whole park."

Tarald leafed quickly through a few pages of runic symbols before coming to his sketches of the stave church. One depicted the portal and the entrance. Another showed all the dragon heads on the roof reflected in the lake. His last drawing showed the whole church and filled a metre-long sheet. It was executed in the greatest detail. She suspected he had worked on it for days.

Reluctantly he let his sister see the other work in his folder. Before his journey home, Tarald had set out to sketch all the great Dresden landmarks. The Prinzenpalais. The Art Academy. The Frauenkirche.

But these pictures lacked any vitality. Some were downright lazy.

Then came the explanation: these buildings, Tarald told her, were so . . . static.

"*Static*, eh?" Astrid said.

Yes, he said. Much more interesting were the things he had seen and understood of the current trends in Germany.

"*Trends*, eh?" Kristine interjected.

"Stop teasing me! I said I'm sorry for being late. The stave church was truly magnificent. But more important was the *excitement* it attracts. There was even this whole procession of folk clad in white who came t' visit it every day and danced and curtsied before the runic symbols. It was a summer school, they said, for folk in Dresden who wanted to learn about the runes."

He took a book from his backpack. Astrid spelled her way

through the title. *Heilige Runenmacht: Wiedergeburt des Armamentums durch Runenübungen und Tänze.*

"If they curtsied before the runes, they must all have been girls," said Astrid.

"Oh aye. They were girls."

"Just girls?"

"Aye, just girls! But what I am trying to get y'all to see is that it was o' more worth to observe folk's ways of thinking than stare at the buildings they visited."

"But the Nazis," Kristine said. "Did ye see them?"

"Nazis?" said Tarald. "There were Nazis everywhere." That was what he wanted them to understand. He and the two other boys had witnessed the marches, the propaganda, the parades, and Tarald had, he said, seen through it all.

"What d'ye mean by that?" Astrid said.

"Well, I began to ask myself. How has this happened? How can it be that they're all so unified? How have the Nazis gained all this power, so fast, so effectively? The answer's simple. 'Tis all down to advertising, from start to finish."

Kristine shook her head.

No, she must hear him out. He hadn't become a Nazi along the way. Didn't they understand what he was saying?

"A day or so after we arrived, we cycled straight into a parade. I couldna' help asking myself how – how do they do it? Well, first they keep to plain, fresh colours. Strong contrasts. Nowt wishy-washy. Their banners with swastikas didna' hang from flagpoles like flags here in Norway, for then they'd go limp when the wind dropped. Nay, these were massive, long banners fixed from under the roofs, so the swastikas were stretched out nice and flat. And there wasna' just *one* banner. They had fifty or sixty! So that every building along the parade route was decked in red, like a long corridor, with the swastika repeated over and over, as though everybody agreed that this was how it must be."

A Swarm of Wasps He Could Not Be Stung By

When the official march started, he realised how much had been borrowed from the parades of the Roman Empire. The pageantry, the equestrian banners, the emblem surrounded by oak leaves, the gold and red.

"They've got such bare-faced cheek! 'Tis like they just plumped on these things cos they worked thousands of years ago and still work today! Advertising – didna' I say it was advertising?"

Astrid looked at her brother. He seemed so strangely disengaged. He could just stand and watch everything from afar. As if this power was a swarm of wasps he could not be stung by.

"But that was nowt compared to the night parade."

His two companions had been keen to see one procession in particular. The train ticket was cheap so as to make it easy for the crowds to get there. As they got closer, they could be in no doubt that they were in the right place. Thousands of people were crowded in front of a stadium. The boys had intended to go up on a hill with a view, but had to settle for climbing a tree.

"I have never seen such planning. An orchestra played, searchlights darted to and fro against the clouds, and they had loudspeakers everywhere so the music could reach all the way to where we were. It was dark as pitch down at the stadium, we could scarce see any movement. Then we saw that folk in the middle were lighting torches. As the music got louder, more torches were lit and a swastika emerged. It came in time with the music, and when it was really burning, the torchbearers began to walk in a circle, so it rotated in the darkness below. Afterwards, as the crowd came away, they were in a daze and talking much louder than when they arrived."

"Why did ye go, Tarald?" Astrid said. "Were the other two Nazis?"

"Nay, it was impossible to avoid these events! There were meetings and parades everywhere."

He went on in more detail, and it *was* interesting to hear.

I Shallna' Be Content with Less

Perhaps, Astrid thought, it was for Esther's sake, as he had always pulled the world apart and explained it to her.

"But it wasna' dangerous?" said Esther.

"Nay, we just had to go along with it all. One thing I can say, they have certainly put things in order there now. The trains ran on time. Folk were happy a stop had been brought to all the riots and communist unrest. Though it didna' take long for me to notice that anyone who disagreed kept quiet. There in't exactly any free speech down there. There's sommat ye must understand about Germany. For all the strange things we saw, sommat else strange pasted itself on top, so that nowt strange were visible for long. We talked about it, me and my two friends from Voss. Anyone who disagrees seems to be sent to labour camps."

"Did ye visit Günther down there?" said Astrid.

"Günther? He lives in Norway."

"How d'ye know that?"

"He told me when he was here. They live in Skien."

Kristine said his clothes stank, and he should get some food in him. She opened his backpack to clear it, but Tarald grabbed it back.

"The cardigan I gave thee," she said. "Where has it gone?"

Tarald laced his backpack shut again. He had sold the Setesdal cardigan to a man in Nuremberg. No, it was the man who had approached him. He wanted to buy it because of its traditional Norse pattern. Tarald got enough German marks for four more days' travel.

Kristine shook her head. She clearly could not find words scathing enough.

A farmhand knocked on the door. They could not, he said, get the reaping machine to work. They had tried for two hours. Jehans followed him to the shed, and Kristine went out to the *stabbur* to find something for supper.

Leaving Astrid, Tarald and Esther.

"That brochure," Astrid said. "The one Günther was going to write. Did ye get hold of a copy?"

"Aye and nay." Tarald shrugged. "But take a look at this! This was worth the whole trip, Astrid. I found it in the archive along with Grandfather's student work."

He lifted out a large envelope.

"I sat and copied it onto tracing paper. It took me four days. Pictures of all the churches Grandfather drew on his tour of Norway. But the most important, the most incredible, thing I found was this."

He spread eight yellowing sheets of paper out on the kitchen table.

Astrid stood in silence. At first she thought they were her grandfather's drawings in her brother's hand.

"They're the originals," he said. "I made copies, put them in the file and took these."

"You stole them?" Esther said.

"Depends how ye look at it. They're more ours than anyone's."

Astrid spread out the sheets. They depicted a stave church, but unlike any she had seen before. A *modern* stave church, Tarald called it.

"Come here, Esther," Tarald said. "Touch them."

His sister ran her fingers over the drawings as he explained to her that the church was sublime, majestic in its dimensions, with a keen and resolute spire that soared up to the clouds. He was using words that were new to her. He said everything in this church stretched upwards, like somebody standing on their knees, stretching clasped hands towards heaven. The decorative elements were more restrained than in the old stave church. Dragons still snarled from the corners of the roof, but they were not so . . . *concrete*, as he put it. They were more a nod to the past. Appropriate to a time when nobody seriously believed that a carved dragon could scare away evil spirits, Tarald suggested.

I Shallna' Be Content with Less

"Although this new church d'nay wholly deny that spirits exist. D'ye see it, Esther?"

"Almost," Esther said, stroking the paper. "Not quite yet. Tell me more."

Astrid stepped back.

She left her siblings to it and went into the living room.

She was proud of her grandfather's rich imagination. Yet there was something about this that asked too much of her. This was what Kai had fought against during the Silver Winter, and now she could see why he had lost. The drawing was titled *Die Astridkirche* – the Astrid Church.

"So now," Astrid said when she got Tarald to herself, "now ye want to be an architect, just like him. And build this church somewhere."

Tarald shook his head.

"Nay, Astrid. I can never be like Grandfather. My talents don't lie in that direction. What I want is to reach folk. Ye could say that the Germans have taught me how it is to win the public over wi' charm, wi' propaganda! So, I shall apply to Oslo, to t' advertising course at the School of Arts and Crafts. Poster art and colour advertisements. That's sommat I can be good at."

"But what about Hekne?" Astrid said. "Ye shall take over the farm. Leastways, that's what Father and Mother think."

He shrugged his shoulders.

"Right," she said. "Off on another cycling trip then, are ye?"

"What d'ye mean?"

"That ye are putting me in t' women's shed again. Sort it all out, Sister dear. Ye who got the bigger dollop of conscience when it was handed out. Look after Esther, look after Hekne, look after the shop, look after the dairy, I'm off t' be a poster designer."

"D'ye want to do sommat else, Astrid?"

"Want to do sommat else? Of course I do."

"So say so. And say it now."

She grunted.

"So niggly," said Tarald. "Just cos ye d'nay know what to do with yer own life, doesna' mean ye can deny me from getting a grip on mine!"

Astrid felt queasy. Her brother was right. It was just too bloody painful to hear it.

"I want to go to college too," Astrid said. "I want to be . . ."

Then it clicked. The Hekne Way came with a broom and swept her doubts away.

"I'm going to be a teacher. So ye mun decide what ye wants to do as the *odelsgutt*, Tarald. 'Tis ye mun have that chat with Father."

She got up and went outside.

"Wait, Astrid. Let's talk."

He sprang after her, fringe flopping and shirtsleeves rolled up, leaner than before the summer.

"Over there. We can sit down there."

He pointed towards the *stabbur* steps.

"I've always been different in this family, Astrid. Nobody has ever asked me what I really wanted t' do."

"That isna' true," Astrid said, waving off a fly. "Ye have had every chance in t' world to say sommat."

"Not really. Just think how—"

"There's nowt t' be done about it," Astrid said. "That ye are nay cut out to be a farmer."

"D'ye think I havena' thought about it?" Tarald said. "About how this shall all go?"

The hot August sun was beating against the *stabbur*'s log walls, and all around them was the smell of old farm buildings. From here they could see the stables, the forge, the tool sheds and hay barn. When he had left, the apples on the trees had been tiny green nubs. Now they were almost ripe.

I Shallna' Be Content with Less

"One day when ye were up on the seter road," he said, "I was sitting alone indoors. Father came in and bade me take a broken plough up to the blacksmith for repair. I know nowt about ploughs, and he knew that full well, but neither of us said it. He just hurried off. I wanted him to show me properly what needed doing on the plough. But nay. It was like he scarpered from the problem. And from me too. From having to admit that I can never fully grasp it. And that the blacksmith would understand full well that I could never understand it."

Astrid went and picked two handfuls of redcurrants.

"When I came back from the blacksmith's I opened Grandfather's sketchbook. It was *then* that I felt it. The same courage as Mother had when she worked till her fists bled up at Hellorn. The same curiosity that grips Father when he constructs things. Except I realised then that the things *I* conjured from my imagination, the things I made, would remain on paper."

He scratched his temples.

"'Tis good ye want to be a teacher," Tarald said, gobbling down the berries. "Get started. I too had to search for what I really *could* do. The thing that offers me solid ground. So that I can stand up, like ye, without these doubts, and say: 'This is me, this is what I can do.'"

Die Brüder und das Volk

Two brochures lay on the table. One was thin and old-fashioned, printed in Gothic lettering. The other was highly coloured with a gaudy picture of the stave church on its front cover. The church lay on the arm of a fjord, with a Viking ship on the open sea beyond, the sun shining in between the mountains. In deep red lettering, the title read: *Die Nordkirche: Ein kritisches Handbuch von Hans F. Günther.*

"And he didn't show these to you straight away?" said Kai Schweigaard.

"Nay," Astrid said. "After our run-in on the *stabbur* steps he sat all evening talking to Esther. I went int' his room early this morning. He was going through a few things he'd bought in Dresden. And ended up showing me these brochures. He seemed slightly ashamed. Or uneasy at least."

"Have you read them?" Schweigaard asked.

"With the bit of German I know. I hoped ye might look through them, Kai. So I know if they says what I think they says."

The first chapter of the visitor's guide was a plain description of the architecture with detailed pencil drawings and measurements. Schweigaard looked closely at the photographs. Seeing the stave church again was a mixed pleasure.

They were in the pastor's study, standing near the table on which the Hekne Weave had lain. The window was wide open, and the cool air carried in the fragrance of haymaking.

"How was it?" Schweigaard said. "The stave church?"

"Tarald said she was well cared for. That he reckoned she had suffered some damage with the years, but that Günther and his folk had invested money in restoring her. On retarring her and buying fire extinguishers. And that there was a lot of interest and excitement around her. But turn to page eighteen, Kai."

Schweigaard leaned closer. The illustration showed two beautiful girls surrounded by villainous-looking men with hook noses.

"What on earth? Is this book for children?"

"Not as I understand."

He read out loud: *In the 1600s two beautiful sisters, robust in body and mind, lived on the Hekne estate, where the Norwegian odel principle has ensured continuity for hundreds of years, so that it remains, to this day, in the proud possession of the same family.*

"It says here that the Hekne sisters worked for years on *der Heknische Wandteppich*," he said. "Though in this version the weave doesn't show doomsday, but a kind of idealised society. A *Gemeinschaft* with united farms where a local ruler, or chieftain, rules wisely over all the smaller surrounding farms. Where – and this is so pompous – where the fertile soil, strong soldiers and a hard-working slave class ensure food and peace for all. A kind of nazified version of the old feudal system."

"Read on," Astrid said. "I think they've made more changes."

Soon he looked up at her and confirmed her understanding. In this account, the sisters were not conjoined. No deformity was mentioned. Their prayer to be allowed to die together was removed. Instead, the girls were gaily wandering along one day when one of them was abducted by gypsies. Later, two church bells were cast in memory of their unhappy separation.

"*Zigeuner* means gypsies, is that right?" said Astrid. "But they also use the word *Täter*? Tinkers?"

"Gypsies, yes. But *Täter* means criminals. Bandits."

She shook her head, saying the pictures didn't bear any resemblance to gypsies. The rogues were depicted with hook noses and greedy faces. They had caught one of the girls, who was flaying and kicking out. The next drawing showed the other sister sitting grief-stricken on a rock. Both were pictured in colourful clothes that had never been worn in Norway.

"They've twisted it into a war myth," he said. "In the earlier booklet it says that the bells heralded danger; here it says that they warn when *the enemy is approaching*. And that the Hekne Weave shows how they'll overcome that enemy."

Astrid watched his face eagerly as he read on in silence. Then he pointed to a line in Günther's guide.

"There are other rewrites too," he said. "Small. But like all small rewrites they're even more dangerous than the big ones."

"How so?"

"In the old brochure, the legend is correctly retold. Namely, that only brothers born without any sister in between can bring the Sister Bells together again. In Günther's text there's a sneaky conflation, or blend, of the words *Brüder* and *Volk* – brothers and the people of a nation. Here, the legend's requirement for chain-brothers for the bells' reunification is given a purely symbolic meaning, built on the notion that all Germanic peoples have an ancestral desire to be linked together – that they are in essence brothers."

"So, how does the story go here?"

"It goes like this," said Schweigaard. "That a man from Germany will meet a man from Norway. They are brothers, in that they are *bröderfolk* – born of brother nations – who will become one forever when they bring Gunhild from Norway to Germany and the Sister Bells are reunited."

Gifts of the Mountain

The reindeer appeared.

Eleven animals, half visible on the slope above them, were making their way steadily up. Then stopped.

She crouched down, released the safety catch on the Hekne Krag. Pulled the bolt back and brought it forward again, and followed the brass cartridge on its way into the barrel. All the little noises from the mechanism vanished into the soft heather. She secured the rifle and crept forward.

I Shallna' Be Content with Less

Father's words again.

Never a female! Not if she has a calf! Take a bull or the calf. Or if one is injured or lame, then shoot them.

Astrid understood now what her father meant about the difference between shooting in cold or hot blood. Cold blood was when they had to kill their own livestock. When they hesitated before the inevitable, and the animal knew what awaited it. In hunting, where the surprise was so sudden, an older instinct ruled. An instinct that preceded any agriculture. Then her blood warmed, and she felt no empathy beyond that needed for the shot to hit the mark.

Good shots be those that kill right away. Ye have but one shot, and 'tis but one shot ye need.

She crawled forward in the heather, inching her way past a thicket until she had a clear line of fire. Rested the fore-end against a rock, released the safety catch, and carefully scanned the group through the sight. None resembled the strange reindeer she had seen that summer. The herd were still relaxed, they had not seen her yet. Old Adolf's words, which had in turn become Jehans' words, now came to her.

First comes the varsimla – the matriarch. An old female wi' no calf. She leads the herd, watches o'er them. Ye mun ne'er shoot the old matriarch. D'nay even aim at her. For then bad luck shall follow thee in t' forest for the rest of yer days. She be more than an animal. Shoot her, and your gun will ne'er kill again, and the day shall come when ye shall walk astray and a storm shall descend.

The reindeer came into view on the horizon, first one, then another, until all eleven were in silhouette. If she fired now, the bullet might travel up and over and hit another hunter, so she waited until the herd were down on her side of the slope, forming a row of safe targets where her bullet would bury itself in the heather. They stood in a long line, and she knew they could disappear in the same ghostlike fashion in which they had come, for they were from another time, and could return to this time in a split second.

Only if she shot one of them would it be trapped in her time.

There was the matriarch. Old, quite big. Never at rest, head always raised, always ahead of the others. A grey sculpture between the golden marshes and blue sky. Suspicious of everything, no playfulness in her eyes. That morning Jehans had rubbed the gunsight with soot, his fists smoking from the flames, and now Astrid trained it on a calf, but it slipped behind another animal, and she turned the sight onto a bull that stood tall and proud, but as she went to fire, the memory of the female reindeer by the fence came back to her, and the Krag seemed to twist away, and suddenly the gunsight was swarming with reindeer in an impossible tangle of antlers, fur and hooves, and it felt as though she was among them, in the herd, and that someone was hunting *her*. She saw a flash of metal, glinting steel and evil intent, then the vision vanished, her blood cooled and her chance to shoot was lost.

Her father was coming.

"I couldna." She secured the weapon and laid it down on the heather. "And the Krag, it—"

"It what?"

"I was aiming at a young bull. Keeping my distance from the old matriarch. But it was as though the Krag said it wasna' right. As though she didna wish t' kill."

Jehans took the gun. Looked towards the mountains and said: "She has done this once afore. The Krag. As though she didna' wish it."

Her father told her what had happened with the grey reindeer mother he had encountered many years ago, and the last he said about it was that there were things in the mountains they could never understand, and that was how the mountains should be.

I Shallna' Be Content with Less

She had a sudden urge to tell her father about the reindeer she had met after the dance, but told herself that he should not be burdened with it. It was a feeling she got sometimes. This wish to protect him. A sense that she was older than him somehow, as intangible a feeling as when something had been forgotten but she had no idea what, and was left wrestling with the feeling that *something* had been forgotten.

They lost any desire to hunt and on their way back said very little, so that she wondered if she had disappointed him. She told herself that the Hekne Krag was a Krag like any other, and felt cross with herself for not firing the shot. She had gone every week that spring and summer to the village's new shooting range, which, like most things in Butangen, was provisional and at the mercy of the landscape. It had been built across a river gorge, so that nobody would get in the field of fire. But its range was 218 metres rather than 200, and with the firing bay and targets separated by such steep slopes, the markers and shooters could never shoot on the same day, so they had to be divided into Tuesday shooters and Thursday shooters. Astrid was usually the only girl. She had managed to shoot 214 out of a possible 250, which was a great achievement, being as they shot with hunting sights and not round target sights.

"It narks me," Astrid said, "that when we girls get noticed, 'tis cos we are doing what menfolk do. When we achieve what is expected of a man. Like when I drive the Reo. It in't hard to drive a truck, even when 'tis big."

"This anger o' yorn," Jehans said, "that offers thee nay release."

"It will soon," Astrid said.

"Oh?"

She did not answer at once. But continued to walk along the narrow mountain path.

In an hour they would be able to see over the seters below. A year had passed since the road had been completed, and in

Gifts of the Mountain

many places new, bigger barns had appeared. Kristine had calculated that she would have to employ two or three more women at the dairy. Their payments to the farms were already up, and optimism reigned in the village.

Tarald had been busy all summer. He had practical assignments to complete for the School of Arts and Crafts. Besides which, he had been called up for military training in Jørstadmoen, so it made sense to work on his drawing skills while he had the time.

Astrid and her father sat close to a large rock. She lay the Krag on the heather before them. It had its share of bumps and scratches after thirty-five years in the mountains. The magazine showed signs of wear, and the stock had dents that coincided with the metal buttons on her father's jacket. He too bore the marks of those thirty-five years. His hair had turned iron grey, and when he pushed it from his forehead, his gnarled, suntanned fingers ran like a rusted harrow through ashes, not that anybody puts a harrow in ashes, but that was what it resembled and why she thought it, despite its being impossible.

He opened their lunch pack, passed her a slice of soft baked bread with black pudding and took one himself.

Then they finally talked about teacher training college.

"Ye be wondering about Hekne," said Astrid. "About who'll take care of the farm."

"I ne'er thought it could be anyone but Tarald. And that ye would always be close."

"To sort things out as ever."

"Happen. So, ye shall finish with school in 1942?"

"Aye. May 1942. Ah, how I look forward to that day."

"And I," said Jehans. "It shall be empty wi'out thee, my friend."

They had time on their hands, and it was barely past midday when they came down to the seter, propped the Krag against the cabin wall and knocked on Esther's door.

Everything was starting to smell like autumn. Esther let them in and said she had fetched some water and that she could feel they were thirsty. A gentle warmth came from the soapstone hearth, and they realised that she had, contrary to their agreement, lit the fire herself.

In early September they were out hunting again. They passed Saubua and walked up the ridge that looked over Kvia and the Breia, then walked further up the slopes towards Suleberghøgda, where they sat and surveyed the world, each through their own binoculars, seeing only a raven and two golden eagles. They slept in a boathouse down by Lake Glupen and next morning everything was white.

Visibility was less than fifty metres. Through the dense snowfall they spied an animal. A young reindeer bull, walking unsteadily. Jehans could see in his binoculars that some other hunter must have injured it, making it easy for Astrid to shoot it. She knelt down, released the safety catch, and with no difficult thoughts, pointed her barrel in search of the reindeer, set the foresight in line with its front legs, then raised it until it was centred on its shoulder, pulled the trigger, then reloaded, and as the empty cartridge sped past the corner of her eye, she watched the bull rear into the white eternity, and knew that a second bullet was not needed. The one she had fired was the one that killed. Everything had happened so fast, and this speed was a part of what was right and true.

Astrid went over to the reindeer. It lay in the snow, bright pulmonary blood flowing from its muzzle. She knelt down and felt its warmth and her father let her be alone, so she could apprehend that something beyond the known and knowable had left a reindeer behind in her world. Proof that the moment of the gunshot had been real. A result of a delicate link with creatures whose foremost task was to make themselves invisible.

They butchered the reindeer as the ravens circled overhead, then left the slaughter ground where blood and entrails lay dissolved in the thin snow. Astrid carried the Hekne Krag, the antlers and one shoulder. Jehans carried the rest of the meat, and further down the snow changed to sleet, and they believed the mountain had given all it could give that year.

But the mountain had, it seemed, given more.

Esther came to meet them; it was her last day on the old winter seter. Down here the sleet had turned to rain, and they sat listening as it drummed on the corrugated tin roof and felt the warmth from the hearth and the joy of being sheltered. It was dark in the cabin and Astrid turned up the wick on the paraffin lamp. Then stopped in surprise. Let her gaze search Esther as if she were a mountain terrain that hid a herd of reindeer.

She looked closely at her face, her skin, her belly.

It began as a question. Shifted to a hunch. Ended as a certainty.

Esther was with child.

Consecrated Floodwaters from the Breia

Whenever Butangenites reminisced about the year 1938, the baptism that May would take up most of the discussion around their coffee tables. The church was full, yes, packed to the rafters with folk with little or no relationship to the baby. For a large number of the congregation, the jostling crowd defeated the whole purpose of having come to church that day, namely to see if a stranger might turn up and reveal himself as the father.

I Shallna' Be Content with Less

Rumours of Esther's "trouble" had started in earnest that winter. It was *kakelinna*, the "cake-thaw", a period of mild weather in December that according to legend was caused by the warmth created by all the pre-Christmas baking and vigorous cleaning. Wearing only a dress and tight-fitting cardigan, Esther had risked going for a walk with Pelle. None of the ensuing gossip, however, as to *who* exactly had made poor Esther pregnant seemed of any substance. The women at the Colonial were intensely loyal and gave the brush-off to anyone fishing for hints. But that merely prompted other speculations.

The Heknes? In't it that twins run in t' family?

Indeed so.

Were it nay said—

Oh aye. Conjoined they were. A living fact. 'Tis no legend. That they were conjoined.

Might it happen again?

That'll be sommat to baptise!

If she lives.

If she lives.

Late that autumn Astrid had often stood in the doorway watching her sister. More than once Esther sat stroking a stalk of cotton grass over her cheek.

A memory, perhaps, of a boy and a summer.

All she would say was that he spoke a Midtdal dialect with a touch of Østerdal, had soft skin and short hair without a fringe, and sometimes had stubble and other times not. She and Pelle had sat outside and Pelle had warned of the visitor from afar, and then the voice was there and he asked if it was possible to have some water to drink, so she brought him the bucket and ladle and set it before him and listened to his movements, and when he went his way, she had still not said she was blind and neither, she supposed, had he realised it. Some days later he was back, and the third time he came, she asked him in, and when she noticed that Pelle stayed outside, she knew he was the right one.

Any bitterness? No, for what? Abandoned or used? Me? How would it ever have happened otherwise? Should she have nobody because she could see nobody? This lover was a gift, that at least was what she told Astrid, and she had no eyes to reveal whether or not she meant it, but for the first time Astrid seemed to hear sadness in her sister's voice. Not over a lover's tryst, but her blindness. Over the fact she would never see her child's face.

They were often alone that winter. And more than once Astrid said: "There should at least be a father's name in the church register. Ye d'nay need to tell it to anyone but the pastor."

"I shall nay go about and lie. Who needs a name up on a seter? I didna' even tell him that mine is Esther. Till next spring the littlun will be here inside me. Happen he'll come back then. I shall ask him then what his name is."

"Might he have been a trapper of sorts? Did he smell of fishing nets?"

"Nay, he smelled only of the mountains. O' fresh air when the weather is cold."

"Ye think about him still."

"I think about him a lot. He sits here in my hands somehow."

"He left thee with no promise?"

"He just left me with this," Esther said, stroking her belly. Then she said: "I hope ye will be its godmother, Sister. In case sommat happens to me."

Astrid said: "Happens?"

"Just in case."

"Heavens," said Astrid. "Do ye know if . . . 'tis one babby or two inside thee?"

I Shallna' Be Content with Less

Esther shook her head and said it was probably impossible to tell so early.

She fell silent and took a sip of the broth Astrid had brought her, here in the room where they had sat so many times as girls.

Esther craned her neck now. Was it mere coincidence that she turned towards the corner of the room closest to the seters? As if she had an inner compass. A compass like the animals had when they found their way home?

"I'll be their godmother," Astrid said. "Certainly, I'll be their godmother."

"She be startin'! And I means now!" yelled Kristine. Jehans flung himself out into the truck and drove to get Oddny Spangrud, who had been Butangen's midwife for forty years, and when they saw that she carried *two* midwife bags and shut the front door hard behind her, four men stood outside, pacing the floor nervously: Jehans, Tarald, Giant Isum and Kai Schweigaard.

The day passed.

Eventually all four traipsed into the kitchen, where they listened out for any noises and the comings and goings of the womenfolk on the other side of the house. When the grandfather clock struck midnight, they stood at the door where the birth was taking place. When it struck one and there was still only moaning and hushed voices to hear, Kai Schweigaard found it steadily harder to hide his concern, but managed to keep mum about the fact he had the Bible in his pocket and was ready for an emergency baptism.

Then the scream was heard.

The great scream.

The scream from life itself.

Together the men stumbled through the door, just in time to see the midwife hold up a large baby boy with gleaming blond hair. Jehans went cautiously up to Esther. So soaked in sweat that her linen gown was dark grey. Astrid said all was well, Esther had been so clever and strong.

"Can he see?" Esther asked. "Can ye see if his eyes are . . . if they are sound?"

The midwife just had time to say, "He be sound in every way," before the boy interrupted with another scream, so loud and shrill that Giant Isum could find no outlet for his joy other than to clench his fists and wave them over his head, as he cried: *Hurrah! For our Esther, the best lady ever!*

In the following weeks, preparations were made for the baptism and celebration. Esther was soon back on her feet, and Astrid had never seen her so enthused.

"Ye mun announce his name soon," Astrid said.

"They shall hear it at the baptismal font," said Esther. "Not before."

"There are limits. To how stubborn ye can be. Even ye."

"At the font," Esther said.

This secrecy surrounding the boy's name was the subject of many a heated discussion around the kitchen table. As usual Tarald backed Esther in her defiance.

"I canna' fathom it," said Jehans. "Shall know it when ye say it? I ask thee again, Esther. Has it sommat to do wi' who the father be?"

Tarald broke in: "The only thing ye can be sure of, Father, is that his name canna' be Adolf."

Father and son were more direct with each other now that Tarald's life plan had fallen into place. Tarald was in his final month of military service at Jørstadmoen. Since he was left-handed, it was decided he should be a machine-gunner. He was given the rank of corporal and learned to fire six hundred rounds a minute from a water-cooled Colt m-29. Whenever

I Shallna' Be Content with Less

he came home he sat so they could see the red corporal stripe on his sleeve, as though to counter the effete profession he had chosen.

As a christening gift, he chopped, sanded and painted a set of an incredible three hundred building blocks, and a wooden case for them all to be kept in.

"Whate'er name ye take, Esther," said Astrid, "folk will think ye named him after his father."

"Folk can think what they like," Esther said.

Three weeks later Esther got up from the front pew in a pale blue dress with her son in her arms. Never in Butangen had so many people held their breath at one time. Never had so many side glances been exchanged.

But not one man behaved in such a way as to fuel more rumours, besides which, nobody could take their eyes from Esther in the moment she rose to her feet.

Schweigaard had of course practised with her in secret, and she walked now like royalty at a coronation. She held the boy in swaddling clothes and moved with unbelievable surefootedness towards the steps of the font, and mounted each so resolutely that some folk thought she had regained her sight or had pretended to be blind.

"What shall this child be called?" said Kai Schweigaard.

Esther gave him her answer and guided the boy's head over the old soapstone font.

Kai Schweigaard cupped his hand, dipped it into the baptismal water, and poured the consecrated floodwater of the Breia three times over Eirik Hekne's brow.

Only until May 1940, Pastor Schweigaard!

Schweigaard was in his study changing the line on his fishing reel, a slightly scuffed Penn Senator with a brass frame. It was May 1939, and he would soon put out in the Priest Boat, as the locals called it, to go trolling again on Lake Løsnes. Earlier that winter, he had put new hooks on the spoons and repaired the landing net. These were the activities to which an angler must turn when it was snowing outside his window. Through his cherished fishing gear, he held the summer in his hands. But increasingly often he heard old age whisper its cruellest question: when will be the last time I change the line on my reel?

Downstairs in the living room he heard Herr and Fru Røhme. They exchanged a few words, then it went quiet. Moments later there was a knock at the door, and he was surprised when they both walked in.

"What's happening?" Schweigaard said.

Herr Røhme handed him a letter. From the diocese of Hamar. The circulars from the bishops – the Shepherd Letters – were usually something Schweigaard just skimmed. But here, his name was not typewritten. The envelope was addressed in Bishop Hille's own hand.

They exchanged glances. "Stay a moment," Schweigaard said, cutting the envelope open.

He was summoned to a meeting at the bishop's office on Thursday, May 18, 1939. *I would like, on behalf of the diocese, to thank* – hmm, such an unnecessarily long greeting – *almost sixty years of service* – worrying so early on in the letter – *the time is come* –

No. He did not want the time to have come. The time should last.

– to prepare for your retirement, and to see that the relevant practical arrangements are made.

He handed the letter to Fru Røhme so that she and her husband could read it. The couple shared a pair of spectacles, and suddenly Schweigaard saw how much they had aged, all three. But *he* was well past his best.

It was a reality he had pushed aside. He had counted on Hille letting him continue until he keeled over. But now. He had been rumbled. No longer useful or fit for work. His experience no longer valued, a new skipper was needed on the ship, even if the seas were the same.

Or were they no longer the same, these seas?

Schweigaard got up and went out into the orchard. Everything was grey and brown after the winter. So austere. Last year's leaves crunched on the ground. Røhme always preferred to rake in the spring, said it was better for the grass. Kai stood by a moss-covered tree. It had borne no fruit that year.

He walked around the corner of the house to be out of Herr Røhme's sight. From here he could see the telephone poles and the overhead power lines.

What a joy it had been when they were erected.

All his life he had been a man of progress. But lately he had begun to wonder how all the changes at the turn of the century had seemed to the older folk back then.

For those who were then as he was now.

Oldfrue Bressum hadn't wanted electricity in the house. She was terrified that it might run out of the wall sockets and over the floor, so she would step in it and drop dead.

Something new had arrived every few years, and every few years something was rendered obsolete, including those with knowledge and experience. Things had been so different when he had first come to Butangen. Back then the knowledge of grandparents was the most valuable asset of all, because life was

Only until May 1940, Pastor Schweigaard!

as it had been for centuries. How important then to learn from an elder how to predict the weather. To really understand your cows. To fell timber trees in the right phase of the moon. Or to strip the bark from birch logs after the first thunderstorm. In the old days there was nothing old. Everything was a reiteration of the world as the world had always been and always would be.

But now? Nobody needed to forge a sickle curved at precisely the right angle to harvest the crops. Nobody needed to know that, in the dry weather, water must be fetched from the stream to fill the postholes to prevent the hayracks falling over. These lores that had once determined whether folk starved or ate during the winter were superfluous now. Superfluous because two men with a reaping machine could harvest the wheat faster than ten men with sickles.

He had always trusted that such changes were for the better. He had felt empathy for those in his community who lacked any aptitude for farming, who starved or lay shivering in their crofts because they lacked the skills of husbandry, the knowledge of the land and forest. Technology would surely offer them a way forward.

Now he shared the village elders' sense of mourning over the wisdoms that had been rendered useless. When he was dead, someone would stand by his coffin and say: *For every little step the world moves forward, some will fall in its path, and these some must be somebody, and this time Kai Schweigaard was that somebody.* No, it would have to be the new pastor, and it was inconceivable that the new pastor would say such a thing. Nobody would or could before they had lost someone dear to them.

He went up to his study and looked around. At the black wood burner. The clock. The greyed lace curtains.

Something *greater* had begun to tug at him. Forces within the walls, forces outside the walls. From under the floor of the new church. He had felt them before, together with the knowledge that his last working day was fast approaching. Had the Hekne Weave's prophecy of how the last pastor in Butangen would die got it wrong? If he was no longer a pastor, the prophecy could not apply to him.

Or did he have just months left before his death?

He began to grapple with the biggest question of all. The question of who had created whom. Of whether a tapestry might create or show reality. Of who spun the Norns' thread. Of whether someone, or something, had approached the Hekne sisters and whispered that they should weave their yarn into an image of him.

The morning after Independence Day, Herr Røhme drove Kai Schweigaard to the railway station by horse and cart.

The pastor felt dejected on the drive down and on the train. Hamar's streets were swept clean after the big May 17 parade. He had arrived with two hours to spare before his meeting was due to start, and he walked around feeling ill-tempered and miserable. Until, that is, he found a copy of the *Russeavis* – the oft-satirical student newspaper – left on a street bench.

A little humour was exactly what he needed right now.

A clever cartoon of Hitler dominated the front page. Above it the headline declared that Norway and Denmark had been invaded by Germany two days ago, on May 16.

Now Hamar is under threat! Hitler invaded Denmark at midnight. Oslo fell after a surprise bombing raid a few hours later. Are we celebrating Independence Day tomorrow for the very last time? Will this May 17 be the last day when we can come out on our streets proudly wearing our bunads and with our flags flying high?

The students had of course placed Hamar at the centre of world events. And this fantastical story was written with wit and elegance. The invasion was imagined hour by hour, and central to the enemy's plans was the seizing of the *Skibladner*, the old paddle steamer, because a certain alcoholic beverage was served aboard: schnapps!

Schweigaard's humour was tickled further when he read the name of the article's author. Of all people, Arnoldus Hille. The bishop's son. Of course, he would be graduating from the Cathedral School this year.

A plan began to take form in Schweigaard's head. Not the best plan perhaps, but the only one he had time to make.

He headed straight for the bishop's office, arriving long before their meeting was scheduled to start. As he had hoped he was ushered to the green sofa in the corridor, which all the clerks had to walk past. There he opened and read the *Russeavis* so that the front page was on full view. At barely a quarter to two a secretary slipped into Bishop Hille's office, shortly after which the bishop himself emerged, looking somewhat ruffled. Schweigaard waved the newspaper at him, and before Hille could shut his door, called out:

"Dear oh dear! A lively piece this, Hille. If youth but knew, and old age could!"

The bishop looked as though he could do without this attention. And during their conversation, Schweigaard gave him nothing for free. Hille had doubtless intended to dismiss him with a few well-chosen words, but his son's outrageous public show seemed to have taken the wind out of his sails. He leafed through his diary, stood up, held out his hand and said: "Very well, Pastor Schweigaard, you'll continue for one more year. There'll be a suitable recognition of your services, don't you worry. But from May 5, 1940 you're a pensioner."

A Pastor's Departure

The calendar showed April 8, 1940. It was late Monday evening, and he was standing in his study feeling rather lost.

In a few weeks it would be over. Over and out, he would be thrown on the scrap heap. Farewell parsonage, farewell room, farewell to the village's respect, farewell to the memories of Astrid Hekne in this house. Farewell to everything, actually. Most of all to his dominion over the situation.

He should have started to clear his things, but had never got down to it. The more unpleasant the task, the longer he put it off. The piles of papers covered decades of activity, and with every letter or document he picked up, he relived memories. The only solution was to put it all in the wood burner. Or fill a hundred boxes and hand everything over to poor Fru Martinsen in the archive.

He looked at the sculpture of Christ on the cross and murmured: "I expect you'll manage on your own. You always have."

But the Saviour's gaze seemed to reveal doubt tonight. As though He too wanted to say that nothing would ever be the same from now on.

Schweigaard's replacement had been appointed. He had visited Butangen in February. Wet behind the ears. With a dialect from the south. His suit one size too big. Over-eager, polite, doubtless a nice singing voice. Unmarried. Forever fumbling with his spectacles. Chaplain Kåre Karlsen. "Morning!"

The villagers were going to eat him alive.

Karlsen was given a tour of the parsonage by Herr Røhme. Yes, the building was in good repair externally. New slate roof in 1927. Inside it was – yes, *intact*, as Herr Karlsen could see. Truth was the wallpaper and furniture hadn't been changed since Schweigaard's predecessor had lived here. It wasn't said out loud, but the fact that the parsonage looked like a museum of pre-1850 interiors was only partially due to the durability of linseed paint. The main cause was Schweigaard's lifelong lack of interest in all things domestic, and his equally lifelong thriftiness that had with time bordered on meanness.

But more than anything it was a monument to the absence of a wife.

Perhaps he guessed this, Kåre Karlsen. That there were things unsaid. He peered up the stairs, but no, he didn't need to see the pastor's study.

Kai Schweigaard tried to see himself in this young man. Impossible. Where was the ambition? The will to do battle? Neither was needed any longer. Norway had become a better place after 1879, and Butangen a *much* better place. Telephone, radio, electric lights, a reliable postal service, a seter road, a co-operative dairy factory and shop, a transport service, car repair shop, school library, representatives on the district council. People could even wear shoes, rather than boots, with most of the village gravelled now.

And it was easier to get down into the valley these days. To access secondary schools. The railway. Doctors. Dentists. Caesarean sections. Aspirin and vitamin tablets from the pharmacy. A kinder government system that saved folk from the misery and dire poverty he had spent sixty years fighting. Were there any grim serpents left for Chaplain Kåre Karlsen to slay with the Almighty's sword? No! Young Karlsen was a mere song thrush! He wouldn't wield a sword but a silver cake slice! He didn't even say *good morning*, just *morning*, the puerile short form that was invading everyday speech. The only good thing was that he would never be a pastor, just a resident chaplain. Butangen had been a separate parish when Schweigaard had taken office, but was later made subject to Ringebu county. According to Norwegian administrative custom, however, a pastor retained his title and authority until he resigned.

What would life be like after May? He hadn't even sorted out somewhere to live. Where would he put all his books? Or the threadbare tapestries he had bought out of politeness when searching for the Hekne Weave? The yellowing newspaper archive that filled half the loft? He was welcome at Hekne, but to pad around there, like some lonesome crow? No, he did not want to be a bother. He was useless with everyday practicalities. All his life he had had his meals served, his shirts ironed, his chamber pot emptied and his bedroom cleaned, while he ruled the village in accordance with the vague contract he had made with God. No point in reading anymore or staying informed now that Sundays were taken from him. He was suited to one task only: to preach, to enlighten, to comfort!

Schweigaard would never go into the church to hear Kåre Karlsen, who would not be the least bothered that he stood on the foundations of an ancient stave church and the Hekne sisters' grave. Karlsen was too young, too stupid – as stupid as he had been as a young pastor, it was irritating to watch! Worst of all, Karlsen would be an easy target for Günther. Karlsen would sell the church bell and use the money for good causes, and then any memory of the sisters would disappear, and when memories were lost, forgetfulness would set in, and then the unbearable would happen: the Hekne sisters' fate would be erased.

Schweigaard went to the wooden chest that encased the Hekne Weave. He did not open it. He felt strangely betrayed. Surely it was impossible that Kåre Karlsen, this milksop, could march in on the legend? Would *he* be the priest to die that gruesome, yet somehow glorious death?

Schweigaard went over to the window.

It was so dark he could not even see Lake Løsnes. There was little to take pleasure in tonight as he stood before the last calendar page of his working life. Even his fishing rod and smoking apparel lay untouched. The winter had been long and dull, full of concern about events in Europe. One morning that September there had been a radio announcement that the Germans had invaded Poland. Three months later, the Soviets had attacked Finland, and anger against communism swept over Norway.

Months had passed without Germany invading more countries. The fighting in Finland continued.

Maybe that was it. Hitler said it was at least. Nonetheless, foreign ships kept popping up along the Norwegian coast. In February the British had boarded a German prisoner of war ship deep in a fjord, and in March the British Navy lay mines along a stretch of Norway's coast.

The clock in the dining room struck twelve.

He often felt a connection with Astrid, the old Astrid, when it grew dark like this. And often wondered what she would think about the way he had started to put himself into her mind.

What would she have said tonight, had she grown old with him? That the lights across the village shone as brightly as the gas lamps in Dresden that she had always dreamed of seeing?

"Yes, let's take a stroll," he whispered, going into the hallway and putting on his winter coat. "An evening stroll."

But . . . an evening stroll? No, this was a nocturnal ramble, he realised as he came out onto the driveway and saw that the moon was no more than *one* finger wide. A nocturnal ramble in a dark that was dark no longer, for darkness had been banished by her own son and his power station at Hellorn.

The snow crunched under his shoes. He pulled his hat down over his head. Stopped and turned.

"Look," he murmured.

Shining pinpricks up the valley sides, one for each farm. Lights behind windows in living rooms and kitchens. Lit

I Shallna' Be Content with Less

pathways between farmhouses and barns. Outside the church a lone lamp cast a yellow glow over snow-covered tombstones.

He walked to the bell tower to get a better view over the village, and was sure he felt her arm in his. He tried to be bright and cheerful; it was important not to be glum when she was around.

So, this is how it would be, his departure from Butangen. An aged man's thoughts in the End Times. Out in the night, walking arm in arm with a ghost.

Kai ambled on without thinking, until he realised he was standing before a gravestone, shivering. Herr Røhme had replaced the gold leaf on her name, and it glinted in the light from the lamp on the church wall.

He looked around. Did he hear the bell? Did he hear Gunhild?

He was wide awake. The April night must surely have made an April fool of him, in the cruel April cold. With the wind in his face. Snow against his brow. Wet feet, icy fingers.

There it was again. A heavy, warning clang.

Second Story

Runes and Warplanes

An Ordinary Tuesday in April

WAR DOESN'T LIKE ON-THE-HOUR SCHEDULES. INVASIONS do not start at eight o'clock on a Monday morning. Or at midnight on January the first.

No, war prefers to follow the dictates of the moon.

So that April 9, 1940 had something in common with the Battle of the Somme and countless other surprise attacks throughout history.

They all took place on moonless nights. Nights when the Earth feels alone. Nights that precede days that nobody expects anything of. Nights for headaches and draughty trips to the chamber pot. Nights for walking arm in arm with a ghost.

Astrid Hekne was up early. She had planned to study for an hour before leaving for teacher training college. From her tiny window she could see the frost-smoke rising over the Glomma. When she had moved to Elverum that spring, she had been delighted to have a view over the river, but in November she looked at the thermometer and understood why these lodgings were so cheap. Mari Slåen was in the next room. They shared the rent and eventually secrets, for Mari had a fair number of admirers. She had let her hair grow long, and it was now a spring flood of red.

Elverum was a wonderful town. Hedmark's most beautiful, where elegant timber buildings fought static fencing matches to outdo each other in grandeur. Each one a testament to the great wealth of the forest landowners in Østerdalen. The finest was the Hotel Central, a white fairy-tale castle, with a roof like a chequerboard, topped with keen spires and weathervanes, a vision from afar and close up. Inside, the hotel was adorned with exquisite wallpapers and elegantly patterned floors. It had a café that made students welcome, where they could sit outside on large, covered balconies to drink hot chocolate and know that life was bountiful.

Astrid turned back to her textbook.

Suddenly she heard hurried footsteps on the stairs. The landlord was an old forestry worker with a bad axe injury to his leg, so it came as a surprise when hearing his voice she realised it was him.

"The Germans," he called out from the landing. "The Germans are here!"

Astrid opened her door. "Here? What do you mean, *here*?"

"Along the coast. Down in Oslo and in Bergen and Narvik. Huge warships. Planes. People are reporting shootings everywhere. Come downstairs. You've got to come down and hear this. I'll wake Mari up."

The wife of the house was sitting in her floral dressing gown in front of the radio. The newscaster's voice was shaking. Warships had fired at the fortress in the Oslo fjord. German troops had landed in Bergen and Trondheim. There had been an air battle over Fornebu. The radio sputtered. Then just hissed. The landlord carefully turned the tuning knob, but all they heard was more crackling. Everyone else stood motionless, as the slightest movement could interfere with the reception.

Mari Slåen stood halfway up the stairs. Astrid met her gaze.

Outside the window the Glomma flowed on its way south.

In just ten minutes everyone was fully dressed and listening to a familiar voice on the radio. This was not a regular newscaster.

An Ordinary Tuesday in April

It was Hartvig Kiran. A presenter only known until then for hosting entertainment programmes.

Denmark was also under attack. Kristiansand had started an evacuation. Kiran sounded strangely calm, but Astrid imagined that a captain on a sinking ship might speak with a similarly calm voice.

The reception was suddenly lost, and the voice disappeared amid crackling and hissing. The last words they heard were "the Chief of Air Defence and keep them filled with water".

"What did he just say?" whispered the woman.

"That – that folk in Oslo mun fill every bucket and pot they have with water," said Mari Slåen. "And put them at the top of the stairs. If they have bathtubs, they should fill them to the top too. Only on the upper floors."

The upper floors, Astrid thought. That means the water's not for drinking. It's to extinguish the fires if they get bombed. Tarald – he lives in a garret at the top of an apartment building in Bjerregaards Gate.

The crackling stopped, but now all they heard was some incongruous, blustery band music. Then both the crackling and music disappeared, and Hartvig Kiran's voice came clear again. He was issuing instructions about the evacuation of Oslo. Anyone who owned a car should take as many people as possible when they left the city. Taxis must drop people off three miles outside the city, then go back to pick up more. The music overlapped with the news again. It grew louder, and a male voice choir began: *Kamerad! Kamerad! Ran an den Feind! Mit Blitzen und Bomben und Brand!*

The four of them looked at each other.

Remembering her father's radio, Astrid realised that the Germans had adjusted one of their transmitters to the same frequency as the Norwegian broadcasting service.

Hartvig Kiran was clearly unaware that his broadcast was

being disrupted, as he went on calmly issuing instructions which Astrid and the others struggled to make out. All able-bodied young men should report for military service. In the event of an aircraft alert, all activity must stop, and everyone should take cover in a shelter, or, at the very least, inside a house. With that it seemed Hartvig Kiran had no more to say, and in the silence he left behind, the choir started up again, singing about fighter planes flying up to the sun and heading for the land of the enemy. About lightening, and bombs, and fire, and how soldiers baptised by fire would crush everything in their path. *Das wird unser stolzester Tag!*

Their landlord did not have a telephone. Astrid and Mari flung on their coats and ran along the river path to get to the telephone exchange. When the main road came into view, they stopped.

"Do that many folks live in Elverum?" Mari said.

They ran into the stream of people, and the noise of distressed and disjointed chatter. Some said it had been announced on the radio that the government had gone to Hamar, less than an hour's drive from Elverum; others thought that was a bluff. A warship had been sunk, but rumours alternated between the ship being German and it being English.

There were about sixty people in the queue at the telephone exchange, and half an hour later there were sixty more behind them. A switchboard lady repeated again and again that nobody could talk for longer than two minutes. They failed to get a line to Hekne or to the parsonage, and when Astrid tried to reach Tarald at his lodgings, there was no answer.

"Let's go to the military camp at Terningmoen," said Mari. "They might give us a better idea of what's happening."

The girls elbowed their way through the crowd. The snow had turned to slush with all the coming and going, and everyone they met had wet shoes and mud all over their ankles and shins. Posters about air raid sirens had been nailed to telephone poles and tree trunks. Short blasts would warn of imminent attack. A long tone meant the danger was over. Driving along the road from Hamar came a stream of cars with luggage tied to their roofs. A woman was almost run down, the car did not stop, and a suitcase of clothes crashed into the mud. As the girls approached the camp, they came across increasing numbers of young men, often hastily dressed. One or two came leading workhorses. Doubtless requisitioned for the war.

There, at last, was Terningmoen. The Norwegian military flag was flying. Along the fences were rows of machine guns, barrels pointed up at the sky.

Men and horses thronged at the gates, with more arriving by the minute. The guards, it seemed, were not letting them in.

"We shan't find anything out here," said Astrid.

They returned to their lodgings. Two announcements had been made on the radio to say that Oslo must be evacuated. But now there was doubt as to whether that applied to the entire city, and there was nothing about the rest of Norway.

"We mun go home to Butangen," Astrid said. "We in't any use to anybody here."

"First train or bus to Hamar," said Mari. "Then north from there."

They were told at the station that the next three trains to Hamar were cancelled. The only services running were to Kongsvinger or northbound with the Røros line. They walked to the main shopping area below the hotel, where they spotted a solitary policeman tearing down the posters and nailing up new ones.

Observe change! Air Raid Warning is a long tone.

A cardboard box filled with the new posters was standing aslant in the slush. Already on its way to being waterlogged.

"Do ye need help?" Mari asked.

"It's a long tone, I said!"

"We asked if ye wanted help putting these up," said Astrid.

"It's a flaming nightmare," he said. "Why couldn't the army guys let the sirens sound with a short tone when I've already hung these ones up?"

The policeman continued hanging up his posters alone.

Around them the chaos had settled a little. The disorder seemed to be taking on its eventual shape. Everyone was heading somewhere, each carrying a suitcase or rucksack. Whole families were making their way with children in their arms and belongings in wheelbarrows, while a steady flow of young men with scant baggage asked for directions to the military camp. Eventually the talk was only about trains and buses and mobilisation. The Germans had, it seemed, already taken Oslo, and soldiers were pouring in by the thousands. The farmers they had met earlier were walking back with their horses. The radio announcement about mobilisation had apparently been wrong, although some companies had already been sent to fight. The others should go home and wait for a summons in the post.

"In the post?" Mari said, looking out over the chaos.

She ran her hands through her hair as though to keep them busy. A futile gesture. But everything seemed futile today. One of the old posters about the sirens was still hanging from a telephone pole. Mari tore it down.

It was unthinkable to go back to their lodgings now, so they squeezed into Café Gråberg, where a radio was playing. It stank of cigarette smoke and sweat. The floor was grey with mud. Mari and Astrid got a seat on a window ledge. Forty-odd conversations were going on at once. Whenever an announcement came on the radio, the noise died down, but started up again just as quickly. The girls asked for soup, but were told they were only serving stew now, as it was impossible to carry soup through this circus.

An Ordinary Tuesday in April

Astrid felt a tingling sensation in her fingers and arms. She had noticed it before when really bad things happened. Now it was there the whole time. She began to picture all the ways Tarald could get hurt. Crushed between brick walls in a bombed apartment building. Or shot down in the street.

Mari seemed to be having similar thoughts.

A man in a red-checked flannel shirt, whose job it was to keep his ear to the radio shouted, "*Quiet! A broadcast!*"

He turned the radio to full volume, and a murmur went round the room as everyone recognised the man giving a speech.

Vidkun Quisling?

The chairman of the far-right Nasjonal Samling Party, which had devoured itself with internal squabbles and chaos. How had he got into the national broadcasting studios? Some of the crowd in the café started to get rowdy, but were promptly shushed.

Astrid sat with her bowl in her lap. She put down her spoon. It was as if Quisling was reading from a manuscript in giant capital letters. He was trying to sound masterful and strong, but sounded affected and shrill as he described any resistance against the Germans as an *aberration* and *criminal*.

Then it came. Quisling declared himself Head of Government and Foreign Minister.

Lots of people shook their heads and walked out. It was enough for one day.

Getting to sleep was impossible. They had brought their mattresses down to the living room and gone to bed in their coats and shoes. Earlier that evening their landlord had told them that the Germans had reached Hamar, and that someone thought they'd seen two black cars with licence plates A1 and A2. This would mean they were the royal household's vehicles. And there were others who thought something was going on at the Folkehøgskole, since the school caretaker had seen a man in the hallway who looked like the secretary of state, but then again, she had only seen him briefly.

Astrid finally dozed off. She had no idea how long she had slept when she sat bolt upright.

What had she heard?

In the semi-darkness she could see the mean furniture in the living room, and on the mattress beside her she saw Mari lying with her back to her.

There it was again.

Shooting.

She went out on the front doorsteps. The shots were muffled by the forest and snow, and only the deepest notes reached her.

But she was sure now. There were gunshots coming from the direction of Hamar. Then a series of long volleys rang out, as though giant woodpeckers were working in the forest darkness.

They must be machine guns. She had thought about Tarald all day. Now she saw him in her mind, dressed in his uniform behind the machine gun he had told them about when he was on his military service at Jørstadmoen. The machine gun he must never abandon no matter what approached.

Astrid jumped. Mari was standing behind her. Her hair wasn't red in the shadows. They were both as grey as ghosts that night.

The next day they heard that the soldiers had managed to halt the Germans along the road to Hamar. Everyone in Elverum was told to evacuate. But where to? Anywhere. Even if it was just to a tiny forest hut. But why the hurry to evacuate? Nobody knew.

"Our skis," said Astrid. "In the college basement. Remember? We had to have them for the gymnastics class."

Mari nodded. "Go home via Østerdalen?"

"We can take the train to Koppang or preferably Imsroa. Pick up some food, then ski to Imsdalen, stop off at my mother's folks, then cross the mountains."

There was no time to reflect, and they changed into their ski boots. Their landlord said he would have given them skis if he had any, but sent them off with eight cans of food, a spare ski binding with screws and glue, a compass and his old axe.

"Please, send us a letter to tell us how it went," said his wife.

At the college they were told by a soldier to sling their hooks, this was now an army barracks. When they tried to tell him about their skis, he called a sergeant who repeated that from now on this was a military zone, and why hadn't they evacuated, as all civilians had been instructed?

"Cos we need our skis to get home," said Astrid. "All we're asking is for somebody to take us down to the basement. They're our skis!"

The sergeant was about to relent when he was called away. They waited an hour, but he did not return, and the guard got cross and told them to go.

Elverum was turning into an abandoned town. An increasing number of civilian men were signing up, but their transformation into soldiers was slow and patchy. The Terningmoen depot clearly did not have enough equipment to go round, so that some wore army jackets with breeches and socks, while others wore military trousers and knitted cardigans. Occasionally an officer came along sporting a trench coat, with a gun in a holster and his face in grim folds.

The girls had no choice but to go to their lodgings again. Next morning, they put on their backpacks, went back to the college, and tried to talk sense into a lieutenant who was by the stairs smoking. He waved them through, pinched out his cigarette, and said that of course they could have their skis.

They had them in their hands at last. Two pairs of fine laminate skis, with Kandahar bindings and tarred soles. Bamboo poles with leather grips. Good enough to take them across the whole country if needs be. Mari and Astrid came up from the basement and walked quietly along the corridor so as not to wake up the soldiers who were sleeping under the windows. Suddenly the building shook, causing all the windows to instantly shatter. The young men came abruptly to, but, still groggy with sleep, cut themselves on the broken glass. Then another explosion rang out. The electric wires along the cornices flashed before it went dark. The girls held tightly on to their skis and headed for the exit. Out in the cold, they heard the fading hum of engines. And low in the sky they saw a dark silhouette moving into the distance.

A huge airplane.

A long howl sounded from a siren someplace. The air raid warning. Soon it echoed through the city.

"They're going to bomb the station!" someone shouted. Mari and Astrid followed everyone else in their flight towards the town centre. They ran through the shopping streets, past the cinema, the public baths, the hat shop and photography studio, they ran so the mud splashed, and stopped in front of the Hotel Central, the white angel in all this.

An officer had climbed up on a trailer to get a better view.

"The station?" he said. "Who said they're bombing the station? Nobody can know that!"

"There's a shelter under the slaughterhouse!" someone shouted.

The crowd changed direction, and Astrid and Mari Slåen followed them. In front of a brick building stood a portly man in a bloodied, white apron. The front door stood wide open, and they laid their skis aside and ran towards him. He pointed towards the cellar stairs. The girls hurried down. There in the cellar a glaring electric light bulb lit about forty people, all in heavy winter clothes and tightly packed. Soon they were part of this steaming human mass, sitting shoulder to shoulder. Everyone twisted about. Some to make room for others. Others to make themselves more comfortable.

An Ordinary Tuesday in April

The door upstairs was closed.

Minutes passed. It got harder to breathe. The electric light blinked and went out. Somebody cried. An old man began to sing a hymn, but was told to shut up or he'd use up what little air they had. The light returned.

No bombs fell.

Eventually the sirens went off. Short blasts. Danger over.

They came back up the stairs and inhaled the cool air. A lorry honked for people to step aside. It stopped at a concrete ramp. Four men carried out some boxes of already cut meat. Somebody said that all the butchers had been called in to secure food for the soldiers at Terningmoen.

A crowd had formed outside the office of the local paper, *Østlendingen*, eager to read the news telegrams that were displayed in a glass case on the wall. A cocky young lad, wearing only shirtsleeves, asserted that the Germans were heading for Gjøvik and that the Hamar trains would run as usual from tonight.

"Idiot," said another lad of like age. "False rumour. The Germans are heading every which way, don't you get it?"

The girls stood there, taking stock. Astrid looked at her watch and said they must go to the station right away if they were to catch the Koppang train.

Mari didn't answer. She stood motionless, her face turned towards the sky.

Her topknot had come unpinned in the commotion, and there she stood with her tousled hair, anorak and skis in the bright, spring sunshine, but her expression seemed disconnected to the sunshine.

"Nay," she muttered. "Nay . . ."

Astrid could hear the hum of engines, but could see nothing until she discovered they were much closer than the sound suggested, and they were flying much lower and were bigger than she could ever have envisaged.

217

Three massive planes in formation. Their bulbous fuselages shone in the sun, and now something happened in the belly of the front plane. Two hatches opened. Then from a shadowy space within came a shower of dark-coloured lozenges. So small, so light, so numerous, like sweets spilled from a paper cone by a kind grandmother, before the bombs straightened up and took a vertical path down through the air, a path nothing would divert them from.

"Run!" Mari shouted.

Astrid dropped her skis and just had time to hear them clatter to the ground before there was a thud and she too fell. When she came to, she was lying on her back, looking straight up at the sky, where more planes were approaching, strangely slowly. The iron cross on their fuselage and wings. Swastikas on their tails. Glass dome above the nose, glinting in the sun.

Strangers. Coming here. Through the air. To kill and to burn. To chasten. We here below, you high above, in the sky. Such an unjust division.

A calm descended on her. As if she had reached the last page of a book.

Today I shall die. Because I was here when you came. Without your ever knowing me. Without your wanting to know me.

Silently one bomb fell after the next.

Damn the lot of you. May you never again rest peacefully in your beds. You up there in your planes. Indestructible because our bullets cannot reach you.

She looked and she looked, up until the moment she was flung in the air. When she regained consciousness, she found herself lying in a pool of mud, and heard moans from among the bricks and timbers that were flying about. The ground shook again, and then she heard nothing more. Aware only of the smell of smoke and that the explosions vibrated through her. When she could finally get to her feet, all the things she had

An Ordinary Tuesday in April

admired were gone. The roof of the Hotel Central had collapsed, and flames flicked out from between the fine trelliswork on the balcony.

Mari.

Where was Mari?

Astrid stumbled towards the slaughterhouse, but tripped over something. A person wearing a blue jacket. Dead. She pushed on, but could not find the shelter. Nothing in the town was recognisable. She tried taking another direction, but still she saw nothing but ruins and fires and screaming people all around her, and she retraced her steps, only to find that she had been standing in front of the slaughterhouse all along.

Half the building had come down. Astrid climbed over the broken brick walls and looked down into the basement. Among the concrete and planks she caught sight of a brown shoe, and then saw the other shoe on a bloody foot. A tall man emerged from the ruins. The brick wall behind him started to crack, and he just managed to run away before it collapsed. When the dust had settled, Astrid spotted something white. A butcher's apron lay beside a box of chopped-up meat. The man himself was nowhere to be seen. Again and again, she called out Mari's name, and others arrived and called out, and nobody found who they were looking for.

In a crater, sprinkled with exploded earth, lay a pile of slaughterhouse waste. She edged around it and continued to shout. Then stopped. Oblivious now to the fires, the screams, the sirens.

She went back and knelt down.

This was not slaughterhouse waste.

It was Mari Slåen.

Our Lord's Decommissioned Warship

Hekne stood there as Hekne had always stood. She was relieved that the evening had brought sub-zero temperatures, and that her skis picked up speed on the harder snow down towards the farmhouse's forecourt where she caught sight of her father. He was out in his shirtsleeves, carrying a bundle of firewood, but must have been scanning the landscape in the hope that she might come, come at last from wherever she was, for he suddenly dropped his logs and broke into a run, waving his hands and wading out into the deep snow. He stumbled up towards her with open arms and Astrid let her skis glide on under her, so exhausted she nearly ran him down.

"We ha' been so afeared for thee," said Jehans.

"I – I was there. When the planes came."

He squeezed her harder.

"Tarald," said Astrid. "Is he in Oslo now?"

Jehans shook his head. "Came back yesterday. The war hasna' reached here yet."

They stumbled out of the deep snow. Now that she had lost momentum, the snow cracked under her with every step. He took her ski poles, and carried her more than supported her.

"Where have ye come from?" he said, gesturing towards the ski tracks.

"Across the mountains. From Imsdalen."

"In this weather?"

"Aye, in this weather. Walked below Kvia. Slept in the Saubua cabin."

Kristine came out, saw the logs in the snow and looked around, and in seconds understood what was happening. She lifted her skirts and ran in Jehans' tracks. They practically fought over who should help Astrid down to the farmhouse. Jehans unclipped the bindings on the skis and stood them in the snow.

"The skis," Astrid murmured. "Nay. We mun take the skis."

"I shall come out for them later," Jehans said.

Astrid yanked herself free. "We canna' leave the skis here. Take them now. They are Mari Slåen's skis."

Her parents didn't understand, and Astrid didn't have the strength to explain.

Then Tarald came wading through the snow.

And Tarald understood.

He pulled the skis gently out of the snow, scraped them clean, put them sole to sole and walked behind. Down in the forecourt he propped them nicely against the wall, along with the poles. Esther and Eirik were already inside in the hallway. Tarald walked past, saying that he would prepare some food. Bread and cheese, it won't take long, Astrid.

"Not food," Astrid said. "I want t' wash myself. Esther, please help me. Fetch the soap. Wash my hair. Get all the soap we have, Sister. *Get me soap!*"

Tarald was ready, for once, to listen to her whole story before starting on his own. She observed that he shared a similar degree of anger, and that their parents seemed to take a back seat, perhaps because they had to recognise that here were two children who were suddenly adults.

Tarald explained how on April 9 he had been woken up by a commotion in the apartment above his. A man had stormed down the stairs shouting. Looking out of the window, Tarald noticed folk wandering about, far more than would usually go to work at this time. He remembered his military service, grabbed his conscription book, and three hours later he was on a crowded train heading north towards Jørstadmoen, where he reported for duty.

"We were walking gormlessly about for two whole days. Several hundred of us. The officers didna' know whether they were meant to mobilise us or not. Exactly as ye described in Terningmoen, Astrid. It was mad at the depot. They had no system for issuing uniforms or weapons or cartridges. They must have had two thousand rifles, but no bolts. Somebody had transferred them to another camp in case the Norwegian communists broke into the weapons store and started a revolution!"

"Unbelievable."

"Aye. A few Krags was all that were in working order. It hadna' dawned on them that if things got so bad that the communists were after the weapons, we should have some to beat them back. And the serial numbers on the bolts have t' match those on t' guns, so ye can imagine the chaos."

Astrid sat with a blanket round her, chewing on a slice of buttered bread, while Esther stood behind her with a towel, drying her hair.

"So, I didna' get a uniform but was finally issued with a Colt machine gun. She weighs almost fifty kilos, and needs two men to operate her, cos she's fed with a gun belt. But then they couldna' put together any teams cos the lists of soldiers were missing. Then the rumours started that we couldna' mix civies and uniforms, as that would mean we were unprotected by the Code o' War. Meaning that the Germans could shoot us on the spot even if we surrendered. They only took a hundred soldiers in the end. They got ten cartridges each. And here I am, at home, waiting for my call-up papers."

He was unable to sleep. Woke up arguing with himself, and often got dressed and went out into the night to walk off the anger. Kristine found his bed empty more than once, and stood on the doorstep looking for him in the darkness.

Astrid began to nod off. The room grew hazy, and the voices drifted into each other. She barely noticed when she was carried to bed.

Next morning, she found Kai by the radio. He rose on stiff legs and gave her a smile that came straight from his heart. He told her how worried he'd been about her. That Tarald had come down to the parsonage late last night and told him about Mari Slåen.

Then Astrid told Kai more than she had told the others.

About how the bombs found their path and whistled through the air. Audible between the explosions and the cries of folk for their dead friends. Children so scared that the safest thing was to wrench themselves free from their mother's hand, or whose mother's hand had let them go because she was herself dead. And finally, about Mari Slåen's mangled body.

"I have no idea where she is now," Astrid said. "She was put into two sacks and lifted onto a truck with some other dead bodies."

"Mari will come here," said Kai Schweigaard. "She must be buried here. By me."

"The state highway is closed to traffic. Everything's been brought to a standstill. But soldiers everywhere. The Germans are making their way up the valley. So, Mari's lying out there alone somewhere. Wi' strangers. Who are dead too."

She went on with her story, and when she had told it all, she sat breathless. And now in the quiet, she could feel how broken she was. She was enveloped here by a sense of safety and order. The red-painted living room with its linen cupboard and silverware and the Røhme family nearby. Such a contrast to the chaos up at Hekne, where everyone was always battling with or for something.

She sat for a long time, and for a long time Kai let her.

"When Tarald was here yesterday," he said eventually, "we talked a bit. I saw another man in him. One with the will to fight."

"He wants to go back to Jørstadmoen," said Astrid. "To get a uniform and weapon."

"The way I see it," said Kai Schweigaard, "he wants to avenge you and Mari Slåen. What could I say to him? Should a pastor invoke caution when a fight is justified?"

She didn't know what to think. There was a difference between brothers and soldiers, though soldiers were often brothers.

Gripping the armrest, Astrid stood up.

"The Hekne Weave," she said.

They went upstairs, and when he let her into his study, it was already rolled out on the table. It had, he said, been there for three days.

Astrid ran her fingers over the threads. Felt the wool pricking her fingertips. Studied the firebirds. Stepped to one side to see the patterns in a different light.

"I canna' say," Astrid said. "This is very like what I saw, and yet not."

"Sadly, I think you're right," Kai said. "What we see here . . . will come later."

She turned away. She couldn't bear to look more. Not now that Mari Slåen was dead. This was not how death was. Not how war was. War must be viewed from below, from the ground. The ground where the blood mixed with the mud. The ground where the slaughterhouse waste was, and the slaughterhouse waste was them. Don't show me war from above, not now that Mari Slåen is dead.

"I must go and see her mother and father," said Astrid. "Tell them what happened. I spoke to a police officer and gave him her name. But the news canna' have got through yet."

"I'll go," Kai said. "Tidings like that are *mine* to bring."

"I must tell them myself."

"Not before tomorrow. Or later this evening. And gild it a little. The dead are always dressed in their best. For a reason. No, sit down. You must calm yourself now."

"Calm myself? They're coming here! They'll probably warn of their attack by flying warplanes right over the treetops and shooting in t' air. To chase the civilians away. But where should they all go? They have cows in barns. Babbies in cradles. Grandparents sitting by the stove."

He had no answer.

She watched him roll up the weave. Patterns and colours slipped into hiding. Silver-coloured threads glinted as they folded themselves into the cloth's dark vault. Then he put the weave in the chest, on top of the two pillows and the rusted knife.

"The day you went into the bell tower," he said, "I said you would take charge of the Hekne Weave when the time was right. That time is come."

Astrid got up and stood before the chest. He closed the lid and stepped aside. She didn't move. Kai fetched a tartan travelling rug from a cupboard. "And take this as well. I was given it by my mother."

"But—"

He waved away any objections.

"I'll be moving in a few weeks. I'm not sure where to. Sometime in May I'll cease to be the pastor here in Butangen. It's strange, but . . . this house has never really been mine. Still I . . ."

His expression darkened and he slumped down on a stool.

"What is it, Kai?" Astrid asked.

"No-one shall bury Mari Slåen but me."

"But of course. What do you mean?"

"I shudder when I think of all the deaths that will come in the months ahead. And that this new-baked curate will be the one who'll go to my villagers and give them the news."

She put a hand on the lid of the chest. It was as though she had shut something alive in it.

"There's a war," said Astrid. "We've work to do. I've been thinking about Günther. The German who was here that Easter. If he comes back here, Gunhild won't be safe in the bell tower."

"I've been wondering whether she should be sunk in Lake Løsnes again," Schweigaard said.

"Nay. Folks watch it too much."

She went over to the map of Butangen that hung on the wall. "There," she said, with her finger on the map.

"*There?*"

"Aye. Naybody ever goes there."

"Hmm," he said.

"We mun find a way to move her," Astrid said.

At first he seemed to agree with her. Then he quickly grew strange and dismissive and refused to say what he was thinking.

"Leave this to me. You should know as little as possible. Your task is to hide the Hekne Weave. Don't mention the bell to anyone."

She tucked the tartan rug under her arm, flipped up the chest's two cast iron drop handles and lifted it up. It was impossible to decide on its weight. Perhaps it had no need to answer to gravity.

Astrid hesitated in the doorway.

A change seemed to be happening in Kai. He straightened up. Rubbed the backs of his hands against his eyes as if he had just woken up. Turned away.

For a moment she glimpsed who he had been when he was young. The self-assured man, one of the Almighty's hardiest warships. Year after year she had seen him weighed down by arthritis, poor hearing and, in periods, agitation.

But now, in this moment, it was as though somebody, perhaps

God himself, had rearmed Pastor Schweigaard. The coals in the old ship's boiler had been relit, the worst scratches had been given a lick of grey paint, a sun-bleached flag had been run up the mast, and this old relic of the Kingdom of Heaven's war fleet had been relaunched. A ship with rusted weaponry perhaps, and with a poor-sighted captain. But which, with a measure of luck and experience, might yet strike a blow at the enemy before it sank in flames.

The Ice on Daukulpen

Kai Schweigaard got up. He felt surprisingly little stiffness and went down the stairs without holding the banister. A couple of hours later he was back, rather shaken after his meeting with Mari Slåen's parents.

Three big tasks awaited him now, and they were urgent. First, he must hold a Mass that gave the villagers strength. Probably his most important before Curate Kåre Karlsen pootled in. Second, he must find a hiding place for the dynamite in his barn. The third was more difficult, but Astrid was right. They must take seriously the drivel written in the tourist guide about the Nordenkirche, and hide Gunhild.

The Germans who were rolling into Norway did not come from Germany. Not from Gerhard Schönauer's Germany. Not Thomas Mann's Germany, or Bach's Germany. The country might be Germany, but only on the map.

He took Herr Røhme quietly aside.

"We're taking a wheelbarrow out tonight. Norwegian soldiers may need our dynamite. Too many villagers know it's here.

Among them Ola Mossen and his sons, who support Quisling. We can hide it in the new church."

"Nay, but . . . we canna' store it *there*!"

"There are only three boxes. The fuses aren't attached, and that, according to Jehans, means it's no more dangerous than a basket of laundry. If the Germans come, we'll pretend to hold a funeral, and take the dynamite out in a coffin."

"And then – then it'll go in't ground?"

"We'll manage. But you don't breathe a word to that whiny little canary!"

"Canary?"

"*Kåre Karlsen!*"

He apologised for being abrupt, asked Fru Røhme for a strong coffee, and went upstairs to his Underwood to type a rousing sermon. But the words seemed to float together, sentences quarrelled with each other, and paragraphs failed to reach a conclusion, so he let them end with three dots. Eventually he ripped the paper out of the typewriter, causing the roller to emit a sharp grating sound.

It was Gunhild, of course, that was troubling him. Røhme could help him move the dynamite, but not the church bell. If the Germans came to take her away, Røhme would be the first to be put under pressure, and he had a wife and children, and grandchildren too. Astrid was already more involved than she should be, especially since her suggestion for a hiding place was so good.

Jehans had raised the bell. He knew all about hoists and lifting heavy weights, and had some sort of moral rights over the bell's destiny. But, then again, this would instantly mark him out for suspicion.

Kai felt his head go into a mush. This whole enterprise demanded a sort of practical physics and exertion that was beyond him. Not even his pipe and coffee were any help.

But wait. How about? Could *he* help?

Kai Schweigaard mulled the idea over. It had never occurred to him that he might entertain anything so bizarre. But perhaps bizarre times demanded bizarre ideas.

A weekend drinker with amazing arm strength.

Either this man was the perfect choice, or he would immediately give the game away.

An axe rang out through the winter forest. Kai Schweigaard broke into a sweat as he ploughed through the snow on his skis, wearing a blue anorak and the gabardine breeches that Konow, his old tailor in Lillehammer, had made for him years ago. He stopped and leaned on his ski poles. Deep sledge tracks had led him to this rather inaccessible copse of birch and aspen on the Hekne estate.

Further ahead the axing stopped. He heard the swish of a falling tree, then the snort of Svarten, Isum's loyal companion.

Schweigaard knew of course what the locals said. Svarten, Hekne's biggest Døla horse, and Giant Isum were inseparable, and the locals joked that it was hard to tell which was the stronger, and which had the bigger brain.

Between the trees he saw a man dressed in loud colours. Summer or winter, Isum wore knitted hats, gloves and stockings straight out of the last century. He had acquired them at the auctions of the estates of various spinsters. Sold by the boxful, these were known as *vonapjank* and were the product of a bygone custom. After her confirmation, a girl would start knitting vast quantities of hats, socks, scarves and more. These would be put by for the day she was keen on a young man, for then she would give them to his relatives as gifts, so they might take her side and talk him into tying the knot. It was vital to have a good supply, so they could be given away at will. Some girls who failed to find husbands never let their hopes die, and went on making stockings, hats, sweaters and gloves. Their stacks of lovingly folded hopes grew bigger and bigger, until they filled coffer upon coffer, as the chances of marriage faded by the year. Some went on knitting till their dying day.

As for Isum, he was too huge and strange, too fierce and too unpredictable, too *much* everything, to be married. He had a constant cold and went through the winter with what the locals called his *Arctic drip* dangling from his nose. As far as Schweigaard knew, he had never had a girlfriend, which possibly explained why he liked wearing these *vonapjank* knits. He invariably got them very cheap. Hardly anybody attended these auctions, since the old spinsters rarely owned more than a battered old coffee pot, their knitting needles and the yarn that was left on the ball when they pegged it. Isum wore these clothes proudly, and the blue and red bobble hat, bright yellow gloves, shocking green stockings and striped scarf that Schweigaard saw him in now had doubtless been made by a hopeful maid in about 1860.

Schweigaard leaned on his ski poles and asked himself if there was any sense to what he was considering now. This, after all, was a man who often betrayed himself. But if there was one thing that Kai Schweigaard had learned over the years as a pastor, it was that the man who betrays himself does not necessarily betray others.

Giant Isum had managed to strip half the branches from the birch tree before Schweigaard came up, but when he called out his name, Isum dropped his axe in mid swing. He pulled off his woollen hat, clutched it to his chest, and said: "It were me, Herr Pastor! But I promise it shall be the last time!"

Schweigaard had no idea what Isum was talking about, but managed to maintain a solemn demeanour. He stepped forward, pulled off a mitten, and laid a comforting hand on his shoulder.

"I understand, Herr Isum. But tell me in your own words what happened."

Through much stuttering it emerged that Giant Isum had gone to the dance up at the village hall on Saturday, April 6. He had drunk a lot, but also been generous with his companions. At the end of the party, he had picked up his jacket and set off home. Sweaty and happy, he walked in his shirtsleeves to let the April breeze cool him down. Not until he was a good way down the road did he feel cold, which was when he discovered that the jacket was a few sizes too small. He rushed back up to Høgvang, only to find the hall locked up and deserted. Since then, Isum had tortured himself about the jacket's rightful owner who might have frozen half to death, but he did not have the mental wherewithal to deal with the situation, not on Sunday, not on Monday, and his nerves got more and more ragged, and then war broke out the very next day.

"Herr Isum," Schweigaard said, taking a moment to think, "if the jacket you took isn't hugely expensive, there's no reason to think yours was inferior. We often think like that when we're feeling down. That we are, in ourselves and in our actions, more odious than others. I suggest that the opposite is true here. Nobody in Butangen has a jacket bigger than yours. If anybody had missed theirs, they'd have gone straight to Hekne to get things sorted. Besides which, since your jacket was bigger, the other man can't possibly have got cold. And you must have been among the last to leave the party, because the hall was already locked up when you returned. So, it's probable that the *other* man took *your* jacket first, perhaps even with evil intent. His wife may have cut it up to make it into two jackets. Whatever the case, he who enters Høgvang never comes out his old self. We all know that."

Isum wiped away an Arctic drip. "Bless thee, Herr Pastor."

"Tell me, Isum. You're happy up there at Hekne, yes?"

"Oh, aye. Allays have been."

Isum went over to the sledge and fetched a large fistful of hay. He stamped down the snow and laid the hay in front of the huge horse, which bowed its head and started to munch. The air was filled with the smell of newly felled birch trees and the fresh sweat of man and workhorse.

"Aye, they be kind. I comes there with my fine friend Svarten here, and there be food enough and ne'er fuss or fits o' temperament. Esther and her littlun be so good, and I ne'er feel dafty in that house. I have a room to myseln and I be putting wages aside for a radio o' my own. And Kristine lets me eat with them on weekends, cos I takes a bath the night afore. And I tasted some o' that new fancy spread on my morning slice – Sunda they calls it – tastes like honey."

"You'd do anything for the Heknes then?"

"Aye, they has been like family to me."

"And you want to stop drinking?"

Isum looked down at his feet. The spring sun was warm, the twigs and bark from his tree-felling were already sinking into the snow, and everything here was achievable with his horse, an axe and a sledge, but the pastor had pointed to the one tree that was too big to fell.

"I *wants* to give up the liquor, truly. But 'tis hard. My mind be too frail, Herr Pastor."

Schweigaard looked at him. Somewhere behind the uncertain smile he saw something else. Perhaps there was a deeper reason for this man choosing to wear *vonapjank*.

"Herr Isum. Be down at the church at eleven o'clock tonight. All the lights will be off. Bring your timber sledge and park it by the bell tower. Go up to the church. The door will be open."

That night, one terrified giant stood quaking in the church. Schweigaard was dressed in his cassock and led him along the shadowy aisle, up to the altar, where the only thing visible was one lighted candle and a dented silver cup filled to the brim with a copper-brown liquid.

"Lift the chalice with your left hand and place your right hand on this." Schweigaard held out a large, black book with a gold cross embossed on the front.

"This is the altar book, Herr Isum. One of our church's most precious objects. Swear on it that you will never reveal any of what we do tonight."

His hand was so big it covered the entire altar book. He took the chalice. It spilled a little. He trembled and sipped a little and tried not to show how vile the altar wine was, something Schweigaard had made worse with a dash of vinegar, in the belief it might cause Isum to hesitate next time he saw a bottle of liquor.

Isum drained it, requested another and received it, and they went down to the bell tower. There, Schweigaard lit an oil lamp. Standing on the floor by a handcart were the dusty coffins intended for tramps or outsiders who suffered a sudden end.

He told him what they were going to do.

"'Tis Gunhild ye speak of?" Isum said. "The Sister Bell herseln?"

Schweigaard nodded solemnly. "I've removed her hammer. There's a pulley system up there that they used when she was hung up in 1918. The ropes and iron hooks they used are still there too. You'll see a hatch up there for Gunhild to pass through. Do you think you can work it out and bring her down, Herr Isum?"

"Is't true, Herr Pastor, that no man mun set eyes upon her? And naybody but a maid from the Heknes may look upon her, or they shall be struck down and die of some dreadful disease?"

"Yes. That's why I've wrapped her in sailcloth."

233

Half an hour later the church bell came swaying down through the dark. Wooden beams, pulleys and ropes all creaked. Gunhild rocked slowly, unable to ring, but demanding the same gravitas as if they were moving a loaded cannon.

The floor groaned as she came to rest on the handcart.

Schweigaard coiled up the bell rope and put it in an empty coffin. Then he opened the door and looked out.

Nobody.

Soon the bell was fastened on the timber sledge. Schweigaard helped, as lumps of snow clung to the hem of his robes.

"Happen she be goin' back to Lake Løsnes?"

"No. To the place called Daukulpen."

"Up o'er the hill? She be going o'er the hill?"

"That's right."

"But the pastor should have said that. We needs a horse. We needs Svarten. 'Tis steep, and this bell is as heavy as a load o' timber!"

"People will notice a horse going past in the middle of the night. You must, Herr Isum!"

Giant Isum took hold of the rope and pulled so hard that the sledge creaked, but the runners only dug deeper into the snow, and it refused to budge. Schweigaard wedged a rod in at the back to try to free it. To no effect.

Then a change came over Isum. It was as though he had summoned up some other creature, a creature more animal than man, and stepped into its body. He loosened the fastenings, grasped the church bell with both hands, and let out a roar as he rocked the bell to the front of the sledge so that its centre of gravity was further forward. He took a plank, placed it across his thigh, and broke it in two with a sound like a rifle shot. Then he cracked his knuckles and loosened his shoulders, stared into the snow, and placed the short, splintered plank against his chest and the rope across it, so it now served as a harness. He leaned forward so hard that he almost fell over, and he exerted so much weight and muscular power that his very skeleton seemed to grind, and the harder he pulled the deeper he sank into the snow, and the rope grew so taut it sang. At last he yanked the sledge free, and without a pause he started to pull the bell up the hill and past the church. He tugged, heaved and hobbled as his boots slipped under him. There was nothing Schweigaard could do but follow behind. A battle was taking place before his eyes, he was witnessing an exorcism, powers greater than any invocation on an altar book, this was Isum versus Isum, a wrestling match against inner weakness, the most fearsome battle a man could fight.

Onwards. Onwards. Grunting and gasping.

Finally, they reached the forest. Here they stumbled out into deep, wet snow, and Schweigaard grew fearful that Isum might die in this battle. But he pulled, and kept on pulling, until they came to a stretch of snow that had been in shadow all day, and here the snow's crust was strong enough for the sledge to glide smoothly without sinking. Suddenly Isum fell. He lay on the ground so long that his body's warmth melted the icy crust, but then he just turned onto his back and lay panting as he sank deeper into the snow.

A quarter of an hour went by with nothing said. Somewhere nearby they heard the cawing of ravens.

Isum eased himself up and sat on his backside in the snow. His coat was shiny and worn to a thread where the rope had been.

"This war," he said. "Has Herr Pastor heard owt more on t' radio about what he wants with us, this German?"

"The gods only know," said Schweigaard. "And the gods get bored from time to time."

"Slow 'n' steady wins the day," Isum said, lifting the tattered rope again. Man and sledge stumbled on through the winter darkness. The moon was quite large and offered them some visibility. It was a little past one o'clock when Schweigaard said they were getting close.

They came to a stream that they could hear trickling under the ice here and there, and whose twists and turns were marked by the absence of vegetation and trees.

There was a change in the weather. He felt a light, spring breeze.

"'Tis there," Isum said, pointing to the small clearing by the river. "Under the snow there lies the sittin' rock, and beyond that the forest pool. Daukulpen. But how can we bring her out over the ice and in t' water?"

Schweigaard hesitated. All his life he had been used to giving unequivocal answers. Now he had to say: "I've not thought that far."

"Ah."

"Isn't it enough just to loosen the ropes and push the bell out over the ice? No. Of course not. Then you'd fall through the ice too."

"Happen we can pull her out on t' sledge," said Isum. "And when the ice starts to give way, I can haul the sledge out from under her. But then the problem be the rocks at the bottom. The bell may crack when she comes down on 'em. Even with the buoyancy o' the water."

Buoyancy? Schweigaard hadn't expected a word like that.

"I don't think there's any other way, Isum. We can't slow it down – the sinking – not without some big apparatus or machinery."

"She'll crack, Herr Pastor. That be too sad to think on. Stay here a while and watch o'er her. I shall be back as quick as I can. I shall run down t' Hekne and fetch sommat to help us."

"But what?"

"I canna' yet tell, Herr Pastor. I shall think on't as I go."

Then he was gone.

Schweigaard sat on the sledge. He was freezing and his feet

were soaking wet, and he couldn't help wondering what difference it would make if Isum thought for one minute or a whole hour.

Time passed. He munched on some snow. Leaned back against the bell and sat and pondered.

Perhaps Gunhild could ring of her own accord and warn of danger. In which case, if she were in danger *herself*, because somebody wanted to take her – might she ring then too? And thus reveal her whereabouts?

He saw clouds overhead. The moonlight dimmed; visibility was dropping.

Noises below. Something dark coming this way. Something that refused to assume the form of either animal or human; it was too round, too unwieldy, but walked on two legs.

Isum was carrying four huge sacks. Breathing heavily, he set them down on the snow, and through a miasma of altar wine, he said: "Sawdust and wood shavings. It were meant as insulation in t' walls o' a house we be fettlin'. In that fourth sack, I have a reindeer skin."

"Wood shavings?"

"Wood floats, Herr Pastor. Till it be sodden with water. So I be thinkin' thus: Herr Pastor loosens the canvas, I tip the bell on her side, ye crams the bags o' sawdust and shavings in t' hollow. Then we tie the canvas back, so she be full o' wood, and then she can float nice and slow down t' the bottom."

It turned out to be a more difficult task than they hoped. The bell proved as unwieldy and heavy as a boulder, and they were hampered by poor light, snow and arthritic knees. The gurgling of the water under the ice was overlaid with the sounds of grunting and heavy breathing. In the end, Isum managed to hold Gunhild on an angle while Kai Schweigaard put the hammer back in place and stuffed the bags around it. It was like feeding the mouth of a whale. As Isum tipped the bell back down again,

Runes and Warplanes

he nearly squashed Schweigaard's fingers, but the canvas was now firmly knotted. Out on the ice, Isum transferred Gunhild onto the reindeer skin, which he had spread out fur side down, its hairs lying in the opposite direction from which he would pull her. He tied a rope to the reindeer hide, threw it over to the other side of Daukulpen, walked round to it and started to pull the bell out onto the ice.

Sweat and snow. The sounds of the night and smells of spring. Bronze beneath sailcloth. Reindeer skin beneath bronze.

Gunhild was in the middle now. The ice cracked.

But she failed to move. The ice was too thick.

Isum went out and rocked his body back and forth.

"Watch out!" shouted Schweigaard. "You could—"

There was a loud cracking followed by a roar that sounded as though it came from the heavens and the bowels of the earth. Snow rose from the ice and whirled in a white, indistinct mist in the dawn light as the bell disappeared between large, upturned icefloes. Time went slowly, the snow settled again, and then a ringing sound was heard from a place deep below, as though from a church under the ice.

The icefloes turned slowly. Water ran into the snow around the gap and turned it to slush. The disruption ended, and Daukulpen was peaceful again.

Kai Schweigaard looked about him in the growing light. Snow sparkled around the pool and stretched like a silver carpet to the edge of the dark forest that enclosed the glade while the tops of the spruce trees pointed towards a grey sky. It was as if this place had always hidden a mystery and was wishing another one welcome.

They headed back down, but now all strength had left Kai Schweigaard. He stumbled, fell and flailed in the snow. Then he felt two fists under his armpits, dragging him up from the snow's grip.

"If it please ye t' sit upon the sledge, Herr Pastor," said Isum. "Then I shall allays know that I drew a church bell uphill and a pastor back down."

Kai held on tightly to the frozen sledge while Isum pulled him home. Apart from their tracks and the cracks in the ice, they had left nothing that might lead anyone to think they had sunk a church bell there.

Suddenly Isum stopped. They were on top of a small ridge. Schweigaard turned. This was the last place from which Daukulpen could be seen. Schweigaard waited for Isum to continue, but he had wandered off and was looking down at something in the snow.

"These d'nay belong to us," he said.

Schweigaard got off the sledge and walked over to him. In the pale morning light, Giant Isum pointed at a set of footprints alongside their sledge tracks.

Major Sprockhoff

They were sitting in the living room eating a raspberry sponge. Herr and Fru Røhme and Pastor Schweigaard. A sense that the end was nigh had hung over them in the last few days, which could only partly be blamed on the war. Schweigaard nursed such a visceral antipathy towards leaving the parsonage that he had failed to pack so much as a pencil.

War or no war: his last service would be on the first Sunday in May. Herr Røhme had put all his skill into making two large, beautiful altar candles for the pastor's farewell Mass. Bishop Hille would come, Karlsen would be introduced as the new curate. There had to be a festive meal, and Fru Røhme had planned a menu of roast veal and apricot compote. Kåre Karlsen would then move in and take over.

Jehans had said that a room and a made-up bed were waiting for him in the farmhouse. They would offer him houseroom at Hekne for as long as he wanted.

But of course.

"We has a drop more coffee in t' pot," Herr Røhme said, getting up and going into the kitchen. Children's voices could be heard from the Røhmes' wing. Yesterday their four grandchildren had been picked up from Fåvang station in the milk truck. Their parents felt it was safer for them here than living with them in Trondheim.

A week had gone since the church bell was hidden. With each day that passed, the Germans moved closer. Rumour had it they lacked any winter camouflage, and were forcing their way into houses and taking white sheets and crocheted bedspreads to wrap around them during the fighting.

Tarald Hekne and three other men from the village had left for Jørstadmoen to fight. The following day brought big news. British soldiers were coming to Norway to beat the Germans back. They would advance in their thousands, with cannons before them and planes above. There was talk that a big battle had taken place at Tretten, further south along the valley. At Hekne, Esther sat in the hallway by the telephone in her woollen cardigan and fingerless gloves, waiting for news from her brother.

End Times.

Schweigaard looked at Fru Røhme. She was always kindly, always knew how he was without a word being said, she tolerated him when he was ill-tempered, but was never servile, just thoroughly . . . good. A wise mother and grandmother.

He was gathering strength to tell her this as they sat here,

Major Sprockhoff

one-to-one, at this tiny round table with its lace cloth, but although words came easily to him in the pulpit or at a deathbed, he found it hard to say the right thing to anyone close, and he realised, with such a jolt it hurt, that there were very few people to whom he actually felt close.

Herr Røhme shouted from the kitchen: "Herr Pastor! There be folk out in t' yard! Germans!"

Through the window they saw two trucks. They both slammed on their brakes by the *stabbur* so muddy meltwater splashed about their wheels. Soldiers leaped down from the pickup bed, rifles in hand. A third truck drove through the gate. Rapid commands sounded.

Then someone hammered on the front door.

"It's probably best that I open today," said Schweigaard. "Put the church register somewhere safe, Herr Røhme."

There he stood, clean-shaven, in an impeccable uniform, even though he had probably been fighting for days. An impressive figure, nearly two metres tall, with the rank of major, a soldier on either side of him, both with sub-machine guns. The barrels pointed, for now, obliquely upwards.

Schweigaard leaned out to get a better view. A chilly April day. Grey-green uniforms everywhere. Soldiers behind the *stabbur* and outbuildings, kneeling with rifles at the ready.

The Norwegian flag was fluttering from a white pole, as it was on most farms in the village now. During last Sunday's Mass, Schweigaard had reminded his flock of the little-known custom that Norwegian flags could even be raised at night if the country was at war.

The officer asked in German if anyone in the house understood German. Or English. Or French.

Schweigaard replied, in his somewhat formal German, largely uncorrected since his student days in the late 1870s, that he could speak all three languages, but assumed from *der Rummel* – the revelry in the forecourt – that their guests would prefer to converse in German.

The officer gave a half-smile. Then introduced himself as a Major Otto Sprockhoff. He had to seize this building for an indefinite period. They had an hour to get out.

Suddenly Schweigaard heard the voice of a Norwegian. A bareheaded man in a knitted sweater got down from the truck parked furthest back. He pointed up at the flagpole, and in a shrill city accent yelled that the Norwegian flag must be lowered this instant. And that went for the other farms too!

The Norwegian failed to say who he was or why he was with the Germans.

"Planes might fly over here," he yelled. "You must take down all these flags, or you'll anger the soldiers! They don't want to be bombed by their own men! Be sensible now!"

The major walked over to a truck. The two soldiers remained in the hallway. Strangers, armed men with expectant glances.

Schweigaard went up the stairs to his study. Through the window he saw three Germans walking towards the flagpole.

An unexpected calm descended on him.

Was there still time? Was today the day it would happen? If so – he must change his clothes.

He tore off his shirt and started to change into his cassock. He stood by the window following events as he fastened his ruff around his neck.

The soldiers were hard at it. They must have discovered that the rope was gone. Two others came. They were all pointing to the top of the flagpole, clearly indicating to each other that the rope was wound around a nail just under the flag. Herr Røhme and the tenant farmer's son had done this earlier that morning with the aid of a very tall ladder.

A ladder they had then sawed in half.

Major Sprockhoff

The major joined them. He did not appear angry. A toolbox was brought from the truck. Someone unravelled a rope. They did not, it seemed, have a ladder.

Ten minutes later they were still no closer to solving the problem. They tried to unbolt the flagpole at its base, but were again thwarted, because the bolts had been filed down so there was nothing for the spanner to grip. Schweigaard had now brushed his cassock and put on his black shoes. He looked in the mirror.

Tried to get his breathing under control.

Is this the moment? Is this how it'll happen? Is it now that I shall step into the Hekne Weave? Back into it?

Tempers were rising below. Schweigaard watched them bring a saw. He heard swearing in German. A soldier was gesticulating at the saw and then at the pole. They must have realised now that big nails had been hammered criss-cross through the pole's lower section, and then painted over, so that their saw kept running into iron.

He and Herr Røhme had been filled with patriotic malice as they did this. Now Schweigaard wondered if he had gone too far. These men had been in battle. They had seen their friends die.

His call to raise the flag all over the village. Had it been rash? Maybe. Who was he to incite war and resistance? He was a priest, not a general. Over on Gildevollen's estate and the farm beyond, he saw the flags being lowered. The Norwegian renegade must have spread the word.

Down in the forecourt the soldiers were still hard at work. The major stood watching, his hands at his sides.

They had finally had enough. A rope was flung over the flagpole and fixed to a truck. It spun in the mud, then reversed and accelerated. On the second attempt the entire base was uprooted. The pole came crashing down, and the Norwegian flag spread itself prettily over a snow-decked raspberry patch.

Runes and Warplanes

Sprockhoff issued further orders. The flag was neatly folded. Eventually they managed to raise the flagpole again, albeit lopsidedly.

And now. Now a German war flag flew over the parsonage.

A cross on a red background like the Norwegian flag, but with a swastika in the centre surrounded by black stripes.

Sprockhoff tucked the Norwegian flag under his arm and went inside.

"So, you claim to be the priest here?"

"I don't claim. I was posted here as the village pastor in 1879. On Monday, May 5, 1879, to be precise. At nine o'clock in the morning, to be even more exact, something you Germans are known to appreciate."

"So that makes you . . ."

"I'm eighty-four," Schweigaard said. "A great deal has happened in my time. A stave church was in fact moved from here to Dresden in 1880. So yes, we've had Germans visit us before. I think I liked you better last time you came."

"Well," Sprockhoff said, "whatever you might or might not think . . . I'm afraid you must get out of this office."

"No. *You* sirs are going to get out of my study," Schweigaard said loudly, settling back in his swivel chair.

The soldiers looked between him and Sprockhoff, and Schweigaard thought that men who liked to shout and goad others did so because they'd been shouted at and goaded, but that they also respected those who could shout louder and goad even more.

"It's like this, Herr Schweigaard – did I pronounce that correctly?"

"Not too badly. Better than I'll pronounce your name when this war's over."

Sprockhoff was about to reply, but Schweigaard interrupted.

He was, he said, going to report the major to the sheriff. Even though war had now been declared, the country had not surrendered, so which took precedence? Civil Norwegian law or German military law? Under whose jurisdiction did he have permission for such actions?

"That's enough now," said Sprockhoff. "You two, assist this gentleman outside."

Two privates walked around the desk and grabbed Schweigaard. He refused to get out of his chair. Held on tightly to the armrests and stared straight ahead.

A soldier grabbed a ruler and slapped it across his knuckles, but Sprockhoff interrupted. "Consider this man's great age!"

In the end, they carried the pastor out in his chair. The landing outside the study was narrow. Schweigaard continued to hold on to the armrests and leaned to the side, but these fellows were strong, and they got him down the stairs and finally set him down on the snow in the forecourt, still in his own chair.

Sprockhoff followed them. Brushing dust from his jacket, he said:

"Now, let's you and I deal with this like adults. I've investigated this place and understand it to be connected to the farm over there." He nodded towards the parsonage's farm cottage. You'll move in down there and fetch bedding and clothes over the course of the day."

Schweigaard got the sense, on the basis of this measured brutality, that beneath the military jacket was a judicious man. Visible only in the split second between his barking orders at his soldiers and then observing their actions. His gaze neither cold nor blind. A vigilance, perhaps even a passing concern, in his eyes. Checking whether he had applied the right level of force.

The split second was now over.

Sprockhoff and his soldiers left for the servants' wing. Soon Herr and Fru Røhme came out with their grandchildren. They were crying. The soldiers were unmoved. One of them pointed his gun towards the farm cottage to indicate that that was where they should go. Meanwhile, more uniformed men piled out of some newly arrived trucks and thundered into the parsonage.

Schweigaard was still sitting outside. His chair sinking into the snow.

They were no doubt trampling in, flinging themselves down, without a care for the spirit or substance of these old rooms. Jehans' childhood room. Oldfrue Bressum's bedchamber. The bedroom where Victor Harrison had begun to suspect that he was Jehans' brother. They would trample through all these with their hobnailed boots. Officers would smoke and drink in the drawing room where Gerhard Schönauer and Astrid Hekne had been married.

Could it ever be itself again, the old parsonage?

A light snowstorm had set in, large flakes tumbled from the skies, but the air was so mild they melted on their way down and became indistinguishable from rain.

Schweigaard got up from the chair. Fru Røhme's kicksled was parked by the front steps. He strolled past two guards. The double doors stood wide open, and he was able to see into the hallway. The drawing room was full of soldiers. The fireplace before which they had been sitting was still alight, and the raspberry roulade was still on the coffee table.

Schweigaard tugged the kicksled loose. He rubbed the ice and rust off its blades and set off through the parsonage gates over the drifts of snow.

And as he sped off, he couldn't help thinking there was more glamour to being kicked out by the Wehrmacht than by Curate Kåre Karlsen.

Out on the forecourt stood an old swivel chair, worn-out by sixty years of ministry.

An Unmarried Hekne Woman

The bell over the door jangled and the chatter was silenced. Two soldiers, barely more than twenty years old. Polite bows from each. Shy smiles. They waited their turn politely, but since nobody was in the shop to buy anything, everyone stepped aside, and Astrid stood alone behind the counter before them.

Smart uniforms. Clean-shaven. Side partings. They had probably cleaned themselves up at the parsonage, in battered tin basins, standing with bare chests and braces, looking out over Lake Løsnes.

"*Zigaretten, bitte?*"

What now? Did they intend to pay with German marks? Did they have the right to get them for free?

Folk looked from Astrid to the Germans and back. Never had it been so quiet in the Colonial. Widow Fløter must have wondered what was happening, because she came out from the back room, but stopped in silence like the rest.

The soldiers smiled and waited. Two young men who, for all Astrid knew, might have shot Tarald. He still hadn't returned.

Rumours were rife about the violent battle that had taken place in Tretten, so close that folk in Fåvang had heard the cannons firing and the general clamour of war. It was there, further south, that the valley was at its narrowest, and where more than a thousand Norwegian and British soldiers had held fort. Against them seven thousand Germans had come with dive bombers and tanks and broken through their lines.

And now here they were for their cigarettes.

Astrid snatched two packs of Medina down from the tobacco shelf. One of the soldiers, with a chevron on his sleeve, slapped a krone piece down on the counter.

Where did that come from? Had they exchanged some

money? Or had they thundered through town with caterpillar tracks and armour plating, shooting and burning and killing, before somebody said, no, don't set fire to that building, it's the bank, so they had stopped at the door, gone in and helped themselves to some Norwegian kroner, put their helmets back on and shot the next people they met?

The villagers turned to see what Astrid did. Would she profit from the Germans' presence here?

One of the soldiers cleared his throat. He must have been practising his Norwegian because he asked for *fyrstikker*, but Astrid had run out of matches: her customers had been hoarding them for weeks. She was about to answer in German, but shook her head and handed them their change. They left and disappeared towards the parsonage.

The villagers exchanged glances, but said nothing. They were sown now, the seeds of gossip.

"What should I have done?" Astrid said.

Widow Fløter came up to her. "We canna' keep that sort o' money. Leastways nay the profits."

"Quite right," said Astrid. "We'll put it aside."

The chatter was soon on the boil again. "Be there any news about the pastor?" asked one woman.

"Went off on a kicksled. Naybody ha' seen him since."

"Be he under arrest?"

"Surely he canna' have . . . been shot?"

"Somebody were taken from the parsonage yesterday and put on a truck. Happen it were him."

Fru Røhme raised her voice: "I would o' seen that. The pastor be alive and kickin' I swear!"

"Aye," said another. "Ye knows all that goes on down there, Fru Røhme. Being as close as *ye* be."

"Can nay fathom how ye bear to live wall t' wall wi' them Germans!" said another.

"We hasna' any other house t' stay in!" said Fru Røhme. "They ordered us out, then ordered us back in and demanded feedin'!"

The talk went from irritable to angry. Astrid went into the back room. Paced back and forth.

Where had Kai got to? She had gone down to the parsonage one day to ask him if he had managed to hide the bell, but Herr Røhme had told her that the pastor had overworked himself and had only just got to sleep.

She gathered herself. A sack of pig bristles had come in, and she began sorting them into bundles. Halfway through she gave up and left it all lying there. Widow Fløter and Ada Borgen took over the delivery.

It was so good to have them, these two stalwart women. They had been in her life for as long as she could remember. Widow Fløter was over seventy now and knew every corner of the shop, but she was stubborn and stern. Ada Borgen was a good deal younger, not much over fifty, but plagued with watery eyes and poor sight. They each had a large, dark blue pinny. The two aprons were almost identical, but Widow Fløter would get very grumpy whenever Ada, always the first to arrive at work, accidentally took her apron.

Astrid slipped out of the back door. There was a sharp northerly wind, cold for May. Jon Mossen was there with his head under the Reo's bonnet. He straightened up and wiped his forearm across his brow. In his hand he held a wrench.

"Any news o' Tarald?"

Astrid shook her head. Remembered the Mossen family's sympathies for Quisling.

"Nay, not for a while," she said. "Have ye been called up yet?"

"Were in t' camp for three days. Same messin' as wi' Tarald. Were packed home again."

She turned and trudged around the corner. The ground was muddy and the air damp. German vehicles were constantly driving to and from the parsonage. Brash foreigners with all kinds of equipment. Here. In their village. Working on a big project, about which they said nothing. A lot to get done, clearly. Yesterday they had driven a caterpillar truck up the seter road and erected a guard shack with a stove near the treeline. Where the materials had come from, nobody knew. Rumour was that there had been a dreadful battle further north, that the Germans had won and had now reached as far north as Lesja.

It was the same everywhere. They rolled forward. Shooting and burning. *From here on, we decide.* Dominant in numbers and purpose.

Astrid noticed that she was always on the watch. With a heightened awareness of sounds and movements. An eye for anything out of the norm.

As last night, when the chairman of the shooting club came to Hekne. Her father had let him in. Then thirty minutes later Widow Fløter's son – known by most now as Fløteren – had come down through the forest. Fløteren was her father's oldest friend and the head telegraph operator at Ringebu train station. Astrid suspected that whatever they were planning involved long-distance messages.

They sat behind closed doors, and Jehans would disclose nothing to her. Her pain and her grit and determination needed an active outlet, but there seemed no place for it here.

Astrid pulled her jacket tightly around her. Further down the road she heard the hum of an engine.

A passenger car. Black, but grey with mud. It skidded on the slippery road and turned in – towards the bell tower?

She walked down to get a better view.

The door to the bell tower was open. There were two soldiers outside, but they were in different uniforms from any Germans she had seen before. These were jet black with knee-high boots. Beside them stood a man in a suit.

At six o'clock Fru Røhme came to Hekne.

"The Germans, Astrid. They be looking for thee!"

"Get inside," Astrid said, closing the door behind her. Esther and Jehans rushed towards them.

"They has this *interpreter* sort with them," Fru Røhme said. "Reckons he be from the valley, but talks like a stationmaster, a bit highfalutin. He came upon us of a sudden. Says we mun *Fetch Astrid Hekne*. Or else they would send soldiers to find thee."

"How do they know my name?"

"I canna' tell. Yesterday there were two men from Butangen in the living room, but we has orders to hang up these blackout curtains and turn off the outdoor lights, and we canna' look out on t' yard. We just recognised the accent."

"What has happened with Kai?" Jehans said.

She shook her head. "We has no idea. That interpreter fellow asked me too – angry and rough he were – but I said what was true, that I didna' know."

"How be things there now?" said Jehans. "At the parsonage."

"'Tis a sad business. They has taken over the pastor's study, and all the upstairs bedrooms. Herr Sprockhoff be so tall he keeps knocking his head on t' door frames, and then cusses in German. The first night he moved in, he bade us make supper for the officers. There be clear boundaries between 'em. The common soldiers makes food in t' back kitchen. The officers gets terrible drunk sometimes. Wi' loud singing in t' parlour. Once, in t' middle of the night a full-grown man came to us crying and wanted to play with our little grandson. Quite overcome. Seemed he had bairns back at home and had seen sommat bad early in t' war. Sprockhoff came in and gave him a bawling. He didna' apologise, but looked at us and nodded as if to say it wouldna' happen again. Nor did it."

"How many soldiers be there?" said Jehans.

"About thirty. Comes and goes. They has built bunkbeds in yer old room."

"Fru Røhme," Astrid said, "it doesna' look good when ye do their bidding. The gossip was bad enough before the war. Imagine it now!"

"Aye, but what can we do? They has weapons! But ye better go now, Astrid, afore they come for thee."

Jehans reached for his jacket on the hook, but Astrid caught him by the arm and said she would go alone.

"Ye have had the chairman o' the shooting club here, and 'tis best the Germans d'nay know about thee."

The hallway stank of foreign tobacco. A soldier led her towards the once-familiar drawing room. She could hear men's voices speaking German, and music coming from a gramophone. A pretty melody led by a piano. In the room, sitting at the round table that she had sat at so often herself, were three men. One wore a grey-green uniform and was very tall, so had to be Sprockhoff. Another sported a resplendent, jet-black, heavily decorated uniform. And the third, who sat with his back to her, wore an elegant suit of marled blue. And there she stood in her thick cardigan, old wool skirt and damp shoes.

They saw her and stood up.

"Ah, at last!" said the man in the suit, in Norwegian. A clipped pronunciation being all that revealed him as German.

His face was fuller than when they had met last, but she remembered him. The man from the guesthouse. The man Mari Slåen had pointed out. The man who had visited Hekne. The man to whom Tarald had shown their most sacred treasures.

Hans Friedrich Günther did not seem to recognise her, however.

He introduced the others. The man in the black uniform was Jankuhn, Herbert Jankuhn. Professor of archaeology, and an

An Unmarried Hekne Woman

officer from something he called the Allgemeine Schutzstaffel. Sprockhoff also gave his name and rank. His uniform seemed intended for parades, bearing, as it did, six medals.

Introductions complete, Günther launched on a description of his skiing holiday in Easter 1936, and how he had enjoyed a most cordial conversation with Pastor Schweigaard in this very drawing room. Not a word passed his lips about his visit to Hekne.

Jankuhn addressed Astrid in German, Günther translated. "We are honoured to be in the very place where the Nordenkirche originally stood. Such a wonderful example of ancient Nordic architecture. We have all visited it in Dresden. As we understand your brother Tarald has too."

Astrid's fingers went cold. Her stomach knotted.

"Did he succeed in his artistic ambitions, your brother?" Günther asked.

She swallowed and nodded.

They invited her to sit down, but, pretending to misunderstand, she remained standing. Their strict social conventions thus broken, there was a moment of awkward silence, and after much humming and hawing, Jankuhn said: *Eine Jungfrau aus der Familie Hekne.*

The shivers ran from her lower back and up to the nape of her neck. *A young girl from the Hekne family.* Her fears were confirmed. She blinked hard, and blinked again, but the shivers persisted.

It was clear to them now that she understood some German.

Günther said she had absolutely nothing to fear. His friend had perhaps expressed himself clumsily, and he apologised. He pulled out one of Kai Schweigaard's best chairs, and with an extravagant gesture asked her to be seated.

It was as though Kai was sitting there. Filled with an inner calm, pastoral dignity and warmth. Don't think about the Sister

Runes and Warplanes

Bells. Pretend you believe Gunhild is still in the bell tower. Pretend that the Hekne Weave disappeared in 1820. Think of the bomber planes. Think about Mari Slåen. Keep on thinking about Mari Slåen.

Sprockhoff and Jankuhn sat back down. Eyes trained on her. Günther remained standing. Then, with his hands resting on the curved back of Kai Schweigaard's old chair, he embarked on a monologue. He and Jankuhn had arrived in Norway on April 13 to undertake a carefully planned project. They had come in their own plane, on the direct orders of the Ahnenerbe's supreme commander, Reichsführer Himmler, who had given their plans in Norway his personal approval. Also on the plane was "a princely" number of soldiers from the Allgemeine SS, who would protect any ancient monuments and archaeological sites that might otherwise be destroyed in the fighting.

"You may be asking yourself, Fräulein Hekne, why we would devote our time to this in the midst of a military offensive. Well, it's quite simple. The Norse and Germanic cultural heritage are twin sisters. A Norwegian monument is a German monument. But . . . it is in times of chaos and war that invaluable treasures are destroyed. Under the Wehrmacht things will be different. From day one, we deployed sentries at the Antiquities Collection in Oslo. We have approached the National Antiquarian to offer him our assistance, secured the Viking ships on Bygdøy and placed guards at rock carvings and excavation sites, and we have a decree from Himmler allowing us direct access to Central Command, so that we can redirect an airstrike that could destroy a priceless artefact or building. The war is now, cultural treasures are forever."

Günther took off his glasses. He rubbed the bridge of his nose, put his glasses back on. "You're a clever woman, Fräulein Hek – Frøken Hekne. You realised a long time ago that our errand here concerns the church bell that hangs in the bell

An Unmarried Hekne Woman

tower. Pastor Schweigaard lives up on the farm with your family, correct?"

She shook her head.

"No?"

"He's gone. We reckoned as he'd been arrested."

The three men looked at each other.

"The fact is that Major Sprockhoff did not receive adequate instructions," said Günther. "Pastor Schweigaard should have been handled with . . . greater delicacy."

Astrid began to see how well prepared they were. They had known, before they had even left Germany, that Schweigaard was still the pastor here.

Jankuhn's splendid officer's cap lay on the table. Under a skull ran a braid of silver thread. One of the badges on his jacket bore a runic symbol. He reached out now for a large envelope from under his cap. The fabric of his black uniform was so finely woven that the folds that appeared fell out instantly when he turned to her again. The envelope was covered with rubber stamps and in the left-hand corner was an eagle. He took out a small pile of photographs on glossy paper with white trims, and, without a word, held them out to Astrid. Günther asked whether she had heard of the Snartemo Sword.

Astrid shook her head.

The top photograph was of a sword. The blade was rusted away, the shaft was intact. The next showed an ancient, threadbare bandolier, with faded swastikas woven into the chequered fabric.

One by one she looked through the photographs. Rock carvings. Small artefacts bearing swastikas or sun crosses.

"I'm showing you these," said Günther, "to reassure you that we are protectors. What I'm about to show you here is the official list of irreplaceable Nordic-Germanic cultural monuments. Note, Frøken Hekne, which artefact stands at number six."

Runes and Warplanes

He handed her a typed sheet. Number one was the Snartemo Sword. Then came Viking ships and rock carvings. The description of "Cultural Artefact No. 6" read thus:

Kirchenglocke aus Butangen in Gudbrandsdalen. "Gunhild", zweiter Teil der Schwesterglocken der Nordenkirche in Dresden. Gegossen 1620–1630. Ungefähr 380 Kilogramm, Diameter 85–95 Centimeter, Tonart unbekannt. Im schwarzen Holzturm 52 Meter von der weißen Hauptkirche.

Astrid tried to hide how fast she was breathing. She looked over at the red armchair by the stove. The fabric was worn where Kai's elbows had rested in contemplative moments. Surely he would have mentioned it if he hadn't managed to hide the bell? So what was going on now? The door into the bell tower had stood open earlier that day. Had they gone up, as she suspected, and seen that Gunhild was gone?

Günther continued. "It's quite simple, Frøken Hekne, we're here to secure the church bell and to eventually transfer it to Dresden. It is in point of fact our property. You might perhaps think that there are nicer ways to deal with a breach of contract than to send the Luftwaffe and thirty thousand troops. This war is not a war over territories. It is the final battle for the soul of Europe. Give us a chance to be your benefactors, Frøken Hekne. We're Germans. We want to do this correctly. The legend of the Sister Bells exists in several versions, the strictest demanding that only an unmarried woman from the Hekne family may look directly upon them. Anyone else is destined to die of a stroke or some awful illness, isn't that so? A beautiful tradition that we'd like to uphold. We opened the door to the bell tower, but out of respect for the bell we didn't go up to look at it. So, Frøken Hekne, we'd like you to come with us now, and do what your grandmother did in 1880, when she covered both bells with canvas, in readiness for them to be transported from here. Naturally, the canvas she used has been preserved in Dresden, and I have it here now. It's in *there*," he said, nodding towards a suitcase on the set of rose-painted drawers.

She handed the document back to him.

"That in't quite right," she said. "The legend says a great deal more than that. The legend says that only seven chain-brothers can reunite the bells."

She knew, of course, that the legend sometimes said two and sometimes seven. But at a coffee social such as this, it seemed only right to say seven.

Günther nodded gravely. "Quite so. Quite so. We are prepared for this. When the fighting's over and we no longer need to worry that British planes pose a danger, seven brothers will indeed come to take the bell to Dresden. I can see you're surprised, Frøken Hekne. The fact is that Germany has honoured fertile mothers for years. We award the Ehrenkreuz der Deutschen Mutter to those women who have many children. Bronze for four babies, silver for six, gold for those who have brought eight into the world. And we have records of these families. Let me remind you that Germany has a population of sixty-nine million, five million in the military. We have eighteen families to choose from in Germany who have seven so-called chain-brothers. At this very moment, we have seven such brothers serving near their home in Frankfurt, not that they know why."

A side door opened. In came . . . Fru Røhme. Servile. Almost creeping. Carrying one of the parsonage's silver trays. On it a plate of her best *krumkake* wafers and three elegant stem glasses filled with sour cream, cloudberry cream and raspberry jam.

Fru Røhme placed it on the table without even glancing at Astrid. She went over to the old wooden dresser for the tableware. Astrid could see she was afraid, and as she crossed the room the china rattled; delicate, blue-patterned porcelain cups and saucers that brought memories back of hot chocolate with Schweigaard.

Fru Røhme curtseyed and was leaving when Sprockhoff coughed and said loudly in Norwegian: "Pour!" She spilled the coffee as she filled his cup, making a stain that spread quickly across the snow-white linen. Mortified, she bowed backwards out of the door, tears rising in her eyes.

Astrid looked at the three men. Günther was clearly the charmer among them, Sprockhoff the executioner. So who – Astrid wondered looking at Jankuhn – are you? Who is this man who dresses in black and embellishes himself with skulls and runes? Are you the wizard, perhaps?

Sprockhoff cleared his throat and nodded towards the silver tray. Exquisite *krumkakes* and glossy red jam. Fru Røhme was known throughout the parish for her cake-making, and her *krumkakes* were particularly famous. Her secret was not only to give these wafer cones a wide opening so that guests could fill them with generous spoonfuls of cream and jam, but to make them as thin as Christmas wrapping and uniquely crisp.

This, however, made them tricky to eat elegantly.

With his very first bite, Jankuhn's cone broke, and a blob of cloudberry cream landed on his freshly pressed trousers. When he tried to wipe it off, it just sank deeper into the fine fabric and left a shiny patch on the crotch. Sprockhoff also ventured on a *krumkake*, but was unaware that you had to tilt your head and attack the cone from below on the first bite, and he was so infuriated when it started to crumble that he became even more heavy-handed and tried eating it quickly to hide his defeat, with which it collapsed entirely, fell onto his chest and wedged itself between two medals. Günther did a little better initially, but then made a cardinal mistake: he upended his cone and tried to eat it from the bottom, but since he'd overfilled it, the raspberry jam and cream spilled out of the top and ran down his shirt.

Astrid leaned over the table.

The time had come for the riskiest party trick known to all Norwegians. To eat a *krumkake* with no plate underneath, just as she had learned to do from Fru Røhme herself.

Astrid took a wafer from the plate. It weighed almost nothing. She filled it with lashings of cloudberry cream and turned it so the delicious golden cream slipped to the bottom of her cone. The secret now was to wait just long enough. The wafer must absorb enough moisture from the cream to make it slightly chewy but not soft.

In the meantime, the three men were fumbling about with their napkins, trying to wipe their clothes clean.

Astrid turned her *krumkake* so any loose bits would fall back with a helpful nudge from her lower lip, and took a bite from the wide end of the cone. After each bite she breathed out and then ate on an in breath so she could secretly retrieve any crumbs.

Jankuhn gave up on getting his uniform clean. Soon all three were watching her intently as she continued to turn her *krumkake* so that the cream remained equally distributed. When a third of her cone was left, she placed her middle finger on the end, popped it into her mouth, and ate it with delicately closed lips, before finally taking a tiny sip of coffee and setting her cup quietly down.

Not a single crumb had fallen on her knitted cardigan. Not a blob of cream was to be seen on her wool skirt.

They glowered at her humourlessly. Jankuhn was particularly irate, since the cloudberry cream showed up so clearly on his black uniform and made his fingers so sticky. *Krumkakes* would certainly never appear on any list of celebrated Nordic-Germanic cultural artefacts.

"Well, well," said Günther. "We clearly have a thing or two

to learn about Norway. Let's hope that the fighting can end soon. That's something we all hope."

They drained their cups. Jankuhn stood up, rummaged in his jacket pocket and held up a large, wrought-iron key.

A key Astrid had once held herself. A key that, as a sixteen-year-old, she had unhooked from Jesus' bloodied big toe.

"No," said Astrid. "No. I can't give the bell away."

"I admire your perseverance," said Günther. "But we really can't delay things any longer. You must get the church bell ready for removal."

Major Sprockhoff went out into the hallway. Two soldiers came in and seized Astrid by the arms. Jankuhn took the suitcase from the chest of drawers. Then she was out in the bright, chilly May evening, a dog and four soldiers following her. She hoped that somebody in the village was witnessing this, that she was going under duress, but they led her down the shortcut that was only intermittently visible. Down at the bell tower were two soldiers, their eyes hidden under helmets. Jankuhn unlocked the door, and they were inside the dark and draughty bell tower.

"Here," Jankuhn said, taking a roll of greying sailcloth from the suitcase. Sprockhoff gave her a battery-powered torch.

"Get to it then. We've no wish to be struck down or die, as they say here."

Astrid looked towards the steep staircase. Rarely had she felt more despondent. How did you feel, Grandmother? What did you think as you climbed up to the church bells when you were going to cover them up? Was similar pressure put on you too?

She was halfway up the staircase when she sensed that something was wrong. Something they had said jarred, but what? There were footprints in the dust on the stair treads, but had they been made by Kai or the Germans? When she was almost at the top, she turned to look at the three men below, who stood by the open door, silhouetted against the grey evening light.

An Unmarried Hekne Woman

With the sailcloth under her arm, she climbed the last few steps, pointed the torch into the space and looked around.

Gunhild was gone.

She stood there and collected herself.

Below she heard the door slam shut.

She took a step back down, and tried to act surprised. The three men had come to the bottom of the stairs, their expressions quite altered.

Astrid understood. This was theatre. They had known the bell was gone.

"Game over," said Günther. "You knew about this. We can see it in your face. Where is the church bell, Frøken Hekne?"

"I have no idea," said Astrid. "I had no part in moving her."

"That may be true. But you know perfectly well where it is."

She shook her head.

Günther took the torch from her. "You can start by telling us where Pastor Schweigaard is. Otherwise you'll be eating cake with us all night. But a very different kind of cake. One that makes you tell the truth."

Günther and Sprockhoff went out. Jankuhn stood, looking up at the shaft where the bell ropes had hung. Then he too went out, and she was left alone in the bell tower. The door was ajar. She could hear them talking quietly in German.

Two soldiers entered, slammed the door and tore off her cardigan. They shoved her to the floor. She twisted round and tried to kick them. They slapped her face, then one of them put his knee hard between her breasts, gripped both her wrists with one hand and clamped the other over her mouth. He looked straight into her eyes. Moved his hand down a little, allowing her to breathe through her nose. She tried to wrench herself free, but he pinned her head to the floor. The other sat on her feet to stop her wriggling, and she saw a knife flash. One soldier cut her shoe straps and pulled off her shoes and woollen stockings. She

261

could smell their bodies and breath. Jankuhn had come back and held the torch to her face. The light burned into her retina and formed yellow circles that did not go when she blinked, and between these shifting circles she saw men moving around.

They turned off the torch and let her go. She scrambled backwards until she reached the wall. Heard heavy footsteps. Glimpsed more movement. Then the door slammed shut.

Time passed.

She got her breath back. Stood up. Felt the cold from the floorboards against the soles of her bare feet. Her night vision began to return.

"You thought everyone had gone, eh?" said a man's voice in Norwegian. A city accent.

Astrid bolted backwards and banged into the wall. She could not see him clearly.

Then she was blinded again by a bright torch. The stranger prowled around her as he shone the light in her eyes.

Suddenly the light went out and she felt her cheek sting from a hard blow.

"Where is he? This pastor of yours?"

Astrid struggled to stay upright. Touched her face. Said she didn't know.

"And we're supposed to believe that? We've had people up at your farm. And he wasn't there. Your pastor."

He switched the torch back on. The beam zigzagged towards her eyes.

"The old tapestry. The Hekne Weave. That used to hang in the church. Where is it?"

She tried to get away, but he followed her.

"Why don't you answer?"

She mumbled that the three others hadn't asked her about any weave.

"No," he said. "*I'm* asking about the weave."

"Who are ye?" Astrid said. "What d'ye want o' me?"

He grinned, went over to the corner and placed his torch on the floor. It made his shadow loom huge. He had his back to her and was rooting in his pocket for something. She could not see what he was doing. Only now did she realise how cold she was and that she had a shooting pain in her foot. She must have got a splinter in her heel.

"What a pity things went as they did for your brother," he said.

Astrid lowered her arm. "What's happened to him? What's happened to Tarald?"

"A real pity," repeated the man. "He had such ambitions. Listen carefully, Astrid. Just sit a while and have a think. If you tell us where the bell is, you get to live. Tell us where the Hekne Weave is as well, and you get to live unharmed."

He turned off the torch. She saw a sliver of light at the door, felt a gust of cold air and stood trembling, terrified that he might still be there.

Time passed. She used it to stoke up anger rather than fear. The ladder to the belfry was visible in a faint glimmer of light, and she climbed up and pushed open one of the small shutters. There below, in the evening light, she saw a group of men heading for the parsonage. One of them walked at a distance from the rest. Judging by his height, it had to be Sprockhoff.

She couldn't see if the man with the torch was among them.

If they tortured her, would she be able to hold out?

She paced back and forth, thinking about Tarald. She must prepare herself for the possibility that he was dead. Kai too, judging from their treatment of her.

She went and sat against a wall. She was terribly cold. If he came back, this man, and did his worst, she wanted the guards to hear it.

The sailcloth.

She groped around and found it on the floor. Was this really the cloth her grandmother had used in 1880? When she covered the Sister Bells?

Astrid wrapped it around her and shivered.

Time passed. Although she doubted that time even existed in a bell tower.

The soles of her feet stung with the cold, and her teeth chattered.

It was bad to curse in a church. Was it also bad to cast an eternal curse upon someone in a bell tower?

Well, it would be on them.

His Right Hand

She lay in bed all day with Esther and little Eirik close by. Jehans threatened to go down with the Hekne Krag and finish the enemy off.

Astrid was still not warmed through by the heat from the stove. Two soldiers had come to the bell tower at first light and thrown in her shoes and cardigan. One was the man who had bought cigarettes the day before.

They led her to the parsonage.

Jankuhn and Günther were nowhere to be seen. Sprockhoff was in the pastor's old study, sitting in Schweigaard's swivel chair. Behind him a photograph of Adolf Hitler. The carving of Our Saviour still in the same place. Next to it a map of Butangen and its environs. Under that he had hung a little painting in a thin frame. A slightly naive but very precise depiction of a battle in the last century: *Die Schlacht bei Metz*.

He asked Astrid in German where Pastor Schweigaard was. Where the church bell was.

Astrid shook her head.

She was waiting for him to ask about the Hekne Weave.

He did not. She wondered why the Norwegian stranger had asked her about it. As though he took it for granted it had been found.

Sprockhoff said nothing more. He glanced at his watch, opened the door and shouted an order down the stairs. The two soldiers led her out. A new guardhouse had been erected by the gates. Manned by soldiers with rifles over their shoulders. They weren't unpleasant as she passed, but nor did they offer any sympathy.

It was about two when she managed to get up.

Esther was sitting by the telephone in the hallway, while Eirik played at her feet. Astrid reached down and took her little nephew on her lap. He had a mop of soft, blond hair that smelled so good, and there was both a strength and fragility in him.

Mopsi padded over to them soundlessly. Eirik stretched out to her and she sprang onto his lap, and thus the three of them sat enjoying one another's warmth. Eirik had a unique way with animals. He had given Esther a fright once by disappearing, until they found him in the sheepfold snuggled up with a lamb. Now, he buried his nose in Mopsi's fur. The war did not exist for these two.

Later that day, an unfamiliar car drove up to Hekne.

Jehans said everyone should go down to the cellar, including Kristine. There was a hammering on the front door, and they heard their father shouting. Then they heard Tarald's voice. When they rushed back up, they found Tarald, his uniform covered in so much mud it clung to his legs. On his feet he had his old skiing boots. Both arms were bandaged. His right arm was in a sling. The bandage that poked out from the sling seemed . . . strangely flat?

He murmured something indecipherable. They followed him into the kitchen where he sat down but didn't want anyone near him, nor did he have the strength to explain why the Germans had driven him home. *Get out! Everyone get out! Nay, not ye, Esther, stay in here with me.*

After a while Esther came out into the living room. Little Eirik was sitting on Kristine's lap, and she went over, took her boy in her arms and sat on the divan.

"He's lost a hand," she said. "He'll be in here soon."

She had closed the door behind her, but Astrid pushed it ajar to save her brother the humiliation of struggling with a door handle. From the gap came cigarette smoke and the sound of somebody sitting restlessly in a chair. Eventually Tarald appeared and told them he had been in Lillehammer Hospital. He took off his military cap. His hair had been shaved off in patches and he had a bandage over one ear. They asked him about his hand, but all he said was that the doctors had discharged four men earlier that day and they had all been driven to the station.

"I was the only soldier to get off the train at Fåvang, and I was arrested there by the Germans. A junior lieutenant and two privates. I thought they were taking me as a prisoner of war, but then they drove in the direction of Butangen, and I had no idea why. And when they turned into the parsonage, I was even more confused. Then none other than our friend Günther leaped out and said he was sorry for my loss, or sommat like that."

Tarald was leaning on the door frame. Astrid got him a stool, and he sat down.

"I told him he'd betrayed us. That all the Germans had betrayed us Norwegians."

"And what did he say?" Esther said.

"Oh, just a load o' hogwash. Must have found out that I go to the Arts and Crafts school. Said that he was thinking o' offering me a place at the Art Academy in Dresden."

"Just like that?"

"Nay. In return he wanted me to tell him where the church bell was hidden. I glowered at him and said that I didna' even know the bell had gone, and that I couldna' care less. I pointed to my hand and said that the place he was offering at the Academy was o' little worth to me now. Then they drove me here."

Tarald wanted another cigarette, and Astrid had to get one out of his pocket and light it for him. After that it wasn't her brother who sat there. This man who sat in the middle of the living room, smoking with his elbows on his knees, was a stranger. The right sleeve of his jacket was ripped all the way up to his corporal's stripe and lay in brown strips over the bandage.

"I can bear it no more," said Kristine. "Those church bells shall be the ruin o' us."

"It doesna' come as a surprise. I've been to Germany. I've seen first-hand what they're like, Mother. With Germans it doesna' do to think like a dairymaid."

"Mind yerseln now," said Jehans. "War or no war. She be yer mother."

"Naybody talks badly about dairymaids here at Hekne," Esther broke in. It was difficult to say whose side she was on. The room went quiet.

"There's sommat strange here," said Astrid. "When I was down in the bell tower, they knew ye were wounded. And how could the soldiers know about thee if Günther wasna' at the station?"

Tarald blew smoke through his nostrils.

"You're right. They must have had help. From someone who knows us."

"He knew that ye had been to Dresden too," Astrid said.

Suddenly Tarald stood up. He stumbled, his voice choked with tears.

"Why don't any o' ye ask?"

"About what?" said Kristine.

He waved his bandaged arm in the air.

"Do ye not want to hear what happened?"

"We did ask," Astrid said.

"Hush, Astrid," said Kristine. "Canna ye see he in't himseln?"

Tarald began to talk. The story had clearly been buzzing around in his head and was so fragmented that it was the next day before Astrid could piece together what must have happened.

There had been no more Colt machine guns at the depot, but he was given an old Madsen, which he taught himself how to use. The soldiers were driven to Tretten, where they started to build barricades and trenches. Two British planes flew over, and hopes were raised.

Then came the train carrying British reinforcements. Out stepped some rather aged reservists in summer uniforms. They had only the usual Lee-Enfield rifles and a few Bren machine guns. They were already shivering from the cold, just from standing on the platform. An officer yelled over a radio transmitter that this was not going to end well. Field rumours spread. Further down in the valley, a barn had caught fire during the fighting. The Germans had freed the cows but shot the crofter.

Some hours later, far below in the valley, a low rumbling sound told them that a large number of vehicles was on the move. The sound grew louder, but there was nothing to see. In the distance, they could hear scattered firing and the rapid clap of light machine guns. Then silence, followed by a loud bang, issuing perhaps from a mine.

By now they had given up all hope that the British planes would come to their rescue.

Dull bangs indicated that the Norwegian positions across the river had been hit by artillery shells. Then the hum of planes sounded above them. They seemed to be coming at lower and lower altitudes. A lieutenant ran in a crouch towards Tarald, and asked if it was true that he was trained to use a Colt machine gun. He said he was, and followed the lieutenant to a Colt without a gunner; where the original gunner had gone he never discovered. A very young lad came to feed the ammunition belts.

Shortly afterwards the dive bombers came. Or what they later understood to be dive bombers. They had a kink in their wings, could dive suddenly and drop firebombs. The sirens on these planes wailed so it hurt your ears, louder and louder as they approached. Some soldiers were so frightened by the noise alone, they abandoned their positions.

The planes then climbed abruptly into the sky and sped away from the trail of explosions and damage they had caused. House after house was engulfed in flames. One belonged to a family Tarald knew. Then the ground began to shake, and they heard the rattle of steel belts coming closer.

Still, all they had seen of the enemy was their planes.

Then, rolling along the high street, between two grocery stores Tarald had often shopped in, was an armoured tank. Tarald could not believe how big it was. Flames spewed a metre out from the cannon's mouth. Tarald aimed the machine gun at the tank and heard the clang of his bullets as they hit its armour plating. And it rolled on as the enemy's bullets whistled around him. More tanks appeared. Trundling between these familiar buildings, they were otherworldly. They were there to kill them and were bigger and noisier than he believed possible. Soldiers who had taken positions near timber buildings had to escape because they caught fire and the heat was intolerable. A car was set alight and sent a column of burning petrol into the air. There was a smell of burning, every kind of burning. One of the tanks changed course and accelerated as if to drive through loose snow, and mowed down a rifle position. A soldier was run down. Tarald watched the man's arms thrash about before he was crushed into the ground and his mangled body left behind as the belts rolled on. Tarald spotted some infantry men behind a tank and fired at them. The machine gun ran empty, and he waited for it to be reloaded. When this failed to happen, he looked down and saw that his companion was dead. His helmet had a large bullet hole from which a strange mixture of blood and hair was oozing.

That was the last thing Tarald saw.

He assumed that he had been hit by a grenade and lain unconscious for some time before being one of the many men tended to by German medics. An incongruous act of kindness so soon after the noise of war had ebbed. The Germans seemed almost surprised that their fireworks could inflict such damage. He had come round when he felt fresh air on his face, and realised that he was lying on a truck, watching the valley sides of Fåberg roll past. The Germans drove through the centre of Lillehammer and stopped at the hospital. There, the doctors put false names on their bed ends and hid their uniforms in case the enemy returned to arrest them as prisoners of war.

But nobody came. They were busy fighting their way north.

"The doctor cut off my hand with a fine-toothed saw," said Tarald, lifting the stump of his arm.

Nobody said anything for a while. Esther walked over to him and stroked him gently over and down his shoulders, stopping when her hand reached the bandage.

"'Tis lucky it wasna' yer drawing hand," she said.

Tarald shook his head, saying that he had lost all desire to draw.

"See t' it that ye rest," said Kristine. "There be nowt else we can do now."

He wanted another cigarette. They let him have his way. It was the least they could give a son who had lost his hand.

Suddenly his temper rose. "The planes that were meant to back us up. The British planes. They were on some frozen lake further up the valley. Parked in the floodwaters, so their wheels got all iced up. We didna' stand a chance. 'Tis shameful! A goddam mess from start to finish."

He had been sent home with a brown bottle of tablets. He lay in his room all the next day with this bottle on his bedside cabinet. Jehans regularly came in to check on him. Twice he went down into the hallway and rang someone, without saying who.

That evening Fløteren stood in the hallway. This thickset man with kindly eyes had come in without knocking. He too went upstairs to see Tarald. An hour later he and Jehans left together without a word of explanation.

Astrid went in to check on her brother. He was asleep.

On the floor lay a map of Tretten. Beside it a red pencil and a roll of baking paper.

Jehans returned at dark, and still he refused to tell Astrid and Kristine what was happening. Astrid grew angry, Kristine grew fractious and Jehans dug his heels in.

"I have seen more war than ye, Father!" said Astrid. "Tell me what is going on!"

He shook his head.

"Tell us now," Kristine said, "why ye were in 'n' out o' Tarald's room today. If there be plans for more o' this family t' risk their lives, we has a right t' know!"

"'Tis nowt for thee," said Jehans.

That did it. Kristine screamed at him so the tiles nearly fell off the roof, and Esther had to take little Eirik over to see Isum.

In the end Jehans had to tell all. Since April 9, his old friend Fløteren had been helping Norwegian soldiers to send messages via the telegraph lines down at Vålebrua station. He had taken it upon himself to circulate a message from a Norwegian general. Help would soon be coming from England. Not just a few reserve soldiers this time. No. Thousands. A serious counter-attack to drive the Germans out. When this offensive started, the Norwegians must be armed and ready to participate. Masses of military equipment had been left behind after the Battle of Tretten. Rifles, machine guns, field radios and ammunition. The weapons that were left on the streets had already been gathered in by the villagers, but what Tarald had shown Jehans and Fløteren were the machine-gun positions and depots they had been forced to leave behind. Every cross on the map of Tretten marked loss, defeat and death.

"So what's happening with these weapons?" Astrid said.

"We canna' be sure yet," said Jehans. "We mun go out and fetch 'em one night. Then they mun be hidden. We be thinking t' move the shooting club's bullets from the Colonial, too."

"But how?" said Astrid.

Jehans had no answer.

Kristine was thinking. She ran her knuckles under her chin, pushing the loose skin back. It was a habit she had developed of late, annoyed that her skin was no longer as elastic as when she was young.

"Happen we could put the cartridges in t' milk churns that goes through the village," said Kristine. "They be marked each wi' a name. Naybody thinks twice about the milk truck when she goes back 'n' forth 'twixt dairy and farms every day."

They went quiet.

Astrid looked at her mother with . . . was it admiration? Yes. And her father's gaze, did that reflect . . . devotion? Nothing had been said, but Astrid saw now that her mother was touched.

"Nay more on't," said Kristine. "If us mun, then us mun."

"Stop a moment," said Astrid. "Jon Mossen will notice that the milk churns are na' empty. And his father supports Quisling."

"Might it be him that tattled t' the Germans?" Jehans said. "The Mossen boy?"

"I canna' believe that," said Kristine.

"He knows that Tarald went to Dresden. And he also knows that he goes to advertising school," Astrid said. "*And* that he went back to Jørstadmoen t' fight."

All three looked at each other.

"Nay, 'tis impossible," said Kristine. "Jon Mossen has driven for us for nigh on five year. Wi'out one single delay. Ne'er a day shirking."

"That means nowt," Jehans said. "Not now."

"Does we have other work we can put him to?"

"Nay. We mun dismiss him. We can say that Astrid needs the work now, with the war on."

"For shame," said Kristine. "Now there'll be still more trouble."

"I d'nay have a licence," Astrid said.

"Drive wi'out," said Kristine. "'Tis war."

We Too Must Draw Strength from Nothing

Sunday came and still nobody had seen Kai Schweigaard.

Fanciful rumours abounded. Some thought they had seen him going past the Gildevollen estate on the kicksled at breakneck speed, but it eventually became clear that it had not been the pastor but Ingeborg Braastad out delivering honey, in a long black skirt borrowed from her sister. Patriots and pessimists were convinced he had been executed on the Løsnes Marshes, where a series of shots in quick succession had been heard early one morning. More moderate folk presumed he was in custody at Lillehammer, where the Germans had set up Central Command. Jehans had denied that he was on the Hekne farm, but this could be a bluff. And then, what about the guards in black uniforms outside the bell tower? Mightn't they have locked him in *there*? Without any stove. Or was his corpse lying there in a coffin?

Unlikely, said others. The guards in those special uniforms had only been there for two days. But rumour had it that Astrid Hekne had gone down there with the Germans that evening. Some said she went willingly and had led the way, others thought she had a gun to her back – but then again, it was getting quite dark.

And talking of the Heknes, it was a waste of time, they said, to try to get anything out of Astrid Hekne. She was so surly and unpredictable of late, and her brother was maimed for life, when he'd been so good at drawing. And like them or not, it was best not to get too close to the Heknes, they were an ambitious, self-seeking lot, who could turn in a moment.

But whether Schweigaard was alive or dead, it was over with him. The new chaplain was starting on the Sunday after next, it had been announced by the parish council long before war broke out. The weekend's farewell Mass had been cancelled because the guest of honour had either been arrested or executed.

As always, folk gathered to hear the latest, and, as always when the Colonial was closed, they stood around the telegraph pole at the village crossroads on which notices were pinned about ski-jumping and auctions, and which many considered the true centre of Butangen. Today thirty or so villagers were gathered there, busy discussing this and that, when they suddenly fell silent, and looked at each other in astonishment.

Wasn't that the sound of church bells? Not the Sister Bell in the bell tower, but the bells in the new church?

An elderly villager noticed that the ringing sequence was like that used in the old days to call for Mass. Back when very few folk had watches. In those days the first round of bells would ring well ahead of the service, giving even the villagers who lived high up on the hills time to come down, and when there were ten minutes to go, the bells were rung again, signalling that folk should hurry.

When the bells rang that morning, Astrid was in the back room of the Colonial. She had drawn the curtains and locked herself in unseen. The door to the iron safe stood open. Out of it she took some small packages wrapped in grey paper and tied with twine.

Cartridges for the Krags. About four thousand rounds.

She left some for appearances' sake, as well as the shotgun shells and cartridges for rifles of other calibres. She allowed herself one more look before she closed the safe. They were so beautiful, these cartridge boxes. They had meant freedom and adventure before the war. The cartons of Winchester ammunition reminded her of the cowboy and Indian books she and Tarald had read as children. The flat, red packets of Nitedals Special held the promise of autumn mornings and grouse shooting.

She carried the cartridges into the cheese-making room. They weighed a good three hundred kilos, and in this weight she felt a pledge of revenge.

Her first trip with the milk truck would be early tomorrow. Her father was going to sit next to her and go over some of the Reo's quirks.

Hurriedly, she started to put the cartridge boxes into the milk churns.

It felt good. Because it was dangerous.

She had nearly finished when the chiming of the church bells joined the hollow sound of the ammunition cartons landing in the milk churns.

The bell ringing awakened her grief over Kai Schweigaard. Day by day, just as blood congeals and dries minute by minute, she had faced up to the fact he was gone forever. And that "Never mention the church bell to anyone" had been his last words.

So why were they ringing now? The new curate must have already come to take over. In which case it would fall to him to bury Mari Slåen. Her coffin was expected this week.

She would have to go to see him.

Outside she felt unsteady and fearful. A new kind of terror had lodged itself in her body. Whenever she saw a German soldier, she would search his face to see if it was he who had pulled off her shoes and clothes.

They had not gone any further, but had made it clear that they could, even there, in the bell tower. And they all looked the same under their helmets, these Germans, making them all guilty. They had *all* torn off her clothes, every soldier she saw.

She slipped into the crowd that was streaming towards the church. Winter refused to give way. The heaps of cleared snow at the wayside were beginning to sink, and yesterday the sun had warmed their cheeks, but the wind was still cold and folk held their jacket collars between their fingers and walked with a forwards lean.

The church door was wide open. Røhme was nowhere to be seen. She hurried in and sat near the front.

The church was freezing cold. Why had nobody lit the stove?

The congregation filed in. Nobody seemed bothered by the cold, and the silence that usually filled the minutes before Mass was replaced with chatter about the war. Everyone was turning to talk to everyone, until all the pews were buzzing with gossip.

And still the church was getting fuller and fuller, and only when it was nearly eleven o'clock did she notice that something was missing.

The organ wasn't playing.

Why was there no organist? Herr Røhme appeared at last, and there was a momentary lull. But why was he standing there looking so bewildered?

The chatter rose again. Norwegian fighters had returned home to the surrounding farms. One had been so sweaty and dirty his uniform could have stood up on its own. The news was bad on the whole, but could it be true that there were a few hundred British soldiers up in the mountains? But where were the king and crown prince? And what were Quisling's intentions?

The talking stopped. A man came into sight near the altar rail.

Pastor Schweigaard.

Grey and haggard, in a crumpled cassock. Hair unkempt, using his walking stick indoors. He must have wandered in with some notion of introducing the new curate, thought Astrid. She got up to tell him to leave and seek safety, because the Germans were after him, and he was so frail he looked as though he might die at any moment. He clearly intended to go into the pulpit now, and the church went as quiet as only a church full of quiet people can be. Unease hung in the air. The tiny necessary sounds – the rustling of clothes, muffled coughs that could be held back no longer, little sneezes – these waves of trifling movements revealed the reigning sense of anticipation. Everyone's eyes followed Schweigaard as he plodded towards the pulpit, in fear, perhaps, that he might fall over. An infinitely long time passed before his shaggy mop of grey hair came into view above them. He gripped the edge of the pulpit like a ship's rails in a storm, and Astrid felt awful for him, it was unbearable to watch him make a fool of himself, and now he couldn't find his spectacles, and suspense had long since changed to embarrassment as he cleared his throat, then cleared it again, and said, in a frail voice:

"We all want a family. We all want a home."

He coughed. Tried to muster some strength, but went on in the same frail voice. "But it takes effort to make friends, a family and home. And the moment this is granted us, a yet more onerous task is laid upon us, to hold it safe, day in and day out. The easiest thing is to destroy. A home. A friendship. And in such times as these our homes and our friendships are at their most fragile."

He coughed again. A hawking cough that would barely have passed in a hut full of old elk hunters. But having cleared the phlegm from his throat, he went on:

"For the storm will shake and the storm will tear, and we will freeze and go hungry. And the storm will rob us of the peace we need to apply wisdom. For the hungry always seek to satisfy their own hunger first."

His voice grew clearer and stronger with each word. He spoke without any notes.

"Many people believe that savagery exists only in other races. Here, the winter cold has always been our enemy, and has perhaps cooled our temperament. We have fought against hardship and adversity, but rarely against soldiers. It is easy, therefore, to think we are kinder and more reasonable than others, and that we will, when called to battle, fight with blank weapons. But cast your minds to the Middle Ages. Remember how we burned women at the stake because fear got the upper hand. Remember the battle of Kringen in 1612. Remember how the battle was won honestly on that first day. But then cast an unflinching eye on what happened the next morning, when 150 unarmed men were slaughtered. One after the other. They were killed by men from *our* villages because they were filled with hatred. I say this because we seldom recognise this danger. It is sly and prefers to come in a shape we have never seen before. We cannot learn from history, because evil always returns with a new face. What we must recognise is the hatred in our own hearts."

There was a pause in his sermon. His skin might be old and wrinkled, but the Kai Schweigaard of the Silver Winter had returned to Butangen, stately and magnificent, in his pastor's robes from bygone days.

His voice rang out once more with all the fullness of a church organ.

"As a young man I chose the wrong path when the church bells were sent away from Butangen. I did something irreparable because hatred was aroused in me. Now I stand for the last time in this pulpit and see that war has come to our land. The trials we shall endure will be many and various. For the enemy is arrived, and the enemy wants to enter our houses. He also wants to enter our thoughts. He will come with promises, and it will be hard to know what is right and true. Hardest of all, perhaps, will be to see who really *is* the enemy. The lie will find its way through devious, seductive words. Many will stumble and many will fall. Some will walk into snares, others will set those snares. For our beloved Butangen will be laid waste. The frosts will bite into our bodies and our thoughts. Until a raging fire will bring everything to an end and the rain will extinguish the flames and we will stand upon bare rock and be called to judgement.

"It is May now. It has been a cold winter, and the snow still lies upon the ground. In peacetime we would be looking forward to the summer, but this summer and possibly the next will be struck by drought and hail. Not in our fields, but here in our souls. So, look at the birch trees as you wander home today. Remember how their leaves will burst forth even though the earth is barren and grey. Like the birch trees, we too will spring forth again. And just as the sap rises in the birch, it will rise in us, even though our soil is also barren and grey. A spring shall come. A spring in which we stand free. Then we must open the door for Christianity's most precious gift. Forgiveness. When this dreadful moment is past, our honour will not be measured by the size of our fields. Nor the weight of a coin. But by the strength of our handshake. By the firmness of our promise. And the sun will no longer bring drought. The sun will bring warmth. And the rain will not bring floods. It will nourish the fields and wash away our resentment. But this will take time. For they will have shot our children and lowered our flags. Let us now therefore sing the national anthem. And as we do so, let us raise the Norwegian flag within us, for no man can stop us from waving this flag in our hearts. God bless the government! God bless King Haakon!"

A Suitable Job for a Pensioner

The final words of the national anthem rang out: *Dets fred, dets fred slår leir* – for its peace, for its peace will encamp. They sang all eight verses, although Schweigaard had descended from the pulpit after the first verse. Many had formed an excited line at the altar rail to shake his hand, but he seemed to have disappeared. They looked around in dismay, some even searched behind the altar, others knocked on the sacristy door, peeped in discreetly.

"'Tis empty in here," someone said.

"So, where's he gone?" said another.

"Might he have gone out the back?"

"Happen he be outside on the church steps?"

"Nay, he in't out here either," came a voice from the entrance doors.

Astrid slipped into the sacristy. There was nothing there but a pair of black shoes. He could not have gone under the church floor since the vestment cupboard was still standing over the trapdoor. She thought of the Hekne sisters down there. The peace that reigned down there, despite all the commotion up here. The dried hands clasped around the dried flowers.

She looked out of the window. The weather had changed. Huge snowflakes were tumbling from the sky, and making a deep, fluffy blanket of white on the gravestones outside. The back sacristy door was unlocked, but when she stuck her head out into the icy air, she saw nothing.

The congregation had given up now, and like a slow river they headed down the aisle to the exit. The chatter still buzzed and Røhme stood by the hymn books, looking confused and stuttering, "Nay, it wasna' me that rang the bells."

Astrid followed them, and had just reached the doors when she saw the soldiers. Two, no, three.

Right in front of the church steps. Keeping watch.

She did an about-turn, muttered to Herr Røhme that she had lost a mitten, and squeezed her way back through the crowd.

She headed for the sacristy and opened the back door. More soldiers on their way. Thankfully they hadn't noticed her.

She went back to the pew she had been sitting on and tried to clear her mind.

But all she could think of was the dark bell tower.

She breathed deep.

It was unlikely that they were after her at this point. Unless they had broken into the Colonial and discovered the cartridges.

No. How could that be?

They had snow on their shoulders. Meaning that they'd been

standing there for a long time, so they could not have arrested Kai Schweigaard.

Astrid hurried back towards the door, and, walking up very close to someone, stared at the ground and made herself small as she passed the soldiers. She stayed in the crowd until she was past the tethering post beyond the gate, and then ran to Hekne just as she had run in Elverum.

How would she manage tomorrow driving a milk truck full of ammunition? The village was crawling with Germans carrying loaded guns, and all with the right to monitor any activity. What if she got as frightened as she was now?

In the hallway she kicked off the snow and shouted out that Kai was alive. Her father came down, and she told him about the service. Jehans nodded quietly and whispered:

"Did ye manage to . . . place them?"

She drummed her fingers. Her feet refused to stay still.

"Aye. There be fourteen churns."

"The fellows at Tretten," whispered Jehans, "they found a fair old haul. Two hundred rifles and sub-machine guns. A dozen machine guns. Ammunition aplenty."

"How are ye going to hide them?" Astrid said quietly.

He said that the plan had been to put them on the seters. "But the Germans be operating up there. So, we needs more folk. But I be short on who t' ask. And how t' organise all the instructions we needs to get out before the big fight."

They ate an early supper, and treated themselves to some cod's roe. Astrid cut Tarald's potatoes for him while he sat brooding. They had agreed not to tell him about the ammunition, since his pills made him weak and a bit strange.

Astrid was still uneasy and went outside on the front steps, so she had the old farmhouse at her back. The snow was melting and there were bare patches around the trunks of the apple trees, and under the *tuntre*, the most ancient tree on Hekne. In its branches she counted three crows. If only she could ask them where Kai Schweigaard was.

She wrenched her kicksled out of the snow and sped off down the hill. The sky was grey and still letting forth a little snow. It had been the coldest spring she could remember, but although it was still possible to sledge on the ice at the path's edge, she sensed that the kicksled season was nearing its end. The village was noticeably empty now, the villagers had doubtless gone home to digest the pastor's words. There were only two middle-aged women by the telegraph pole at the crossroads. She dug her heel into the snow to brake. The women looked at her and said nothing. A new poster had been put up, brilliant white against the black creosoted timber.

REWARD
Reward of 10,000 kroner for information about the old church bell which is being unlawfully withheld from the German Culture Department.

The poster was signed by their own sheriff.

Astrid parked the kicksled across the path to stop it sliding down. Then, walking past the women, she tore down the poster, screwed it up and stuffed it in her pocket.

She met the gaze of the two women. She had served them both in the Colonial for years. One always wore the same tatty clothes and never bought coffee. The other ordered half a paper cone of camphor drops every Saturday. She had no idea what she saw in their eyes now. They were the sort to blab because the high-almighty Heknes had sacked Jon Mossen from his delivery job for no reason.

Astrid sped off again on her kicksled.

This anxiety about the future.

She suddenly had the feeling she had lived through it before.

Runes and Warplanes

And it struck her that there was a place here in Butangen where this anxiety could be stilled or at least given a name.

She started up the old seter road, which was no longer shovelled clear of snow. Here she saw the tracks of another kicksled that looked quite fresh. Behind a bush she found the sled, and, from there, footprints leading to the old midwife's cottage.

They sat as Norwegians have always sat in times of trouble. In front of a wood burner with wet toes, cold fingers and empty stomachs, while the spruce logs crackled and sparked.

"I still havena' seen his wrist. He refuses to take off the bandage. Keeps himself to himself."

"And you?" Kai said.

"I cry, but not so the others can hear. I dream bad dreams. About Mari Slåen. About what happened in t'bell tower."

Astrid leaned forward to adjust the damper on the stove. Schweigaard placed a sooty coffee pot on the top.

She showed him the reward poster. At last, his face broke into a little smile. She opened the stove door, and he folded the poster and put it on the flames. They sniffed in the rising smoke.

"The bell is in Daukulpen, am I right?" said Astrid.

"Don't ask," Kai said. "A pastor cannot lie."

"D'nay say that. An untruth is not always a lie. When the truth is greater than the untruth. 'Twas ye that said that once."

"I did?"

"Aye, I remember it so. But not what it related to."

"Very well. You need to know in case something happens to me. It *is* in Daukulpen."

"How did ye get her there?"

"Isum helped me."

"Giant Isum?"

"Yes. He proved surprisingly knowledgeable and skilful. Just one problem," he said, twisting on his stool. "We saw a set of footprints in the snow. Someone else in the village may know where the bell is."

Astrid was lost for words. She had felt hungry on her way here, but she had no appetite now. Just the onset of a headache.

"I'm sorry, Astrid. The tracks were on a spot that overlooks Daukulpen."

"Man or woman?" Astrid asked, after a while.

"Impossible to tell."

"There's sommat strange going on," Astrid said. "The man in t' bell tower talked as if he knew that the Hekne Weave had been found."

Schweigaard shook his head. "He must have been bluffing. It's common knowledge that I was looking for it. But only you know about it. The only thing that might have betrayed me is that I stopped enquiring about it sometime before the last war."

He looked at her expectantly. Astrid picked at a graze on her hand and settled back in her chair.

"The weave is hidden at the very back of the earth cellar," she said. "A good distance from any o' the farm buildings. In case o' fire. D' nay fear, 'tis dry there. But I wonder if I should hide it up at the seter at some point."

Kai Schweigaard nodded slowly.

He rubbed his chin, pondering.

"You know, Astrid, I don't think Sprockhoff poses the most danger ultimately. But Jankuhn and Günther. What they do is as cunning as it is terrifying. Is he in the SS, this Jankuhn fellow?"

"If they're the ones with the black uniforms, then aye."

"I've been thinking. To us Norwegians, and to the British too, a uniform is simply work apparel. The Germans decorate their uniforms with mystical symbols. As a pastor I recognise what they're doing. They're borrowing from magic. Creating a religion for themselves. They see themselves as crusaders on a noble mission. The idea that we can return to an ancient and glorious

285

past, something nature-given in which the Germanic and Norse peoples are united – I suspect a great many people will fall for it. It's a very seductive idea."

Astrid got up and walked around a bit. On the wall hung a 1938 calendar and a tarnished mirror. Adolf and Ingeborg had lived here for a while after being evicted from Halvfarelia. Later paupers had been accommodated here, and Kai must have been surviving on what they had left behind. He smelled of sweat, and his beard was growing through. On a table lay a yellowed envelope on which were jotted some key words for the sermon he had given.

"There must have been some mice in here because the bedding's all chewed," said Kai. "But we've always kept some canned food and firewood here. As a backup for people in crisis."

"You must be exhausted," said Astrid. "Careful you don't get pneumonia."

She was standing by the window. Outside was the forest and the snow-covered path leading to the old seter road. The snow had stopped, and something told her it was the last of the year. An icicle dropped from the roof.

She could see no soldiers. But any soldier worth his salt would make sure not to be seen.

"In't this where Widow Framstad lived. The old midwife?"

"Yes, she left it to the church. A remarkable woman who – who foresaw her own death. And your grandmother told me she had a vision here. A vision that told her she would give birth to two sons."

Steam rose from the kettle on the stove. Schweigaard struggled to his feet, and, somewhat unsteadily, made the coffee. Astrid swept some mouse droppings from the kitchen counter. Then took a sip of coffee. The best she could say about it was that it was hot.

"This coffee must have been standing here for years," she said.

"That's a relief to hear. I assumed it was my lack of coffee-making skills."

They drained their cups. He went to empty the grounds into the basin.

"Nay! Ye'll block it!" she said, leaping up. She took the coffee pot from him and cleaned up the mess. "Ye mun scrape the grounds in t'bucket with a spoon before ye rinse it out!"

Outside, Astrid brushed the snow from a bench. The afternoon sun came out from the clouds, and they sat against the wall and listened to the stream burbling on the slope behind them. The fieldfares chirruped in the bushes.

But it felt as though the spring was behind glass. As though it had nothing to do with them.

"The British are coming back," said Astrid. "There's hope. But we need help. Can ye point me to some menfolk? Men ye trust."

"Jehans knows everyone," Kai said.

"Not like thee. Ye know all about folks' drinking habits and such. Pick four or five men. Put their names in a sealed envelope. Preferably one that in't covered with notes for a sermon."

"And what will these men be doing? I need to know."

"Transporting weapons. In batches. To be picked up from Tretten, taken up int' mountains by sledge and hidden on the seters. I am trying to work out a way to pass messages on."

Kai Schweigaard nodded. His familiar pastor's nod. The nod with which he had received the news of deaths, and joyful and dubious wedding plans. Eyes lowered, head tilted, in repose for a few seconds, conveying acceptance of the decision, then his head lifted to signal that *yes*, he would take the matter in hand.

"That's a risky undertaking. When the Germans find civilians with weapons, they shoot them on the spot. Even if they surrender. These men have to be willing to risk being shot and left in a ditch."

"Quite. Which means they mun be quick-witted. So, they d'nay get shot and left in a ditch. They have t' know the mountains, and the seters, and they canna' be disloyal."

"I'll pick out a few," he said. "It's a fitting job for a pensioner."

And they went on sitting against the weathered log wall.

"Round the back of the cabin here," he said, "up by the rhubarb patch. There's a flower meadow."

"Oh?"

"It's a graveyard. Widow Framstad buried the babies there that died at birth. I've consecrated the ground. Just wanted you to know."

The sun continued its journey. Suddenly Astrid leaned forward.

"Kai. Tell me, who is the last person in the church before Sunday Mass?"

"Herr Røhme. He goes in at four o'clock every Saturday afternoon and puts up the hymn numbers listed for the service. Sets out the altar candles and sweeps the floor. Then, at ten o'clock on Sunday morning, he unlocks the church ready to ring the bells."

"I need the church key," Astrid said, and before he could ask, she said, "Hush. Ask no questions, Kai, and ye shall hear no lies. You're a pensioner now."

A moment later he pointed towards the hallway and said that the key was on the peg behind his cassock.

His eyes followed her as she fetched it.

"It feels strangely sad to hand it over. Don't go making too many problems for Kåre Karlsen."

"We shall see."

She clasped his hand and held it. Young and firm it rested against his wrinkled skin, flecked with age spots and slack over his knuckles. In her other hand she held a church key that he no longer needed.

Four Trusted Men

Kai Schweigaard was standing in the doorway.

The afternoon sun still hung above the tops of the spruce trees. Pale, but warm.

He had, at this advanced age, got the status of a *wanted man*. This amused him rather, but the promised reward dampened his mirth.

Ten thousand kroner was a fortune. Isum would never be tempted. A better life than with Svarten and a room at Hekne could not be bought with money. But there had been footprints along the sledge tracks. He had to assume that someone in the village knew where the bell was hidden. And they were waiting to step forward.

He went back in. Noticed how bad it smelled inside. Opened the door to air it.

This place was hardly equipped for waging a war. A wind-blown log cabin with a rusty old stove, with no electric lights or telephone, with no horse-drawn carriage, and no Oldfrue Bressum or Fru Røhme to slice him some bread and cheese, and yes, he even had to empty his own chamber pot.

But he must get down to it. Astrid needed some trustworthy men. It was a difficult assignment. The war had been going on for just a matter of weeks, and a patriot in April might turn traitor in May.

From the log basket he pulled a dry, crumpled edition of the local paper, the *Gudbrandsdølen*. Brushed off the mouse droppings and loose bark. And with a pencil jotted some names down in the margins.

He was soon shaking his head.

No. One man had had an affair with the wife of a hare hunter who was politically radical, the other tended towards depression.

Runes and Warplanes

Schweigaard closed his eyes and imagined he had the church register before him. He leafed through its pages in his mind's eye. All the village surnames, all the village heroes, all the village sinners. All of them recorded in his own hand. He weighed up each character, rejecting the periodic drinkers and any loose-tongued braggarts.

Which did not leave many.

The stool he was sitting on was hard and had loose joints, what Astrid called *sliddery*, and he stretched his back. It was impossible to remember everyone. If only he had his old archive. He had never thrown anything away, not even the accounts book from when one of his duties as pastor was to issue the bounty payments for the shooting and trapping of vermin. The village youngsters had regularly blagged their way into getting him to pay unjustly high bounties. They came with mountain fox pelts and said they were wolf skins, and even tried to get the bounty for a wolverine by presenting him with the skin of a Spæl sheep. But with Astrid's help he had eventually seen through their scams, although, since these boys came from such poor families, he often paid for a hawk when they came with the claws of a common rooster.

Hmm.

These lads were now mature men. They had formed teams that hunted elk, an animal that had been rare to see back then – so rare that the villagers believed they were the cows of the mythical Hulders – but whose numbers had vastly increased as the coniferous forests had been allowed to grow with modern forest management.

He was excited. His hand groped for his pipe in his desk drawer, but there was no drawer and certainly no pipe, because of course he was not sitting at his old desk.

It was an inspired idea. These were men who knew their firearms. Strong walkers. Used to surviving in the mountains and forests. Who from their youth had been acquainted with every byway and seter cabin – in particular the bedchambers – better than any respectable folk. These old elk hunters would be able to pick out younger patriots, as any political sympathies would have been long since laid bare on drunken evenings in their hunting cabins.

Yes. He had found them. They were perfect for the task.

They mustn't be crooks themselves, but know a crook when they saw one.

He wrote their names above the headline of the *Gudbrandsdølen* from 1937.

Røen. Asphoug. Evensen. Brenden.

These ageing miscreants would finally make good for his past generosity in the handing out of hunters' bounties.

At evenfall next day, he heard voices outside.

He hurried over to the wood stove. There was a knock. *Yes*, he said, holding the newspaper near the flames and looking towards the door.

It was Fru Røhme.

"Are there any soldiers out there?" he whispered. "Are you here under duress?"

"Nay. Be just us two. Herr Røhme be by the gate keepin' watch."

Kai put the newspaper down and closed the stove door. Fru Røhme unburdened herself of a carrying frame. From a cardboard box she lifted his Underwood typewriter.

"Astrid said ye had need o' some office equipment. And we has another backpack too. Wi' some food, a change o' clothes 'n' yer shaving things. There be some cheese and speke ham – I cured it myseln."

"And my tobacco? I had three boxes left."

"I snuck everything from yer drawers when I were up there

cleanin'. And I has underclothes for thee too. Were Astrid reminded me."

He looked away as she brought out his long johns, vests and pants and saw to his chamber pot.

"The parsonage," he said. "Have Günther and that archaeologist fellow in uniform been back?"

Fru Røhme was already busy with the broom and cloth. "We in't seen nowt o' them since Thursday. I has a notion they instructed Major Sprockhoff to get the church bell. But the major has more important fish to fry, for they be teachin' the soldiers to ski. Happen there be sommat going on up in t' mountains."

"This Norwegian man who tormented Astrid in the bell tower – who was it?"

"We has no idea," said Fru Røhme.

"Hello?"

Herr Røhme was standing in the hallway. Unable to hold back, Schweigaard shook his hand and slapped him on the shoulder, and soon all three were tucking in to delicate slices of speke ham with flatbread and sour cream, and when Fru Røhme fished out a bottle of malt beer it was as though nothing had changed.

"It's a shame Oldfrue Bressum isn't still in charge of the cooking at the parsonage," Schweigaard said. "The Germans would have left weeks ago."

"Or surrendered," Herr Røhme ventured.

"The sheriff were round askin' after the church bell," said Fru Røhme. "Wanted us t' understand he were only doing it out o' duty. Asked where ye be. We said we didna' know, which were true at the time. I asked if ye were to be arrested. He hummed 'n' hawed. Said he just wanted to question thee. Nowt else. That he had sent some clerk round to pin up a poster about a reward. But seems like he only ever put up one."

"So there's still a bit of the old sheriff in him," Schweigaard said. "That's good to hear."

"There be sommat more important," said Fru Røhme. "We both wanted to be here when we told thee."

She bent down and picked up a large book wrapped in grey paper. Schweigaard recognised it immediately.

"The church register?" Schweigaard said. "But surely the new curate needs that?"

"That be just it," said Fru Røhme. "We has news from the bishop's office. Chaplain Kåre Karlsen doesna' wish to leave his old mother wi' this war on. And they canna' find a replacement."

"And?"

"Happen Herr Pastor mun be our priest a little longer."

Schweigaard could not hold back a gravelly *hah!* as he took the church register in his hands.

"At last something good has come out of this war!"

The Poor Souls who Languish in Paganism

He was holding services again. They buried Mari Slåen through tears and rain. Nothing noteworthy happened. He was not arrested by Sprockhoff's men, and the bailiff did not seize him along the old seter road.

The snowmelt gained the upper hand. The patches of snow were soon outnumbered by the bare patches. Surface water lay grey on the ice across Lake Løsnes.

May turned into June.

Every day brought with it the feeling that there might be a

shift. The moment when the British would come like a hurricane and sweep the Germans out.

But every day the Germans strengthened their defences, dug themselves in deeper, both in the earth and in purpose, and there was a constant flow of trucks driving up to seters and mountains. Jehans barely had time to mourn the fact that this heavy traffic might ruin his road before he discovered that the Germans were actually improving it. Military engineers reinforced the bridge, smoothed out the frost heaves and other winter damage, and a few days later they had erected a bigger guard station deeper in the mountains, with sleeping quarters, woodsheds and an observation tower with tall antennae. Local farmers commented on how the Land Management Committee's tardy processing of applications was no more.

Astrid still had the church key and Schweigaard blithely assumed that the messages she left for the hunting teams were cunningly hidden. A note under a pew, or in a hymn book slipped discreetly from one man to another. Or the like.

Another Sunday dawned, as Sundays do. The voluntary sounded from the organ, and Schweigaard, wearing a white surplice over his cassock, stepped once again from the sacristy and approached his congregation.

He realised that something was brewing even before he walked past the altar rail.

The service was rather too well attended.

Røen and Evensen were near the front. Further back he caught sight of a man from one of the other elk hunting teams whom he had picked out. None of them had been to church since their confirmation, and they were clearly unsure as to how to comport themselves.

"Let us pray silently," Schweigaard said, kneeling on the prie-dieu. He felt a shooting pain in his knees. The old midwife's cabin was cold and damp. Terrible for his arthritis.

The organ started up again. The hymn-singing was a shambles even by Butangen's standards. He had sent Røhme the hymn list yesterday, and since there were rarely any lead singers now, it consisted of familiar and easy-to-sing staples. As the opening hymn, he had chosen "Jesus, frelser" – Jesus, our Saviour – and he had sung the first lines before realising that the organist was playing a different tune. The congregation were also singing something quite different, so while the organ droned on, Schweigaard was left unable to lead the singing, for he had no idea which hymn it was.

Not until the end of the verse did he recognise it. One of those hideous missionary anthems they had not sung since the turn of the century, about *the poor souls who languish in paganism*.

Mistakes happened every other year when Røhme misread his handwriting, but such a mix-up seemed impossible: Røhme was meant to have put hymn number 9 up on the board, while all the missionary anthems had three-digit numbers, running from 770 upwards.

He flicked through his hymnal and found the lyrics, and then on the second verse something unexpected happened.

The mood lifted.

A few elderly ladies got into their stride and started singing rather loudly. This clutch of deeply religious womenfolk always sat together on the front pew. Thrilled at being reunited with this hymn, they sang to near bursting, raising the battle cry against the *black souls of the hellish night*. Meanwhile, wrapped like a woollen blanket around their rather shrill voices was the tentative mumble of the rest of the congregation.

Schweigaard sweated his way through the fourth and fifth verses.

At last, the boil was lanced. He set about the sacrament of penance. His voice was steady now, and his old, great schooner-like Mass was on course again. After the next hymn he read from the Book of Romans as his epistle. He had chosen his reading with care. Appropriately fortifying for wartime, but not too stirring. He had selected number 314 as a suitable epistle hymn. But when the organist started to play, he shivered.

Again, the organ was playing an altogether different melody from the one he was expecting. Eventually he realised that the congregation were singing one of the gloomiest hymns in the entire *Landstad's Hymn Book*. With the words *Min død er mig til gode* – my death is my blessing – the pious old ladies were moved to ever greater enthusiasm. These were churchgoers who asked to be buried with a hymnal in their hands. Now they had something to dispel the fear of war, and they sang with a passion close to intoxication. Halfway through, in a manoeuvre that looked a little deranged, Schweigaard wandered down the aisle, far enough to be able to turn back and look up at the hymn board.

Most of the hymn numbers were wrong.

He could see from the number of digits that these hymns would be totally out of place in the liturgy, as they were either missionary or confessional hymns.

It suddenly occurred to him that Astrid Hekne had been here in the night and changed the numbers into some secret code. And now – well, he could hardly stop the service and change the hymn board! Not only would the codes be lost, but he might unveil her plan, whatever that was.

If it hadn't been unveiled already. Folk must be wondering. The elderly women led the way despite their voices cracking on the high notes. And now, to his despair, the hunting teams joined in. Hard of hearing after a lifetime of shooting, they sang out of tune and rather too loudly.

Still, Kai Schweigaard battled through. When he finally went into the sacristy to take off his surplice, he had to lean against the wall. From the nave came yet another missionary anthem, a roaring cacophony that collapsed here and there into mumbling.

It was time for his sermon. In which he would speak of the brighter prospects for humankind, that better times would surely follow if they held close to their faith, and that all wars eventually came to an end. Naturally the evangelical hymn was meant to support this message, which was why he had chosen "Vår Gud han er så fast en borg" – Our God, He is a strong fortress – a discreet nod to his support of the king and his government.

Instead, a simple, mealtime grace followed. *Our table*, the congregation sang, *is laid with cloth of linen*.

From here on it was just a matter of muddling through. The closing hymn had of course been swapped too, this time for a sombre confessional hymn. The voices of the devout were overstrained now, but their joy at being reunited with "Uverdig er jeg" – Unworthy am I – was intense, and they gave it a last big push.

The hymn-singing in the village had never been good. In periods when the few God-fearing farms had more daughters, it had been passable, but he had often lamented the shrill tones from both the old wooden organ and confirmands whose voices were breaking.

But the Mass on June 2, 1940 left Schweigaard certain: never, *never* had the hymn-singing in Butangen been worse. Teeth gritted, he forced his way through the verses, while the women on the front pew reached a state of ecstasy that was almost impolite.

The Simplified War Liturgy

"Astrid! We can't have this!"

"Aye, Kai! We have to!"

"Impossible! If you'd been there you'd have seen the havoc you caused!"

"We have to!"

"*Now listen to me!* Can't you see why I'm angry? No? Because you put people in danger! Somebody could have twigged that the numbers up on the hymn board were codes, and then—"

"They couldna'. Or, anyways, they wouldna' know who—"

"Yes, they *would*! The church was overflowing with elk hunters and heathens! If you'd just bothered to familiarise yourself with the liturgy, Astrid, you'd—"

"The liturgy! Ye mun realise it was done in a hurry! We had *no choice*!"

Astrid slumped down on a stool. The last few weeks had been tumultuous. She had driven ammunition in milk churns past the Germans, visited Fløteren and hatched plans for the transport of weapons, only to be scolded now by Kai Schweigaard.

"It wasna' my intention to change *all* the hymn numbers. Just the middle ones."

"And!"

"Hear me out, please! I let myself in t' church last night. Røhme had hung up the numbers ye had given him. But the stool I stood on was unsteady, so I knocked the board and all the numbers fell down. Well, it was dark. And I tried to put them back up from memory. But at least I managed to get the coded numbers up in the right slots."

"What was the code?"

"'Tis best ye d'nay know."

He was cross. "I'm the parish priest here in Butangen, Astrid! If this is to be permitted, I must know!"

"Alright! The hymn numbers stand for the farm and unit numbers o' the seters to which the weapons are to be transported. Number 735 is Hilstadlykkja."

Schweigaard slumped into the cane chair. "Heaven help us. So, because the farm and unit numbers are 7/35, we had to wade through some morbid hymn about the blessing of death! And a totally unsuitable mealtime grace – number 691. What farm is that?"

"Mork. Weapons are to be delivered there too."

"Really, when?"

"Are ye really asking me *that*?"

"Yes, I am. Because I think there's a change of guard in the mountains on Wednesday mornings and Saturday afternoons."

"Oh?"

"Fru Røhme told me. The Germans are obsessive about the cleanliness of their vehicles. But she's noticed that every Wednesday and Saturday a truck comes with its wheels plastered with the red mud unique to the seter road. The soldiers they bring in that truck always seem exhausted."

"That's useful," said Astrid. "I shall pass it on. But, I should tell thee . . . folks are saying all sorts."

"About the Røhmes?"

"Aye. The officers make her cook for them sometimes. But the villagers believe she cooks for all the soldiers."

Schweigaard shook his head. "A terrible misunderstanding. It was I who asked her to carry on with that. So, she could keep an eye on what they're up to. You must try to stop these rumours."

"Wi'out letting on what she's actually doing? That shan't be easy."

Schweigaard got up. Paced the room with his hands behind his back.

"This thing with the hymn numbers," he said. "Despite my qualms, I have to admit it's clever."

"Doing it like that, right under folks' noses, removes any need to write our instructions on bits o' paper. It means the hunting teams never have to be seen together. Or ever use the telephone, for who knows what the switchboard ladies might come up with. The men can just go in t' church. Then they know where they mun . . . do whatever."

"How did you come up with this?"

"'Twas sommat Tarald told me. The churchwarden in Dresden was superstitious. Believed a ghost from Norway liked to make mischief in the stave church. It was Klara Mytting."

Schweigaard had to sit down.

"Klara. Old Klara? Over there? In Germany?"

Astrid nodded. "The churchwarden believed Klara would swap the numbers on t' hymn board. So she could hear her favourite: 'Thy little ones are we'."

Schweigaard had gone white.

"What is it, Kai?"

"Ah, just . . . a memory. Although no memory from that time is *just* a memory. Hymns. They seem to be the subject of the day. Yes . . . it wasn't until after Klara's death – when she froze to death during that New Year Mass – that I realised how much she loved that hymn. I thought it rather childish, then. Until I studied all the verses. Saw the darkness within it, and how sharply it conveys the smallness of human beings in the grip of the greater powers."

He fell into thought again. He seemed to be tussling with old memories, pushing them into a cupboard and trying to shut the door on them as they thrashed about inside.

"You know, Astrid," he said at last, "it might actually work. It's so outrageous and in such plain sight as to make it invisible. But it needs refining."

"I wanted to tell them t' time, place and date," said Astrid. "But that is impossible. Hymns only have three numbers."

"Maybe. And maybe not," he said. The floorboards creaked as he wandered around with his hands behind his back.

"Oh, come on!" she said. "D'nay' play-act!"

Schweigaard sat down, and began somewhat theatrically:

"If one of the digits means the day of the week, we can signal *when* something is to take place. Another could mean time, but then we only have one digit left to indicate location. Furthermore, we can't use the first numbers in the hymn book too freely, because they're grouped by occasion and church year. The Christmas carols, for example, run from 106 to 150. So if the mission is to be carried out on a Monday night, we could end up with Christmas carols in the middle of summer. We have the same problem if the first digit indicates a location, because most farm and unit numbers in Butangen start with a 7 or 8, and unfortunately the hymns from 700 to 899 include all sorts of oddities – from missionary songs to hymns for funerals at sea and cemetery dedications, and, not least, all those gruesome hymns about sickness and death."

He continued to pontificate on problems she had long since considered. From her rucksack she took out a loaf of rye bread and some coffee, and suggested they needed some sustenance if they were going to solve this.

Later that evening, in the draughty old midwife's cottage, they had sketched out the Simplified War Liturgy. Only two hymns could contain codes. One of these had to be the closing hymn. Nobody would notice if it was odd because everybody just wanted to get home anyway.

"The second code number," said Schweigaard, "can be played as a melody without lyrics. On the violin or organ. They often do this in towns, but rarely out in the countryside. We can call it *Down Memory Lane*. The organist can play the most obscure melodies to the delight of the ladies in the front pew."

A mouse ventured out onto the floor for some crumbs while they continued to plug the holes in their plan. Eventually they found that it was surprisingly sympathetic to the liturgy, and that it was better and more secure the stranger their hymn choices. The last figure in the number would be the day of the week on which the action was to take place, and the two first digits would indicate the location. Thus hymn number 315 "Naglet til et kors på Jorden" – Nailed to a cross on Earth – would indicate an action on Friday at location number 31. They also agreed to make it clear that some hymn numbers had no special meaning, so that patriots didn't set off for Gråhøgda every time they played hymn number 309. Spies might also be uncovered by occasionally choosing hymns that led them to a place the resistance had under observation.

But no matter how hard they wracked their brains, it was difficult to achieve safe and accurate localisation through the 1926 edition of *Landstad's Hymn Book*. Location numbers had to signify something solid: farm and unit numbers in the seters. But what if they needed to go into the forest or above the treeline in the mountains? A list of positions was the only possible solution, but that would be fatal if it ended up in German hands.

"I was thinking," said Astrid. "Before the war, when tourists came here to hunt hare and grouse, we sold hunting licences at the Colonial."

"Oh?"

"The Butangen Land Association could never agree on hunting rights, which is why the hunting grounds are divided int' thirty-four zones. To stop arguments when tourists shot game on other folks' land, my father stencilled copies of a hunting map that covered all t' forest and mountains. Every hunter has one. They're dated 1938, and naybody would find it strange t' see a mountain huntsman with a map in his pocket."

"Do they have coordinates?"

"I believe so. Or we could take baking parchment and draw numbered points on't. Then they could lay that over their maps. And maybe several numbers could refer t't same place."

He nodded eagerly. "That'll be less suspect than if the same unusual closing hymn is played over and over again."

"In which case our men'll have to keep their hunting maps and baking parchment in separate places in t' house," Astrid said.

"Hmm, that troubles me," said Schweigaard. "Maybe it's better with coordinates after all."

They continued. Then Astrid went quiet. It was all very easy *now*. Like a parlour game. But when it got serious, when the military turned up, when soldiers aimed their loaded Mausers at folk, at villagers she knew, at her customers from the Colonial, when her terror of the bomber planes and the fear she had felt in the dark bell tower returned, what then? Would she be up to the mark? Would her comrades?

"What's bothering you, Astrid?"

"Is this getting overcomplicated? Ought we t' just paint the numbers outside t' Colonial or sommat?"

"No. It's not overcomplicated. Remember what strange times we're living in. Nobody can be arrested simply for going to church. I'm the one who chooses the hymns, and if this is uncovered and I get interrogated, it stops with me. I shan't ever give anything away."

"That's easy t' say."

Schweigaard cleared his throat.

"Well, that's how it is. I shan't ever give it away."

She shook her head. Went quiet.

"There are times I reckon I'm going mad."

"In what way?"

"I can go to visit Mari's grave and hide away and sit sobbing wi'out a tear. Then seconds later I can remember the bullets in t' milk churns and want to burst out laughing. And then, afterwards, I just feel confused."

"Perhaps that's what war does to us," said Schweigaard. "But never deny laughter. It comes to our rescue in the darkest of times. How's Tarald, by the way? Does he ever laugh?"

"Well. He went to Oslo a day ago. To check on his lodgings. Told Esther it was hard to call us, having to wedge the receiver between his chin and shoulder while cranking the phone to get the exchange. When it hit him that was how using the phone would be from now on, he burst out laughing."

It was getting dark, and, thinking she heard a noise outside, she crept over to the window. He waited until she was back, lit a couple of candles, and soon they were talking in normal voices.

"Fru Røhme brings me food here twice a week," he said. "She shops for me every Friday. Make sure you're the one who serves her. Write the codes on the back of the receipt. I won't know which locations they indicate. Fru Røhme will come here with my shopping, blissfully unaware that she's our courier. Then I'll check the receipt, finish the service schedule, and hand it back to her to give to Herr Röhme. Who will, equally unsuspecting, hang the hymn numbers up on the board, just as he has for years. The only person who might wonder a little is the organist, but like most organists he has a phlegmatic, near indifferent nature."

They got up.

"I shall try t' repair the damage to the Røhmes' reputation," said Astrid. "One way or another."

"Good. And by the way. Instruct your couriers *not* to join in the singing. The biggest risk, the thing that'll arouse most suspicion, is if Evensen and Røen come to church and start singing missionary hymns."

Six Dead Pheasants

"We must get our own food," said Victor Harrison. "That's what these are really designed for. For circumstances like these."

He and his sons, now fifteen and sixteen, were standing in the gunroom at Finlaggan. Before them was a large gun case whose contents had begun to acquire some patina. The walls were decked with stuffed animals. The pride of their forefathers. Above the double doors of frosted glass hung a reindeer head with a long beard and magnificent antlers.

A memento of peacetime. A memento of an autumn hunt and a brother in Butangen.

The two boys should soon have had the chance to fill this room with their own mementoes, but the war had put everything on hold. They were too young to be called up. But if, like the last, this war continued for four years, then Edgar at least would be caught up in it.

Victor looked into the reindeer's glass eyes. The instant Norway had been invaded, he had been filled with regret. Regret at not having sent more letters to his niece Astrid. Or a proper invitation to Jehans. The silver christening spoon decorated with Celtic patterns they had sent for baby Eirik's baptism, what use was that? What would a boy care for such things? No, Victor should have written: *Listen, Brother. I'm inviting you all to come here. You, Kristine, Astrid and Tarald. And of course Esther and Eirik. I've visited Norway six times, and you've never travelled abroad. So please come. We've got plenty of sporting guns and fishing rods. I'll pick you up in the Fokker from the nearest passenger ship.*

It was too late now. With the war on, there was no postal service between England and Norway, and the newspapers barely covered anything that went on in his second homeland.

If only he could be sure they were safe!

"Well now, let's get started," Alastair said, opening the gun case.

Through a haze of gun oil they came into view, nestled in narrow compartments with partitions covered in green felt. The barrels and stocks of two shotguns. Arcane craftsmanship had made the honey-coloured walnut so shiny it could have been glass, and the deep blue-black of their barrels was matched only by the sea. This weapon – for it was one, although there were two of it – was the most beautiful he and the boys knew. Not just because of its craftsmanship and elegant line. Greater than these were the promises such trustworthy instruments held. Expectations of wild birds flying into the air, of long walks on foggy or rainy days, of heightened awareness before a thicket that glistened with raindrops, and the weight of red cartridges in a jacket pocket.

From this day on, a tool to defeat hunger.

Edgar handed his brother a cleaning rod with a pad of sheep's wool at the tip. Their communication bore no exclamation or question marks. Just a confirmation of what the other had already thought. With agile movements Alastair wiped the Rangoon oil from the barrels. This was an oil that could prevent rust in even the wettest jungle, but it was running out and was now unobtainable.

They were still at the school near Alnwick, Elsa still played the piano in the drawing room, Gisela still managed one of the offices of Harrison's Air Lift. But the Royal Air Force had now requisitioned their reserve aircraft. Victor's own Fokker Universal had been on the list, but the inspector had realised that no RAF pilot would be familiar with the American model, and it now stood, gas tanks empty, on a nameless lake in the foothills of Northumberland.

It was Edgar who had flown her there. A last trip before fuel rationing put paid to their flight training. They were all but fully fledged pilots anyway. Alastair had landed in rough seas just off the Orkney Isles aged only fourteen, and both boys could tune a star engine before their thirteenth birthdays.

Victor glanced back down at the shotguns and his thoughts ran to Jehans. They lay head-to-toe, separated only by a thin partition. Carved from a single tree, a many-centuries-old walnut tree, in which every major event in its life could be read in its rings. The patterns ran to and fro on the stocks in a seemingly bewildered flurry, for the two had been one until they were split apart by the saw's blade and by a moment's happenchance in the gunmaker's workshop, when it was decided which would be shotgun No. 1 and which No. 2.

Victor's sons had been introduced to weapons and aircraft when they were nine, and he had taught them the difference between a sidelock or boxlock shotgun, and that a Westley was neither, but a *droplock* – with an exquisite mechanism that could be removed for cleaning and lubrication in a few simple moves. But since the action was at a right angle to the stock, the untrained eye might mistake a droplock shotgun for an inexpensive boxlock, and below many inexpert eyes noses were turned up, since prejudice dictated that only a sidelock shotgun was good enough for an English gentleman. The only advantage of the sidelock was that it was seen as a technical descendant of the flintlock, giving it *pedigree*.

For many of Victor Harrison's acquaintances, pedigree always trumped technical quality. But for him it was the detail that offered a sense of meaning. Notions of pedigree and heritage had rankled with him all his life. He was content to have weapons that looked cheaper but were superior in ways that these so-called connoisseurs would never understand.

"Right, let's pick a hand," said Alastair.

Edgar took the initiative. He hid both fore-ends behind his back and swapped them round a few times before Alastair touched him on the left shoulder. The fore-end Edgar handed to him was marked "1", meaning he would shoot and Edgar load. Alastair went to a cupboard and rattled two cartons of cartridges. "Twelve left, Father," he said, without even looking in the box. "And four or five in this one."

"Which tells you how economic you'll have to be," Victor said.

They assembled the Westleys and went out, a father and his two sons in shabby attire. Alastair had stretched out in the past year, and the old jackets the two boys had taken from their foster grandfather's wardrobe hung loose on their lean bodies.

Meanwhile Elsa and Gisela were on their way to the thicket with Pidge. The plan was that Victor would enter from the opposite side and scare the birds so that they flew to where the boys were standing, ready to shoot. People might assume that the most effective way would be for them to stand slightly apart and each fire their own gun, but that was not for the Harrison brothers. They stood close together, but not out of desire to keep to the well-tested way of shooting pheasant, where two guns were shot alternately and passed between a shooter and a loader.

These two young huntsmen were dependent on each other. Four eyes focused on where the wild fowl emerged. They always shot with greater accuracy when they were together. Victor had never witnessed anyone with a rate of fire that compared, a skill built with practice when cartridges had been in plentiful supply.

The drive went badly. There were barely any pheasants, and those he did scare out of the undergrowth flew the wrong way. When he came back out from the thicket, he saw his sons. They were still poised to fire.

Elsa called from their position. She or Gisela must have managed to flush some out in the right direction, because there was a sudden rush of birds, far above the treetops, pheasants on stiff wings, maybe forty yards up, at the limit of their shotguns' killing capacity.

In a flash, Victor's sons switched guns. Although it was not regarded as good form, Edgar always held two cartridges with coarser and longer-range shot between his teeth, being a master at judging the situation and changing cartridges according to how high the birds were flying, and to what he predicted his brother's next move would be. Alastair swept the barrels skywards and the first two shots rang out, and a second later shotgun number two was in his hands and firing, while Edgar reloaded shotgun number one.

The pheasants spiralled down towards the ground. Loose feathers hung a while in the air as they fell, as though the birds were flying out of their own plumage. Once more the boys exchanged guns, and the fifth and sixth shots rang out. Moments later Victor heard a thud as the first pheasant hit the ground. Then another thud. Then four more.

The birds had flown so high and the shots had been fired with such rapidity that the first pheasant had not hit the ground before the sixth pheasant was hit. During this near invisible rotation of two guns, six shots had been fired in close succession, a four-handed virtuoso performance driven by one consciousness, or as though by one person with four arms.

Victor could hardly believe what he had witnessed. He felt it in his gut. A sense of exhilaration but also unease. Never before had he seen such intuition and synergy.

Six shots fired.

Six pheasants stopped in mid-flight.

There were always debates in hunting circles over which were Great Britain's greatest shooting achievements. First place was accorded to Lord Ripon, who had fired with such amazing rapidity that he had seven dead pheasants in the air at one time. Ripon had had three shotguns and two men to reload them.

Runes and Warplanes

This morning at Finlaggan Victor had witnessed a performance about which the world would never hear. In another time, following a day's shoot with spectators, a debate would have raged, the columns of *The Field* would have buzzed, with the question of which was the greater feat: six dead pheasants in the air with two guns, or seven with three?

But with his rush of pride came a memory. The memory of his own plane crash in 1917. Like a pheasant, a warplane could not change course mid-flight, as the air-defence soldiers on the ground well knew. He had flown in a squadron of six planes that day. All six had crashed.

For a split second he thought he had seen a pattern in the feathers up there. Against the dark blue sky, a new bird seemed to take form from the dead pheasants' plumes, before they returned to being feathers floating to earth.

The Fly in a Clenched Fist

Hymns were sung. Weapons were hidden. Hunting maps were stencilled, and baking parchment bearing mysterious numbers was distributed in secret. Decisions were made in silence, followed by glances at loved ones: this may be the last time I see you.

But the British did not come. The German clenched his fist, hard and without mercy. Then he loosened his grip a little, as a man who has caught a fly opens his fist enough to see if it is still alive, but not so much it can fly away.

Eventually the German opened his fist fully, and, lo and behold, the fly did not move. Either it had nowhere to go, or it had lost the will to fly.

The Fly in a Clenched Fist

During the summer of 1940, Sprockhoff and his men had less to do. They left their Mausers in the parsonage, went around in shirtsleeves and helped anyone who would accept help. Most of the soldiers had grown up on farms and were keen to show this. They were kind to the cows, understood horses and were good with a pick and shovel.

Young lads much like the lads in Butangen, had the latter washed, worn clean clothes and talked politely.

Later, engineers arrived with a diesel-powered machine with big wheels at the back and small ones at the front. It could pull, push and lift just about anything, and they widened the road to Fåvang, in the process helping the local farmers to pull up tree stumps and shunt away boulders that had been an obstacle for years.

In the evenings, music sounded from the open windows of the parsonage, and the officers who had instigated the drinking sessions early on in the war were presumably posted elsewhere in the country.

Life was convivial.

So convivial, in fact, that Hitler himself came to visit Butangen the following year, on his birthday no less. The soldiers celebrated the day with extra meat rations, accordion playing and singing, and at midday the Führer arrived, dour, hair smoothly greased, in a long, leather coat. He marched past the guards' shack at the parsonage, and the soldiers dropped their rifles and stood to attention and saluted stiffly, then picked up their dropped rifles and stood to attention again, whereupon Major Sprockhoff yelled at them and demanded to know what was going on, by which time Herr Hitler had disappeared into the forest.

It was of course Reiulf Stangenes they had seen, a local farmer who had made a fortune in the local revue in Høgvang before the war by putting on a moustache and parting his hair to the side. His resemblance to Hitler was so great that the audience fell about laughing. He had now donned the costume again, saying afterwards that he felt safe because the soldiers would never shoot Hitler, but also that: *We can only do such a thing once.*

One villager did not laugh at this joke.

He never laughed. Neither did his sons, and those who never laugh are usually quite comical, but not in wartime.

It came as no surprise to anyone that Ola Mossen took on the role of chief Nazi in Butangen. It would have made the first page of the story of his life, had there been such a thing. What did surprise many was the power he gained, how quickly he was given it, and how efficiently he put it to use.

After the building of the seter road, Mossen had extended his barn and reared a fine herd of goats. The land on his croft was poor, but he was clever and hardworking; attentive to his livestock, he utilised every patch. Yet, like so many others, he had big debts, and in 1938 his farm was threatened with foreclosure. His family came close to losing everything, but the Butangen villagers all agreed that the bank had treated them unfairly. Nobody entered a bid on the farm, and the Mossens stayed put.

Despite this Ola Mossen became increasingly resentful and angry about everything. Angry at the town council, angry at the government, angry at the newspapers. And especially angry with the Hekne family, who had their "vulture claws" in everything in the village. The dairy paid too little for his milk, the prices at the Colonial were excessive, and the cost of electricity from Hellorn power station was far too high. He was an atheist and was angry at Schweigaard, who was a washed-up nobody who had far too much prominence in the village, far greater than his office deserved. This was no longer 1880, so the pastor should keep to his fairy tales about Jesus and not strut about playing mayor.

The NS Party had won barely any votes before the war, and had as much political clout as a folk dance society, but the

The Fly in a Clenched Fist

time had come for another meeting up in Høgvang village hall. Ola Mossen took to the rostrum, and, quoting Vidkun Quisling, declared that the old Norway had fallen. The new Norway beckoned. The old politicians had earned everyone's contempt. Their shame made them dead to everyone. There was only *one* path forward, and that was with the NS, especially since all other parties were prohibited.

The Mossen family were catapulted to the top, which in Butangen was far from high, but high enough. Ola Mossen was the local NS branch leader, Jon Mossen was made treasurer, and his brother Odd was made section leader, despite there being only one section. It was time to bring order to disorder. Norway must be like Germany, Europe's most efficient and enterprising land. There had been too much shillyshallying and chatter for chatter's sake. The path must now be laid towards the future, great works awaited, and under the circumstances it was essential that the death penalty be brought back. Most importantly, every citizen at the grassroots must pull their weight.

While Mossen pontificated from the rostrum, his sons Jon and Odd sat at a rickety old table offering subscriptions to *Fritt Folk*, the NS newspaper. In the months that followed, new regulations came piling in. Anyone holding a position of authority was meant to be in the NS, whether on the parish council or in the philatelic society. The same applied to teachers and to employees of the municipality and state.

Few folk, however, paid any attention to this. Then came a stroke of genius: a national decree allowing NS members to keep their radios and hunting guns. At the next Thursday meeting up in Høgvang, it emerged that half the subscriptions to the NS in the village had been paid by toothless old greybeards, whose only ambition in life was to shoot capercaillie on their springtime mating grounds, and who waggishly raised the wrong arm when they said *Sieg heil*.

But even an idiot can tighten a knot when the rope is already knotted.

And now they were given more power.

As Hirdmen.

Political soldiers, they called themselves. Their uniform resembled that of the police, but they were of higher rank and were permitted to carry truncheons.

Ola Mossen and his sons did not thrash anyone, not at the start of the war, at least. They knew the limits of the village's patience. Instead, they adopted the habit of strolling about, hands behind their back, observing folk. When they were later exempted from petrol rationing, they acquired a reasonably new Ford in which they sped around, enforcing the constant stream of new regulations. The ban on public dancing. A heating limit of 18°C in houses and shops. A ban against picking lingonberries that were less than two-thirds ripe.

Astrid had to stop outside the village hall one Thursday evening, because the Reo had gone off course when she put her foot on the brake. She was crouching by the front wheel when a young man came out of the hall, locking the door behind him.

"Broken down?" he said, dropping the key into his jacket pocket.

Jon Mossen.

Their former milk truck driver. The young man who had once sat alongside her on the back of the truck, in a thin, checked flannel shirt and shiny, brown belt, who had rocked in time with the bends in the road, and was as much a part of the view towards the seters as the spruce trees and the Breia.

He was now a Hirdman in uniform, with a bandolier across his chest, and a wooden truncheon in his belt.

He pointed at the Reo he had driven for so many years. She told him what was wrong.

"Brake shoes," he said. "Comes out o' alignment after a time.

Used t'happen t'me too. Right on this spot. They overheats on t' slopes before Fugleslåa. Where ye slams on the brake before the hump below Fjellstad. Rubs against the drum, most likely."

He walked over to the grey box near the rear fender where the scissor jack and tools were kept. All at once he seemed to get a pain in his back. Then it was gone. Lifting the hemp cover on the toolbox he rummaged in it, then turned and came towards her. The massive old jack had lumps of black grease along its shafts and looked odd against his clean, new uniform. His boots crunched on the gravel.

"It were an injustice," he said. "A gross injustice, and ye knows it. Time'll come ye shall lose everything."

Jon Mossen came so near that the jack made a greasy mark on her coat. He circled the truck, walked to the steep edge of the road where the menfolk pissed during dances, and flung the jack into the nettle thicket below.

One morning Tarald got up and said: "'Tis enough moping about."

He went out to the *stabbur* steps and smoked a cigarette. His technique, developed with practice, was as follows: squeeze the cigarette pack against his chest with the stump of his arm, push one cigarette up, wet his lips and catch it with his mouth, then flick a flame from his lighter.

Astrid watched him as he sat there gazing out over Hekne. As though he was holding a little funeral for himself. When he came back inside, he pulled the sleeve of his sweater over the stump of his wrist.

"I had better get a move on."

The School of Arts and Crafts was to reopen for the autumn semester. Tarald's landlord had let him keep his room in Bjerregaards Gate because he had fought the Germans. Tarald left, and Astrid missed him, just as she missed life before the war, and missed Mari Slåen. He got himself a night job in an advertising agency, finishing the work of the company's permanent draughtsmen. His boss gave him the freedom, or, as he said with a wink, "a free hand", to choose the colours and type of shading. Not that there was much work. There was little use for advertising in wartime, with the shop shelves being emptier and emptier. There was a shortage of everything, and when a product came into the shops, it was sold that day.

He was home for Christmas, and Astrid thought that he had made his peace with the outcome of his life. He lived on the memory of having fought as a machine-gunner. A girl had knitted him a sweater with extra-long sleeves, but he said that introducing her would have to wait. He hardly talked at the supper table, but when Jehans came down on the Germans, he woke up: "Father. Ye must distinguish between the Germans and the Nazis. The Germans are yer father's folk. Have ye forgotten that ye are half German? And that we bairns are a quarter German?"

Some weeks after Tarald had left, the war deprived the Reo of its fodder, as petrol rationing got ever tighter. Eventually Jehans fitted her with a *knottgenerator*. He never called the unwieldy apparatus on the back of the Reo anything but a gas generator, but it was essentially a stove that burned hardwood chips, known as *knott*, in a large metal barrel. The smoke it produced flowed from this barrel through pipes to the part of the engine where the carburettor had been. Soon every Norwegian vehicle had a similar contraption at the back. They were hard to start, but ran reasonably well, because, as Jehans calculated, wood gas had half the power of petrol.

On the Heknes' parlour wall there was a light patch where the Hekne Krag had hung. Astrid and her father had removed the bolt and the magazine parts and greased it. It was now hanging, barrel down, in a dense spruce above the farmhouse. Packed in a waterproof bag were the cartridges, cleaning equipment and solvent. The gun could be cleaned and ready to fire in only fifteen minutes.

But this was just a pale dream. A frost had gripped them. An inertia like the winter-frozen grease around a Krag's mechanism. Jokes did not come as easily. News reached them slowly.

Fløteren said that they could do nothing now but prepare for a long war. "Can ye keep watch?" he asked Astrid. "Take note o' what they does? The Germans? If ye pull over for a convoy o' trucks, count 'em and look for their department badges and what sorta' weapons they be transportin'."

She began to memorise the new German postal codes. Trained her memory and her capacity to make connections. Noted the quantity, direction and type of vehicles. Learned to scrutinise the unfamiliar, to superimpose her own ideas on it to see if that might reveal its purpose to her. Gathered information on the ground, picking up the gossip, including the information that Fru Røhme was passing on to Kai. She reported everything back to Fløteren when she drove the milk truck down to the railway station where he ran the telegraph office.

"Ye be a canny lass, Astrid, sharp as a razor," Fløteren said. "The apple didna' fall far from yer mother and father. And such an ear for gossip!"

Astrid laughed. "What do y'expect, I'm a Butangen girl. The pastor once said that if gossiping had been an art, Butangen folk would have decorated cathedrals."

But whatever Fløteren said, she never thought the things she found out were of much consequence. Until finally, on a particularly grey, war-weary day, along with the endless stream of post about new regulations and rationing, each more loathsome than the last, a thick envelope arrived from the Department of Health in the Ministry of the Interior. It contained ten posters in both Norwegian and German. They were to be displayed on the relevant front doors.

Verbot zum Besuch von Unbefugten in Meireien und Käsereien
Prohibited: Unauthorised Visits to Milk and Cheese Producers

Astrid stood up with the posters in her hands.

Was this true?

To avoid the spread of infection, it was now forbidden for unauthorised persons to enter any dairy-related workplaces. She read the accompanying letter. Looked at the ink and paper quality. At the grammatical errors in the German text.

Yes. It really was from the Department of Health in the Ministry of the Interior.

Astrid went through to the office. Her mother was sitting before an accounts book with her reading spectacles and pencil. Over her greying hair she wore a faded scarf.

Kristine looked from Astrid to the posters.

"That strict, eh?"

"No Norwegians can come in. Not even the Hirdmen. Not even the Germans. Unless they have a *special assignment*, it says."

"So Mossen canna' barge in wi' his thermometer anymore?"

"Nay. And t' soldiers will need permission from t' Reichskommissar Herr Josef Terboven himself to come in t' our humble dairy factory."

Her mother brought her knuckles to her chin. She was wearing the same expression as when she had suggested they transport cartridges in the milk churns.

Astrid went into the staff cloakroom, and a memory from childhood came to her. From the day of Ingeborg's funeral. The factory had been closed for half a shift, so all the womenfolk could attend. Widow Fløter and Ada Borgen had held Astrid's hands as the coffin was lowered and Pastor Schweigaard had said a few last words about Ingeborg. Then the two women had led Astrid back to the factory, and to this cloakroom in which she now sat. Here they had changed from their black mourning clothes and into their white overalls. They were shy as they got undressed, standing close to the cupboard doors with their backs turned.

Astrid had always thought that the ladies in white who magicked up all those creamy delights looked like angels. But standing here in their white overalls after the funeral, they were still so sad. That darkness never seemed to have left them.

Now this thought gathered into an idea.

The German officers were used to good food. Those who thought a lot of themselves liked to have their little extras. And the things they craved most were the most difficult to obtain. Cheese, butter, soured cream. Ada Borgen and Widow Fløter were the same age as the mothers and grandmothers of these soldiers, and what they most associated with home must, without doubt, be a glass of milk and an old woman's wrinkled face.

"Ada," said Astrid, when she got her alone.

The other looked at her. Wiping away tears with her handkerchief. She had picked up the wrong apron again this morning, and had suffered another scolding from Widow Fløter.

"What be ye after now, my lass? I sees it in yer eyes!"

"Ye can do a bit against the Germans."

"Me? This old bag o' skin?"

"Aye. Thee. Because ye are so . . . well, advanced in years. I d'nay quite know how we'll do it yet. But we have got to find out what they are doing up there in t' mountains."

"And?"

"When soldiers come in to buy odds and ends, and the shop's empty, spin out the time."

"Uh-huh."

"Ask where they've been and whether they're staying long. Ask if they're moving on. If an officer comes in, then try saying *Milch*, *Butter* or *Käse*. See how he reacts."

Ada Borgen shot a glance towards the counter where Widow Fløter stood.

"Does *she* know?" she whispered.

"It was her who more or less suggested it," said Astrid. "Ma and I shall arrange it so we always have butter and cheese over."

"What wi' the Supply Board?" said Ada. "They keeps careful check on t' milk quota."

"We'll bring some milk straight from the milking shed at Hekne."

"That be trading wi' Germans, Astrid. Worse than the black market. What if the villagers see us? That be riskier even than if the Germans catch us fishin' after information."

"We shan't do anything big. We'll wait for when 'tis worth it."

"Alrighty," said Ada, glancing over at Widow Fløter. "If we canna' fight wi' guns, we shall fight wi' cheese."

The Second Most Powerful Man in the World

Then it happened, the thing that silenced the doubters who had believed it was just another Hekne yarn that a plane load of archaeologists had come in the first week of the war to protect Norwegian cultural artefacts, and that they had even travelled to Butangen to seize a church bell.

For in January 1941 Himmler visited Norway.

Not in the shape of a revue star. No, this was the Reichsführer himself, flesh and blood. Hitler's number two. Commander-in-Chief of the civil and military SS and the Gestapo, and, as the newspapers pointed out, despite being barely forty, he was a pan-European cultural personality who consulted astrologers before making big decisions, a man with extensive knowledge of medieval history and Norse mythology. This busy man had set aside two whole weeks for his visit to Norway. Yes, he would inspect a few companies of soldiers, but the war was going so well now that time could be devoted to the most important thing, namely the common cultural heritage of these two countries. The Department of Culture ensured that Himmler's visit would be filled with guided tours, with traditional dishes from the creamiest *rømmegrøt* to *lapskaus*, and folk singing accompanied by the *langeleik*, the table harp in whose soft tones he claimed to hear the ancient voices of the Germanic race. Not least he must see a large farmstead far north in Gudbrandsdal, where the unsuspecting farm owner opened his front door one morning to the village's bailiff, who told him to expect a visit from Himmler. Yes, Himmler. Today. There he stood, out on the forecourt, smiling and bespectacled, in the snow in his jet-black coat, cultured, engaged, surrounded by elite soldiers from the SS. Just go out and say hello, and by the by, somebody should put the coffee on.

Something that did not appear in the papers immediately, but which Astrid and Schweigaard would, to their horror, find out later, was what the intended highlight of this state visit had been. A grand ceremony had been planned at which Gulbrand Lunde, the Nazi Minister of Culture, was to present Himmler with the ancient Snartemo Sword. A newly woven bandolier would glitter with scarlet and blue swastikas. But Anton Wilhelm Brøgger, the legendary archaeologist and director of the Antiquities Collection, refused to reveal the sword's whereabouts. He was sent to Grini detention camp, and Himmler boarded his plane without the Snartemo Sword.

Minister Lunde was furious.

There must be some other gift he could offer the world's second most powerful man? This friend of Norway who was placed to decide whether the country be governed harshly or leniently? A gift that would signal true brotherly intent?

Telephone calls were made. Then late one February night three large cars with Oslo numberplates made their way slowly through a snowdrift along the Løsnes Marshes.

Somebody hammered on the front door.

Astrid came out onto the landing.

"What can that be?" Kristine said, standing at the bedroom door in her nightgown. Jehans crept barefoot down the stairs in his pyjamas. Astrid followed him. The house was in blackout and the outside lamps were off. Her father opened the front door, and was immediately pushed to the floor by some large men who forced their way into the hallway.

An electric torch was lit.

Astrid felt her heart race. The cold sweat came. The horror of the bell tower. The man with a torch.

Blinded by the light, she felt somebody grab her arm. A man yelled an order: "Get the others! Upstairs!"

They dragged Astrid through the kitchen and ordered her into the living room. More men followed. In the shifting light of the torch, she could see they were Hirdmen.

She could hear tramping and screaming from the floor above. Kristine and Esther were dragged down the stairs, half-dressed, frightened and angry. Then two Hirdmen came back with Jehans. His nose was bloodied.

To save on firewood the Heknes had allowed Isum to live in the farmhouse with them, and now she could hear his heavy footsteps on the landing above. More shouting. Then he too was forced down the stairs. He appeared in a yellowing nightshirt, patched with old sheeting and reaching only as far as his heavy calves that had never seen the sun. She could see the terror in his eyes, the eyes of this giant who had always seemed so invincible.

Astrid gathered herself. From their dialect, she knew these men were not from the village.

"Where's Eirik?" Esther shouted. "Where have they taken him?"

They heard Eirik screaming out in the hallway. Jehans wanted to go to him, but two Hirdmen blocked his path.

"Don't move!"

More waving of torches. They could not find the switch for the ceiling light, but when they found a cable on the floor, the room was finally lit by a lone table lamp.

A civilian stepped forward and said he was from the Ministry of Culture. Slamming his fist into the table, he roared that Germany was a friend. How could they be so disloyal to Norway by withholding the Sister Bell, which was clearly German property, and whose whereabouts they knew?

Jehans said: "Let the lad in here now. Or we shall—"

"Do what, Jehans?" said a voice from the hallway. The door opened. There stood Ola Mossen in his Hirdman's uniform, together with a man in breeches and knitted sweater, who had Eirik by the hair.

"Ye ought t' at least let bairns alone!" cried Kristine.

"Ma!" screamed Eirik. He tried to run to Esther, but the man tugged him back by his hair. Then, just as quickly, he released his grip and sent the boy flying. The three-year-old scrambled away and clung on to his mother's legs. A small puddle had formed where he had been, and a wet stripe marked his path.

The man ambled over to the curtains and dried his hands as though on a guest towel. Then lit a cigarette.

Astrid observed him move. His gait.

It could be the man in the bell tower.

Mossen paced around the living room. Took his time. Lifted a wooden dish made of burr birch, gazed at it as though it held some deeper meaning, then placed it on another table. He stopped by the grandfather clock, then shrugged his shoulders.

"Admit it, Jehans. The bell were rung when ye baptised this bastard bairn." He nodded towards Eirik, who was crying. "The sheriff should ha' come down on thee harder last year. 'Tis clear as day that ye took the bell to help the pastor, for in't naybody in t' village has a truck but thee."

"Pastor Schweigaard has never asked us for anything!" Astrid said.

The man who had been holding Eirik laughed at her. He seemed to be mimicking something he had seen in the movies, as he made a show of dropping his cigarette in the little pool Eirik had left behind. It sizzled a bit. And smelled a bit.

He walked over to a Hirdman who had kept a low profile, and the two men stood side by side and leered at Esther. They whispered something and made gestures that seemed to relate to her from the waist down, in a game that meant they knew she was blind.

"The weave," said Ola Mossen. "That hung in the old church. Folk be saying that Herr Pastor found it in the end. So where might it be now? It wasna' in the parsonage."

The room fell silent.

"We've time aplenty," said Mossen.

The clock ticked.

"Oh, and we has men with the pastor this minute," Mossen said.

"The pastor! Ye shall never lay hands on our pastor!"

It was Isum. He went for Mossen, nightshirt billowing, with such force it felt like a whole kitchen dresser was rocking across the floor.

Weapons were drawn in the Heknes' living room. Somehow Jehans managed to stop Isum, who stood there snorting heavily.

Mossen smirked. "So, Herr Isum! We mun nay lay hands on yer pastor, eh?"

The two men in front of Esther sniggered.

Then, through all the chaos and nerves in the room, and unaware of the weapons, Esther freed herself from her son. She walked slowly towards the two men who had pleasured themselves looking at her. She stopped right in front of the man who had held Eirik and said: "Give me yer hand. I shall put it where 'tis warm and moist."

He froze, as if hypnotised or under the control of another's will. He held out his hand. And everybody stared.

Esther took his wrist, and without effort guided his hand up and pressed it to his forehead. He broke into a sweat.

She took a step back. The man went red. Was unable to take his hand from his forehead. Calmly Esther backed away, while large beads of sweat collected on the man's brow. When he finally managed to bring down his hand, a white mark remained on his reddened skin.

The pistols were lowered. It was a while before the man from the Ministry of Culture gathered himself and tried half-heartedly to re-establish order. Ola Mossen was so stunned he simply left.

Astrid took Esther's arm and pulled her close. It was like touching an animal. Tiny lightning-quick shudders. Their mother stared at them open-mouthed.

A shot rang out in the forecourt. The Ministry of Culture's emissary and the Hirdmen exchanged glances and hurried out.

Another car had pulled up, and stood with its lights on and engine running. Some men were arguing with a dairymaid, whom they were refusing to let into the cowshed. It seemed the shot had been fired accidentally.

The uniformed men took over. They forced their way into the barns, outbuildings and brewhouses, pulling down piles of materials and tools. The cowshed filled with the bellowing of cows who could have no idea there was a war on. The strangers opened the trapdoors of the cellar, fired their pistols into the darkness, and listened for the sound of lead against bronze. All they achieved was to put the livestock into a frenzy and make Kristine even more furious.

They searched the *stabbur*. They searched the forge. Then a Hirdman walked to the edge of the forecourt and stared out over the snow-covered landscape. Twenty metres in front of him was a gentle mound that indicated an earth cellar. In it was the Hekne Weave.

Astrid held her breath.

He just wanted a piss.

For three hours the Hirdmen searched.

For thirty hours the Hekne family cleaned and tidied.

For three hundred hours little Eirik was inconsolable.

Astrid went up to see to Schweigaard immediately the strangers had left Hekne. They had smashed the few coffee cups he owned and tipped his log basket out over the floor. He had played the confused old man. Was informed that the Ministry of Culture had reported him for theft of public property, and that he had been summoned before the new, party-loyal bishop.

"Green soap!" Astrid said. "And green soap here too. The only thing that gets rid of the stench of disgusting men."

When the floorcloth was wrung out and stretched to dry over the zinc bucket, Astrid made her way back to Hekne. She fetched a shovel and waded through the untouched snow below the stable. She cleared away the snow in front of the small mound, and reached a frozen, wooden trapdoor. She looked around cautiously, tugged the door open and crept inside. She took out a greying wooden chest.

Soon she was standing before the extra-wide door in the house's oldest wing. Afterwards she fetched Esther.

Her sister ran her fingers over the wool threads, gently and lovingly, as when she stroked her son's hair.

"D'ye know what this is?" Astrid whispered.

"It must be it. *It*."

"Ye can say that about anything, and it'll always be right."

"No. Because this is the only *it*."

Astrid had hoped for another answer. Once more, she questioned Esther's abilities. Ingeborg had told her that, according to Butangen folklore, anyone with a defect would gain another sense, usually rare, in its place.

Astrid sat closer to her sister. The Hekne Weave was on the table in front of them. In some places ragged and torn, in other places as richly coloured as if it had been woven yesterday. She contemplated this awe-inspiring communication from another time.

"'Twas woven right here," said Astrid. "Here in this room."

Esther did not answer. She moved her fingers. The yarn she now touched shimmered so brightly it appeared to be spun from the thinnest silver threads. It was woven into the image of a sheep, standing on two legs and eating from a tree.

"Tell me, Esther. What do ye sense?"

"Has it been back here since it was woven?"

"I d'nay think so. Does it tell thee anything?"

Her sister was silent for a long time.

"About us?"

"About us or anyone," said Astrid.

"Oh aye. It wants sommat. Though I canna' work out what. We are not like them. The sisters. Even if ye think we are."

"Ye must know something about them to say that."

Esther grabbed her hands. Astrid's mind raced back to the dried hands she had touched under the church floor. She shuddered at the thought of the sisters' empty eye sockets.

"I saw them," Astrid said. "I touched their hands, their

Runes and Warplanes

knuckles. They are buried beneath t' floor o' t' new church. Under a layer o' stones."

Esther nodded. She let go of Astrid's hands and began to trace her fingers over the weave again. Stopping at the oval shape that encircled the Hekne sisters. That Astrid thought resembled a face.

"Astrid," Esther said. "Astrid."

"Aye?"

"Ye mun take good care now. There's sommat evil outside and it wants to come in. It didna' leave with Mossen."

Farewell to Svarten

In June 1941 they had a new enemy. That, at least, was what the propaganda said. For some it was an old enemy, for others an old friend. The papers reported that the great showdown between worldviews was underway. This was a war within the war. A second front. The front against the Bolshevik threat from the east.

The propaganda posters were soon bringing colour to telegraph poles and the walls in the village. Young men with smooth-shaven chins and upturned gazes fixed upon the thousand-year Reich. *Join the Waffen SS Combat Battalion with the Norwegian Legion's Ski Corps. Help guard the border to the east! Fight for everything you hold dear.*

They were printed in the tens of thousands. They were put up outside railway stations and inside waiting rooms, in train compartments, in the doctor's office and outside the post office. They even appeared on the wall outside the Colonial, because a rule about compulsory posters had been introduced, and

Farewell to Svarten

Astrid could not tear them down without being reported by the Mossen family.

She despised these posters. Warped messages conveyed in a style she had so admired before the war, namely that of the artist Harald Damsleth, the children's book illustrator and magician of Norwegian advertising, the man who had brought colour and joy into every Norwegian home. Damsleth was now a sworn Nazi. And it seemed to Astrid that he had a monopoly over everything – stamps, posters, adverts, magazine covers – and, most annoyingly of all, his work was as elegant as ever, if only she could overlook its message.

A boy or two from the village went to the enlistment office. It only took one boy or another from each of the country's many villages to add up to almost four thousand soldiers. Soon he was wearing a German uniform. Soon he had a Mauser. Soon he was sent to Germany to a training camp. Soon he watched his friends die.

He would go voluntarily. But in August, during the haymaking season, a different sort of recruitment took place in Butangen. The Mossen boys were not in the village at the time, but they must have had a hand in it. How else could the Germans have selected the best, so quickly and efficiently?

The first warning sign was when Fru Røhme saw three trucks full of soldiers pull up at the parsonage. Sprockhoff welcomed an officer with military badges she had never seen before, and, as she cleared the coffee things, she glimpsed the registration list for the 1939 Stavsmartn Horse Show.

But it was already too late. The visiting officer was a certain Oberst Reißner, who, despite being in Butangen for only two days, would come to be more hated in the village than Mossen and Quisling put together.

At six in the morning the village was shut off. Soldiers with loaded Mausers were posted at the driveway to every large farmstead. Trucks blocked the road to Fåvang and to the seters, and Major Sprockhoff accompanied Oberst Reißner in a light grey car that drove from farm to farm.

At first glance, Reißner seemed like any other grumpy, rotund, middle-aged man. He wore a large leather apron outside his uniform, and the villagers would soon learn that he was the *stabsveterinær* – the Chief Veterinary Officer – and a man who really knew about horses. On every farm, soldiers led out the horses from their stables for Reißner to inspect. With a keen eye he assessed all their qualities and faults. Word spread quickly of what was happening. From Oppigard Flyen they took Graupsvarta, the village's best dray horse. She had rhythm, speed and a fine temperament, and always attracted attention. Now she was led away with her head bowed, together with Molyna and Hilding.

At half past nine they came to Hekne, and the soldiers went straight to the stable. Major Sprockhoff appeared stern and cold, looked nobody in the eye, and merely sent a soldier over to Kristine with a notice of requisition written in Norwegian.

They would collect at least one horse from each farm. Two if there were four in the stable, three if there were six. The compensation came to little more than the value of the horses' shoes.

"What o' a farm that owns but one old yaud?" said Kristine.

Sprockhoff, who now understood their dialect quite well, shook his head.

Kristine shouted: "Ye canna' do this! Ye might as well just shoot folk! How can anyone fend wi'out a horse?"

Out of the car stepped the *stabsveterinær*. He leafed through some papers, barely noticing the civilians who were standing out in the forecourt grumbling. Then Astrid heard the soldiers say something about *die Ostfront*.

Suddenly she understood what the *stabsveterinær* was here for. It wasn't just the young Norwegian lads the Germans wanted in their service. Døla horses were exceptionally strong and good for pulling heavy timbers through deep snow. The Germans must have realised they would be equally good for hauling artillery through the snow on the Eastern Front.

The two soldiers came back out.

The horse they had on a leading rein was Svarten.

Had she had the Hekne Krag, Astrid knew she would have used it. She knew now what it felt like to hate, and how it felt to want to kill, but all she could do was clench her fists.

Astrid remembered what Tarald had told her about the fighting at Tretten. Dead horses had lain everywhere.

In a flash she saw it all. They would be transported on a goods train to a foreign land, they would stand cheek by jowl with other unknown horses until they arrived somewhere deep in the Soviet Union, where they would go out in the white daylight, harnessed to a cannon. These gentle, home-loving beasts who had pulled ploughs and lumber for years would now drag cannons that thundered so loudly they would be deafened, and be beaten by rabid soldiers, ignorant of why they had been taken from their farms to this desolate, snow-covered, endlessly flat landscape where men shot at each other. And being so large and such an easy target, they would die.

Now Isum tried to push forward and was blocked from going to Svarten by the soldiers. As Svarten turned at the gate and whinnied, the giant fell to his knees and his face grew so contorted it was beyond recognition.

Astrid tried to stay calm. Svarten had been a part of her life for as long as she could remember. When she was little and read adventure books, she had wondered why this horse did not have a loftier name, Svarten meaning simply *the black one*. Now, as she watched him being led away, she thought: Svarten is grand enough. He had no need for a grander name. He was not a stallion that galloped across the horizon in the sagas. He was a Døla horse, a workhorse, and he was black, and therefore Svarten, and nobody could come and say that wasn't enough.

Then Svarten was gone.

Isum could not work. He sat in his tiny bedchamber. Astrid brought him food, but when she came to fetch the tray he was lying curled up with no quilt over him. He said nothing and ate nothing, even though she had spread his beloved Sunda so thickly on his bread.

Later that day Jehans had to go down to Fåvang with a delivery from the dairy factory. He had taken Esther along, and when they returned home they were both ashen. They had passed the horses along the road, a group of thirty or more. "We drove past them," Jehans said. "They looked like prisoners o' war. I saw Svarten were among them, so I pulled the milk truck over t't side and got out wi' our Esther. But then t' soldiers pointed their Mausers at us. But – I reckons Svarten saw us. Leastways, I hope he saw us, our Esther and me."

Everybody knew Ola Mossen was behind this. Who else could have advised the Germans so that they went to Nordigard Sylte first, to drag off Draupner, the pedigree stallion traded and bought at such a high price, or knew in which stall they would find the offspring of Galdebrona, one of the best broodmares the valley had ever produced?

When the horses arrived at Fåvang, they were tethered outside Tromsa Farm along with some workhorses from Brekkom. The next day they were to be taken down to the train station.

Whether Svarten could see grief from afar was something Astrid mused later. If the Heknes had been sentimentally inclined, they might have believed that Svarten knew how Isum cried that whole night. To weep demands exertion, and a violent release of energy takes place when such a giant as Isum sobs. Usually, such tears act as a powerful sleeping potion, leaving the body exhausted, so that sleep descends even in the greatest sorrow. But Isum was strong in mind and body, and he wept all night without stop.

Just as Isum had abilities he kept to himself, including the ability to keep the location of a certain church bell secret, so Svarten must have had a hidden ability.

Because, when the southbound goods train left Fåvang the next morning, Svarten was not on it. A horse from Brekkom had also disappeared. The two had gnawed themselves free in the night and headed home. Svarten had presumably gone into the forest on the upper bank of the Laugen and continued south as he recognised the familiar murmur of the streams and smells of the forest and fields. At Fåvang church he must have climbed the steep slopes up to the Løsnes marshes, and as the sun rose the next day he walked through the gateposts at Hekne and straight up to the farmhouse, where he stood whinnying. Isum suddenly woke up. He was so overjoyed he ran barefoot out into the muddy forecourt, where he embraced his horse and cried again, but this time from happiness. What Svarten thought when he saw Isum again nobody knew, but there were many who would have liked to know.

A Layer of Grease in the Milk Churns

Astrid had driven over the Breia when she spotted the truck in her rear-view mirror.

That truck. The truck that the villagers had learned to fear since spring. With six wheels, a spare wheel on either door, and soldiers sitting under the tarpaulin at the back.

Runes and Warplanes

The Reo's windscreen was spattered with insects. She was driving along the seter road with her window rolled down, and life might have been good were it not for the fact that it was the summer of 1942 and the country was still occupied.

After a year-long pause the Germans had begun driving up into the mountains again. It was still impossible to find out what they were up to. A new spur road had been built close to the crossing she was now approaching. A high barbed-wire fence had been erected. Whatever was behind it was hidden by spruce trees, and there were no elevated positions from which she might get a view through her binoculars.

They worked fast. In the first year of the war alone, they had seized land and built an ammunition depot along the railway line north of Ringebu. It was so big it could have kept a major war going for months, and an ingenious cableway carried mysterious cargo down into huge concrete bunkers.

Fløteren said he would have given *an eye and a foot* to find out what was going on. All he knew was that construction had gone slowly to begin with, because the Germans had got villagers, voluntarily or involuntarily, to build barracks and erect fences. But they had a better workforce now. Russian prisoners of war.

Which was why Astrid had learned to fear the six-wheeler, because it didn't carry the ordinary soldiers who stayed at the parsonage. These were hunters.

A couple of weeks ago they had caught a Russian who had escaped. He had hidden in a fisherman's boathouse. Meanwhile two villagers were asleep in the fishing cabin after pulling up their nets at sunrise. They were arrested, despite knowing nothing about the man in the boathouse. The Gestapo beat the Russian till his face was black and blue, and when they came for the Norwegians, one of them clung to the door frame, but they kicked him until he could no longer hold on. They shot a hole in the boat, then forced the three men to walk single file down to the roadway. There they ordered the men to put down their catch and stand in the middle of the road with their backs turned.

They stood there for ages.

Then the soldiers shot the Russian.

He fell forward and lay twitching until he died.

Behind them a gun was cocked. They waited.

No more shots came. The villagers were put on the back of the truck and sent for questioning in Lillehammer. Three days later they were freed.

It left a deep cut in the village, this incident. The Russian was not buried. He merely disappeared.

And *that* six-wheeler seemed even bigger now in the dust behind the milk truck. Those rugged wheels could carry it over any terrain. It had tarpaulin over both the pickup bed and cab, but she had seen them drive with it pulled back. The soldiers had stood up there, shirtsleeves rolled up, bareheaded with the wind in their hair, and standing like a sculpture among them had been a machine gun that could be pointed at enemies both in the air or on the ground.

Astrid did not have a full load today. Just the milk churns she was delivering. A young boy on his way to see his grandmother, who kept goats near Saubua, who had wanted to sit at the back to feel the rush of the wind. A new windowpane for the Tromsnes seter, where an argument over barley sowing times had got out of hand.

Astrid pressed the clutch, put the Reo through neutral and into second gear. The engine was running poorly today, the wood was probably damp. She shifted back into first gear. More than once on this slope she had had to ask her passengers to get off and push.

The truck behind her, and the other German vehicles, ran on diesel, and left a dense, greasy smell of exhaust that seemed to hang around long after the car itself had gone, as if to say: *We are here, even if you can't see us.*

This side of the war. The continual presence of fear. Every flavour of fear. Fear of what might happen today. Fear of what your neighbour might do. Fear of the great fallout, of the years that must surely come.

The truck now filled her entire rear-view mirror. The driver had his hands high on the wheel and was trying to skirt round the potholes.

The Germans were in a hurry. Here, on their seter road.

Astrid came to a passing place. She would usually have pulled over and let them overtake, but instead she drove on. They honked behind her.

She must delay them.

Something had happened up in the mountains last night, beyond the treeline – where the mountain was covered with snow even in summer. That much she knew, because they had put up hymn 453 at the last service.

Three digits to ensure that the mountain's gifts came down to the village.

The first airdrops from England had arrived that June. Containers filled with weapons. Agents by parachute. She was never there herself. Wasn't supposed to know who was up in the mountains to receive the goods. Merely relayed the messages. Kept her eyes open and told Fløteren what she saw.

The truck behind her honked again.

The lad on the cargo bed tapped on the cab window and stared in at her. He was frightened. Understandably. The Germans were close behind them. Like hunters behind a squirrel.

It was becoming impossible. She pulled in at the next passing place. The military truck roared past. Thick dust swirled in through her window. There under the tarpaulin she could see the faces of some of the soldiers, eyes hidden beneath helmets, an impenetrable shell over their thoughts, Mauser rifles between their knees.

She started up again, entering a cloud of exhaust fumes, the milk truck like an old horse on poor feed. Come on, Reo. Do your best.

She drove fast from milk churn stand to milk churn stand. Tried not to get caught up in chitchat with the dairymaids, who were always desperate for company up here on the seters. The churns from the morning still retained the body warmth of the cows. Those from the evening's milking had lain in streams and were cold.

The young boy got down from the truck.

"Nay, keep yer coppers," she said. "But ye can help me with this glass pane."

The pane was protected by sheets of plywood. After checking it hadn't been broken on the way, she put it on the Tromsnes milk stand and hurried on. Where could the Germans be now? The road was dry, so it was impossible to see any tracks. And not even at the northernmost stand did she detect any smell of exhaust.

Something didn't feel right. There was barely a soul to be seen. She was halfway through her round, without anyone asking for a ride. Then came Widow Modal, the old dairymaid who never brought a shopping list like the others, but insisted on Astrid writing it all down, and Astrid knew it was because she couldn't write, something she hid behind endless talk, which it paid to navigate carefully so as not to embarrass her.

"Aye, and then we needs a wick for t' paraffin lamp. The wider sort. Oh dear, be there so many diff'rent wide ones? Ours be the common sort o' lamp. The kind that were common afore. What do they cost nowadays?"

"I shall bring thee a few up tomorrow," said Astrid. "So ye can try. Or clip them to size. But tell me. Did t' Germans drive past just now? A big truck with spare wheels on the doors?"

"Germans? What Germans? Spare wheels?"

"I shall be off," Astrid said.

She rounded the bend and Dokken seter came into view.

The milk stand was empty of churns. Standing by the woodshed was a stranger wearing a dark blue windcheater.

Two more men came out of the shed. Villagers from one of the hunting teams. Their trousers were black, drenched in water. They must have waded across a marsh. Very recently at that.

These were not the kind of men to step into a marsh by mistake. They must have gone there so as not to be seen. Astrid stopped the truck, and leaving the door open walked through the seter gates. "There are soldiers close by," she said. "In a truck. Lots of them."

The two men exchanged glances. Astrid spotted three milk churns standing outside the barn door. Two others were cooling in the stream.

"Where's the dairymaid?" Astrid asked.

No answer. Something had happened. Something they did not know how to handle. There were two sets of fresh footprints in the grass from the barn to the forest, set wide apart. The men may have carried something between them. Astrid edged forwards so she could see into the barn. There in the shadows stood the dairymaid. Only when Astrid stepped closer did she grasp that the girl had a pair of scissors and was cutting up her costly apron.

Over by the wall lay a young man. Even in this light, Astrid could see he was injured. His knee was swollen, and he had no shoes. Blood had run out over the hay on which he lay, and now she glimpsed a sub-machine gun with blood on it. Three backpacks stood just inside the door, and from the jagged bumps she could see they contained weapons.

"How d'ye tie a bandage?" said the dairymaid. "Like this?"

"I don't know," Astrid said.

"He needs a lift down t' village," the dairymaid said. "Say he were fettlin' a roof and fell from t' ladder."

"No seters under repair now."

"He be bleedin' hard. Why in't the menfolk comin' t' help us?"

Astrid ran out of the barn and over to the Reo. *Knott-generators* hissed and spluttered, so she went further up the road to hear better. She stood and listened.

No trucks nearby. For now, at least. If this man was caught, the seter would be burned down, the dairymaid shot.

Then it occurred to her. The ban on visits to dairy producers. It was their only hope.

She ran back down, lifted two empty churns from the truck and hurried to the barn. The men were still standing gawping at the dairymaid bandaging the injured man.

Astrid pointed to the backpacks by the door.

"Are those weapons loaded?" Astrid said.

"Nay."

"Are there cartridges?"

"In one o' t' bags."

"Will they survive getting wet?"

"They?"

"The cartridges! Do they tolerate water?"

"Aye. Although, I in't too sure. Happen, for a time. They tolerates the rain. What o' it?"

"Fetch the three milk churns by the barn door. Bring them here!"

She explained the plan, and they complied. Astrid unlaced the first backpack. It was full of pistols, Colt 1911s, as she had learned. Another contained the sub-machine guns called Sten guns.

She knocked open the lids of the milk churns and started to

transfer the guns into them. They clattered in, and the echoes from the hollow cavity changed tone as each milk churn grew full.

The light crept through the gaps in the barn's timber walls and fell on the young man. He lay there gasping for breath. The dairymaid was trying to bandage him again. He said nothing.

Soon one milk churn was full, and the men from the hunting team opened another. The Sten gun stocks barely fitted through the necks of the six-gallon churns.

All of a sudden Astrid froze. She felt a rush of blood to her head. She stood there, paralysed. Her fingers tingled and her chest pounded.

The others stared at her. Slowly her fear melted.

Then it was over.

"Now fill them – pour the milk over them," said Astrid.

They started pouring milk over the weapons. The creamy white liquid trickled past wooden barrels, past blued steel, until bubbles rose as their mechanisms filled. She was reminded of the legs of lamb that she put to marinate in a giant pot of milk when she made *surstek* before the war. The churn was nearly full now, and the last thing to be visible was the muzzle of a Sten. When the milk finally reached the neck of the aluminium churn, what she saw was an ordinary, very full, milk churn. They worked on. The barrel of one gun poked up too high, and they shoved it into another churn. The earth floor of the barn turned to mud with blood and milk.

Five minutes later, wet with sweat, Astrid was driving the Reo to the rest of the milk stands. The wounded man was curled up in the footwell under the passenger seat. His blond hair was matted, and there was dried blood on his temple. She kept the truck windows open so she would hear any foreign vehicles or gunshots.

Nothing.

A Layer of Grease in the Milk Churns

Two boys passed by and waved. She watched them in her rear-view mirror to see if they turned round.

"Think up an excuse," she said. "Ye fell down a steep bank along the Breia. Ye lost yer fishing line. Right below the seter. 'Tis steep enough there for ye t' injure yerself badly. Who ye are and why ye are here in Butangen, I hope ye have an explanation for yerself."

He said nothing. Revealed neither his voice nor dialect.

She put the Reo into third gear and they continued along the fences, but at a bend near the forest he struggled up.

"Stop. This is too risky for you. Throw out the churns with the weapons too."

Astrid stopped the truck. The man opened the door and flung himself out. Astrid had to walk round the truck to slam the door shut. She watched him stagger along a fence and disappear down the slope towards the river.

Astrid could drive no further. She just sat, clinging to the steering wheel, as a prickling sensation crept through her whole body.

Standing at the last milk stand were six milk churns. As well as three bairns aged between ten and twelve. Regulars. They weren't headed for the village, they just wanted to hitch a ride to the crossroads and then walk back home. The girl wore a dress that had been mended multiple times, and one of the boys had odd shoes. Before Astrid had even opened the truck door, they leaped onto the cargo bed, and they were now sitting among the milk churns, laughing and screaming.

"Get yerselves over t't milk stand!" Astrid said. "Ye canna' have a ride without helping a bit!"

They ran over instantly and helped her lift the churns over to the cargo bed. Three with yesterday's cold evening milk, three with warm morning milk. Astrid went to the cab, but hesitated.

They oughtn't to come. Absolutely not.

But it was impossible to refuse them. This was the milk truck after all!

She drove on. Just a couple of hundred metres, and she would reach the crossroads that led down to the village. It had been a rash decision! They should have dragged the backpacks into the forest and returned to them later. Now these weapons had to go down to the factory. She must pick up her father and leave it to him. He could wipe the guns dry, oil them, and then—

Astrid did not have time to complete her thoughts. Now, through her open side window, she smelled diesel exhaust.

A group of Germans were standing at the crossroads around two trucks. A couple of soldiers emerged from the forest buttoning their trousers. A few others jumped from their pickup bed. Some were walking about without helmets.

Her pulse pounded in her ears as she drove on.

A soldier quickly stepped out into the road. He held his palm up towards her.

What now?

She saw that these trucks were not like the one that had driven behind the Reo on her way up. One had the tarpaulin pulled completely over it, and standing next to it were two soldiers with guns.

What now?

The gravel crunched beneath her wheels as she slowed down. She pulled on the handbrake and the Reo juddered to a halt.

Between the cargo bed and the driver's cab was a small, sliding window. She shoved it open and told the bairns: "I d'nay know what these Germans want. Hop off now. Slowly and calmly. Go straight home. Do *not* run."

Astrid got out and stood beside the truck. A soldier started towards her. He had no gun, but a bayonet hung from his belt. He loosened the hemp strap on its sheath.

A Layer of Grease in the Milk Churns

The youngsters jumped down from the back of the truck and tried to walk calmly. After just a few metres they broke into a run and raced up the gravel road.

The German strode up to her confidently. She could see from his uniform he was a *Feldwebel*. A sergeant of sorts. He eyed her up and down, then stared into the driver's cab for a long time. He said nothing. Strolled round and opened the door on the passenger side. She jumped when he slammed it shut again. Suddenly he was back in front of her. A steady, inscrutable gaze. Taking off his cap, he studied himself in her wing mirror. He smiled at himself and shook his head. Wiped the sweat with his arm. Ran his hands through his hair. Straightened his shirt. Put his cap back on and walked towards the cargo bed.

Six other soldiers approached. Each holding a battered metal cup in their hand.

What was it that Kai had said? That folk who hollered and screamed had suffered such treatment themselves, and had respect for those who also hollered and screamed?

Astrid blocked their way and yelled that they had no right to take any milk, it was *Dieberei* – theft!

"You're quite right," said the sergeant in slightly creaky Norwegian. "But what if we buy it?"

He had calm, brown eyes and a mop of dark hair, and the same dark hair sprouted forth from his open shirt. He was like a reindeer hunter who had just come down from the mountains, in need of a good wash and shave. He had a pungent, though not unpleasant, smell.

The pressure had built up in the *knottgenerator* and a valve started to hiss.

A twenty-five øre coin appeared in his hand. He looked straight at her as he flipped the little silvery coin at the bonnet. It clinked against the metal and lay there. Without waiting for an answer, he climbed up onto the back of the truck. Took his bayonet from its sheath, turned it and struck the edge of one of the milk churn lids.

He was clearly a farming man. Or at the very least a man who knew that these lids could not be twisted off, but had to be knocked loose. Preferably with a small hammer.

Or a bayonet shaft.

The whistling from the valve on the *knottgenerator* was getting louder and louder. Every milk churn was marked with a farm's name, and three of those from Dokken had guns in them. But which? All she remembered was that they were filled with warm morning milk. Added to which, the men from the hunting team had fetched a fourth from the truck, but she had failed to notice which farm it came from. They had, as a precaution, put the milk churns filled with weapons furthest in. But the children often moved them around to make imaginary dens and roads, so that the churn he was now opening might be full of pistols.

Astrid climbed onto the cargo bed. He was still hitting the lid with the shaft of his bayonet. With each blow it eased its way steadily up until it came loose. He let it drip and put it gently aside.

The churn was filled to the brim. Floating on the milk's rippled surface was a rainbow-coloured membrane.

Gun oil.

Astrid took the lid.

"*Nein. Nicht diese,*" she said. "*Morgen milch. Warm.*"

She took his hand and pressed it against another milk churn. "*Abendmilch! Kalt!*"

The footsteps of the other soldiers crunched in the gravel. More came to join them. Soon nine soldiers were gathered around the Reo.

The sergeant stared at Astrid. His expression was hard to make out.

She pointed at the other churn and repeated:

A Layer of Grease in the Milk Churns

"*Abendmilch! Evening milk. Kalt. Gut!*"

The corner of his mouth moved. It took a second, then a smile formed. He flipped the bayonet over and handed it to her, shaft first. She did not take it, and still holding it in the same position, he walked right up to her.

She took it.

She was pointing a bayonet at the stomach of a German soldier.

The other soldiers watched them up on the platform. The sergeant put his hands up in the air, stuck out his belly and pretended to be stabbed, before acting out a dramatic and torturous death.

The soldiers burst out laughing.

The movement caused the milk to slop. Astrid seized the lid and slapped it back on the churn. Thinking she heard a tell-tale clanking from within the churn, she made a pretence of knocking into some others to create an equivalent din.

The sergeant said something in German she couldn't catch, and soon more coins lay scattered on the cargo bed.

She used the bayonet to knock the lid loose from the cold milk churn, and using a beaker as a ladle she filled the cups they stretched towards her. Last, she filled the sergeant's cup and forced herself to smile.

Having drained his cup, he tilted his head back and shook out the last few drops.

"Enough money?" he asked, in Norwegian, indicating the coins.

"Aye." She brushed away a fly.

"*Danke*," he said, jumping down.

She stood there, still holding the bayonet. He started to leave. Then suddenly turned back and reached his hand out with a smile.

She turned the bayonet and held the blade in her hand. It was as sharp as any steel could be. A point made to penetrate, keen edges to slice and separate. Whetted many times and ergo used many times.

Throughout all this, two soldiers armed with sub-machine guns had been standing next to the truck with the closed tarpaulin. Astrid thought she glimpsed some movement behind it, and a man poked his head out. One of the soldiers pointed his gun at him, and the man immediately drew back inside.

"Wait!" Astrid shouted.

The sergeant turned. She jumped down and went towards him.

"Shall ye and yer men be here t'morrow?" she said.

He shrugged his shoulders.

"Are ye staying down there?" she said, pointing towards the forest where the new camp was being built.

"Why?"

"I can arrange more milk. And I can sell thee butter and cheese. *Käse*."

Sunbeam's Martyrdom

His name was Ernst Böhm and he looked rather handsome in his grey uniform. What did not suit him so well, to her mind, was the emblem of the German eagle with its claws clutching a swastika.

"I suppose you shall sell it on for double in the camp," she said in broken German.

"I'll offer it for sale," he said. "But at the same price. It's more likely to be you who doubles the price."

He was two years younger than her, and it was the third time they had met. They stood at the edge of the forest where the barbed-wire fence began. She had left the Reo parked on the Hekne seter, and had walked through the copse with a whole kilo of butter and a small churn of milk under her anorak, and with a ready-made excuse that her dog, who was at her side, had run off.

"Where did you learn German?" he said.

"I went to teacher training college."

"But you never got to be a teacher?"

"No. Your lot bombed the college."

"I didn't finish my training either."

"Which was?"

Ernst smoked a lot, his cigarettes were dry, and he smacked his lips to remove a strand of tobacco.

"Excuse me," he said. "Electronics. I wanted to be a radio repairman."

"So, you fix their radios?"

"No," he said. "I didn't get to attend college for more than a few months. They sent us to France."

"Have you come from there now? From France. Or did you all get some kind of holiday?"

"Leave, it's called. *Urlaub.* Yes. I did. Then we spent three months in the *Übungslager.* The SS training camp."

"In France?"

"No, in Germany. I was in Königsbrück."

"The men in the truck," Astrid said. "The ones I saw behind the – what's it called – tarpaulin. Are they prisoners?"

"Yes and no. They work for us."

"Do they get paid?"

He laughed.

"They're Yugoslavs. Serbs."

"But why have you got them working here," Astrid said, "when there's nothing but forests and mountains?"

He stiffened a little. Drew air through his nose. Stopped being Ernst Böhm.

Then he softened again, took out a bar of chocolate. They ate. She looked at her watch.

"Listen," he said. "I don't like this war any more than you do."

"Then you don't like it at all."

He seemed in no hurry to move on and lit yet another cigarette.

"Ernst," she said in German, "the prisoner I saw behind the tarpaulin was so thin. If I manage to get a sack of potatoes, can you—"

"You really don't know much," he interrupted. "I'd be court-martialled. Do you think we act as we want? None of the soldiers are treated well. I yell at the soldiers in my charge and the *Oberfeldwebel* yells at me and the *Stabsfeldwebel* yells at the *Oberfeldwebel*. When we first came here, we took the direct train all the way through Sweden. Five days. We couldn't get off even once. We were packed together. Diarrhoea spread from wagon to wagon. The toilet was blocked from day two. A friend of mine was the only man to arrive at all rested. He's a little fellow. Climbed onto the luggage rack and used it as a bed."

"At least you're getting enough food now. What do the prisoners get?"

"A quarter of a kilo a day. Cabbage or soup. If I came with potatoes for them – what do you really think?"

"But nobody can work on a quarter of a kilo!"

"Ring the Führer and tell him that. We're not even permitted to give them any medicine."

He moved closer to her, and she did not move. He gave her his hand. It was so big her hand disappeared in it.

"Thank you," he said. "It's good to see a normal person."

I'm not a normal person, she nearly said.

"I hope we meet again."

"Me too," he said. "Although we probably won't. I'm going north the day after tomorrow."

"As a guard soldier?"

"As a sergeant for guard soldiers. We're going to a place called Beisfjord. Near Narvik. Do you know what it's like up there?"

"Narvik? No. I've never been. Maybe a bit milder in the winter. Damp. Lots of cod, if you're lucky."

He wasn't listening properly.

"If we could give them some medicine at least. We're expecting some officers in the new camp up north, with experience from the bigger prison camps in the east. So I'm hoping it'll be better organised."

August came. The month when her father usually asked himself whether this was the year when he would finally get to invite his brother over for the reindeer hunt. The month when plump sheep and stout cows should be brought down from the mountains. The month she might have returned to teacher training. But the war was still the war, and the only bit about the autumn that was autumn was that the leaves were turning yellow and the nettle thicket had begun to die back.

Soldiers came into the Colonial now and then, almost always in twos. Widow Fløter and Ada Borgen rarely sold much to them. A drop of milk, a morsel of cheese. And only to those who they reckoned were homesick, or who had yellow badges at the bottom of their right sleeves from which they could tell what work they did.

Astrid had received two posters showing all the German military insignia. At first the posters had been left rolled up in the wood stove, but then she and the womenfolk at the Colonial made a point of memorising all the insignia pictured. At a glance they could see whether a man was a car mechanic, minelayer, radio operator or saddler. Even the carrier pigeon service had its own emblem: a strangely pointed B, confusingly similar to the emblem for the department who paid the soldiers' wages. She had never seen either. But that summer, Ada Borgen had seen the fortress engineers' badge three times. Although, what they were doing near the seter, or what they were planning, Ernst Böhm had not revealed.

Fløteren was always keen to talk about the things she had discovered. But one day he seemed strangely subdued. He was standing by the storage shed, and she wondered why he was clearly waiting for her, yet seemed reluctant to talk.

"We has a problem, Astrid."

"Oh."

"Ye has been seen. Happen on yer first meetin'."

"Who did ye hear that from?"

"Someone in t' village. The words German trade came up too. And that ye opened milk churns with a German bayonet."

"Oh, hell," said Astrid.

She looked around for something to punch. Asked him whether it had been worth it, this mission.

"Happen we shall never know the answer t' that question," said Fløteren. "Not till this be over. Not even then."

She went to the packing shed and began loading the truck. In the semi-darkness, he said:

"Ye mun decide for yerseln now, whether ye wants t' continue or not. When rumours spread about thee, they spread about the Colonial 'n' Ada Borgen, and my mother 'n' yer mother. Rumours grow bigger, as ye knows all too well. They never shrink."

"Aye, and the worst slander is spread by the very men who work as carpenters for the Germans."

"'Tis the way o' it. Naybody has clean hands after two years o' war. Then 'tis tempting to fling mud at others."

She got up to leave. Stopped at the door and turned.

"That message to England," she said. "For my uncle. Victor. Do ye reckon it got there?"

"A fifty per cent chance. At best. And it'll be hard for him to send thee an answer. How old be those boys o' his now?"

"Sixteen and seventeen."

"They shall be called up," said Fløteren, "if this war doesna' end soon. Which doesna' look likely."

Three women stood at the side of the road one morning with empty berry pails. Astrid knew two of them; the third had to be from outside the village.

Astrid stopped the Reo, leaned across the passenger seat and rolled down the window.

"Ye going up t't pinewood? Hop on."

"Nay," said one. "We gets awful grubby in the back there."

Nobody had complained about that before.

In the rear-view mirror she saw them gesticulating towards the truck. One seemed to say something that got the others shaking their heads.

Up at the seters it became too much for her. She stopped the Reo between two milk stands and walked up to the old winter seter, found the key between rocks in the foundation wall and let herself in.

Several summers had passed since anyone had stayed here. The soapstone hearth had been scraped clean of ash, and the check curtains were drawn. On the kitchen table were two upturned stools. In one corner there was a zinc bucket with a floorcloth stretched over it.

Astrid sat down and thought about the years before the war. When the gossip had been poisonous, but not deadly.

It took time before she could continue her round. The Heknes' dairymaid was standing by the milk stand and had clearly been waiting a while, but she did not ask what had held Astrid up.

"I has a sad message for yer ma. See her yonder? Sunbeam."

The dairymaid pointed to a field where a cow was going round and round on herself, with agitated movements. As though she was being forced to walk in a circle.

"She has the Circlin' Disease," the dairymaid said. "Worms. They settle on t' brain."

"D'nay tell me she mun be killed?"

"Tak' a lot afore we kills a cow."

"So, she's in with a chance?"

"Vet shall know when he sees her. She mun go down t't village. In a fold on her own. She can infect the others, and I has but one barn up here."

Back at home they agreed that Jehans should drive the milk truck while Astrid and Pelle led the cow down to Hekne.

"D'ye really want t' go alone?" he said the next day, as she stood there with the cow on a rope and Pelle dashing around her excitedly. "Happen ye ought t' bring the under-dairymaid with thee?"

"I'd rather go alone, Father."

He looked up at the sky and the treetops. "Weather be shiftin'. D'nay do anything daft now, lass."

The Reo disappeared behind a bend and Astrid started to walk. The cow seemed even sicker today. She was twitching violently and was spinning around biting her own backside. It was hard to lead her and awful to see her in such pain.

Fifteen minutes later and they had not gone far. Sunbeam's behaviour grew increasingly wild. She appeared to be hungry but would not eat the rough grass at the wayside. She continually tugged on the rope and tossed her head, causing the bell around her neck to clank furiously and her spittle to fly. She spotted a gate into a meadow and strained to get in. Astrid tried to grab her by the horns and look her in the eye, but it was impossible to get any communication with her. Astrid ended up with spittle on her hands, and, remembering the worms, wiped her hands on the ground.

"So, ye want to eat the grass in there, eh?" Astrid said. "I understand. That's how 'tis in autumn, but that's not our field, ye knows that. Come on, now."

They continued, and at every gate the cow wanted to go in. Not until they were some distance from the seters did Sunbeam settle a bit. They were on the slopes where the fields ended and the spruce forest thickened. Pelle was still running loose. When they got to the village crossroads, Astrid stopped.

The path to the right was the one she *should* take.

To the left was the path that led to the wire fence where she had met Ernst Böhm.

Her heart was pounding all the way up to her larynx, and her fingers were icy cold as she dragged the cow into the forest. It was a struggle to get her to follow. Pelle scampered about with his tongue lolling out. Soon she could see the rust-red watchtower over the spruce trees. She shoved the cow on and assumed that the guards would hear her bell, realise what was happening and not fire their guns.

Between the tree trunks she saw the guards' hut and two soldiers. One shouted something to the other.

Astrid acted as if she had lost control of the cow, slapping her backside with a willow stick so she bellowed wildly. Pelle barked and she put him on the lead.

Then she let go of Sunbeam's leading rope, and she stormed off in the direction Astrid had shoved her in. Astrid wound Pelle's lead round her wrist and dashed after her. When she reached Sunbeam, she was walking in circles again. Astrid gave a shove and managed to get her to trundle on again. Then some soldiers appeared, presumably to see what was going on. Pelle barked. Sunbeam spotted them, bellowed, and stamped the ground threatening to charge towards them.

"*Nicht schießen!*" Astrid shouted.

One of the guards kept pointing his rifle towards the cow, but another two stepped calmly around her. Her lead rope was trailing behind her, and one of them went to grab it. But Sunbeam had other ideas. She lowered her head and charged on and through the camp gate. This was Astrid's chance, and she set off after her with Pelle leading the way, stopping for a moment in front of the guards.

"Help me catch her! Please!" she shouted in Norwegian, running into the camp.

The cow continued along the clearing inside the wire fence, before she disappeared among the young trees towards the middle of the camp. Astrid kept running, branches slapping her face. In her head she was trying out various excuses that didn't stick.

A siren sounded behind her. Then another sounded from further in.

Astrid and Pelle followed the noise of the cowbell and finally caught Sunbeam again. Then Astrid spied a group of low buildings surrounded by tall trees. She pulled the cow close to her, then pretended to lose hold of her and scared her in the direction of the buildings.

A voice rang out from a loudspeaker. The guards emerged from the copse, fired a shot into the air and shouted *Halt!* Astrid let go of Pelle's lead and put her hands in the air.

She had seen the forced labour that was taking place.

And she could not process what she had seen.

Pelle disappeared, his lead trailing after him. She heard loud shouts behind her. A soldier grabbed her arm, another ran after Sunbeam. She was by a grey shed, leaping around herself again as if she wanted to bite her own tail. As the soldier reached her, she trampled him down. The soldier who was holding Astrid, let go of her and raised his Mauser. A shot rang close to Astrid's ear. The cow bowed her head and bellowed. Astrid knew it was a belly shot. The man on the ground crawled away. A second shot sounded, and Sunbeam ran a few metres before she came crashing down headfirst.

"Nay!" Screaming, Astrid sprinted down the hill. The soldier did nothing to stop her. Trying all the time to register everything around her, she knelt beside Sunbeam. The cow lay there with wet earth and heather between her hooves, tongue hanging out, gulping at a froth of blood. Random twitches ran through her, and the gurgling turned to wheezing. Then her carcass came to rest.

The shouts fell silent behind them. More soldiers arrived. The soldier who had shot the cow secured his Mauser. Another helped up the man who had been trampled. Soon five soldiers were standing in a ring around Astrid and the dead cow. Young uniformed men. Freshly shaven versions of Ernst Böhm. Nothing was said. Their faces notably free of anger. As though she had just fallen on some ice and they wanted to express their willingness to help.

They came from farms, like her.

Astrid looked out of the corner of her eye. There must be a hundred Serbs working here. She recognised the smell of wet cement.

The soldiers led her away without a word. They led her towards a tall, red barracks. From behind it she heard barking. Then howling. Then a shot rang out, a sharp crack, probably from a pistol. Then another.

Pelle was nowhere to be seen.

"This has gone too far," Fløteren said.

"I had to do it, or I couldna' rest."

Around them was the burnt odour of railway tracks; they had taken to talking when the freight trains went past, so that nobody could hear.

"Were ye seen by anyone this time?"

She shrugged.

"We canna' be seen together," he said, looking quickly around.

"Oh?"

"I shall explain." He looked at his watch. "Meet me at home."

Soon they were at the kitchen table, a half-drawn map before them. Astrid stood with a rag polishing an ignition cable from the Reo to make it look new. The cable was fine, but she needed it to back up the note she had put on the milk truck's window: *Delayed departure: 4 p.m. Engine problem.*

"I canna' forget how they looked," she said. "The Serbs. I've never seen owt like it. Some were just skin and bone. With clothes so ragged they were barely worth wearing. Here. Right here. In Butangen. In our seters!"

"How long were ye there?"

She put the ignition cable aside and sat next to him. "About a half-hour from when they shot Pelle. They led me away from the work site, but I managed to observe a fair bit. The prisoners walked about like sleepwalkers, even with the heavy labour they were put to."

Astrid clutched her hands together.

"But it bothers me that I canna' get the numbers to tally," she said. "When they started building the camp, the trucks carried prisoners up to the seters and down. They were hidden behind tarpaulin, aye, but we had a good idea of how many there were. And the trucks often transported men *up* but brought timber *down*."

Fløteren continued drawing his map and asked her if things were in the right place. Then he suddenly put his pencil down.

"When they d'nay come back down, 'tis because they has died up there, Astrid."

"Died? They work them t' death?"

"Aye."

Sunbeam's Martyrdom

It was too painful to talk more, so they concentrated on the map. Eventually he asked:

"So how did it end with Pelle?"

"The vet amputated his paw just below the joint. He's all bandaged up now and he has a limp."

"Mercy. What did Esther say?"

"I didna' tell Esther the truth of course."

"Nor yer father?"

"Nay. But I reckon he knows."

"I reckons so, too. Tell me. Did Pelle really cover that German Shepherd?"

"Well, he got on top of her. So, probably. The first shot I heard was a warning shot. The officer who owned her didna' dare shoot while both dogs were prancing about. Then I shouted out, and Pelle limped back to me."

Fløteren laid his hand on hers and smiled.

"'Tis good he came back alive. And ye ought t' be proud o' yerseln too."

He turned back to their map and pushed his glasses up over the bridge of his nose.

She described how she had seen the prisoners laying bricks to make structures that looked like cellars, but whose roofs were level with the ground. Between them were paths, laid with rocks.

"They left nearly all the trees standing, even though that must have slowed the building work down. Further along there were long barracks with iron bars in front of the windows."

"Can ye draw them?"

"Ay, of course. Now that my hands are steady."

Astrid took the pencil, made a sketch on a piece of notepaper headed with the letters NSB, the logo for the Norwegian national railway.

"They might be underground bunkers for ammunition or explosives," he said. "Set fifty to sixty metres apart t' avoid any secondary explosions if they be bombed. The trees were left t' make it hard to spot from a plane. But why the devil would they build a small ammunition depot deep in the mountains? 'Tis a mystery t' me. But one thing I know: when the Germans do sommat, they has good reason and often a very good plan."

He went on quizzing her about distances and materials, and she made more sketches and descriptions. Fløteren nodded more and more excitedly.

"'Tis a blessing the Germans likes t' standardise things. They build large sheds wi' concrete floors like these as workshops, and this kinda building for fuel tanks. They be working on sommat that requires labour and heavy machinery. Ada Borgen saw six Germans wi' engineers' badges, right? But only two were fortification engineers."

He leaned back in his chair.

"I reckon they be plannin' a road," Astrid said. "A road over the mountains."

"Aye, makes sense. And it tells us sommat about their grander plans. Very important plans maybe. For the Germans d'nay care about county borders. Down near Våler in Hedmark, in the old potato fields along the Glomma, work has begun on a new airport to serve the south. And they be planning a huge harbour town up in Trøndelag. A road here would join all the valley roads. And there be a still grander idea behind this again. Ye did well, Astrid. This be invaluable information. They'll be interested in this."

"Milorg, ye mean?"

Fløteren balanced his pencil between his thumb and middle finger.

"I in't working for Milorg anymore," he said.

"Oh?"

"I did afore. Likely they reckons me a coward now. But our work be o' far greater consequence, Astrid. Milorg barely know we exist. That be the whole point. We d'nay carry weapons. Or blow up bridges. We collect and pass on information to our allies beyond. We reckons this be o' far greater use in the end."

"In what way?"

"'Tis easy to think that the war be happenin' far away. That this place is just a little station town in Gudbrandsdal. That there be nowt we can do agin the Germans here. In truth we find ourselves at the heart o' it. The war traffic through our valley has been massive. The Germans avoids sending their soldiers and equipment by ship, cos the English are waiting for them out at sea with bombs and torpedoes. Which be why all the transport o' soldiers and equipment goes by rail and road."

He told her that in five days seventy-eight trains had gone south, carrying 1,300 soldiers. But that just fifty-two trains had gone north, with 270 men. They had marked the trains so the soldiers could find their correct carriages, meaning that he could tell her which artillery regiment went south yesterday, and that they had ten trucks.

He lifted his spectacles to rub his eyes.

"When they took the Døla horses, we were forewarned, for they had requisitioned animal transport wagons from each station along the valley. But we could tell naybody, cos then the Germans would know we was spying on them. This in't to save ten or a hundred folks, Astrid. This be to win the war."

"So who are ye passing information to, then, if not Milorg?"

"'Tis not for ye t' know. But we tries to be one or two in each village. We receive orders. If sommat be urgent we reports it to London via radio transmitter. That be all I can say. Or should say."

Astrid refrained from asking more. She looked at her watch. It was coming up to four o'clock. The villagers would be standing round the Reo by now, gawking and impatient to get home. The gossip would start. She must rush down now, open the bonnet and flash the "new" ignition cable at them, and come up with some story about how she had got it soldered, in case someone asked where she had managed to buy a new one.

"The captain was about to shoot Pelle in the head when I arrived with the soldiers," said Astrid.

"And?"

"Made myself difficult of course. Ranted about the cow and the dog. He gave in. One of their paramedics bandaged Pelle's paw and gave him a drop of morphine from a syringe. They'll give a dog medicine. But not a prisoner of war."

"That be how they are. Or rather, how they has become. Which cow were she?"

"Sunbeam. Named after the old cow at Halvfarelia."

"Well, I shall nominate Sunbeam for a medal if I ever has a chance."

"I got two hundred kroner for her."

"*Ye didna' sell her carcass?*"

"I did indeed. The Chief Rationing Officer came along. By the name of Neutzner. He offered me a hundred, but I said she was our best milking cow."

Fløteren sat and shook his head. "How much meat were on her?"

"She'd got thin, but I think there was about 120 kilos ready cut, 140 at most."

"Not such a good price, then."

"Happen, but when ye consider that her brains were wormeaten, it was quite generous. She wasna' even fit for mink feed. So, for once, 'tis good they d'nay give meat to their prisoners o' war."

A Bible and a Kicksled Stand

Kai Schweigaard would occasionally pause along the road and look at his old home. At the white house and the flagpole from which the German war flag now fluttered. The parsonage, which for centuries had been the hub of civilisation in the village, with its gentility, its orchard and bathtub, its Sunday roasts and books in Gothic script.

And now?

The old midwife's cottage. A cramped old box bed, a smoky paraffin lamp and mice in every corner.

And a battered old Underwood, with a threadbare ink ribbon.

For Kai Schweigaard – prompted by his great age, experience and slightly imprecise self-image – did not neglect to write a large number of letters to the Church's leaders. His style was dramatic and full of righteous anger. In particular, he supported the suggestion that the Church break away from the occupying government. *It is*, he wrote, *impossible to have a state Church, when the state itself has been transformed into a violent police regime!* The problem was that his letters, which he always franked with pre-war "Official Document" stamps, also contained attacks on colleagues whom he found either passive or self-obsessed. His tone was too excitable to be referenced in any episcopal meetings or printed in any secret circulars – despite his providing theological proof that the occupying government's founding ideas could be logically defined as *evil*, thus constituting an impossible basis for any Christian involvement. Such involvement was like a pact with the Devil himself. *It is time*, he wrote, *for us to stand up and be counted! Let us break with the Quisling state!*

And – it happened. Without the old man's influence, no doubt, but in 1942 his hopes were fulfilled. Pastor Kai Schweigaard stepped up into the pulpit and announced that he, like most other pastors, had resigned from his office, on the dictates of the bishop's Shepherd's Letter. He would no longer take instruction from the state, and he renounced his salary. He would however continue to be their pastor, and would hold Mass and preside over confirmations, baptisms and funerals.

Schweigaard felt his blood rise as he made this declaration, doubtless because he delivered it during Easter Mass, always the highlight of his year. He felt oddly liberated afterwards. For decades, the primacy of his position had been diluted by decrees and bureaucracy. He had even had to endure the occasional petty objection from the parish council. But now he was freed from such formalities. Now he stood alone with the sword in his hand. Battle awaited.

It was not long in coming.

Quisling's government immediately accused the priests of disloyalty. Hille was thrown out of the Bishop's Residence in Hamar, was stripped of his office and then had his bank account seized. NS members with some theological know-how were allowed to take clerical robes and move into the larger parsonages. They proved a dull and ineffectual bunch in comparison to the country's real priests, men who had developed an assuredness and obstinacy over decades, like the protective bark of a *tuntre* – that most ancient and revered of trees.

Nor were there enough of them, these "loyal" priests.

A tacit agreement was reached. The pre-war pastors could stay on, so long as they did not talk politics.

Ola Mossen never humiliated himself by talking with Schweigaard. Instead, he sent a keen young NS man to sit at the back of the church every Sunday to ensure this unwritten ruling was upheld. The flaw in his plan was that this young man was a bachelor. He was soon captivated by a hearty young blonde who attended church devotedly each Sunday, and it ended with the NS man finding God in just three months, renouncing the NS

A Bible and a Kicksled Stand

and being married by the very man he'd been assigned to watch.

In the neighbouring parish of Ringebu, the pastor was ousted and replaced by a bizarre figure named Haffergård, who preached to empty pews. Ola Mossen suggested that the parish of Butangen be placed under Ringebu's jurisdiction, but discovered that an old rule made this impossible until Schweigaard, who had the title of parish pastor, was either dead or dismissed.

The cash box was empty and Kai was forced to accept the few coins that Herr Røhme discreetly collected. Then, to the Mossen boys' delight, came the ban on giving priests alms. Soon Schweigaard had to acknowledge that the only things God could equip him with were a Bible and kicksled. He received a sprightly letter from Widow Stueflaaten, who wrote that she was proud of him. Three weeks later came a sweater knitted from leftover yarn, its stitches a little loose, but warm because it was made of Spæl sheep's wool and by her own arthritic hand.

He lived on potatoes and rabbit meat from Hekne, but was worried by the change in mood on the farm. Jehans seemed so in on himself, Kristine was always cross, and Astrid was increasingly hard and cold, less trusting, as though she carried a vial of bitterness inside, to be bitten open if they had to concede the war. She did not come into full blossom. He had observed the same in *his* Astrid towards the end, filled with spirited defiance, but also a resignation that this was unlikely to end well.

Kai Schweigaard continued his regular trips between the old midwife's cottage, Hekne and the church. He got holes in his shoes, and his winter coat lost its well-brushed elegance. With the winter came bronchitis and back pain.

"Heavens, ye look at death's door," said Fru Røhme, when she dropped by on her weekly visit and found him lying there, pale and covered in sweat.

"No," he said, and she must have thought the fever had got him when he went on, "I shall not die in any bed."

Runes and Warplanes

He rallied again, but the screws were constantly being tightened on the Norwegian clergy. One intransigent pastor after another was interned in a place where complete control could be had over them. To Schweigaard's surprise, this was near Butangen, namely in Lillehammer. He took the train there from time to time, because the priests met every day at midday in an old bank. But whenever he went, he noticed that they saw him as a relic of a bygone era. Many even assumed he no longer held office, with his threadbare clothes and walking stick, and fire in his eyes, and phrases that belonged to the last century. His mind wandered when they discussed theology, and it always struck him on the train home that he could never be one of them, could never think like them. He had grown to be a part of Butangen.

Kai Schweigaard woke up one morning and saw Grocer Engstad patter across the floor. He had stopped by last night too. They had shared Fru Røhme's pastry. What made Kai think he could distinguish Grocer Engstad from Fru Odden and all the other mice?

His new interest in intuition, he realised. Here in the old midwife's cottage, he often felt a whisper of Widow Framstad's ancient wisdom. The echo of her rituals that lent form to the invisible.

He fetched some crumbs and sprinkled them on the floor. Engstad stood up on two legs and looked him in the eye.

What he saw there in the mouse's gaze made Kai realise why he could never really talk to the theologians. They would think he was crazy if he told them he had opened his mind to the ancient faith. When Jehans and Victor had been mortally ill in 1919, he had taken the Hekne sisters' dwarf-forged knife to the inside of Gunhild and scraped off the Holyblight. He recalled how this action demanded he suppress all common sense and his scientific knowledge that the verdigris scrapings could not have any medicinal effect. Yet the brothers had recovered. The Holyblight had cured them because it forced him to believe. To have *faith*. True faith demanded submission to the unprovable, in that which was impossible in the exterior world, otherwise it was not faith. It was in the word itself. In true faith, two plus two could never be four. Perhaps five, or three, or nine and three-quarters. But never four. And in that moment of submission, he seemed to touch another kind of consciousness. Himself, perhaps, in another form. A kind of web in which everything and everyone from all time was connected. Or a weave, for that matter. Something. Something that might achieve something greater. Among the living here on this wretched earth.

These were his thoughts in the midwife's old cottage, while the question with grimy sorrow beneath its nails clawed its way ever closer: when will it come, *my* end time?

The Past Demands No Interest

The blow of a hammer on the outside wall. The banging continued and silenced the chatter in the Colonial. The corners of yet another poster or announcement must of course be nailed firmly down.

Astrid looked out. Ola Mossen could be seen outside the window. He stared back at her with a hammer in his fist. His expression was impossible to interpret. A grin of sorts? A kind of... recognition?

He nodded before getting into the Ford and disappearing, heavy blue smoke pouring from his exhaust pipe.

Astrid never went outside when the Mossens were nailing something up. She had no interest in seeing what bans had been introduced that week, or the latest nonsense folk were to be convinced of. Throughout the spring of 1943, she had been reasonably well informed about the progress of the fighting abroad, and that the Germans had to retreat increasingly often, but the war had become something that just *was*. Like the weather. It was always there, had its shifts, quiet days that were never many before some new catastrophe hit.

A couple of weeks ago, Fløteren had passed her a small, crumpled note. A message from England. Probably sent in the post to an embassy in Sweden, then brought into Norway by one of the border couriers. A reply from her uncle to the message she had smuggled out several months ago.

All alive here. Little food. Sad news about T's hand. E likely to be enlisted as a pilot. A too. We think of you all every day.

"What be that fuss outside?" said Ada Borgen, leaning forward to see out of the window. She had misplaced her spectacles, and when she squinted, her face wrinkled. Widow Fløter looked up. She sat struggling with the ration lists. Last month they had managed to get hold of some paper curtains and bedsheets, and this morning eight pairs of fish-skin shoes had come in, all of which proved to be size 36. Ada Borgen wondered if they should send them back, or let eight village bairns choose a pair each.

A crowd had gathered outside. Folk started to stare in.

Astrid flung on a jacket.

"What's happening?" she said, going over to the corner.

The crowd fell silent. Some looked at each other. Others looked at her.

Finally, a man's voice said: "Happen ye can tell *us*."

A corridor formed to let her through.

It was a new recruitment poster for frontline fighters. *The Joint Front Against Bolshevism!* A Norwegian coastal landscape bathed in sunlight. Three men, one behind the other on a diagonal. A full-grown man in German uniform in the fore, then a young boy in a summer shirt, and behind him again the hazy image of a helmeted Viking, with a shield bearing the sun cross. All in sky blue, corn yellow and white.

The same Nordic man in threefold. At different ages, in different eras. One with a full beard, one clean-shaven. But always the same man. The will and spirit of the past recast in the young. She saw that the style and vibrant colours echoed the illustrations she had so loved in those pre-war children's books and Christmas pamphlets.

A door closed for her.

Until this moment, the war had meant hunger, fear, anger, anxiety. And just sometimes the exhilaration of getting your own back. A tingling through the body: I'm alive, I got away, I tricked you.

But from hereon, from this day, she would know the sting of being branded, of wearing a mark on her forehead, always visible to others.

The poster was signed *T. Hekne*.

Every detail of the image was fixed on her retina. Impossible to blink away. As when she stared into a candle in the dark. When she blew it out, the flame was still there.

Nobody said anything. Everyone saw how she took it.

But none could see that what hurt her the most was that the poster was beautiful. She knew her brother. Knew how he strove for perfection. This poster represented days of thought, of experimenting with line and colour. It was executed in the style of Damsleth, but it was no mere copy. Its originality was what pained her most. This was Tarald's own creation. A product of his own talents. But was it also an expression of his thoughts, his own will?

They stood with eyes turned upwards and forwards. These three men. Towards a common, great goal. A goal placed high up, outside the poster's parameters and beyond the viewer's grasp. A trick of perspective that pulled the observer in and demanded something of them.

She knew how he had achieved it. She had heard him explain it to Esther when he was talking about what he had learned on his advertising graphics course.

"If we draw a figure from below," he had said, "then, whatever the angle, that figure will appear to be taller than the viewer. 'Tis an ingrained memory from when we were bairns and admired the all-powerful adults. 'Tis that simple. The viewer becomes small and wants to be accepted by those who are bigger. But ye, Esther – ye canna' be fooled by such things. That's why ye are so secure in yerself, because naybody is above thee and naybody is below thee."

It was as though her blood vessels were fit to burst.

She recognised Tarald's way of drawing from when he had drawn the stream and goat that would become the dairy factory's trademark, namely the arrangement of his subjects on a diagonal. A yellow sunbeam ran obliquely through the entire image, imbuing everything with a sense of movement and intent. Stretched out in the background was a fjord. The sun came in between the mountains and lit a glassy sea. On it a Viking longship.

The past lends out its riches to everyone, she thought, and demands no interest. The typeface was identical to the one on the front of the Nordenkirche brochure. It evoked the Viking Age because, like runic signs, it had no curves. Just straight dashes, from a time when words had to be chiselled into rock or carved into wood.

A man spat out his chewing tobacco.

"What say ye t' that, Hekne-wench?"

Astrid had no answer.

She might have tolerated the sun crosses, the longship, the Viking.

But not what she forced herself to look at now.

Because down on a plain by the fjord, he had drawn something else from Norwegian history. Something that had seemingly wandered here from Grandfather Gerhard's pencil.

A stave church.

Death is Quick for the One who Dies

It was rare for Jehans Hekne to behave like an old-fashioned farm owner, driven to exercise control over family and labourers. It was known that in his youth he had formed such distaste for Uncle Osvald's brutal management of Hekne that he resolved to be the opposite. When work was poorly executed, Jehans would often redo it himself rather than bawl at anyone.

Now, as he stood before a torn poster on the kitchen table, it was as though he tried to cling on to his old ways. Under his family's gaze he fought and lost the battle against himself. Twitches crossed his face, and when he finally turned to Kristine, they could see his sad realisation that another Jehans was needed this time.

Two days later Tarald was suddenly there. Unannounced for supper. Jacket off in the hallway, through the door, to the kitchen cupboard from which he fetched a bowl. Pea soup. Looks good, Mother. Hello, Eirik.

Jehans leaped to his feet. Father and son stood in the middle of the floor. Pelle limped away.

"What were ye thinking?" said Jehans. "The Eastern Front. 'Tis a wicked swindle, Tarald."

Esther ushered Eirik out.

"Our boys'll be shot, Tarald. Shot. Die upon their knees in a marsh some place, not even knowin' where they be. They'll be shot in the back as they swims away 'twixt ice floes in the spring melt."

Turning towards the kitchen clock, Tarald said: "That's how it is now. The war. Stalin is more dangerous than Hitler. If the Russians come, it'll be *us* getting shot in the back as we swim between ice floes in the spring melt."

Jehans shook his head.

"This can never be right. However ye tries to explain it. What youngsters do be one thing. But these lads has parents. Death be quick, for those who die. But a dead bairn hurts for life. Day after day, year after year."

Tarald put the bowl on the table. Avoided his father's gaze and shook his head dismissively too.

"Truth be, Tarald, they shall be going around in German uniforms. Looking nay different from the Germans that kills our folks here at home. How can I look them in t' eye when ye have tricked their lads o' seventeen into believing this Germanic-Viking claptrap?"

"I am not tricking anyone! The war of 1940 isna' the same war we are fighting now. Has it nay dawned on thee yet? That the Russians have Norway and Sweden in their sights? So, parents will just have to take it. Stomach it as ye had to stomach it."

Jehans fell silent. Tarald sat down. Jehans sat down. Kristine sank the ladle into the pea soup and filled her son's bowl.

Astrid watched on. For a moment she thought that was it.

Then Jehans got up and snatched Tarald's soup away.

"Nay, they shall nay take it. When 'tis nowt but a shameless swindle. 'Tis agin my will now that ye take over Hekne, Tarald. Nay, Astrid shall have the farm, as well as the shares in t' dairy, in t' Colonial, in t' power station and all that follows."

Tarald stared at Astrid.

"Out, Tarald! Out! No Nazi shall ever own Hekne."

"I am not a Nazi," Tarald said, rising so the tableware clattered. He punched the air with his arm stump. The stump that had the power to end any debate over the war. That could seal any pact.

"Sit back down, Tarald," Kristine said. "Jehans, ye canna' make such decisions alone."

Tarald shook his head and marched out into the hall. He shoved on his boots, making a show of how impossible they were to lace with one hand, and left the front door open as he stormed out, laces flying. Astrid took her jacket and followed him out. She caught up with him below the *stabbur*.

"Where'll ye go?" she said.

"Oslo, of course."

"Today?"

"On the evening train."

They walked on without a word. When they got to the gate, he stopped. Astrid bent down to tie his shoes. "About all this," she said, pointing to the barn and the *stabbur* and all the farm buildings that were Hekne. "I knew nowt. Father has scarce spoken to us these past days."

"The farm's not the issue right now," said Tarald, looking down at her. "Ye must start to see things from a wider perspective. Look reality in the face, Astrid. And stop hiding bullets in milk churns. 'Tis futile."

She flinched and looked up at him.

"Aye. Of course, I knew," he said. "And I shall, of course, keep my lips sealed."

His laces were done. She handed him his jacket. A suit jacket with a high collar that she had never seen him wear before.

She lagged behind him as they passed the guards outside the parsonage. Then, moving closer to him, she said: "Sometimes ye are so bloody daft. Ye didna' have to go and sign that poster."

A young boy with an empty wheelbarrow came towards them on the road. Tarald looked at the ground. On the shore of Lake Løsnes they passed four men repairing their boats. They stared at him so long, it would have been rude in peacetime. Their glances triggered Astrid's old defiance.

"I shall row thee over. Come on, Tarald. We shall take our boat."

Soon they were out on the lake. The oars creaked against the rowlocks, and with each stroke the village grew further away. Tarald had waded into the mud as he pushed the boat out, and now he sat with wet shoes.

"D'ye remember when we came out here as bairns," he said, looking down towards the end of the lake. "On winter nights at the first sign of ice. To play polar explorers."

Astrid nodded. "Ye were Otto Sverdrup. And I was Amundsen."

"The ice was so thin," Tarald said, "it cracked open as we rowed."

The sun was low now. Its rays, broken up here and there by the trees on the horizon, threw shards of colour over the water. As they drew closer to the other side, the shadows lengthened. The boat slipped gently between them, and the temperature shifted to the same rhythm. There were no other boats out.

"Believe me, Sister dear. I canna' stand the Nazis. But I despise t' Bolsheviks even more. They d'nay tolerate any culture at all. No art. No religion. They see human beings and civilisation as nowt more than machinery. They hate anything ancient or great. Hence the poster."

"Tarald. Whatever the explanation, 'tis right what Father said. They'll wear German uniforms, these boys. They'll wear the executioner's uniform. The uniform that abused me in the bell tower! That killed Mari Slåen!"

He dipped his fingers in the water so they made tiny, short-lived waves.

"The war will end, Astrid. But the problem, the thing that ye d'nay seem to grasp, is that *one side or the other* will have won. Nazism will die out. It is too ugly and hateful to do otherwise. In a few years, Germany will return to being itself again. To the Germany that took the stave church to Dresden. To Grandfather's Germany. In the meantime, it behoves us to be flexible and adapt. Fight the right battles and get in with the right folk."

They were approaching land now. She stopped rowing and let the boat drift. All they could hear was the murmur of the nearby stream. Astrid breathed in the cold, damp air. Tarald stared at the mouth of the stream and the place where the Sister Bells had lain. Everything was mirrored in the water's surface, which shivered lightly in the wind.

The men over at the boatyard had lit a fire to soften the tar for their repairs. Despite it being so far away, the fire cast a yellow glare across the water. The men had been watching the rowing boat all this time, and Astrid knew that here, in full view of the entire village, a story was taking shape.

Tarald lifted his fingers from the water. She started to row again. Let her gaze rest on the wake, watched how it divided itself behind the boat, and then slipped back into its original smooth form. And she thought how nobody, not even the most powerful person, could leave a trail behind them on Lake Løsnes.

Only moments later she wondered if she was mistaken.

They were almost there. Tarald seemed to have entirely forgotten the incident at the farm. His thoughts were elsewhere.

"The easiest thing is to keep dreaming," he said. "Soon ye shall look back on this day, Astrid, and say, 'Thank heavens, it was here that it turned.'"

"What d'ye mean?" she said, lifting the oars.

"Wait and see."

"Wait and see? D'nay be like that, Tarald."

The boat lost speed, and Lake Løsnes rocked them. He did not answer. It felt as though he had poked her in the eye with a sharp pencil. "Believe me, I shall win. History has chosen *me* to understand."

The boat scraped on the gravel, and he jumped out. Stood with his feet in the water, steadied the keel with his forearms and pushed it free, and as she rowed away, he finally met her gaze.

Astrid could not free herself from the look on his face. The look he had always had when he entered on big thoughts. Laced this time with bitterness from the incident with the plough, when his father had made his inadequacy so plain.

She lost the strength in her rowing. Far in the distance she saw Tarald. A tiny speck of a brother crossing the Løsnes Marshes.

Dead Woman's Will

Kai Schweigaard had heard the Sister Bells ring of their own accord three times. In 1880, when the church was to be demolished. Before the Spanish flu in 1918. At the outbreak of war in 1940. And yes, he had thought on occasion that he had heard ringing from the bell tower or the depths of Lake Løsnes, but accepted this had been a figment.

Now, in July 1943, he got up from his bed in the midwife's cottage and listened. Was Gunhild really calling him?

Kai Schweigaard listened harder. He heard the church bell ring as he would have heard her if he were deaf. Seen her if he were blind. With the knowledge that she wanted him to do something.

The sun was rising. He went to the nettle thicket to relieve himself. The ringing did not fade. Its echoes chased away any thoughts that tried to take hold.

Without having eaten, he set off for the village on the bicycle Herr Røhme had got for him. On his first trip on it, he had swerved into a ditch and spent half an hour getting back up. Because he had told nobody, the chainguard remained twisted and the wheels scraped the mudguards, so the bicycle emitted strange noises that grew louder as he picked up speed down the forest path, his walking stick strapped to his back.

Outside a log cabin stood a car and a man in city clothes and a beret, and an old-fashioned handlebar moustache. Schweigaard met his gaze, but it did not invite him to ask why he was here at six thirty, when the grass was still wet with dew. He looked like the distant, intellectual sort. A very bad sign here in Butangen.

Kai continued towards the forest. There, he put his bike down. A fine, large hare darted away as he entered the forest. The summery landscape was gently rolling and untouched, with crooked birches and flowers and trickling streams. Yet it was a strenuous walk. Sweaty and short of breath he reached the little clearing. An area of good sheep pasture with a peaceful stream and a flat sitting rock.

He walked over to Daukulpen. Leaned on his stick and contemplated his image in the still, black water. An old, old man. With an old, old hope.

Only a forest pool could be so silent. So secretive. Although . . . it was only secretive if the observer had some expectation.

What is it you want, Gunhild? Why are you calling me?

He suddenly had a flashback to the moment when he and Isum had spotted the footprints in the snow in 1940. When they had realised that the moving of Gunhild had been witnessed.

Runes and Warplanes

Now, on the other side of the stream, was a set of wheel tracks. Deep tracks, made by tyres with an unusually rugged tread. The water in the pool tugged on a red-painted float. It must be attached to something on the bottom.

He sat down on the rock. It was cold.

He heard voices. Men passed by the trees on the other side of the stream. Some in German uniform. Five civilians, one being the man with the handlebar moustache.

They stopped. One of them pointed at him. They walked towards Daukulpen, and he heard the roar of an engine in the forest.

They made no effort to give the moment any solemnity. They had no doubt been here yesterday to plan all this out, because they now backed the truck down to the water's edge and unloaded the timbers that soon formed support pillars for an iron beam across the pool. From it hung a pulley with hooks and chains.

More soldiers came out of the forest. One was Major Sprockhoff.

Schweigaard stood up and made his presence known.

Sprockhoff walked down to the pool. Schweigaard said nothing. Like a statue with no name plaque that wanted nothing more than acknowledgement from the initiated.

The two men stood on either side of the water, staring at one another. Then Sprockhoff lifted a hand to his cap in greeting and ambled over to the others.

Kai Schweigaard climbed onto the rock to watch. Only in 1881 at Astrid Hekne's deathbed had he felt so powerless, and never had he felt such power from a dead woman's will. He would have liked to stand there in his cassock, a solitary figure, black and menacing in the mists, a messenger from the spirit kingdom, but the dawn light revealed him as a bushy-haired, old man in patched clothes. Nobody was bothered by his presence.

It was as though he did not exist, or was watching something happening in another time.

Two soldiers cranked on a hoist. Something moved in the forest pool below. Something large that made its surface tremble. The iron beam buckled slightly. A dark dome rose slowly from the water. A church bell much bigger than Schweigaard remembered.

The shape of the bell was so alien to the nature here. Voiceless she came up. Voiceless the soldiers who brought her up.

Gunhild was still wrapped in sailcloth. It clung to her like wet clothes to a human body, so she was at least permitted a modicum of modesty and remained under the legend's protection. The water that trickled down glittered in the sun. She was pushed over the iron pulley, put on an old cart and from there hoisted onto the back of the truck.

Still voiceless.

Also about who had betrayed her.

Who?

Who!

Who had been standing up on the slope and watched her being hidden?

To whom could he direct it, this anger that must surely match the anger Astrid had felt towards him when he betrayed her in the coldest month of the Silver Winter?

Major Sprockhoff shouted his instructions. The soldiers dismantled the hoists and pillars, and in a surprisingly short time Schweigaard was alone. The only signs of their presence were some tyre tracks, a dirty, frayed rope, and an empty tin of lubricant with a German label.

He sat there for a long time after the sound of the truck had died away. The flat rock at Daukulpen had retained the night's cold and was no help.

Not a Word to Yer Father

Tarald, Astrid thought, whatever became of you? You who read aloud to Esther. You who rowed our boat through the ice. What was it stole you away, Brother? Was it the Battle of Tretten? Was it your trip to Germany? What was it you bore, what was it cut so deep under your skin?

Their parents had made two small gestures. Kristine insisted that Tarald's room be left untouched, while Jehans took Tarald's military jacket and hung it on a peg in the hall, arranging it so that the right sleeve, the one that was rolled up to the red corporal stripe, faced outwards.

Gunhild was transported from the village without fuss or fanfare. All Astrid saw was a truck proceeded by a few cars with Oslo licence plates. Nevertheless, when it stopped at the parsonage, she realised what had happened.

She phoned her brother in a rage.

He said: "It had to be done."

During one of his sleepless night wanderings in April 1940, Tarald had spotted Giant Isum in the dark and followed him. He had kept his lips loyally sealed. Until, as he said, the war changed direction.

It had not been an easy decision. It required him to take a wider view. To look at the story from another angle. To expose an old legend for what it really was. A childish fairy tale. Gunhild was now, with the help of the Ahnenerbe, a symbol of brotherliness with Germany that would soften its rule of Norway.

"I can just picture it," Astrid said. "Himmler and ye taking a stroll with yer hands behind yer backs. A heart-to-heart chat, so ye can both be wise and straighten things out. Revenge on Father, that's what it was."

"Astrid," said Tarald, "ye had some fancy about the bells

being reunited. It was never going to happen. Should the bell be a hidden curiosity that only ye and a soon-to-be-dead pastor knows about? Naybody else in t'village cares!"

She hung up. Pictured the unbearable moment when she would tell Kai that her own brother was the culprit. Asked herself if she could have prevented it.

Astrid wished her grandmother was alive, so she could have asked her: "What was it like when you lost the battle, Grandma? The battle against these vainglorious men who impose their will. Who are so certain of the supremacy of their ideas. Even though these ideas are only the *day's special*. A plateful of notions and machinations. Did you think as I do, Grandma, that it should be unlawful for men to hold any office higher than mayor?"

In the weeks that followed everything went dark.

The fact that the church bell had been carried off never quite gripped the village's attention. It was Tarald's poster and the boat-crossing over Lake Løsnes that tore the wrapper off the gift of local gossip. Rumour spread that the Heknes were turncoats. That they were war profiteers. Nazi stooges.

The milk truck had been seen near the military camps once too often, the women in the Colonial were too nice to the Germans who came in. Ada Borgen's daughter heard a rumour that Astrid had sold a good, frisky cow to the evil guards who tortured prisoners of war, and that she had sold food to one of them, and it wasn't long before some swore Astrid Hekne had been seen with a German soldier in a seter hut. For money no doubt. Her grandmother had bairns with a German, remember that? Aye, Jehans was half German. And the electrics in the village had worked wi'out any hitch throughout the war, perhaps he had gotten some new dynamos. Wasn't it in Germany they made the best?

Many villagers started shopping down in Fåvang, taking the

long way home with a backpack. Others revealed their true colours. They waited until Astrid was alone behind the counter, and said: "Aye. It all makes sense now, what Tarald stands for."

Jon Mossen included. He came in, leaned against the door frame, and looked around his old workplace. "We be older now, me and thee," he said to Astrid. "Older and wiser."

He looked at her as he had on the back of the Reo, on the day the seter road had been opened. She crossed her arms.

"Aye, well," he said, and left.

In the days ahead Astrid would be forced to concede that the things she had risked her reputation for had made no difference. The camp near the seters had suddenly been demolished, the materials transported elsewhere, and the barbed wire rolled up. All that remained were some mounds of earth, a few concrete bunkers, and an unknown number of dead Serbs under the lingonberry patch. The road the Germans had planned was never built. According to Fløteren, they had diminishing manpower and resolve. Everything was going into the war on the Eastern Front.

Less was said at the supper table at Hekne.

Winter.
New Year.
January 12, 1944.

It was seven o'clock when Astrid and Eirik hurried down from the farmhouse in the blue-dark morning. Blackout rules meant there were no outside lamps shining anywhere, which was, as Jehans and Kristine said, how Butangen had been for centuries before the arrival of electricity. Astrid and the boy walked in light snowfall to the Colonial, where she brushed their shoes and unlocked the shop door.

She switched on the light and looked around at the gaping shelves. Eirik sneaked through the curtain and into the back room to play with the building blocks Tarald had made for him.

Before the war.

Astrid put a massive kettle of water on the wood stove. The thermometer by the door had shown −24°C, and the Reo would only start if she took out the thermostat and poured hot water into the radiator.

Eirik began to build a castle with his bricks. He placed guard huts outside. The blue blocks were, it seemed, cars. The black ones were soldiers. Astrid had tried to build ordinary houses with him, but he always ended up playing war.

It turned eight o'clock and the stove had started to warm up the shop. They were due to open at nine. Not that there was much to keep open for. Or much joy to be had in shopping.

Sewing thread was rationed to one reel every six months. Families with small children could get one small chocolate bar a month. Ersatz goods were often all that were available. Substitute flour. Substitute coffee. There was now a mandatory order for the collection of hair, which was Widow Fløter's responsibility. She paid out a few øre for each little bag handed in, collected it in a sack and sent it to a factory that made it into insoles and thin duvets.

At last the water came to the boil. She carried the kettle out to the Reo and in the light from the doorway poured the water into the radiator, steam rising all around her. She blew the snow off the top of the *knottgenerator*. Put the wood into the burner and lit the fire beneath it. It was like lighting an ordinary stove. In half an hour the pressure would be high enough for them to drive down to the village.

Astrid pulled her jacket around her. She stood for a moment in the half-dark and falling snow, and looked at the store and the truck. She was fond of the slightly battered Reo, just as Giant Isum was fond of Svarten. A truck, though, suited her needs more than a dray horse. Especially now in wartime. It only stopped with good reason. It never had moods. If something was broken, it could be unscrewed and repaired.

It took a good hiding, too. One morning somebody had let the air out of its tyres. Another time a swastika had been drawn in the dirt on the door, the wrong way, and with a small finger, so it had clearly been done by children.

The snow on the road down to Fåvang was rarely cleared this early in the day, and she was putting chains on her rear wheels when she heard footsteps in the snow.

"I can help thee start her up."

Ada Borgen emerged from the darkness, dressed in a worn-out coat and a blue scarf. Her eyes watered when the *knottgenerator*'s smoke came her way. She climbed up into the driver's seat and sat ready to slam her foot on the gas as Astrid turned the crank under the bumper to start the engine. It sputtered and coughed, and Astrid went back and forth between the generator and the cab to adjust the smoke mix. At last the engine was running smoothly. She drove the Reo up to the door of the Colonial, placed a stepladder up to the cargo bed and left the engine idling.

It was fifteen minutes before departure and still dark. Dark in all its varieties. It was mandatory to dip vehicle headlights, and she had to drive slowly to be sure not to go off the road, since the narrow strips of light barely reflected off the snow poles.

At nine o'clock three men and two women sat on the back of the Reo. One had a blanket wrapped round her and was probably going to see the doctor. Astrid invited her to sit inside the cab with her.

"Nay, I shall sit here. 'Tis better company."

"Right," said Astrid. "Listen, 'tis such a cold morning none of ye need pay. The truck's going down anyhows."

"Grateful, I'm sure. But we shall pay. We canna' sit for free."

For free *with you* were the words that were left unsaid, but that everyone heard.

Five clammy fifty-øre pieces were put in her hand. They had been held ready in their mittens.

This scant offering was enough for certain folk to say that they had done their bit towards winning the war.

The station was like all stations outside train times, strikingly quiet and orderly.

She parked the truck by the goods shed, and by the time she got out, her passengers had already abandoned the cargo bed.

Astrid walked into the waiting room. Grey-painted walls with worn benches, a calendar and a ticking clock. The only things on which to rest the eyes were the public information and propaganda posters.

Blackout! Your responsibility!

Our cause is your cause! Join the Women's Hird!

And *that* poster.

She went to the ticket office. On the counter lay some instruction books, an inkpad and various rubber stamps, and a cash box. The back wall was covered with timetables and a kind of panel dotted with tiny lamps. She assumed the red lights marked how near the trains were to the station.

Fløteren sat with his back to her, his hat hanging on a peg.

He turned to her and signalled where they might meet. Not long afterwards she had completed her errand.

"Let me handle the radio transmitter. Father taught us Morse code when I was little."

Fløteren was shaking his head before she got the words out.

But she continued: "Ye said yerself that ye can no longer transmit messages from down in t' village. Because o' the new receivers."

"Have ye lost yer senses, lass?" he whispered irritably. "Have ye nay seen what it says on t' poster? *Shot on the spot.*"

Naturally she knew the penalty for being taken in possession of a radio transmitter was death. But there could, she said, be no safer messenger than her. "With the milk truck I can send messages from a different location every time. I am here at set times, and in the summer I drive all the way up to the goat seters in the mountains. And the higher I go, the better the radio connection. I can wire the radio battery to the truck to charge it up, and I can—"

"Nay, Astrid lass. Ye has done yer bit. Ye has been taken out. By village gossip. Our government-in-exile says that black-market activity counts as treason now."

"Happen we can exploit the suspicions."

Fløteren shook his head again.

"Nay, lass. Ye be my best and oldest friend's little girl. So, nay. Messages on the hymn board – aye. Trade with the enemy and rumours – done is done. A radio transmitter – nay. Risking yer life won't bring the church bell back from Germany, Astrid."

"It in't that. Or not *just* that. I must have sommat t' fight against or I shall go mad. I keep reliving the bombing. Over and over. The blood. The screaming. The explosions, they go round my head. And what's worst is that it all gets clearer wi' each night. Only when I feel I'm doing sommat, taking action, do I escape t' dreams."

Fløteren looked at her. His entire friendship with Jehans was in that glance.

"It in't ye asking me," said Astrid. "'Tis me askin' thee."

He took off his NSB cap. He was starting to go bald. He brushed a speck of dirt from its brim and put it back on.

"Not a word to yer father," he said.

Next evening she was sitting in the byre with a backpack

marked *Lost Luggage*. In it was a small, brown leather box. When she opened the lid, a childhood came flooding back.

Two meters, one round, a row of black knobs labelled in English. Headphones. A box of spare parts. A little lever with a Bakelite handle that gave a distinct click when she pushed it down.

She remembered a childhood with her father. The dynamo master who was always so busy. An alphabet that she and Esther and Tarald knew by heart. A word that ended the day.

-.... -.. - .. -- .

Bedtime.

Eighteen Cassocks to Helgøya

Kai Schweigaard was on his way home to the old midwife's cottage. The calendar showed June 1944. Mass was over, and he was leaning on his bicycle more than sitting on it. He had a headache, and his arthritis was now a daily torment, because he had been saving on firewood all spring.

That was the way of things. The firewood ran out, food ran out, soon life would run out.

On the slope past Romsås he met a couple carrying a rabbit in a cage. He called upon his well-practised pastor's kindly yet scrutinising gaze. They had not attended church and were a little embarrassed.

"A tenacious little creature," said Schweigaard, peeping in through the chicken wire. The Trønder rabbit sniffed the air, whiskers aquiver. These small animals had provided meat for many a family. They were tough, fast-growing, and also provided a soft, glossy black pelt with grey speckles. They could survive on leaves and rowan twigs and withstand the extreme cold. The downside was that they were touchy.

"A pregnant doe," the man said.

They stood there a while. It was rare for villagers to take the lead when talking to the pastor, but now they were almost mute. They soon said their goodbyes and went on their way.

Turning the corner, Schweigaard's back was a little more stooped.

The carefully measured words. The little gestures that signalled a preference to walk on. The respect that had crumbled.

For sixty-five years he had watched the villagers of Butangen, and four of those had been in wartime. He knew their moods and anticipated the workings of their minds.

Two weeks ago three men from Butangen had been arrested and sent to Grini detention camp. They had had weapons in their houses and could, in the worst-case scenario, expect the death penalty.

More and more villagers had been reported on this year. And in the most diabolical ways. Infiltrators talked their way into the resistance groups under cover of being good Norwegians. They secured their access by taking big risks and thus building trust. They helped folk escape at the last minute, got refugees out of danger, one even blew up a bridge.

Then, suddenly one night, the Gestapo would come and arrest everyone, all except the mysterious outsider.

Nobody had news about the three arrestees from Butangen. Someone had turned them in, but who? All they knew was that the Gestapo offered bounties of five to ten times the annual wage in exchange for naming prominent members of the resistance.

The rumours grew vicious. Reputations were blackened. As usual they aimed their attacks at the Heknes, and at the Røhme family.

And he had been tarred with the same brush.

Although that was surely the reason behind the colour of a cassock. So that a priest could mingle freely with those who were blackened.

Those who were quickest to slander others were never those who helped to smuggle out refugees or who took in weapons or hid undercover agents in the mountains. They, of course, had to hold their tongues. That was the nature of slander. The difficulty was that nobody was honourable every day, or a sworn Nazi all around the clock.

It was all so muddled. Herr and Fru Røhme constantly had insults thrown at them. Fru Røhme no longer cooked for the Germans, but earned a few coppers cleaning, which she mostly did to prevent the parsonage's rooms and fixtures being completely wrecked. Their grandbairns were still living with them, but that winter they had come home with snow in their satchels. At first they refused to say what had happened. Then it came out that they had been cornered in the schoolyard and told that they were so big and pudgy because they were being fattened up on schnitzels.

Røhme was still a dutiful churchwarden. Over the last year, three young Butangen lads fighting on the Eastern Front had returned home in coffins. Ola Mossen had hailed them as Nazi heroes and demanded they be buried in the best place in the cemetery, next to the silver birch tree near the church doors.

So Røhme dug.

In full view of everyone.

How could the villagers have known that Fru Røhme's floor-cloth was as dangerous a weapon as the best artillery? Being slow to read when she was young, Fru Røhme was still thought a bit backward by some villagers, and it was likely that somebody, Mossen perhaps, had told this to Sprockhoff. Whatever the case, the Germans assumed she was harmless. But Pastor

Schweigaard had taught her a little German, so she listened in without Sprockhoff having the least suspicion. Schweigaard then passed anything of interest on to Astrid.

Schweigaard could see the top of the slope now. A little further, and he could have a lie down on his narrow box bed. No, there was no denying that his powers of oratory were waning. His Sunday services relied on routine and sheer determination. But he kept at it, and whenever he was in the church, he let himself believe that the Hekne sisters gave him renewed powers from beneath the floor. Not until the end of today's sermon had he shown even a dash of spontaneity. His congregation had perked up, so it must have fallen on fertile ground, even if he could not quite recall what he had said.

The road flattened out and he forced himself onto his bike.

He sensed trouble the minute he turned the corner. A newly washed car stood in front of the midwife's cottage, its tyre marks in the grass. The front door stood wide open. The buckets under the gutter, in which he collected rainwater, had been overturned.

"The old man's coming!" came a voice.

A stranger filled the doorway. Wearing the Hird uniform. Armband with the sun cross. Ski hat. "Stop there!" he shouted. "House search!"

Schweigaard got off his bike and asked what was going on.

"Tell him it be because he talked politics in t' service," someone shouted from inside the cottage.

Schweigaard recognised the voice. Ola Mossen.

"It's because you talked politics in the service," said the guard.

Kai walked up to the door, leaned in past the Hirdman and shouted: "Mossen? What on earth are you doing in my house?"

Furniture had been knocked over. Some of his glasses were broken, not that he had many. Mossen did not answer. Schweigaard asked the Hirdman: "To which service are you referring?"

From inside, Mossen shouted: "Today's! Just now!"

The Hirdman was about to repeat this, but Schweigaard walked away. He sat down by the grindstone, from where he could see down to the old seter road.

Politics? Had he talked about King Haakon again? In an attempt to relive the magnificence of his Jubilee Mass back in 1940? Or had he given a critical reading of the letter to the Romans? *Whosoever therefore resisteth the power, resisteth the ordinance of God.*

He couldn't remember.

Ola Mossen came out. Behaving as though they had never met.

"Yer name has been reported to t' county governor with a request t' banish thee from Butangen. Ye has been unloyal to the Church o' Norway's ordinances. Ye may talk all ye likes about Christianity, Herr Schweigaard. But nay agin t' government. Ye knows that full well."

Mossen's sons came out too now. Jon Mossen was holding a garment of a heavy black material not unlike that of his own Hird uniform, apart from it looking so worn.

It was the cassock Schweigaard had worn when he first came to Butangen as a young pastor. The only one he had kept from his younger days. The one he had worn when he deconsecrated the old stave church. The one he had worn when he buried Astrid Hekne.

"Seized," said Ola Mossen. "We has been in t' sacristy and taken any robes that were hanging there too."

Schweigaard looked into his face. Searched for the humanity and common sense in this man. True, he had come from a poverty-stricken croft in the village, but how many Norwegians came from poor beginnings and turned into 24-carat human beings?

"What's got into you, Mossen?" Schweigaard said. "What

happened to the two of you?" he continued, reaching his hand out to Mossen's sons. "I baptised and confirmed you, I—"

Jon Mossen straightened his armband. "Confirmed us, huh. Ye should ha' heard what we boys used t' say about thee. Standing up there, so self-righteous in yer pulpit, gibberin' away."

"Ye be a danger t' this village, Herr Schweigaard!" Ola added. "Haffergård, from Ringebu, shall take o'er in t' church here. He can stay with the Røhmes when needs be. Hold Mass every other Sunday."

Schweigaard had to lean on the grindstone for support.

Jon Mossen went over to the car, opened the trunk and flung in the cassock like a wet rag.

The car wheels skidded on the grass, and they almost tore down the gatepost. Then they stopped abruptly. The back door opened. Jon Mossen leaped back out and grabbed Schweigaard's bike, saying it was seized under the paragraph on materials used for subversive activities.

They lashed the bicycle to the roof rack and drove off.

The noise of the exhaust died away.

His typewriter lay on the floor inside. The roller was dislodged, and the ink ribbon lay in a tangled mess.

He hid the church register safely each evening, so it had not been found. But they had emptied his crock of money, leaving a receipt. NOK 37.60 seized.

Kai Schweigaard sat down on the box bed. Too weary to begin clearing up. His body gave in to age, his mind gave in to the war.

Fifteen minutes later he felt there was still some life in him. No more than an ember in ashes, but an ember at least.

He went out to the grindstone again. Sat down and looked along the old seter road.

The sun was peeping through the clouds. Then he heard footsteps on the gravel. With quick and firm footsteps, she came.

"Did they strike thee?" she said, as soon she was within earshot.

He shook his head but could not stand up.

"They – they have burned yer cassock. Nailed it to a stake. Poured paraffin o'er it."

He stood up now as she reached him.

"'T'was awful," she said. "Like watching thee burn."

"I'm unscathed," he replied. "But I can see you are not."

A long time passed before she said anything more. It was as though she was struggling with something formless inside her, something that wanted to burst out, but must at all costs be left unsaid.

"I feel so dreadful," she said. "I have t' go about lying. Lying t' everyone I love. I say I'm just popping out a while, and it in't true. Then I come back and have to make sommat up about what I lied about. And when Mother says something nice or kind t' me, it bounces off. Like I'm eavesdropping on't. Then I hear what I'm saying, and it sounds fake. As though I'm a sort of actor pretending to be the person I really am."

"You could tell me *why* you have to lie, Astrid. If it helps."

She had to catch her breath after this speech, and her gaze wandered between the ground and the sky before she said, "I've got a radio transmitter."

Schweigaard frowned.

"But don't – don't they have equipment, the Germans? That can track down radios in less than an hour?"

"An hour? A quarter, more like. They've got some antennae overseas that are so big they can detect a signal in Norway just seconds after it's sent. Then a message goes from a central exchange t' the nearest German station. When the alarm goes off, they send folk out with location sensors. Worse still, the Abwehr surveillance station has been moved to Lillehammer."

Astrid went over to the grindstone. The axel sat in a bed of iron and was rusted in. She shoved the stone back and forth until it could spin freely again.

"Mother and Father . . ." she began. But her voice cracked at these two words, and she had to gather herself before continuing. "Both o' them. What should they say? About their own son? Should they say Tarald is disinherited? Should they criticise their own bairns to strangers? Stand and explain sommat we can barely talk about ourselves at the kitchen table?"

Astrid stood and looked at the old seter road.

"Sometimes I just want t' give up," she said. "Hang my head. Sit and wait."

"I doubt that'll ever happen," he said. "But your strong will can prove your greatest enemy. I've seen it before."

He joined her, and they took turns in pushing the grindstone. The moment gave way to a silence that in turn took on a warmth.

"Grandmama and thee," said Astrid.

"Yes," said Schweigaard.

"On one hand I want to know all there is to know about it. On the other I d'nay want to know anything."

"It's a long time ago," Kai said. "But certain things in life will always have happened yesterday. And that's how I feel it is with her."

They sat outside until darkness fell. When she had gone, Schweigaard stood and contemplated the old midwife's cottage.

A battle had taken place on that doorstep today. A fight for dominance in the village.

A fight between two men in black.

A fight that was not over.

Early next morning he got a lift from the cottage to the railway station, ignoring the restrictions that had been laid upon him. Borrowed a few kroner for the train. Arriving in Lillehammer he trudged up the slopes to Lilletorget, the old town square.

Eighteen Cassocks to Helgøya

Tailor Konow's shop was closed. Raw timbers covered the display window. The panes appeared to have been broken from outside. Kai peeped in through a gap. Its contents were in disarray. Gone were the rolls of fabric. The tailor's dummy lay in pieces on the floor. The heavy sewing machine had clearly been used to help in the destruction, for it now lay damaged in a corner.

"They did him over because he was a – one o' *them*," said a voice behind Schweigaard.

He turned and initially saw nobody, until he discovered that the voice had come from a small boy. An hour later he had tracked Konow down to a squalid little room in Emma Gjelens Street. Konow averted his gaze as he spoke. It was five days since his shop had been ransacked, but Konow still had black eyes and could barely walk.

"I doubt I'll ever sew again," he said, showing Schweigaard his bandaged hands. "The iron was on when they came."

Schweigaard told him about Mossen and the cassock.

"That's how it is now," said Konow. "There was a council meeting in Gjøvik last weekend. They all sit up there in the great hall spurring each other on. Then they go back home to *clean things up*."

"Have you reported them?"

"There's no point. Two police officers came when they broke my window, but didn't dare get involved. The Hird leader took out a red book and said they were acting in accordance with Paragraph 6 on restitution rights."

"Restitution?"

"It's a word I've had to learn. They shoved the book up in my face and I remember what it said verbatim. 'The Hird may exercise its right to restitution on the spot in case of insults against the NS or the Hird. In the event of such actions the police shall not intervene.'"

"I'm losing hope," said Schweigaard.

"It's the Hirdmen themselves who decide whether they've been insulted. All the police can do is get the traffic moving again and restore order when it's over."

"And had you offended them, Herr Konow?"

"Well. Needles can of course prick. I'd been given a remnant of lace, and being in a good mood I made a little blouse and put it on a doll. There were no customers, so I made her a bonnet to match, a frilly *baby's* bonnet. Then for fun I put a brown ribbon across the doll's chest, so it looked like a Hird bandolier, and sat her in the window. People pointed and laughed. Someone warned me, but I think by then it had already been reported."

"So, they wrecked your premises?"

"They were unstoppable. They whipped each other up. It wasn't just the doll it seemed. It was my character too. That in itself is a standing offence to the NS. Although whether it's *standing* is questionable at my age."

"Oh come on, Konow!"

"I'm just trying to keep my spirits up, Pastor Schweigaard. To be honest, I'm choked up about it. The shop's one thing. I don't actually live here, you understand. I've lived all my life in a rather overpriced apartment uptown, but now – I daren't even go home."

"I came to ask if you'd make me a new cassock," said Schweigaard.

Konow said neither yes nor no. He started pacing the room, then loosened his bandages and tried to move his fingers. His knuckles were bruised and the backs of his hands were burnt, but the joints in his right hand were working. He went out into the entrance hall and returned with a dented pocket flask.

"May I dare ask if Herr Pastor takes a nip in the middle of the day," Konow said, shaking the flask. "It's nearly empty. But it's White Horse."

"Well, in that case," Schweigaard said.

They drank from cracked egg cups.

"To think they call themselves Hirds – the old king's guard!" Konow said.

"They don't know what they're trampling on," Schweigaard said.

They had a last half-cup each. Tailor Konow seemed perkier now. Not so much from the whisky as from the company.

"Sadly, I don't have any rolls of fabric left. They confiscated them. Meaning they'll sell them and drink the money."

He stood up, and Schweigaard thought he saw the seeds of fight in him.

"We can pop quickly home. I've got scissors there and pins and a roll of old-fashioned floral gabardine for summer dresses. But I could dye it black. And I can take the curtains. Question is where I'll sit and sew."

That evening a rather surprised Astrid Hekne collected two elderly gentlemen from the station, one battered and shy, the other deep in thought. Schweigaard said nothing, but craned his neck as they drove past the parsonage. It was late by the time they were settled in the midwife's cottage, where they had a supper of flatbread and ersatz coffee. Schweigaard lay on the narrow bed and Konow took a straw mattress on the floor. The oil lamp had been broken during the raid, so their only light was from the fireplace.

Schweigaard, who had barely ever shared a bedroom with anyone, stared into the flames, sure that Konow was doing the same.

The fire turned to embers. Both men were clearly waiting to hear snores, but none came.

"Can't you sleep, Herr Konow?"

"No."

"That's hardly a surprise. After what you've been through."

Konow was clearly feeling the cold. Schweigaard watched him fumble his way over to the fireplace and fetch the socks that were hanging there to dry. He pulled them on and returned to his mattress.

"The punches weren't the worst thing. It was the contempt. And that I knew many of the men from before the war. Two of them were always loitering on the Mesna Bridge with no work. Another was my customer for years." Konow pulled the blanket over him. "Good night, Pastor Schweigaard. Tomorrow I'll take your measurements for your new cassock."

"Good. One thing this war has taught me, Konow. A sword is forged in embers and hardened in water. Heroes are forged from ordinary people and hardened by injustice."

Neither man put more logs on the fire and it was almost dark, but the singular peace that sleepers usually bring to a room did not come.

After a long silence, Schweigaard cleared his throat. "Tell me, Herr Konow. Do you want to talk about the *burden* you've had to carry all these years?"

More silence. The floorboards creaked each time Konow turned.

"That's not easy to talk about," he said.

"I understand."

"Eventually I accepted it about myself. That I liked men. Mostly as close friends. And one or two in other ways. One particular man I liked both as a very close friend and – in other ways."

"You know something, Konow. I wonder if it's really so different from conventional love? From love for a woman?"

"The love is perhaps the same, but I think the desire is different somehow. Simpler perhaps."

"Right. I was thinking more of the spiritual and intellectual attraction. Admiration. Friendship."

"I admired men in so many ways – including you, Herr Schweigaard – but with the admiration one might have for a painting. One knows there'll never be anything more. But you know, Schweigaard, I often wondered why it was you seemed to stop ageing. Sometimes I thought the Good Lord had condemned you to immortality. Like the Flying Dutchman, who craved his own demise, but could only die if he was kissed by a woman who truly loved him."

It was Schweigaard who was silent now.

"As I understand it," Konow continued, "you visited Widow Stueflaaten. And yet . . ."

"And yet?"

"I think you've always loved another. Deeply. It's in your eyes."

"It's too dark in here for you to see my eyes, Herr Konow."

"I've known you for years, Pastor. I've seen you when you think nobody's looking."

Schweigaard cleared his throat and did not contradict him. A spark flew from a spruce log in the hearth. A miniature shooting star, whose presence in the night sky has, throughout time, prompted people to make wishes – wishes that must be declared to greater powers in the brief time in which its glow is visible on its path – and he sensed they were both making wishes now, and that their wishes tonight were humble and small, but borne on the wide wings of that great word *love*.

"Is it many years since he left, this man you liked?" Schweigaard said.

"It'll be sixteen years soon."

"And there's been nobody since?"

The embers before them were faint now, and Konow's movements could be heard but not seen.

"No. And there weren't many before him, either. And not much, even when there was anything."

"So, there's been something at least," said Schweigaard.
"Something. Yes."
"I think we'll settle for that, Herr Konow. That we have been love's small investors, we two."

A week later the cassock was complete. The dye was only partially successful – in bright light the floral pattern shone through – but that could be forgiven, not least because Konow had, on Schweigaard's request, managed to re-create the cut and detailing of the robes of his youth.

Konow took his stay as a holiday in the country. His injuries had still not healed, but he made breakfast and lunch in the doleful little one-room cottage, cleaned the windows, even went outside with a hammer and saw, and thought he would have passed muster as a carpenter too. He cut up two bed sheets to make the pastor's ruff. It took three whole days. First Konow had to hammer an old tin plate to make a pleating-iron, which he heated with an iron bolt made hot in the stove, and then used to press each pleat. There was no starch to be had in the shops, so he made some by repeatedly soaking grated potatoes in water to extract the starch. The result was almost to pre-war standards.

The cottage was cramped, and both men were used to living alone. Their companionship eventually reached a healthy saturation point, but not before Konow had initiated Schweigaard into the secret world of tailoring.

"Did you know that all measurement charts for a Norwegian men's tailor have a check box, which, after a discreet glance at the client, and without a word, reminds him of whether his client is PTL or PTR? That is, whether his reproductive organ lies to the right or left. Based on this, we make trousers slightly roomier on the correct side of the crotch. About fifteen per cent of the male population are PTL, Pastor!"

Schweigaard blushed a little and suddenly had an idea. He

headed down to the village and rang Bishop Hille. Konow's curiosity was aroused, but he received only the vaguest answers.

On the first day of July the two men ambled off with light luggage and a newly sewn cassock in a suitcase. It was raining hard, and by milk truck and train they worked their way south to Ringsaker, where they were picked up by a cab. If they were stopped, they planned to say they were on the way to borrow some freshwater herring nets from Rudolf Sagen – an excuse they thought the guards might find odd, but which would in fact stick, because Sagen had six newly repaired nets at the ready and was waiting for two men by the names of Schweigaard and Konow.

Rudolf Sagen was a small cog in a secret apparatus that had been set up a few days earlier, but which was the culmination of events dating back to the priests' rebellion in 1942. The colony of exiled priests in Lillehammer had annoyed the NS so much that they had sent them to the Helgøya peninsula. But even here the rebels refused to simmer down, and they had invited two hundred churchmen to a missionary convention. Among these were eighteen young men whose interest was not in the convention itself. They were theology students who had cycled all the way from Oslo through the rain, and who planned to sneak out in the dark of night to the remote chapel, where a bishop and three pastors would be waiting to ordain them by candlelight. Such a catacomb ordination could land them in a prison camp or before a firing squad.

It was here that Schweigaard and Konow were now headed.

For security's sake Konow was blindfolded towards the end of the journey, still unaware that he was to be the solution to a large problem: how to get cassocks for eighteen men. It was a criminal offence to sew any official dress without NS authorisation, and the tailor risked looking into eight rifle barrels if he was caught.

It was this that Schweigaard had rung about some days before.

Early next morning, Schweigaard led Konow, who was still unaware of what was happening, into a basement room with drawn curtains. His blindfold removed, Konow was confronted with eighteen young men in vests and long johns, and told he was expected to make each of them a cassock.

Every man's measurements were written in a code that corresponded with his cover name, which was kept in another book. Numbers were converted into letters to prevent the measurements being used to identify the priests later.

Schweigaard left Konow there on the peninsula.

Where he spent the rest of the war Schweigaard never knew, but the tailor was given a place to live, where, with his usual flair, he sewed many a cassock that was secretly delivered to its proud owner.

What followed Schweigaard home, and what stayed with him as he cleared away the mattress and noticed the little improvements his companion had made in the midwife's cottage, was Konow's calm and steady gaze. His smile, the tape measure, the pins and notebook, in the moment that would be the master tailor's finest.

Greetings to Fru Ro

The freight train stopped with a screech of brakes. A good thirty flat wagons with grey tarpaulins covering cargo. Two passenger carriages. One at the front, the other at the rear. The doors were open as it pulled in, and in the corridors she could see German soldiers. They leaped off the train now, ran along its length, dividing up so that in mere seconds all the carriages were guarded by soldiers with sub-machine guns.

Astrid was sitting on the platform with a small suitcase. She stared impatiently at the clock that hung out from the wall. She rubbed her eyes. Standing around her were six other travellers. She recognised one or two.

The load on each goods wagon was apparently identical. The tarpaulins hid something egg-shaped and fairly big. The train must have come a long way, as it was covered with dirt and ice, and the snow had only melted on the parts of the wheel arches that got hot.

The speaker crackled. "The 10.23 southbound passenger train to Oslo has to wait until the goods train has changed locomotive."

The other passengers grumbled and went back into the waiting room.

It was February 11, 1945. No sign of milder weather. The icy wind froze everybody's faces, and their shoes still creaked in the snow. Nevertheless. There *was* another spring on the horizon. Everyone felt it. That the war would soon end. The question was *how* it would end.

Everything was starting to fall apart for the Germans, and in response they grew increasingly bestial. The resistance had shot the national police chief, and as punishment thirty-four Norwegians were sentenced to death. The valley was crawling with Gestapo, and they were being aided by Norwegians. Mossen was housing a group of non-villagers whom nobody had seen, except to say that they were three men and one woman. The giveaway that they were in league with the Germans was that they drove a petrol-fuelled car. A green Opel.

When she heard this, Astrid took even better care of her shoes and always laced them tightly in case she had to run.

She shifted her gaze to the siding further up. Fløteren

appeared among the soldiers who were guarding the freight train. He gave a signal to someone, and clinking noises came from up there. Someone was clearly loosening a jammed coupling. Further up, another locomotive was reversing. A man who must be the pointsman walked towards them carrying an iron rod.

The station smelled of brake lining and coal and lubricating oil.

And perhaps fear.

The time was 10.35 a.m.

The locomotive change was complete. Fløteren was no longer to be seen. Someone blew a whistle, and the soldiers streamed back into the passenger cars. Then the train came to an abrupt halt. A man emerged from a shed, waving an iron rod in the air. Minutes later the train crawled out on the northbound track, gained speed and disappeared.

Fløteren came running. He did not look behind him, just hopped over the tracks and climbed the iron ladder that led to the platform. Astrid got up slowly and went in through a back door.

"Quick," said Fløteren. "Count them. I had thirty wagons. Be that a match wi' what ye saw?"

"Aye. And forty-three soldiers on my side."

"This be sommat big," he said. "There has never been such a heavily guarded train pass through here afore."

"Did ye get to see under the tarpaulin?"

He nodded. "Some kind o' torpedoes. Ne'er seen anything like them afore. Not even on the latest weapon charts from England."

Fløteren took a piece of paper and began to draw. He was midway when he looked up at her and said, "Prepare to send some urgent messages. Happen they be for use against the Murmansk convoys. I shall hold up yer train."

402

He went into another office. Soon an announcement came over the tannoy.

"The Oslo train is waiting for northbound freight trains to pass and is severely delayed. Expected arrival time 10.55."

They had only just managed to prepare the messages before her train pulled in. Astrid got on and sat down, her cardboard suitcase on her lap. The train chugged out and onto the bridge over the Laugen. Through the window, she could see the river rushing south. Soon afterwards, in the tunnel, the carriage went dark, and Astrid got up and made her way to the toilet.

The door was locked.

She knocked.

"Alright, don't nag," came a man's voice.

The train rattled out of the tunnel. It was light again. She was waiting impatiently in the corridor. To her left were the fields down to the river and to her right the mountain wall.

If he didn't hurry now, she wouldn't manage to get off at Fåvang, and her father would be left standing on the platform worrying. Asking questions.

At last she heard the toilet flush. The red stripe on the lock changed to green. An elderly man in grey wadmal trousers and a thick jacket came out.

She went in and locked the door. The man's strong odour hung on the air. Astrid took a thin screw from her pocket, opened the toilet lid, put the screw in a hole on the inside of the seat and prised out a wooden plug that had until then been invisible. Behind it was a cavity. She took a metal cylinder, as thin as a cigarette, pressed it into the hole and replaced the plug. Then she opened the lid of a little jam jar, and with a stick she smeared faeces around the plug and down over the porcelain.

She peered out of the gap at the top of the frosted window. She would be in Fåvang in a few minutes.

She began making a copy from memory of the drawing she

had put in the cylinder. It looked like a cigar with a lump on top and wheels at the front. She described it as some kind of torpedo or one-man submarine.

There was a knock on the door.

Astrid froze.

"Ticket control!"

"One minute," Astrid said. "I'm going to Fåvang. I've got a ticket."

Hurriedly she finished writing her description, almost certain that her comments matched Fløteren's. *30 units. Through transport towards Namsos. Soft tarpaulin over camouflaged iron frame. Car wheels. Circa 8 metres. Various coiled ropes in addition.* She folded the drawing quickly, shoved it down past her midriff and under her petticoat.

Breathless, she got off at Fåvang. Her father was standing beside the Reo, waiting.

"What did t' doctor say?" he asked.

"Everything's fine," Astrid said. "Women's stuff."

Jehans didn't ask why she had a suitcase with her. He probably presumed she had women's stuff in it.

"D'ye want to drive?"

Astrid shook her head. The train picked up speed, and she heard the whistling in the rails fade away. Before it passed Lillestrøm, somebody would go to check if there was anything behind the wooden plug under the toilet seat. That being the case, he would take the message and put it in a toilet seat on the Stockholm train. At the Swedish border, the Germans would search the train and any luggage and chase people out of the toilets. They had never found the postbox in the toilet seat. Once the train had crossed the border, a passenger would get on board and visit the toilet. Find the cylinder and pass the message to a Norwegian office in Stockholm. Everything was organised by the group who had at the start been nameless, but were now called XU, without anyone quite agreeing what it meant.

Talking to her father felt awkward, and she blamed a stomach ache.

"Father. Could ye drive me up t' Hekne on yer way t' the Colonial?"

"Sommat the matter?"

"Just a bit tired."

Astrid could think only about her urgent message. The drawing on the train would not be there before the next day. A lot could go wrong. It could be lost, or clumsily interpreted.

Which was why they had agreed that she should send a message by radio as well. Then a high-ranking middleman would go to Fløteren and get his description of the weapons load. If he found it of significance, he could ask the British Air Force to bomb the train.

He had behaved so oddly, Fløteren. Had seemed so uneasy. He thought there had been people outside his house on the previous night. Before they parted, he had said: "If the middleman doesna' get in touch wi' me, Astrid, ye shall be next in line."

"What do you mean?" she had said.

"Be at t' shop tomorrow. If a man comes in and asks t' buy yellow ski wax and two seven-øre stamps, ye mun give him the drawing."

Ten minutes later, Astrid clipped on Mari Slåen's skis. They were flat skis. Size nine. Too long really, but they did not sink through loose snow. Besides, she had lost weight over the last year, so they carried her well. The transmitter in her backpack smelled of sheep. She had hidden it in the byre, as the warmth helped the batteries stay ready.

Astrid went between the forest and the well-frequented path below, where the snow was tight-packed from other skiers, making her tracks harder to follow. When she reached the slopes, she felt the skis grow slippery, and she was cross with herself for not taking the time to wax them appropriately for the weather.

And what would her excuse be?

She ought to have set up some marten traps to have an excuse for being here in the forest if she was arrested. Ought, ought. Too many oughts.

Her anxiety was accompanied by an increasing sadness. That from now on she would always be alone. That nobody would get near her again. A sort of magnetic field would push everything away instead of drawing them closer. A consequence, perhaps, of this perpetual secrecy, all the little lies. Of keeping a half-metre distance from everything and everyone. Because everyone could be someone other than who they presented themselves as. Because she was other than the person she presented herself as.

The terrain was steeper now. The snow deeper. Difficult to negotiate. She climbed the slope with her skis in a herringbone pattern until she came to the more open plains near the seters, where the radio signals would run freely. She had sent a message from here earlier, and it had arrived safely.

There was a sudden noise, and something moved in a spruce tree. She flung herself down then realised it was a capercaillie. A while later she saw two black grouse high above the trees. They were headed towards the village.

She went out onto a slope, planted one of her skis in the snow, fixed the antenna to the binding and threw the antenna cable down. The snow was blowing. She bent down and raised the antenna towards the other ski. Standing waist deep in snow she wired up the radio with numb fingers. Put on the headphones. A vacuum tube began to glow. The needle on the ammeter moved, chattering sounds changed to hissing. She turned the frequency dial.

All she had to do now was wait for the radio tube to be warm enough.

Now.

She sent the call signal that identified her.

yarrow

And waited.

The headphones crackled. The Stockholm office came in loud and clear.

anemone

Astrid quickly looked at her watch and started sending.

hello

The falling snow went into the Morse key. A Morse code sounded in her headphone, interrupting her transmission.

qsd

This code meant her message had failed. She must collect herself. Transmit dainty, as Fløteren called it.

She started again. Looked at the time. The receivers had picked up the signal now. How fast could the Germans get someone up here, on skis, in this impregnable territory? In fifteen minutes perhaps, if the alarm reached the parsonage.

Hello fru ro

She waited. A few seconds. Then confirmation came in the headphones. Message received.

Astrid got up and tried to snatch the antenna down from the ski above her, but as she did so the ski came with it and slipped past her with a swish. She wrapped the cable around her waist, stuffed the radio in her backpack and waded after the ski, which was caught in a juniper bush. The ski binding was full of snow. She scraped it clean with the spike on her ski pole, put it on and continued. She pulled out the antenna and threw it behind a huge rock. Her heart was beating so hard she could feel it in her throat. Reaching a corridor between trees, she took out the radio, and, on the move, she heaved it towards a spot where she hoped it was out of sight.

It was a bad throw. The radio shouldn't be that close to her ski tracks! She went back to fetch it, and on the next downhill slope flung it behind a tree.

Her heart was beating more calmly now. If only it wasn't for the empty backpack. Who would come up here with an empty backpack?

The terrain was narrower now and she knew she was near the road.

Then she heard a truck. She knew by the hum of the engine that it was petrol-fuelled. A military vehicle. German. They were dangerously quiet because they had good engines and twin exhaust pipes. The noise was getting closer. Between the tree trunks she saw it. A small all-terrain vehicle with a dish-shaped antenna on the roof. She crouched down in the snow. Or should she just move on? So as not to look guilty?

It was so close now that she heard the creak of rubber tyres on snow.

The truck stopped. Left to idle, the engine hummed. Then fell quiet. Astrid heard a door being opened. Hiding behind some snow-laden spruces, she moved her head carefully to see.

Three German soldiers. They had got out, leaving the car doors open. Two men were walking uphill towards them. A soldier and a civilian in a knitted sweater. The soldier held a huge device in front of his stomach. It hung from a strap about his neck. He stopped and clearly adjusted something.

A snowflake landed on her eyelash. She waited a moment before blinking it away.

Snow. The brother of flight. Let it snow. As much as possible. As fast as possible.

Astrid kept perfectly still. Thought about the reindeer hunt. About what her father had said.

It be movement that gives us away. Both hunter and animal.

As he got closer, she saw that the civilian was Jon Mossen. If they saw her and pointed their guns at her, she would have no choice but to stand up. Pretend she had taken a tumble. Say she got scared. Was out checking the marten traps. Yes, in the middle of the day, she'd forgotten to do it this morning. Had a fall, was wet through, so clumsy, yes. Then they would arrest her.

She lay low and listened.

Muffled voices. An exchange in German. Vehicle doors slammed. The engine started, and they drove away uphill.

Astrid got up carefully to check if they had put a guard in place. Nobody. Unless he was hidden from view by the bank of cleared snow.

She lifted her ski poles and sped down the slope, double-poling hard. She reached a vantage point with a view of the topmost farms of the village and the surrounding roads. She had eaten nothing before setting off, and now everything flickered around her.

At last she came to a ski track. She changed direction and headed for the Colonial, where she dashed into the warm back room, tore off her outer clothes and wet shirt and borrowed Ada Borgen's dry sweater. She sat in there for an eternity before she could go out and serve, and continued to sweat despite being frozen through.

Fru Nyfløt came in, wanting coffee substitute and a soup bone. She was wearing a shapeless coat of grey dog fur, a common enough sight in Butangen now. With the winter being so cold and clothes in mercilessly short supply, many a farm dog was given eternal life as a jacket or coat.

Reaching for the coffee, Astrid stopped. Jon Mossen was outside. Still in his knitted sweater, he must have come by car, as there was no snow on his shoulders. He had a stranger with him wearing a blue-grey jacket. They came in and stood by the door. Mossen crossed his arms.

Ada Borgen made a point of not greeting them.

"And milk," Fru Nyfløt said. She had a one-year-old and was entitled to an extra ration of milk.

"'Tis . . . all gone, I'm afraid," Astrid said. "We'll – I'll put some aside for thee."

Jon Mossen stepped forward.

"It in't permitted t' set goods aside," he said. "She mun get in line like anybody else."

Astrid did not answer.

"Where were ye earlier t'day?" said Jon Mossen.

"That has nowt to do with ye."

Astrid felt her body go rigid. There was nothing left of the old Jon Mossen. Nor, perhaps, of the old her.

"But ye went out, I takes it. How else would yer shoes be so wet?"

Astrid swallowed. How could he see her shoes behind the counter?

"Up t' Hekne," said Astrid. "Took a wander up there."

"How d' yer shoes get that wet just goin' t' Hekne?"

The man in the blue-grey jacket joined him now at the counter.

"Because I have t' wear t' same pair of shoes every damn day. There's a war on, Mossen, in case ye hadna' noticed!"

"So how come yer ma didna' know where ye were earlier? I asked her."

"She didna' want t' say," said Astrid. "Not to thee. Not t' a man."

"*Not t' a man?*"

Two more customers came in. Astrid made sure to say it loud:

"I went up t' fetch cloths!"

"Cloths?"

"*The curse, Mossen!* It came on. So I needed cloths, and I had some back home. I couldna' exactly go knitting them here."

Fru Nyfløt laughed. Jon Mossen swallowed and took a step

back. When faced with something as revolting as menstruation even a Hird had to back off.

The stranger stepped forward. He held out an identity card and said he was from the state police.

Customers started to leave. Fru Nyfløt left without her shopping.

"So, ye have your monthly," the stranger said. "I take it ye can give us proof o' that? Join me in the back here and show me the cloth. Or I can arrest and examine thee."

The last customer hurried out. The door slammed, sending a blast of cold air to the counter where Astrid and Ada Borgen stood. A shopping list floated to the floor.

Ada took Astrid by the shoulders. "Ye shall hold off her!"

The policeman did not budge. She was uncertain whether or not she had seen him before. There was something too smooth about him, his features were utterly nondescript, he looked like everybody and nobody.

"Very well," Astrid said. "'Twas true earlier today and 'tis true now. I shan't take off the cloth out here in the shop. Follow me in t' staff changing room. You can take yer pistol out if ye so wish. If ye are that scared o' me. Aye. I can see it there, under yer jacket."

And he did. The stranger took a blue-black pistol out of a shoulder holster and went with her. Jon Mossen opened the door for them, followed them into the changing room and warned her that if she jumped from the window, she'd be shot.

Astrid went into the cubicle, closed the door, and sat down.

She had just about managed to stop her body trembling when she remembered that her skis were standing outside. And skis weren't needed to go up to Hekne.

There wasn't much time.

The idea came to her suddenly, and it was good, but she must do it quickly.

Quickly and quietly she opened the little cabinet where she kept some spare cloths. She was the only one who needed them. Ada and Widow Fløter were "past breedin'", as they often joked. And there were the nail scissors.

Just do it. Skirts and petticoat up. Pants down.

Open up a fold of the thin skin in her crotch, set the scissors against the skin, nip the fold and hold the scream inside.

The pain, it was so damned *painful*!

Not enough blood.

She pinched off the loose flap of skin, opened up another fold, bit her lips and snipped.

The pain ripped through her. She pressed the cloth on the wound to catch some blood. It soaked into the knitted material, but looked less impressive than she hoped. She squeezed the cuts to get more out.

"What are ye doin' in there?" the man yelled. There was a hint of a Trøndelag accent in his voice.

She pulled her skirts down, tore open the door and held the cloth up to the policeman's face. There was only a small bloodstain on it, but before he could say anything, she said:

"Like I said, I changed it not long ago!"

She looked at Jon Mossen and said: "Not much of a world ye are fighting for, when grown men stand and watch o'er a girl wi' the curse."

The policeman opened his lapel and put his pistol back in its holster. Looked at the cloth and wrinkled his nose. Did he know enough about women to tell the difference between normal blood and menstrual blood with its iron-like odour?

"Disgusting," he said. They were turning to leave, but stopped and glared at her. Glaring back at them, she cleared her throat.

"'Tis the only cloth I have," she said. "So, may I go now and put it where it belongs?"

*

Hungry, but with no appetite. Couldn't it all just end?

They stood at the kitchen bench. Astrid's mother asked why Mossen had been looking for her. She lied. Said he had made a mistake. Kristine knew she was lying.

Astrid went to the bathroom, found a bandage, wrapped it around her crotch. Sat on her bed.

Eirik came up and said there was food.

Carrot soup. Flatbread. The last of a pork knuckle. They had plenty of potatoes, thank the Lord, they had plenty of potatoes.

The phone rang in the hallway. Esther got up. A duty nobody must ever take from her, where, helped by the shrill ringing, she quickly crossed the floor, which Eirik had strict orders to keep clear so she wouldn't trip. Out in the hallway, she could tell, by the warmth or coolness of the air she set in motion, whether or not the front door was open. She picked up the receiver, wavelets of brown hair falling over neat, pretty shoulders.

It was usual to call at suppertime, for folk were generally home. And then everyone would sit as they did now. Knife and fork idle, wondering who the call was for, and chewing what was in their mouths, so as to be ready to talk, because it was so expensive to call.

Esther did not talk for long. She stood a while in the hallway shadows before appearing in the doorway.

"Fløteren," she sobbed. "'Tis Fløteren."

Kristine dropped her fork. Jehans stood up. Little Eirik watched.

"Took his own life," Esther said. "This afternoon. That was his mother."

Jehans put his head in his hands. Then he lifted his gaze and stared at Astrid. She tried to hold back. Then had to nod. Nobody moved. Esther coaxed the cat to her and took Eirik out into the living room.

Darkness fell as they cried. Kristine went over and drew the blackout curtains, and sat back down in the certain knowledge that from this time on they would carry a heavy rock with them wherever they went.

The food went cold. Left untouched before them.

The clock struck seven.

Suddenly Esther burst in. She took Astrid by the shoulder.

"Sister, dear! 'Tis starting," she said. "I am certain. 'Tis starting."

Astrid looked up.

"What?"

"Sommat bad. Worse than bad. I felt it when ye showed me the Weave. Ye mun go now. Shuttle as fast as ye may, Astrid. Now."

Kristine turned off the kitchen lights. Went over to the window, pulled the curtain a crack and looked out. Astrid joined her. Nothing but the snow-covered apple trees in the garden, and, below them, Lake Løsnes glinting in the winter moonlight.

Pelle rose on his hind legs, put his single front paw on the window ledge and growled.

"Go! Ye have gotta go, I tell thee!" Esther said.

Astrid saw the headlights of a car further down on the road. Lights that were then turned off.

She hurried to the hall and flung on Esther's white anorak. Opened the breast pocket and filled it with the potatoes from the plates.

"Ma. Tarald's blue sketchbook in the second top drawer. There's a drawing. Ye shall see 'tis not his. 'Tis o' some sort of submarine or torpedo."

Quickly she told them about the man who was coming to ask for yellow ski wax and two seven-øre stamps.

"Clear the plates and set the chairs so it looks like there were only four at the table. Say ye havena' seen me since I was up at the shop. D'nay try to come up with fancy explanations. Just say I have gone. Or they'll burn Hekne down."

There was no time for hugs. No long glances or solemn words. Astrid put on her wet ski boots without lacing them up. She and Kristine ran through the hallway to the corpse hatch. This year, as in previous years, they had dug a tunnel behind it, so Eirik could enjoy their old game.

But also with escape in mind.

"Hurry, Astrid my girl."

Kristine tore open the hatch, and snow cascaded over the floor. Behind it was cold, hollow darkness.

The last thing Kristine gave her was the one thing she could give. A mother's gaze upon a daughter who has done what she must.

It was a quarter past two in the morning when Astrid reached the treeline. She lay down beneath the wide branches of a spruce tree. The mountain ahead was visible as a faint light with no separation between heaven and earth.

In the first hour she had repeatedly turned and looked back at the village to see if it was lit up by a farmhouse fire. But Butangen had remained dark and neither were there any gunshots.

Not, at least, from the distance within which a gunshot is audible.

Next to her was a backpack filled with equipment. On top of it, the Hekne Krag. She pulled out Kai Schweigaard's plaid travel blanket and wrapped it around her. Making sure to pull out her wristwatch. It was vital to know how much daylight and darkness were available to her.

It had taken her seven hours to get this far. Her backpack and skis had been waiting for her at the end of the snow tunnel. A couple of hundred metres away was the tree in which the Hekne Krag was hanging. With this slung over her back, she had started out on the route she had been planning for weeks, before finally lying here to rest, in view of the mountaintop in the distance.

She had worked up a sweat and her back was freezing.

The question was whether this was the right mountaintop. She wasn't quite sure where she was, only that the forest had ended, and that Saubua and Kvia were now somewhere out there in the dark. Beyond them was Imsdalen, and beyond that, far beyond, was Sweden.

The wind was cold.

Astrid waited for the morning light as a new brand of fear came and went. Anxiety for those at home. Remorse over all the risks she had taken. And beneath that a more tangible and immediate fear. The question of whether someone was following her.

At last, it was light enough to prepare the Krag. She unfolded the blanket, laid the bolt and the magazine parts in a row, and took out her cleaning kit. She was cold and had to work fast, but as she turned the tin of paint thinner to dampen the felt, it slipped.

"No! No!"

A large splash of thinner ran over her hand. She plunged it into the snow to get the solvent off, but it was too late.

It had soaked into her skin.

She bit back the swear words. It was minus twenty out now, so the solvent would also be minus twenty. It had gone deep, and she knew her fingers would be frostbitten.

She pressed her hand against her stomach. Managed to warm it up a bit. Worked on. The solvent made her dizzy. She cleaned the grease from the gun parts and mounted the magazine. Cursed the hard leaf springs, cursed the snow that showered over her from the branches above, but eventually managed to draw the cleaning cord through the barrel and twist the bolt into the mechanism.

She clicked it three times.

Each time the Krag made the same sound it had made before the war. She took out six cartridges, and put five in the magazine and one in the chamber.

Safety catch on.

She could still barely see ahead of her, just a strange half-light. Taking her compass, she tried to plot a course.

Her fingers stung.

She wanted to cry. Everything she had done thus far on her journey she had rehearsed in her mind countless times. Including what she would do if she met the Germans. But she had not prepared herself for the grief that would accompany her fear, grief for Fløteren. Nor this anxiety about the others. Having risked their lives for a single radio message that she could not even be sure had arrived!

But: *If we mun, so mun we.*

Her ski bindings were made of fresh leather. The back straps had new springs. Her backpack contained enough provisions to get her to Sweden. Maps. Matches. Ski wax for grainy snow, dry snow and wet snow. Her father's old binoculars.

The big question: go straight over the mountain, in full view of the soldiers on the surrounding peaks with better binoculars than hers and radio communication? Or spend the whole day battling through the undergrowth in Samdalen below, difficult terrain that would drain her of strength and delay her arrival in Imsdalen by hours?

Astrid thought about yesterday. The capercaillie and grouse she had seen flying down towards Butangen. She remembered something her father had said, something he had in turn learned from old Adolf. "When the birds o' the forest head for t' village, it shall be stormy weather. Ye may count on't."

If there was in fact a storm, nobody would be able to see her crossing the mountain.

Astrid scraped the snow off her skis, rubbed them with a softer wax, slowly ate the crumbled potatoes from her anorak pocket, then got up and headed towards the grey mountain. When daylight came, she should be able to see exactly where she was and plot out a new route. If the sun came out, she would dig herself into the snow and lie there until dark. Freeze the day away.

She got into a rhythm and began to warm up. The snow was carrying her well. The skis swished in the small dips. Before her she saw the mountain she knew.

As she went she wondered again at the strangeness of the light this morning, a grey shimmer that was neither one thing nor the other, a curious battle between day and night.

Firebirds

It was a grey morning and standing before them were endless rows of bomber planes. All painted in mottled green and black. The most powerful aircraft built on British soil. The four-engine Avro Lancaster with a wingspan of thirty-four yards. Four twelve-cylinder Merlin engines. More than 7,000 horsepower. A payload of twenty metric tons. Range from Great Britain to all Germany's borders and back.

It was unusual for a civilian to be allowed a tour of an air base, but Victor Harrison was one of the few men alive to have flown with the original Royal Flying Corps in 1914. Now he wasn't sure what to think. These gigantic holds were never meant to carry twenty tons of goods. Or twenty tons of food. Just twenty tons of destruction.

These were warplanes of aluminium and steel. With more power than human beings should have in their control. Long machine-gun barrels stuck out from glass domes in the nose, tail and back, and the bomb hatches looked big enough to drop a railway carriage from. The landing wheels reached his shoulders. An airman sitting in the cockpit was so high up, it was like looking at a man on the balcony of a house. Standing close by were some grey fighters, like wagtails around a heron.

Despite all his warnings, Edgar and Alastair had both joined the RAF Bomber Command. He had doubtless failed to find the right words, the words to describe how it felt to fly a bomber.

"Well," he said at last, "beautiful they are not."

"No warplane is built to be beautiful," said Alastair.

"The Spitfire is beautiful," Edgar said.

Victor wished they would change the conversation. He knew his sons well enough to know this discussion was going to end in a dark place, without their noticing it was headed that way. As much as his sons were agreed on most things, they argued about everything. They debated as though blow by blow, and he knew that soon one would say that a Lancaster wasn't ugly for what it was but for what it did, to which the other would reply that if a warplane was ugly for what it did, then the men who flew them must also be ugly.

He didn't want to hear them say that.

Edgar had left Finlaggan when he turned eighteen, Alastair on his birthday the year after. Alastair had arrived at Bomber Command three weeks ago.

"You should come up in her, Father."

Victor felt regret the second he climbed inside. The Lancaster was dark, gloomy, unwelcoming, brutish in its proportion. A rain-sodden, medieval fortress. With the smell of a musty, cold basement, plus a whiff of new-welded iron, impregnated leather, motor grease and petrol. A smell he knew would always be strong because these planes never had time to grow old. Nor did the pilots who flew them.

The brothers spoke of the plane as they would a motorcycle, but he noted they were holding the greater truth under. Alastair showed him the navigation board and instruments that guided them to their targets thousands of miles into Germany and over the cities thousands of feet below.

"Will you sit at the controls, Father?"

"I suppose I ought."

He tried to play along. There was no point making them anxious. He acquainted himself with all the switches and instruments and nodded as Edgar went through the start procedure that ensured all four engines had equal power.

"We lock her wheels and increase the revs way more than the manual suggests. Have to let the propellers really fight against the brakes. With so much force that she pulls away and *wants* to go."

"Does it ever happen?" Victor said. "That the plane starts to go off course because one of her engines is weak?"

"It's happened once. Ever since then, we have tested her so hard that everything in here shakes."

"Doesn't the problem show up on the tachometers?"

"No, you have to give the engines a proper load. So hard that the fuselage shakes and the navigator's map flaps about."

Victor could not get excited. But he covered it up and did what any father of two war pilots should. He lauded the plane and pointed to all the innovations that had been introduced since he had flown the Bleriot in the infancy of flight.

Back when a plane meant play and acrobatics.

Before two world wars had led humanity to this. To the Lancaster. To something unique in the history of combat and the art of engineering.

A night bomber.

Attacks on ships, tanks, columns of soldiers and any moving target still had to be carried out in daylight. But Europe's cities lay where they had been for many centuries. Destroying them was a night mission. Colossuses like this could fly high above the clouds and drop thousands of bombs through those same clouds.

He looked at his sons. The conversation had dried up.

Edgar ran his fingers through his curly hair. Cleared his throat. Then Alastair cleared his throat too.

All three men knew the tough reality.

Five years of intense fighting had taught Bomber Command that the ideal mode of attack was if 700 planes dropped their entire bomb load in just fifteen minutes. Any more, and a queue would form in the air and they risked colliding or being hit by bombs from the planes above them. If a mission took longer, enemy air defences on the ground had time to home in on them.

The pathfinders came first, flying low and dropping coloured flares that landed and burned in streets and on rooftops. They were harmless in themselves, but anyone who saw them was about to die. These flares were markers that showed the bombers where to drop their load. Greatest damage was done by the incendiary bombs, and they were always mixed with explosive bombs, which smashed buildings and flung bricks into the streets, delaying the firefighters on the ground.

Edgar had said that he did not look down when his bomb load was released. "They go down, whether you look or not," he had said. It was never talked about, but Victor knew they were given amphetamines to cope with such long missions. The Germans used them all the time. Eyes widened, vigilance artificially sharp, fear minimised.

The Fokker. Why, thought Victor Harrison, did I ever take them up in the Fokker? The average lifespan for a crew here is three months. On the other hand, my boys have a better chance of survival because I made them good pilots. I might wish they hadn't been pilots at all. Or, that they were pilots, but this bloody war had been avoided.

Memories flashed into his mind.

One day towards the end of the last war, he had been on the ground and seen a bomber coming in to land, long after the others. The sun was up, making everything too visible. It was a Handley Page on which they had, as a trial, installed a glass dome for a machine-gunner to sit in. The plane was riddled with holes. It came sailing down with a trail of smoke behind it that went in huge loops, mapping the despair of the pilot who had lost control. It landed at an angle, so that the wing hit the runway and snapped. The plane then spun around, and its landing wheels were torn off and rolled and bounced towards the onlookers. The scraping of metal on asphalt sounded as though the plane itself was screaming. Before he died, the pilot must have managed to shut off the fuel, since the fire in the engine went out, and two men threw themselves out and reached safety.

But what they all saw, the men on the ground, was the glass dome with the gunner inside. They couldn't understand it. The sun was making the glass dome sparkle ruby red. Then it dawned on them that they were looking at the gunner's remains. His blood was frozen to the glass. The firefighters smashed the dome and hosed it down. They went over the asphalt with rakes, and what was recovered was what was buried.

That day Victor learned why the coffin lids were so firmly screwed down when a bomber airman was to be buried. So the family would never know there were sandbags in the coffin. To give it a decent weight.

Victor and the boys climbed down from the plane and walked towards the officers' mess. The airfield was busy with mechanics, fuel trucks and trucks carrying bombs. The officers' mess was fairly empty and smelled as empty officers' messes do. Stale air from the day before, tobacco smoke and Scotch. Beyond the canteen they found a little room with a divan. Victor cited his painful knee and said he must take a rest. There was a bookcase beside him, and he noted that the tattiest books were the poetry collections. He was unsurprised. It was easy in any officers' mess to distinguish between the bomber pilots and fighter pilots. The fighter pilots stood at the bar and talked animatedly. The crew of a bomber plane sat alone, in silence.

Some even read poetry.

He hoped his sons would never reach a point where they wanted to read poetry.

Edgar and Alastair carried in two chairs and sat beside their father. Victor pretended to be asleep on the divan, and lay listening while the brothers talked with each other.

A ruse they had always fallen for.

Old Mother Reindeer

She had been going for an hour when she caught sight of two other skiers. Two tiny figures in a massive swathe of snow-covered mountain. Tiny figures that were gradually getting bigger.

Nobody was ever out this early.

They must have stayed the night in the Saubua cabin. She pictured them climbing onto the roof at first light to scout the terrain with binoculars.

The weather was still undecided, the visibility rather too good. If I can see them, they can see me.

She turned and went back in her own tracks towards the

edge of the forest, the two men lagging behind. So they must be skiing on loose snow.

This was also a sign that they were not out on a cosy day trip. In thirty to forty-five minutes they could reach and follow her tracks. The misfortune of deep snow. The hunter always followed in the tracks of the prey, while the prey exhausted itself making a trail for the hunter.

Astrid reached the forest and came across an open stretch. A frozen marsh. She could not recall having passed it the night before.

Not much time to think. She crossed the marsh deliberately so that her ski tracks would be easy to see. From there she went along the forest edge until she was almost back where she had started. If her ski tracks were shaped like a fishhook, she was now in the barb. She found a small hill with a view over her own tracks. She put her backpack down in front of her. Removed the Krag's muzzle cover and lifted the bolt to ensure that the cartridge had not frozen in the chamber.

Her frostbitten fingers had been hurting. Now they began to itch.

Nothing to do now but wait.

Just eat snow. And feel this accursed, unnecessary frostbite.

A colourless winter landscape. Nothing but grades of darkness and white and the blued gunmetal of the Krag.

The wind picked up. A bitter blast. February cold. Still not overcast enough to give her cover.

There.

Movement between the moss-covered birches.

Two men. Both in ordinary skiing gear. Loose anoraks. Wool hats and breeches. One with something sticking up behind his back. A rifle on a strap.

They stopped at the edge of the marsh and looked out across it.

The Krag was resting on her backpack. She trained it in their direction, weighed up the fors and againsts, but could not find a good enough *for*.

They started out in her tracks, and soon they were in the middle of the marsh.

Astrid realised she had lain there too long waiting to shoot. She was unable to control her breathing, and the two figures danced across her gunsight. She took her finger from the trigger, lifted her cheek from the rifle butt and breathed into the snow. Asking herself if this might be for the best.

When she looked up, they were gone. She was furious with herself.

Ye let the chance slip from thee. They have followed thee armed wi' guns, and what do they want with these guns when they catch thee?

More long minutes. Light gusts of wind. Loose snow drifted across the barrel of her gun.

Her fingers throbbed with pain. She shoved her firing hand in the waistband of her ski pants to warm it against her belly.

Then she spotted a man at the outer edge of the marsh, far away from her ski tracks. He might have been standing there for some time. Either the two men had conferred with each other and parted ways, or a third man had joined them.

Astrid followed him with her gaze. It must be another man, since the first two had loose anoraks. This man had a ski jacket, the type with elastic at the waist. Prepared to shoot, wearing no mittens, and holding his gun on an angle across his chest. A short weapon. Magazine at the bottom. Probably a German submachine gun. The British ones had magazines that stuck out to the side.

He raised a pair of binoculars.

Astrid released the safety catch on the Hekne Krag. Placed the butt against her shoulder. Found the man in her gunsight. Breathed out.

A life there before her. A man, a father perhaps, somebody's son at least.

Her father's voice. *Good shots be those that kill right away.*

She took a breath in and held it. Set the foresight on the centre of his chest. The man was aiming his binoculars straight at her. He saw her. Letting go of the binoculars, he reached for his ski poles.

Astrid did not hear the blast from the Krag. Just saw the snow whirl up in front of the muzzle. Reloaded the rifle and tried to find him in the gunsight again.

He was gone.

She looked around quickly. Listened for any sound, but her hearing was temporarily dulled. Something moved where he had stood. The man got to his feet, leaned on his ski pole for support, but lost hold, slid a little way on his skis, then keeled over and collapsed. She thought she saw splatters of blood in the snow behind him. He let out a long howl and tried to drag himself onto his knees, but fell forward again. His screams grew steadily clearer as the ringing in her ears faded. The man lay quivering, and for a time it looked like his clothes were moving on their own. Then he fell silent and lay still.

There was a shout somewhere to her left.

Astrid moved her gaze slowly from side to side. Registered everything, including that a slanting hole to her right marked the place where the cartridge case had melted itself down into the snow.

No more shouts.

There was a rustling over the way, she took aim, but saw that all the surrounding branches were swaying in the same direction, and that it matched that of the wind. Breathing out she took her finger from the trigger.

Which of us can hold out the longest? It's vital it be me. She reached into her pocket for a cartridge. Her father had told her that the Krag was the only rifle that could be fed more bullets while loaded, but he had never imagined a situation where such a thing would be necessary.

Quietly, she flipped the magazine lid to the side and slipped the cartridge into place.

Around her was nothing but spindly dwarfed trees, the February snow and an overcast sky. Everything was as the belt between forest and mountain had always been, nobody had come here except the grouse and the wolverine and reindeer.

But then again, she thought.

Death was always here at the treeline.

The wind blew. Snow began to fall. Astrid felt calmer now, knowing that this weather might offer her some cover. It was cold lying here, poised, ready to shoot, fingers bare. They were white now and had started to peel.

Down at the edge of the marsh, the snow began its slow burial. The dead man was white across his back, but black in the folds of his clothes and where the warmth of his body had melted the snow.

The others were doubtless lying low watching the corpse. Waiting for her to emerge from her hiding place, to check on her victim.

No thanks.

She lay there a little longer. Knowing she had to move on. Soon she would be too cold to shoot accurately.

She waited until the corpse at the end of the marsh was completely white. Rose to crouching, stiff after two hours in the snow. Took the Krag in one hand and her ski poles in the other.

If they were going to shoot, they would shoot soon.

Where had they gone?

She spent a long time soundlessly clipping her skis on. Poles under arms. Hekne Krag in her hands, safety catch off.

She set off in silence. As silently as after a funeral.

She tried to advance calmly. Was no longer too sure of what direction to take. But go she must.

A couple of hundred metres on, she decided to pick up speed. If they fired, she must throw herself down and work out where the shot had come from.

Astrid double-poled with all her strength. She picked out a dwarf birch ahead and got to it before glancing back.

Nobody there. She continued, panting hard, sweating.

At last, she was back at the treeline. The weather was much greyer. The wind made her anorak flap. She stopped and looked about. The loose snow was drifting all around her. No movement. There was nothing to do but ski into open terrain. If a shot came, it would be soon. She put the Krag's strap round her neck, making it easier to get in position to fire, and sped off. Preparing herself mentally to twist down onto one knee in the snow, and use her ski poles as support for the gun to shoot back.

Fifty metres. The Krag thumped into her chest every time she lunged forward.

One hundred metres. Two hundred.

She was safe now. Unless they were extremely good shots.

She took one last look behind her.

Was that two men there at the edge of the forest? She gave it all she had, turned again, and saw them no longer. But then, visibility had lowered with the change in the weather.

Which meant they couldn't see her either.

Astrid followed her compass and found herself on harder snow, which told her she had reached the mountain for real. Stopping to check her compass again, she suddenly threw up. Orange food remains splattered onto Mari Slåen's skis.

Her watch said ten past one now. Fortunately, visibility was still poor. Now that the storm was hiding her, she was grateful for each gust of wind, each flurry of snow, for the frostbite on her cheeks.

Then she heard the noise of a plane. Deep. Steady. It got louder, she crouched down and made herself small.

The plane was close now, but invisible in the grey sky. It must be quite low, because the hum was even clearer than when the bombers had come in April 1940. Or perhaps this was a much larger plane. It stayed over her for a long time, during which she kept stock still. Eventually the noise slowly faded.

Then disappeared completely.

There was a huge German encampment in Koppang on the other side of the mountain, where it was said they had trucks with caterpillar belts that could carry troops over loose snow and up the steep slopes. The best thing she could do now was to reach Orm Setra, or preferably Imsdalen, find a barn and hide there for a day or two.

She got up and went on. Then she sensed a change in the sound of the wind on the snow.

It was no longer coming from the side, instead she felt a rush of cold air from somewhere – from beneath her? She stopped. Was she near a cliff edge?

The weather had cleared a little.

To her left an outcrop began to take shape. Did it have a tall rock marker on top? No, two – but that meant it was—

Nay.

Nay, nay, nay!

This was Suleberg mountain. And the three columns of rock she saw rising along the horizon must be the Suleberg Maidens. Meaning she had gone too far east.

Taking out her compass, she plotted a new course and raced on.

She needed to eat. But this was open terrain, the plane would find her if it returned.

Darkness would fall soon.

Perhaps the plane was not looking for her. She could hope. Though not rely on it.

Food. She needed food. Even though she wasn't hungry. She stopped. Unlaced her backpack and threw the blanket around her. Managed to prise the lid off a can of peas and pork, and ate with her fingers.

The pain was unbearable.

She forced down a few mouthfuls. It tasted of nothing. Onward now. Better to lie half starved in the forest than dead in the mountains. The sweat had accumulated on her back, and she tied Kai's old tartan travel rug over her anorak.

Something stirred in her memory. A presentiment of sorts from another time. Suddenly her skis pitched down, and she fell and landed hard.

A road?

A road for motor vehicles? Up here? In the mountains? With metre-high banks of snow on either side? Surely the Germans hadn't built any winter roads up here? Or had they perhaps started to build a road, but from the other side? If so, where did it end?

She gathered herself, then hope rose.

She had accompanied her father in these mountains, as her father had once accompanied Adolf. He had talked of how good the winter pastures were for reindeer round here. Perhaps this was a reindeer herd's trail. Reindeer travelled in long, narrow processions, trampling the snow down, making a path reminiscent of a snowploughed road. Always along the same thousand-year-old route. The trail would presumably lead down to the forest, where the herd could graze on mosses and twigs.

Astrid headed down. The surface was hard, and she sped along at high speed, so eager now that she put out a ski pole to draw stripes on the wall of snow. Skiing along in this deep gully, she was hidden from anyone who might be there with their binoculars scouting for her.

She went so fast that her ski wax wore thin, increasing her speed still more. A few dwarf birches stuck out from the snow, indicating that she was approaching the treeline again. Imsdalen was close.

Dusk too.

The rumble of a plane.

She stabbed her poles in harder. Crouched low on her skis. The plane grew louder.

And something massive was coming up behind her. An intangible shift behind a veil of something amorphous. Spatters of grey and white in a continually shifting form. Unreal creatures took shape and loomed in on her. A rush of pelt and bone. Creating and re-creating itself in the snowstorm.

A herd of reindeer. Tightly packed, females with adolescent calves, young bulls and large bulls, with the old matriarch at the front. They charged onwards, their fur caked in snow. The only thing not frozen was their eyes.

The whole herd was fast looming towards her. Like rushing water down a dried riverbed. Only animals in a panic would run like this.

Once again the roar of the engine in the sky was audible. She realised that the airplane had scared them from their grazing grounds.

The herd divided in two as though Astrid were a rock in a stream. One or two animals glanced at her for a split second in passing. They were as terrified as her. Carried a kind of recognition. The same fear of the same enemy.

She crouched down so they would not knock her over. She could see the plane directly above. The Iron Cross on each wing. Skis instead of wheels. A Fieseler Storch. She remembered them from Fløteren's sketches. Strange, long-footed, scout planes that could fly so unnaturally slowly that when people saw them they wondered why they didn't fall from the sky.

She wondered that now. It was hovering up there like a bird of prey. She was in this mass movement of reindeer and hoped she was invisible.

The last reindeer passed her. The plane turned and disappeared. Alone on the trail, she slipped through a storm of animal smells and grey hairs.

Then she heard a shot. And another.

She took the Krag from her shoulder and with the rifle in her hands ploughed on down the slope. She saw something move between the trees. The reindeer herd again.

Their ancient trail had ended, and they were scattered and strutting nervously between the dwarf trees. She came out in a whirl of loose snow and animal tracks. Before her lay a massive grey bundle in convulsions.

A female reindeer with unusual, pale-coloured flecks. An old animal. The matriarch. It was her. The mother of the herd. Shot in the belly and spine. Her blood seeping into the snow, turning it to a red slush. Eyes growing dull.

Astrid could see soldiers further down in the forest. She saw now that they could have shot her ages ago. They wanted her alive.

Drawings of torpedoes were one thing. If she revealed the group's methods of carrying information to Sweden, everything would fall apart. She knew how they tortured the truth out of people. Fløteren had known what awaited him. He had crushed the poison ampoule between his teeth.

The choice flickered in her mind.

Them or me?

The hum of the plane returned. It was hanging in the air directly above her. She turned and fired up at it, reloaded and fired again, then sent two shots down towards the soldiers.

The plane remained there, hanging above her. Something was thrown from the plane and landed in the snow next to her, and a grey-coloured gas seeped out.

Again, she felt her fingers smart. Tomorrow the frostbite would be excruciating.

Only there would be no tomorrow.

Astrid turned the Krag so its barrel pointed upwards. She set its butt in the snow and leaned her head towards the muzzle. Holding it firmly against her temple, she used her ski pole to reach down the length of the rifle.

She pushed on the trigger.

Nothing.

Just a muffled click into the snow.

Sometimes the Hekne Krag is like that. She doesna' wish to kill.

A soldier came up behind her. Then another rose from the loose snow. She had no idea where they had come from, but no matter, she managed to reload. The cartridge slid into place, and again she lowered her head to the muzzle and again she reached for the trigger. Then came the almighty blow. And in that moment when everything was blotted out, she understood why the evening light had been so strange.

It would be a moonless night.

Third Story

Night of Nights

Altar Candles for a Farewell Mass

KRISTINE'S BODY SHOOK WHEN SHE SAID ASTRID'S NAME.

"'Tis impossible to say how it has gone with her. Were gale force winds in t' mountains last night, Kai."

"Kristine. I wish I had some words of God that might help. But I have none right now. Sit here. Give me your hands."

They sat in silence, while the aged log walls of the old midwife's cottage tried to keep out the February weather.

Shortly after Astrid had taken off into the mountains, the Gestapo had arrived at Hekne. They had searched the farm and arrested Jehans. That evening, three Norwegian men had paid a visit to Widow Fløter. The old woman had been sitting, trying to take in her son's death.

"He took cyanide," Kristine sobbed. "Fløteren. And they taunted his mother about it. Told her how he writhed while the foam came from his mouth. That were what they said. These Norwegian menfolk. So they mun have come upon him of a sudden."

Kai Schweigaard shook his head.

That was *not*, he thought, how Butangen folk should meet their death. They should be kicked by a horse. Or perish in childbirth. They should be killed by shrapnel from a rifle fired with a reloaded cartridge. Or drop dead of exhaustion on the kitchen floor as they stirred the porridge. They should drown in swollen rivers with a trout on the hook. Or freeze to death in the mountains with a secret lover. They should fall onto the blade of

Night of Nights

a saw. Or rupture themselves lifting heavy timbers in the forest. They should die when they were eighty with twelve children at their bedside and forty grandchildren out in the hallway.

That's how Butangen folk should die.

Not by poison. Not by torture.

"Where did they take Jehans?" Schweigaard asked.

"I hasna' a clue," Kristine said. "There were fisticuffs out in t' forecourt, and they kicked him and put him in handcuffs and dragged him out to a car."

Kai Schweigaard was still holding Kristine's hands. They were no warmer.

"I mun go now, Kai," she said.

"I'll come straight after you," he said. "I can't sit around here."

He downed a morsel of food and set off, following her tracks down towards the village. He could almost read the despair in her footprints. The wind blasted. It began to snow, gradually obscuring the path. He walked faster, but the snow was merciless, and soon her tracks were gone, as though Kristine had vanished from the world while he desperately sought her.

He came down to Butangen, but could barely recognise it.

There wasn't a villager to be seen. The milk truck stood snowed under by the dairy factory. There were soldiers standing guard outside the parsonage.

Schweigaard went to the church and let himself in. It was months since he had come in here. In the sacristy cigarette butts lay in a white saucer. Haffergård must have been in here, smoking Teddy Virginias. Comforting himself, perhaps. Church attendance had fallen to almost nil after Mossen had cleared the way for the Nazi priest.

Schweigaard went out into the nave and paused by the altar rail. There was complete silence. He felt a faint rush of blood in his ears and remembered when Astrid had come up through the trapdoor after seeing the Hekne sisters' grave. He folded his hands and wondered where she was now.

On his way home, he found that the Colonial was open. He went in. There were no customers at the counter.

"You could close the shop today, you know," Kai said. "Even you could stay closed today."

"Not t'day," said Kristine. "Certainly not t'day. Ye should be off now, Kai. Nay let yerself be seen here."

He paused at the door. An unknown car was coming down the road with a stranger at the wheel. The car stopped in front of the shop, but the driver did not get out. Kai Schweigaard met Kristine's gaze and headed back towards the old midwife's cottage.

He woke up to Fru Røhme stoking the wood stove.

"Herr Pastor," said Fru Røhme. "There has been a death."

Schweigaard sat upright. He had collapsed onto the narrow box bed fully dressed. He took out his pocket watch and saw that it was just past midnight. Fru Røhme lit a candle. The cold rose from her coat. Her face was as white as a sheet, and she must have come without a hat, for her grey hair was wet with snow.

"Please don't say it's Astrid," said Schweigaard.

"We canna' be sure. The body were laid out in a pulk. Reckons it were brought down from the mountains."

She said that two Norwegian men had arrived with the corpse. Herr Røhme and she had watched from the kitchen window. "The body were so covered in rime that it were impossible to see if it were Astrid. The Nazi priest mun have been informed, for he rang us at suppertime and bid us prepare his room, make up his bed and thaw the ground out for a grave. Haffergård shall hold a funeral tomorrow evening."

"A funeral in the evening? What kind of nonsense is that?"

Night of Nights

"We canna' make head nor tail o' it. Happen there be some reason for haste. But we canna' tell what."

"But the ground won't thaw in a day! Listen, Fru Røhme. It's been almost thirty hours since Astrid left. Do you think it was her in the pulk?"

"'Tis possible. But then surely they wouldna' make such a fuss and get the Nazi priest here so quick?"

Schweigaard wondered if it could be Jehans who had died, but that didn't match with sending for Haffergård. His confusion must have shone through, since Fru Røhme threw her hands out and said: "Folks tells us nowt these days! We knows only what we sees from the kitchen window. Please come tomorrow, Herr Pastor. At first light. Be a pastor t' us."

She went. Schweigaard stayed in his bed, unable to move. That night strong winds shook the little log cottage. They lasted for an hour. At half past three he sat before the wood stove, lit it and folded his hands. He was unspeakably tired.

It was noon before he managed to trudge down to the village. His shoes leaked, the February wind was icy, there had been heavy snow overnight, and the path had not been cleared of snow. Crows flew over the spruce trees. Beyond that there was no life. A clouded sky and large, lazy snowflakes cast a blue haze over everything around him.

He stopped outside the parsonage and looked up at his old study. Something moved behind the window.

Unusually enough, a light was shining from a solitary basement window in the corner. But surely that was just a potato cellar?

Parked by the *stabbur* was a green Opel.

Kai Schweigaard walked on to the church. So white in the white snow. From the gate and up he recognised Herr Røhme's immaculate snow-clearing. Snow piled equally high on both sides, crisp edges. He followed the path up to the church, then waded out into the loose snow to see Astrid Hekne's grave.

Her stone was gone.

He walked agitatedly around in his own tracks. The stone was nowhere to be seen, even though he knew exactly where it was, this grave he had visited for so many decades. He pulled off his mittens and dug with his hands in the snow, and eventually found something hard.

How had it fallen over? In the spring thaw it might come loose from the frozen ground, but not now, when it was frozen into place? He went down on his knees and swept away the snow. It was lying inscription down.

Schweigaard stood up. Looked around at the churchyard.

Something had changed. He walked around the corner and to the entrance.

The large birch had fallen.

The beautiful silver birch that had for so many years waved proudly at the church doors, welcoming newly-weds with sunlight through shining green foliage. The birch that he had asked his congregation to look upon in 1940. The birch that had stood in the wintertime with frozen branches, reminding the villagers that there was life after winter, and perhaps after death.

The wind must have brought it down in the night. The birch had fallen in the direction of the church, tearing down the eaves and knocking the front doors off their hinges. Now the trunk lay with its bowed branches reaching up the church steps, as if it had invited itself in to take a look.

Next to the torn roots lay a pick and shovel. An electric cable ran from inside the church to the ground-thawing device.

Why was there nobody around?

Schweigaard grabbed onto the branches, struggled up the church steps and peered inside. Hymn books lay around the entrance, jumbled up with broken twigs, splinters and snow.

Night of Nights

Footsteps nearby.

Herr Røhme rounded the corner, carrying a bow saw and forestry axe.

"Is that – is it . . ." Kai Schweigaard said, pointing to the open grave by the tree root. "Is that for her? Is the plan for that to be Astrid's grave?"

Røhme removed his wool hat.

"What is it, Herr Røhme?"

Røhme positioned himself with his back to the parsonage below, as if someone might be up there who could read lips.

"They be watchin' us," he whispered. "She be back at the parsonage – Astrid. Arrived late last night. But she will nay have a grave. They wants to sink her in Lake Løsnes. This grave shall be for the man they says she killed."

Røhme and Schweigaard looked at each other. An outsider could never catch what was contained in their glances. Without a word they went to the corner behind the church steps, where they had always gone to discuss difficult matters.

"I canna' say how long she can hold on in this life," said Röhme. "We – we hear her screams."

He explained that the Gestapo had come to the parsonage. They had trampled around in hobnailed boots and pushed Major Sprockhoff to the side. A car had arrived late that night. In the glare of the headlights against the snow Røhme had seen two men drag Astrid out of a green Opel. She had fallen to the ground, because her arms and legs were tied. But Røhme saw that she was scantily dressed, with no hat or coat, and her face was swollen. A woman got out of this same car, lit a cigarette, crouched down and said something to Astrid. Then they dragged her into the parsonage.

"Røhme! Stop! What's all this about – screaming?"

"An interrogation! What else? They thinks Astrid knows

sommat. I reckons the Gestapo be letting this Norwegian gang do their dirty work."

Røhme fell silent. And collected himself, before going on.

"The sound carries right up to our kitchen. We hears the blows and what they shouts. We hears her try to get them to stop. We had to send the littluns out so they didna' hear it all. But naybody in t' village will take 'em in, not now they all thinks we be Nazis. So the bairns be sat on their ownsome out in t' forest."

Schweigaard leaned against the church wall.

"Has Kristine been told?" he murmured.

Røhme shook his head.

"I – I be losing hope, Herr Pastor."

"Me too," Schweigaard said. "Can't we get in there with a gun?"

"Nay. There be too many Gestapo folks coming and going. Sprockhoff sent several soldiers out in a truck earlier. So we reckoned it were all over, but—"

"But what?"

"The green car were away for a while. Then it came back and parked right by our wall. This woman got out. Drunk a fair bit she had, to judge by how loudly she talked. Said the man our Astrid had killed were her husband. And – and . . ."

"Come on, Herr Røhme, don't waste time!"

Røhme swallowed.

"There were another fellow in t' car. A new man. Seems he were there to learn. A man who were 'rested', they said. The woman were to teach him. She began tellin' him how he might use an awl and a ball pein hammer. And a bicycle tyre filled wi' sand so it were kinda firm. I reckons they talked loudly on purpose. So Astrid could hear them through the cellar window. The woman went on about this rubber tyre. Then she mun ha' pointed to a certain place on herseln, for she said that if he stuck

Night of Nights

the awl up there, Astrid could never have babies. 'Most folks,' she said, 'gives in after a quarter of an hour. But this one mun have all day.'"

Schweigaard clenched his fist.

"So what is it about this funeral? Why the haste?"

"The Norwegians in the Opel wants t' go further and interrogate other folks. There be arrests every blasted day now."

Schweigaard shook himself.

"This man isn't from Butangen," he said. "Yet he's to be buried here?"

"Mossen demanded it."

"Mossen?"

"Came and said that the NS would pay for his gravestone. That I mun open a grave right here. Alongside the lads who came back from serving the Nazis at the front. Cos he were a hero too, he says. Happen the fellow be from Finmark. There be full-on fighting up there, and they hasna' time to send bodies that far north. I told him if we dug the grave that close to the birch tree, her roots would come loose. And the ground wouldna' thaw. 'Do it anyways,' he said. The ceremony were the important thing, the coffin could be lowered later."

"Mossen said that? That the important thing was the ceremony?"

Røhme nodded.

"I fears she has little chance, Herr Pastor. We heard it loud and clear that they would fling her out in t' lake. Weigh her down. Drown her."

Schweigaard looked around at the snow-covered gravestones. He stood for a long time.

Until a light wind from long ago breathed on him. An old woman's words. Widow Framstad's words. *Ye shall live long, Pastor. But ye too shall see the sign. Ye most of all.*

Røhme looked at him but said nothing.

Kai Schweigaard had often doubted the prophecy of his death. He had wondered where it would happen, when, and not least if it might carry a *greater meaning*.

He was in no doubt now. The signs were coming together.

He would die today.

At last the tattered corner of a weave made sense to him. He understood the significance of the fallen birch tree. And he saw how the frozen ground, his old arch-enemy, had in the end come to his aid.

"How deep does the frost go in the earth here?" Schweigaard said, pointing at the roots of the fallen tree.

The question surprised Røhme. "One metre, or so."

"So the earth will be frozen under the church floor?"

Røhme nodded.

"And the funeral is at eight?"

"Aye."

Schweigaard looked at his wristwatch. A quarter past two.

"Herr Røhme. I must ask a service of you. One last service. The greatest I have ever asked of you."

His voice had the firmness of his younger years. "Tell Fru Røhme that she *must* stop Haffergård. Poison him if necessary."

Røhme nodded.

"Can you hurry the funeral on somehow? Find an excuse? Every hour will count if we're to save Astrid's life."

"I shall try, but . . ."

"Well, repair the church doors and remove the birch tree. Then take out those big altar candles, Røhme. The beeswax ones. That you made for my farewell mass."

Røhme inclined his head. Kai Schweigaard went closer to him and whispered in his ear. Røhme took a step back and stuttered.

"B-but – but *who*?"

"Me," Kai Schweigaard said.

Night of Nights

"Nay, Herr Pastor!" said Røhme. "Not thee." He shook his head, not knowing what to do with his hands. "Not like that. In such a way."

Schweigaard gripped his arm.

"Never have I met a more steadfast man than yourself, Herr Røhme. Will you do it?"

Eight Hundred Years to the End

Churchwarden Emmerich stood motionless in the belly of the stave church in Dresden.

A deep sound filled the entire nave. A rumbling sound, deeper almost than the human ear could perceive, so guttural and so powerful it shook him.

The sound issued from the tower. From the Sister Bells. It grew in strength and sank in frequency, and was soon inaudible, but present nonetheless, as the pews began to vibrate.

Over by the entrance a hymn book tumbled to the floor. Then everything went quiet again. As a house when a person has brought news of a death and closes the door behind them.

He looked at his watch. It was six o'clock.

Emmerich went over calmly and picked up the hymn book. The old Norwegian hymn book, *Landstads Kirkesalmebog*.

The old churchwarden looked around him. It had been his life, this stave church with its carvings and painted pews and heavy smell of tar. An existence with a slow pulse and near imperceptible breath. Infinite in its mystery, distinct in its power.

They were united again, the bells in the tower.

One day in 1943 Halfrid had rung of her own accord. Not

with her usual melancholy. She sounded lively and quick that day. There were no maudlin undertones. He did not understand the reason for her ringing, until an unannounced crane-truck came driving down the wide, gravelled path in Großer Garten. It turned onto the lawn, and a trail of thick exhaust fumes described the truck's movements as it reversed towards the church. Tied on the back was a transport crate. The driver had no idea what it contained. Only that it was to be delivered here.

Emmerich had always imagined the reunification of the Sister Bells as an occasion Handel might have set music to.

Instead, here he stood, alone, one chilly afternoon, with a wooden crate before the church steps. No ceremony. No chain-brothers. No chamber orchestra. No unmarried woman from the Hekne family. No bishop or guests. The Ahnenerbe's headquarters had been destroyed by a bomb earlier in the war, and all they had managed to offer was a certificate to say the bell was exempt from the requisitioning of metal for the war effort.

In all his years as churchwarden, Emmerich had never looked directly upon Halfrid. Whenever he had reason to go up into the belfry, he always shut his eyes and hid the bell under a sailcloth before opening them again.

And so it was now.

It had taken him and a helper three days to hang Gunhild, and when the load-bearing beam was finally carrying twice the weight, and two cloaked bells hung side by side, he recalled the rich legend from Norway and was struck by how lacklustre this event was. How un-German.

There was nothing to sense or feel. As though all the spirits were turning their backs.

When the Sister Bells rang together for the first time in sixty years, they were clearly under some sort of restraint. As though something gripped the bronze and refused to slip the chimes

Night of Nights

free. There was no joyous reunion. They sounded tame, no matter how hard he worked with the bell ropes.

Perhaps *that* had been their message.

That this was not over. This was not the legend's fulfilment.

But now in 1945, at the stroke of six on February 13, he felt that the bells' strange murmuring carried the message that they had an important errand.

The last years had taught him a great deal about fear. He had developed a belief that danger could be sensed. Like the smell before rain. Like the clatter of pebbles before a landslide. Or like the murmur of the church bells.

He was still standing with the hymn book in his hand.

He rushed to the sacristy and opened the trapdoor. The whites of three pairs of eyes came into view. The family had been hiding under the church floor for four days, and his helpers had still not managed to find them transport or a hiding place.

"What was that sound?" said the man.

"The church bells."

"Surely those couldn't have been church bells?"

Emmerich waved them closer. "You must go."

"Now?"

"Yes. Something's about to happen here. I don't know what."

The man came up first, crouched down and held out his arm to each of the children and pulled them up. They smelled of earth. For a brief moment they all stood and stared around the church as they listened. Emmerich opened his wallet and gave the man all the money he had. Then, reaching into his pocket, he found some coins and gave him those too. From a cupboard in the sacristy, he gathered some biscuits and filled a bottle with water.

"Hide among the trees at the edge of the park. If you can, try to run across the bridge at Loschwitz and into the forest behind the Weisser Hirsch."

The man seemed doubtful.

"Why aren't you coming too – if it's so dangerous?"

"I have to be here. Right here."

Emmerich opened the sacristy door. Just cool air and the silhouettes of bare park trees. Silence followed them as they left.

Not long after, Emmerich went out too. The moon was elsewhere and the night sky dark. The street lamps that had once been the pride of Dresden had not been lit since the outbreak of war. The city's inhabitants were at rest behind their blackout curtains, and Dresden lay as silent as an unpopulated forest.

He had a good idea of how German soldiers behaved in the countries they occupied. For he had seen for himself how the Nazis treated their own people. When he went to the town square to try to buy food, he would pass corpses swinging from the gallows. Each with their crime written on a sign around their neck. *Protested. Committed treason. Helped Jews. Tried to escape.*

But nobody could watch over every cellar, every attic. Not all the time. And a stave church under the ownership of the Ahnenerbe avoided police searches.

This knowledge was what had set it all in motion. A chain of elderly people whispering. Shadows among the beech trees in Großer Garten. Forty people walking in for Sunday Mass, forty-two walking out. Two new grandchildren, hand in hand.

He often hid those deemed by the Nazis as *Ballastmenschen*: polio victims, deaf people, "retarded" people. Those unfit to become future soldiers or housewives. At night the kids would come up from the basement and play between the rows of pews. Emmerich made them a wooden rocking horse and painted it yellow. They used it so much that the yellow wore off its back.

He was confident they wouldn't be exposed. They had the help of a most unusually vigilant sentinel.

A church bell that could warn of danger. And from 1943, two bells.

*

Night of Nights

Emmerich sat down on *die Fröstelstelle*, the pew where old Klara had frozen to death during a New Year's Mass in Norway.

The day before yesterday he had gone to the Mattheus Cemetery. The headstone was crooked now, and Gerhard Schönauer's name was barely legible under the ivy and moss. Later Emmerich visited the Kunstakademi. The auditorium had been converted into a medieval-style hall filled with monumental artworks. Bare walls painted with eagles and swastikas. Sculptures depicting the most banal subjects. Medieval knights on galloping steeds, their helmets embellished with wings.

Is this really Germany, he thought. Is this us? If not, then where are we?

The endless victory speeches had long since stopped. There were constant rumours now about how far the Americans had come after the Normandy landings in June last year, although most of the prayers Emmerich overheard in the church spoke of fear of the Soviets approaching from the east. The hospitals were full of crippled soldiers, but Dresden itself had been spared from attack. Previously you faced the death penalty if you left your city, but in recent weeks citizens living near the Soviet border had been told that these punishments would no longer be enforced. Dresden was in fact regarded as a safe city, and refugees had arrived in their tens of thousands. Memel, the city closest to the border, had been emptied in a matter of days. For all he knew, they were here in the neighbourhood at this very time, Gerhard's relatives.

The war would soon be over.

Half an hour passed.

A faint chime issued from the belfry, no louder than if a child had struck the bell with a ball pein hammer. It was soon followed by another single chime, similar but more of a base tone. Then the deep humming began again. As if a gigantic swarm of bumblebees were circling in the church tower.

The Sister Bells began to ring.
Emmerich stood up.
First Halfrid. Then Gunhild. Fourteen strokes in two rounds. A sequence not belonging to any liturgy.
Now they began to chime together.
Emmerich went up to the ledge where the bell ropes hung. Swinging back and forth in the semi-darkness, they looked like two cats' tails, and from the way they moved and the delay he knew that the bells were swinging the ropes and not the reverse.
The ringing gained rhythm and fullness. It poured between the church walls and vibrated through the old man who stood alone there.
He ducked through the low portal and walked out onto the church steps. The bells sounded even louder here.
Sirens were sounding in the distance. Followed by some that were closer.
A red sphere tumbled out of the sky. It trailed a similarly red streak after it, and appeared to fall near the Hoftheater or the Semperoper opera house. He heard the hum of a plane and watched another orb tumble from the darkness. Green this time. A third fell close by, and he saw smaller flares shooting out from its glowing centre in gentle arcs, like the branches of a spruce bent under the weight of snow. Soon more fireballs were falling than he could count. Red and green flames shot out, and for the next few minutes the centre of Dresden was illuminated by what looked like tumbling Christmas trees.
Air defence searchlights began to sweep across the sky, outlining the clouds. Like futile brushstrokes on a canvas that refused to absorb paint. Now and then he thought he glimpsed movement up in the furthest reach of the beams, small flecks where the light had lost its strength and become a dusty skin.
Why didn't they shoot them down? Were there no anti-aircraft guns in the city?

Night of Nights

The Sister Bells were so loud now that he felt every stroke in his spine. The ringing was followed by a murmur from the sky, which he soon recognised as the hum of planes.

Then came a loud bang. The ground shook. Over in the city he saw flames shooting up. The tremors reached him, then faded like waves on water. With every blast the church creaked, and the bells took up the rhythm of the explosions, as though they wanted to repeat or answer them. In the sky over the Art Academy and the Frauenkirche the orange glow of the flames took hold.

Leaving the door to the weapons porch open, Emmerich went back into the church. Calmly, he lit the candles down the aisle.

When he came out again, it was as though the sun had risen. Flames stood high in the trees and buildings before him, and Großer Garten was as bright as on a summer's day, but the park's trees had unnaturally long shadows, as the light came from one side.

The carvings on the portal were lit up, and in the shimmering light and fluttering shadows the mythical beasts seemed to come alive. The pupils in their eyes appeared to move, and the serpent bared its teeth.

The searchlights had gathered in the sky above Friedrichstadt, and now he saw something beyond his comprehension.

If those were planes, could there really be so many?

Were they all headed here?

Still no sound of artillery on the ground. He realised that the city no longer had any defences. The anti-aircraft guns must have been sent elsewhere.

A huge pillar of fire shot up by the old palace on Strehlener Platz. A forest fire was spreading on the other side of Lake Carola, and he felt the heat growing against his face, second by second, until he had to turn away.

Then the wind began to blow.

A strange wind, a reverse wind, which he soon realised was a draught from the fires in the city. Stronger than any storm he had known, it found its way into the church, making the church candles flutter wildly.

The explosions stopped. The draught persisted.

A minute passed without any new tremors. Only now was he aware that the Sister Bells were still ringing.

For a moment he thought it was over.

But everything with a name would be erased this night.

A dozen firebombs sailed down into the park and within seconds ignited as many fires in the grass, and through this wall of flames he saw people running towards the stave church. Some in their nightclothes, many with children in their arms. Their cries could be heard in the short gaps between explosions. Each time the ground shook, they fell to the ground, before getting up and running in another direction. Some managed to get away before another bomb was dropped, others vanished in the explosion.

A giraffe came galloping along the gravel path. It changed direction at his workshed and headed for Lake Carola, and with high steps it staggered out into the water, where it was lit by the forest blaze and the light reflected from the lake's dark surface. Two lions leaped into view. One had a torn hind leg and was limping, and the uninjured lion did not wait for its lame companion.

The zoo, Emmerich realised. The bombs had hit the zoo.

Next came monkeys with burning fur. They climbed into a tree with wide, bare branches, and formed a chaotic pattern. Those who had reached a higher branch kicked against those who tried to follow, and they must have got something sticky on them, for no matter how hard they shook themselves, they did not stop burning. The branches of the tree caught light, and one by one the monkeys fell down like so many bundles of burning matter.

Night of Nights

Up in the sky a bomber burst into flame. It plunged towards the ground, tails of fire tracing the spirals in which it fell. It was coming fast, and he thought it would fall near the church, but it suddenly changed direction and disappeared. Seconds later he heard a muffled bang, and new tremors ran through the ground, and tiles fell from the church roof and the stone steps shook.

The bombs were coming so thick now, he could no longer tell them apart. Fires rose from ever more places in the city centre. The noise ripped into his ears. The roar of planes and explosions blended with the church bells. And all the while he felt the unnatural gusts of wind. Heat from all sides tore and shook the burning treetops and stung his eyes.

An old couple hobbled towards him. The man was bleeding from his forehead. The woman's hair was singed. In her hand she held a torn human ear, a gold earring still in the lobe. The ear belonged to neither of them. The man took the ear in his hand as he supported the woman up the steps to the church.

Emmerich said they would die if they went inside.

"Yes," said the woman. "We want to die in a church."

The organist appeared as if from nowhere. He was running barefoot and his face had cuts from broken glass. He told Emmerich how he had seen furniture and paintings sucked through the air towards an insatiable sea of flame. On his way here he had seen people standing with their feet in melted asphalt, being cremated alive. The organist used his last breath to say all this before he bowed his head and went into the church.

A man came up the steps with a child in his arms. He cradled it and said: "It goes quickly in a wooden church." Emmerich saw that the child was dead.

Inside the church the organist began to play Bach's *Ich ruf zu dir*. The melody was just about audible in the din.

The church looked upon her watery reflection in Lake Carola, flames licking all around her. It was as though she had a burning sister. The heat softened the tar on her walls, and it smelled like the hottest of Norwegian summer days, and Emmerich thought: She'll catch fire now.

Then bombs exploded in Lake Carola. The water washed like flood waves over the church. Emmerich curled up and clung to the handrail. When he lifted his head again, he was soaking wet. Water was trickling from the roof.

He staggered inside and sat down against the wall by *die Fröstelstelle*. There was still some evening cool and evening darkness here in the nave. There was a pause in the noise, and for a moment the melody rang out from the organ uninterrupted and pure.

Then flames burst forth in one corner. The light outside shifted colour and shape through the leaded windows and met the same colours within. The 800-year-old wood caught fire and illumined its own timber frame.

A young girl got up from her pew and ran out. The others remained seated. The man was still holding the child in his arms, and the married couple sat close to each other, still holding the ear with the gold earring. The Sister Bells had shifted from their warning clamour to a steadier, more sedate chime.

The sound of the organ grew increasingly contorted before the crackle of fire was the only noise in the church.

Flames crawled across the floor, and a second later the tar-impregnated church was engulfed. The ceiling was ablaze and flames danced around the pulpit and baptismal font and altar, and in the bright light there emerged a rectangular patch on the wall, where a weave had hung for many hundreds of years.

The vaulted ceiling cracked above a pew, then collapsed over the people seated there.

Emmerich saw the timber cladding burn away, so that only the church's staves were left standing. They reached towards the sky like the tall pine trees they had once been, long before

Night of Nights

Norway's Christianisation. They reached up as they had when the stave church was first built in 1170, and when it was rebuilt in 1881.

Above him, Emmerich could see up into the belfry, and for the first time he saw the Sister Bells whole and complete. They swung in the blaze, red-hot against the night into which they rang.

The Last Pastor in Butangen

A coffin stood in the church aisle, like so many coffins before it.

He placed his hand on the lid. Beneath it lay the body of a man whom Astrid Hekne had apparently shot and killed.

How it had happened was hers to tell.

The church was in near darkness. Only the electric lights by the hymn bookshelf were on, and the one over the chancel. Two bronze altar candlesticks stood on the floor at the altar ring, in them the handsome white candles Røhme had made, waiting to be lit at last. A box of matches had been laid by Røhme on the collar of one of the candlesticks.

In the sacristy Schweigaard changed into his cassock. He had not worn a cross since 1881, when he had stood beside Astrid Hekne's coffin. Now he took out a black box. On purple velvet was a large silver cross on a braided chain of the same metal. He slipped it under his collar, felt the weight and coldness of the silver on his skin, and said aloud: "I am in Your hands. Whether Your hands raise me up or cast me down."

He stood at the altar and thought of another church. An

older church, a better church. *This* church, *his* church, had done as best it could.

"We thank this church building," he said, "for serving Christian peace for more than sixty years. We thank God for sparing it from fire and acts of war. We give thanks that it has given shelter to our most devout prayers and humble hopes, that it has housed baptism and liturgy. We thank this church building – for all it has been to us. I hereby deconsecrate it and release it from its duty."

He looked over the rows of pews. The church was sparsely decorated, but a woodcarver had made a large and beautiful relief of shepherds with lambs. The altarpiece was handsome too, as was the crucifix, and the stained-glass window, given by an emigrant on his return from America, was a true work of art.

All this he noticed now.

In this last moment of impossibility.

Røhme had put the church doors back in place. Outside, the big birch tree had been chopped up and removed. Any fragments of bark and twigs had been swept from the steps and out into the snow.

Haffergård was in bed. Fru Røhme had dashed to the parsonage stables and scraped a harness with a knife. She had added these scrapings to the coffee pot and offered the priest a cup of ersatz coffee. Horse sweat was such a potent poison it could be fatal, and Haffergård was probably lying in a cold sweat now, emptying his belly from both ends.

The organist arrived. In the darkened church he had to go all the way to Schweigaard before he could say: "Is that *you*, Pastor?"

"Yes, it's me."

"What will Mossen say?"

"Mossen mustn't know," said Schweigaard. "It'll be a small funeral."

Night of Nights

The organist rolled a cigarette with some homegrown tobacco and put it in his breast pocket. He sat down at the organ and launched into the standard repertoire of funeral hymns.

Schweigaard had heard them all countless times. Now they filled him with rising dread. The moment had come. The inevitable moment. *His* inevitable moment.

It would not be brought about by a stroke or a sudden illness.

Not by a bullet, not by a gallows rope. Not by drowning, or frostbite.

He was to die by fire.

The threadbare corner of the Hekne Weave depicted a pastor in a ruff collar and a demon with the tongue of a snake. The priest was touching the demon's head. They were both surrounded by flames.

Over the years, he had accepted it. Sometimes even cherished the idea that he would die in this way.

But now, now that the moment was come, he had no wish to die. He wanted to live, if only for a few more days, hours! Live, live! He wanted to sit in the Priest Boat out on Lake Løsnes, he wanted to go out and breath in the smells of the soil and the fields, he wanted to sit by the hearth with Herr and Fru Røhme, with Jehans, Kristine, Esther and little Eirik. And he wanted to tend Astrid Hekne's grave.

But the time had come. Astrid might already be dead. Which would mean that this was only revenge, yet—

He shook his head.

There were no rules for this choice. No trial run. He was so alone down here! So small! How could he be sure that *he* was the pastor in a ruff collar standing in the sea of flames? Might the image in the weave merely be the sisters' expression of their revenge wish? A desire that the priest and bailiff who had testified against them should die in the same manner by which they had once tried to condemn them?

Lord, come to me. Come! Come to me and say: Here I am. Step aside, Kai Schweigaard, you shall not have to make this choice.

But he realised, once again, that he must act in the world as if there were no God, for now he heard the door open.

A woman and two men entered. They stood a moment and looked about them before walking down the aisle. Kai stepped forward, making himself seen. The woman nodded at him while fixing her eyes firmly on the coffin. She was dressed in a blue woollen coat with a white embroidered collar. He could see no evil in her. On the contrary. She had a gentle and tranquil face. A mother's face perhaps. The two men seemed rather reserved. In single-breasted suit jackets. Narrow-brimmed hats in their hands. Newly polished shoes. They nodded calmly at him.

The men sat down. The woman walked alone up to the coffin. The chancel lamp threw her shadow behind her.

"Good evening," she said, looking Kai in the eye. "Thank you for your trouble."

Kai Schweigaard felt unable to say anything. They still thought he was Haffergård.

She nodded and laid a red flower on the pine coffin. A begonia, or so Schweigaard thought. One of Fru Røhme's potted plants, no doubt.

Then wiping away a tear, she turned and joined the others. They sat on the left. In the second box pew from the front, with the woman in the middle. Far in. Where those who wanted to avoid shaking hands always sat.

A familiar funereal smell hung in the aisle. The odour of brandy and toothpaste.

Their hands were scrubbed red. To remove Astrid's blood?

Schweigaard bit his lip and closed his eyes.

The doubt! The appalling doubt! This woman – was she really the woman Røhme had heard talking about the bicycle tyre, and where they should jab the awl so Astrid could never have children? She seemed so ordinary, so grief-stricken at the sight of the coffin, and the two men were so polite, he saw nothing sadistic in them.

He hoped nobody else would turn up now. What if some German soldiers were sent here? What if Major Sprockhoff came?

Schweigaard turned away from the coffin and headed for the sacristy door. He needed to get outside, walk round the church, and talk to Røhme.

Then he heard someone open the main door. He craned his neck. Felt the draught from the cold wind outside.

Mossen.

Mossen and his sons. In their Hird uniforms.

There are six of them now, he thought. Six. But are they all guilty, these six, and if so, how guilty? How guilty is Jon Mossen, the village's former milk truck driver? How guilty is Odd, who proved to have such a good singing voice in his confirmation classes? How can I decide whether the sum of his life is worse than the sum of my own?

He tried to let go of the thought. Turned, stepped out from the dim light between the altar and sacristy and went towards the Mossen clan. This was how for decades he had halted any sign of drama during services. Quashed any beginnings of hysteria or disagreement by going straight in with an argument at the ready.

Mossen and his sons stopped in their tracks. Schweigaard continued up to them.

They smelled of tobacco. But not alcohol.

"I know you were expecting Haffergård, Mossen. I'm afraid he's been taken ill."

Mossen looked at him with contempt.

"Ill? Who says he be ill? And who asked thee to take his place?"

"Haffergård himself," Schweigaard lied. "Through Herr Røhme."

The organist stopped playing. He leaned back on his stool to stare. Mossen put his hands on his hips in a display of authority.

"Tell me, Pastor, why it be so dingy in here," he said. "And from where did ye get that?" He gestured limply towards Schweigaard's cassock, but without waiting for an answer, just walked towards the three other mourners and shook their hands. One of the men thanked the Mossens for offering to help bear the coffin.

They exchanged a few words that Schweigaard did not hear. The woman craned her neck and looked at him. Then shrugged.

Without looking at Schweigaard again, Mossen and his sons sat down on a pew to the right of the aisle. Ola in the middle, Jon and Odd on either side.

No more arrivals. There were six all together and him.

The organist started to play Johan Svendsen's arrangement of "Allt under himmelens fäste" – All beneath the firmament – one of the few melodies Schweigaard actually liked.

Schweigaard saw Herr Røhme over by the main doors. The agreement was that he would lock them and do the same with the sacristy door as soon as the organist had gone out. Like all his predecessors, this organist had many annoying habits. One being that he went for a cigarette outside the sacristy between hymns. Today this would hold him in good stead.

Now Herr Røhme locked the main doors. He had, on Pastor Schweigaard's orders, hung them so they would open inwards, as stave church doors had always been hung in Norway before the fire of 1822 in Solør. And just as on that fatal day in 1822, there would be no escape from the church today.

The time had come to light the altar candles for a farewell Mass.

But again, doubt struck. Was he really placed to ... kill?

Night of Nights

With what right? The Mossens had not actually murdered anyone. How could this then be defended as a tyrannicide? Was the sum of evil in these other persons so great that it countered the death of innocents?

He felt the power from beneath him more strongly than ever. Not just the power from the foundations of the stave church and the Hekne sisters' grave. Lying under the church floor was the dynamite and guncotton that was left over from the construction of the seter road. In 1940 Herr Røhme had transported it down the aisle in a wheelbarrow, opened the trapdoor and hidden it in the village's safest place. Since then, it had lain down there in the dark. The ground was frozen through now, and the sisters' burial place would, he hoped, be spared.

On the two tall, newly polished brass candlesticks stood Herr Røhme's handsome white altar candles. Røhme had drilled holes through them and driven a fuse along their wicks.

That, at least, was what Schweigaard had asked him to do.

The final chord of the hymn rang out. Its echoes fading between the walls, the organist left.

The coffin stood before the altar, and Schweigaard was just metres from the six people in the pews.

There was nothing to read in their faces. Nothing! He had thought he could recognise evil when he saw it. Now he saw only human beings. Ordinary human beings! Surely Röhme would have rushed in to tell him if these three weren't *the three*? Or had he been held up in some way?

Again and again Kai Schweigaard sought an answer from the powers beneath him.

But he eventually turned to the powers above for answers.

Kai Schweigaard approached the altar candles. He opened the matchbox, but his hands were shaking so hard the match snapped. As he tried to take a new one, he dropped the box and its contents scattered across the floor.

"For shame," said Ola Mossen. "Ye be a disgrace, Pastor Schweigaard. A right out disgrace."

Jon Mossen stood up, fumbled in his trouser pocket and produced a lighter.

Schweigaard bent stiffly down and picked up a match. He lit it, and despite his trembling held it to the wick of the candle. With the match still burning he walked carefully over to the second candle and lit that too, blowing out the match just as it scorched his skin.

He had always lit the altar candles this way. He felt it as a matter of honour that he bring the same flame to both candles.

Jon Mossen stood and watched him for a while, then stuffed his lighter back in his pocket and sat down.

The flames grew on their wicks and fluttered gently. Schweigaard had no idea how long the wicks would have to burn before they ignited the fuses which continued through the brass candlesticks down into the floor and to the explosives.

He hoped it would be quick.

One of the candles sputtered. The flame flickered.

Kai Schweigaard turned and intoned:

"*Out of the depths I cry unto Thee, O Lord! Lord, hear my voice, let Your ears be attentive to the voice of my supplication! For forgiveness is with Thee . . .*"

He ended the moment of prayer and went to stand alongside the coffin, moving carefully to ensure his robes did not blow out the candles.

"There have always been bonds of friendship between Norway and Germany. A stave church stood here for centuries, a church which, to my great regret, we did not at that time have the sense to preserve. Fortunately, we had friends in Germany. These friends understood, and the church now stands in Dresden. I say this to draw a connection to this young man's actions. He lived believing in his fight to unite our peoples."

Night of Nights

Ola Mossen scratched his nose. The three mourners in the second pew stared at the ceiling.

Schweigaard continued. "There was a portal on the ancient stave church that stood here. It was decorated with carvings that were meant to prevent evil from entering. The church in which we now sit does not have such a thing. Here, in this church, as otherwise in life, we are alone in the task to keep evil from our hearts."

Jon Mossen cleared his throat loudly.

Schweigaard suddenly lost track. He started to mumble. What came next? Had he – the man who had presided over thousands of funerals – forgotten the Bible reading?

He cleared his throat and remembered the words.

"*So when this corruptible shall have put on incorruption, and this mortal shall have put on immortality, then shall be brought to pass the saying that is written, Death is swallowed up in victory. O death, where is thy—*"

It was then that he saw sparks and smoke issuing from one of the candles. He could not continue. He stood and looked at the six people before him.

The woman stood up. Their recent deeds had doubtless made them alert to any deception.

"Oy, what be going on?" shouted Ola Mossen. "Pastor!"

Schweigaard heard a very faint hissing noise travel steadily beneath the church floor, as though the Door Serpent, the great mythological beast from the stave church's portal, had returned.

He could run into the sacristy now. Hammer on the door and beg Herr Røhme to let him out.

But no. He had sentenced them to death and would accompany them. To stand at the throne of judgement, bow his head, and say: *Judge me with them, O Lord.*

"Everybody out!" shouted Ola Mossen, getting up. He

took off down the aisle, his sons close on his heels. While the strangers sat on in bewilderment.

There was a bang louder than any gunshot. The windows shattered. The floorboards tore apart, tipping the box pews up, flinging those sitting on them into the wall.

Then, as the floor fell back into place, Schweigaard watched a dark cleft open up. Pews slid along it and fell into it. The pulpit and altar shook. Beams broke in two, timber loosened from timber. The noise reminded him of when the old stave church was dismantled.

Then it was as though a terrible snowstorm rose. Sixty years of accumulated church dust gathered in a dense haze. Seconds later the nave was filled by a blinding light, a fireball from wall to wall, and Schweigaard just had time to observe his being thrown into the air before everything went blank.

Dark. Very dark.

Blue-black. Dense. Impenetrable.

World before Genesis. Without dimension, distance or measurable time.

A fire of orange and red flared up ahead. Nearby, through the heat, he saw a twitching, writhing form. A diffuse nativity. A person staggered to their feet. As from a sleep or at the resurrection.

The blaze grew in size. A second figure took form in the dust. It evaded the fire.

Flames lit the randomly strewn remains of the church's decor. A crucifix. A woodcut of lambs.

The fire shot out sparks. They tumbled in arcs through the blue-black. The stained-glass window lay broken before him, and in one of its shards Kai Schweigaard saw his face.

He wondered briefly: Was it *from* this place I wandered, or was it to this place I came?

Night of Nights

A splintered beam fell, impaling a man. Someone near the fire hammered on the doors with their fists and could not get out. Flames rose from the crack in the church floor. Paint started to drip from the ceiling and caught fire in the air.

So this is it, he thought. The thread is cut. And without my knowing if I managed to save her this time.

Now he noticed the fire's great heat.

Farewell, then, to the familiar. See me when I come through.

To his left, at the edge of his field of vision, Schweigaard saw a figure. The woman with the embroidered collar.

He glimpsed his old Bible. It lay open on the floor. The fire had caught its pages.

Schweigaard struggled to his feet, grabbed his Bible and crawled to the woman through smoke and dust. He knelt beside her and laid his hand on her forehead.

You Were in the Church When the Church Burned Down

Astrid Hekne was lying on the dirt floor. At first, she thought that the jolt in her body meant they were kicking her awake, but when she finally opened her gluey eyes, there was nobody in the parsonage cellar.

Had the house shaken? Or was this some new form of torture?

Astrid let her eyes roam towards the tiny cellar window with its iron grille. The glass was overgrown with dirt, but she could make out a scrap of sky outside, and to this scrap of sky she murmured a wish to live.

She tried to poke a blood clot from her nose, but in so doing she did not feel the contours of her own face, but a tender, swollen mass. She tried to turn over, but there was no part of her they had not beaten raw.

She remembered the gunshot in the mountains with total clarity. Each one of the man's desperate screams. Her doubts afterwards about whether she had been right to kill him. If he was just a guide, as the woman said, and the father of their two children, a boy of four and a girl of two.

"How old were ye when ye gave birth to yer little boy?" Astrid had asked. The woman had to do the arithmetic in her head, and when she saw that Astrid had seen it, she struck her with a steel ruler.

Astrid heard footsteps on the stairs now. Careful footsteps. She would not let herself be fooled again. Several times they had crept down, only to fling the door open with a bang to confuse all her senses. She crawled over to the corner.

She couldn't take more. The three of them took such pleasure in what they did. They would bring paraffin lamps close up to her face so she felt their heat. Run the length of a hemp rope over the wounds on her neck, and tell her that even an ordinary rope could be a gallows rope in their hands.

Before they turned to something else.

The pains in her belly were the worst. Down over her back. And it was painful to swallow when your larynx was so swollen.

Why had the Hekne Krag not gone off? Why had the rifle not let her die?

The footsteps were further down the stairs now.

The latch clicked. The door was pushed ajar.

"Astrid?"

A woman's voice. Trying to sound so sweet. Oh, yes. I'd kill you if I could. Kill you with my bare hands. Bite off your ears and your fingers.

"Astrid?"

The door was opened wider. A light shone down the stairway and into the cellar.

Somebody whispered:

"Oh, Lord above. Sweet Lord above."

It sounded like Fru Røhme. Astrid tried to get to her feet, but her knee gave way.

Fru Røhme cut through the ropes around her wrists and ankles.

"Somebody ha' blown up the church. The soldiers be o'er there right now. We mun hurry."

They staggered up the stairs. Astrid's head was filled with strange noises that she knew came from the blows to her ears, and whenever Fru Røhme said something, she had to ask her to repeat it.

An eternity later they came up into the hallway, where the German military coats hung. The door to the living room stood open, and through the windows overlooking the churchyard, Astrid could see a dance of huge, yellow flames. Fru Røhme guided her out onto the forecourt, where a wind warmer than a summer breeze eased the pain of her wounds for a moment, before she realised what made it so warm. With each gust came an acrid smell of smoke. They moved forward and saw it all.

The church was on fire. The entrance was in flames, the roof had collapsed, and the building was leaning on its foundations. The timbers creaked as the blaze grew. Restless light flickered between the gravestones.

Astrid saw someone pull out a burning body and roll it in the snow. Others arrived and tried to haul it away from the flames. The fire lapped at the spire now. Then it was engulfed, and for a moment it stood like a glowing tower against the night sky.

People crowded in from the road. One or two tried to get closer to the blaze, they lifted their arms as a shield from the heat but had to retreat. The flames were raging and were soon so high that the parsonage was lit up, and the trees and the outbuildings and flagpole cast shadows at an angle never before seen.

Astrid held up her hand towards the window of Schweigaard's old study.

"The pastor?" she murmured. "Who . . . oversaw the . . ."

Fru Røhme shook her head and held back the tears.

"I didna' realise. That he would take them. Not like that. Not wi' himseln too. It were meant to be the NS priest, but Pastor Schweigaard asked me to stop him."

"Was – was Kai in *there*?"

"Aye," Fru Røhme said. "Happen."

Astrid felt the tears sting on her wounds. It was not the time for it, but she had to weep for Kai Schweigaard and his Astrid Hekne. Weep because she knew she would never, in any time or before any mirror or face, meet a man who could measure up to him.

But he would never get to hear it. Kai.

Down by the church, the yelling had stopped. The fire changed to a redder hue. A gust of wind, still warm, stroked her face. Then she felt something soft land on her skin, and soon the snowy forecourt was speckled with large flakes of ash.

"Hurry now," said Fru Røhme. "We mun get thee up to Hekne."

"Nay, not Hekne," Astrid said quietly. "They shall burn it down if they find me there."

"Aye, but we mun get thee away from here!"

Fru Røhme supported her, and they staggered in the direction of the shortcut behind the *stabbur*. They had not gone far when they heard someone shout out, "Stop!"

Astrid turned her head.

A uniformed man was walking briskly towards them.

Major Sprockhoff.

Night of Nights

It was two years since she had seen him up close. But he seemed more than two years older. There were deep furrows in his brow. His face had no room for levity. He stank of fire and had soot on his uniform sleeves.

When he saw her, it was as though he had to shake himself. But he barely let a second pass, before he said:

"Get back in. Now."

Very gently Sprockhoff gripped Astrid's shoulder, and together with Fru Røhme he helped her back to the house. The flames still threw a flickering glow over the heaps of snow that surrounded the parsonage. He looked around him as they went in.

He pointed them up the stairs and stayed in the hallway while Fru Røhme helped Astrid up the stairs and into what had been Kai Schweigaard's study.

Kai's desk stood as before. But on the wall was the map of Butangen. The little painting of a cavalry charge. A framed photograph of Hitler.

But also, an old wood carving of Christ on the Cross.

Sprockhoff entered with heavy steps and ordered Fru Røhme out of the room. The blood from Astrid's wounds dripped onto the floor. Sprockhoff took a handkerchief from his pocket and wrapped it around the wrist that was bleeding most.

Then he stood in thought. He looked at the clock. Glanced out of the window.

"The Gestapo are due here in four hours," he said in Norwegian. "They're expecting to find three Norwegians who have been told who else they should arrest."

Astrid had to swallow the blood in her mouth before she could speak. "Aye well – it in't any good then," she murmured. "It doesna' help whatever ye says."

"No," he said. "I won't have that laid on me. That it doesn't help whatever I say."

"The Gestapo," Astrid muttered.

He shook his head. "Only I know what's been happening here. I sent my soldiers away when those lunatics were let loose on you."

Sprockhoff looked up at Christ on the Cross. A bunch of keys dangled from his bloodied big toe. She could see by their shape they were car keys.

"I don't yet know what caused the explosion," said Sprockhoff. "But when the Gestapo get here, I'll tell them you're dead. I'll say that the three Norwegians forced you to go into the church with them. That they wanted to torment you further by making you participate in the funeral of the man you shot."

He took the car keys, led the way to the door and said: "You're dead, Astrid Hekne. You were in the church when the church burned down."

A Final Task for an Unloved Church

One might assume that Our Lord, in the turbulence of 1945, would be preoccupied by things other than Butangen. Each day events of such magnitude occurred that they would impact the world for decades, and so much was overturned that even an omnipotent being might find it impossible to keep up. But the faithful believe time is irrelevant to God, and that He can hear all our prayers and follow each of our destinies, and thus they found it plausible that He, between his many duties on February 13, took a moment to turn his gaze towards a backwater of His creation and watch, perhaps with wonder, His unruly servant Kai Schweigaard fight his last battle.

Night of Nights

It was at this moment that the first villagers had drawn back their blackout curtains to see where the loud bangs were coming from, and had discovered the glow which grew into a fire.

The Hekne household had sat in silent angst all evening. Jehans had come home from a half-hearted interrogation in Ringebu. On hearing the noise, he and Isum ran down, with Kristine following after. Already from a distance they could see the impact of the explosions. The walls were folded out and the church looked like a house of cards about to fall. The roof was on fire and the flames were spreading fast. Later they learned that the dust in the church had formed an additional explosive, as powerful as the dynamite itself. Hanging in the air, it had been ignited by the guncotton. Jehans and Isum had arrived in time to see the soldiers making a futile attempt to extinguish the fire, since all they had at their disposal was snow. The church bells then fell with a deafening thud before the spire crashed into the cemetery and the soldiers ran off.

The church looked as though a mighty fist had crushed it between its fingers. Charred timbers and white-painted cladding lay in disarray on the ground, together with the pews and the altar. Here and there they could hear the cries of those who were still alive but either pinned to the floor or buried under planks. As though the unloved church had set itself one last task: to hold the guilty fast.

The organist was found by the gate. He had fainted. A bleeding Herr Røhme called out for Pastor Schweigaard. The soldiers had pulled free someone who was trapped near the door, but with the fire spreading so fast they themselves were burned as they dragged him away. Jehans rushed towards the part of the church where the fire had not yet taken hold, and clambered up onto the foundation wall. Between the window frames and a heavy door with a shiny brass handle lay the pulpit, and in a pile of broken roof tiles lay the crucifix and twisted organ pipes. The smoke was intolerable, and Jehans had to climb back down. The heat melted the snow like a sudden spring thaw, and water found its way among the gravestones. The noises from the fire altered. Loud cracking sounds were followed by rumblings caused by the huge amounts of air the fire devoured.

Jehans knew it was all over.

Then he spotted Isum. At first Jehans thought he had lost his mind. Wearing his usual colourful wool sweater and bobble hat, Giant Isum lay down in the melt water and writhed about. When he was thoroughly soaked, he flung himself into the snow and rolled about to make it stick to him. Then, looking like a huge snowman, he leaped up onto the foundation wall, took a deep breath and vanished into the dense smoke.

Butangen's believers would discuss this moment at length in the future. They felt it marked the exact time when the Lord raised His hand against fate and said: *Wait. Give him a chance, this madman.*

In the ruins, beneath the grey fumes, something happened reminiscent of the clumsy exertions of a bear. A burning cross rose above the surface for an instant before it came crashing down, a cross they realised later was the church's great crucifix. Then there was a loud crack and grunts of exertion as a heavy beam was broken in two, and out of the smoke, steam all around him, came Isum, with a black bundle in his arms.

He had lost his woollen hat, and his eyebrows and hair were singed off, yet he plunged on through torn planks and crushed timbers. The wind turned, driving the flames in his direction, but he fought on and climbed back up. The stave church's ancient foundation wall gave him a strong foothold, and he took a colossal leap out of the fire and let Jehans and Røhme take the bundle as he landed. Then, flinging himself into the snow, he lay there gasping and steaming, for the wet clothes had almost caused him to be boiled.

Night of Nights

Behind them, the church was engulfed in flames, as if someone had loosed their grip and let mankind solve the tangles themselves.

Røhme and Jehans pulled Kai Schweigaard away from the fire. So severe were his injuries that he was almost too fragile to carry. His body was so scorched that it was hard to differentiate between what was cassock and what had been skin. When Herr Røhme carefully peeled away the burnt cloth, a large silver cross was revealed beneath it, and when this cross was lifted up, they saw it had left its mark on his chest, a chest that gently rose and fell, as if it sought to elevate the crucifix, or as if the crucifix sought to help his breathing.

In the night's dark flew a multitude of short-lived flares: the pages of the church's hymn books, thousands of sheets of gossamer-thin paper that hovered in the hot air before they caught fire and fell in a shower of ashes, like words thought but unsaid.

He Could Bear Death No More

Victor Harrison stood by the beech trees with a loaded Westley Richards. On this February afternoon in Finlaggan, 1945, aged sixty-four, he felt the weight of the gun in his hands like the weight of life itself, for a shotgun ideally weighs the same as a newborn child.

Both his sons had now been reported missing after the bombing raids over Dresden.

Dresden.

What must they have thought, these two young men, when

they learned where the pathfinder planes were going? What must they have thought up there in the Lancaster, cold as the grave? With its strangely, static view of the flanking planes on their way through the grey light. Flying on a course so fixed that they looked like a school of fish in an aquarium. All the loud noises that surrounded them in there, the engine's roar, amplified by the hollow metal body. What thoughts lodged in their minds? These lads who were going to bomb their mother's city? The city where their grandfather was buried? The city that held their grandmother's stave church, Butangen's greatest legacy?

A night bomber in the dark, his sons' faces just visible in the pale yellow light of their measuring instruments. Altitude, speed, direction, oil temperature, fuel pressure, more than a hundred switches and warning lights, and scales for everything human beings mastered and understood.

But perhaps there were greater forces at work that night. Forces not displayed on any measuring instrument.

There were no air defences in Dresden that night, and no German fighter jets arrived in time. As a result, the air squadrons had suffered practically no losses. Very few planes had gone missing. Those that did, had probably crashed into other Lancasters because they were flying in such tight formation. Or had been hit by bombs from a plane above them.

Either way, his sons may well have crashed in the centre of Dresden.

He grieved for them. Remembered the years when he and Elsa were their whole world and could satisfy all their curiosity and wonderment.

But now? If they came home, it would be with wounds no bandage could ever fix.

And this sporting gun. Memories of two sons and times of peace. Memories he clung to now with his firm grasp on the pistol grip and barrel.

Night of Nights

Three black birds flew in on the diagonal. Victor Harrison raised the Westley and put his weight on his left foot, so that, with this as a pivot, he could let the barrels follow their flight path, before moving the muzzle ahead of one of them and pulling the trigger. The bird died in the air as the shot passed through its plumage and into its heart and lungs and head, and suddenly he could bear death no more, and let the muzzle lose track of the next bird's path. He opened the shotgun and the empty shell was ejected. One barrel was clean while the other was filled with black gunshot residue, and he knew it was an irrational, superstitious belief, but it was the belief he held in this instant: please let us have one son back alive.

The crow looked healthy enough. He plucked it on the spot and headed back to the house. On the way he met Elsa, who immediately understood it was a crow and not a pheasant.

Hand in hand they walked over the lawn.

"Let's make a Kerala stew," she said.

After supper Victor went up to his foster father's old room. It stood untouched. Towards the end of the Great War the old man had spent his last days here writing letters to Victor in the prisoner of war camp. These letters now lay in a little wooden box, and Victor sat on the bed and read and relived an old man's hope that his son might be alive. Then he went to his study to reread the letter Astrid Hekne had written in 1936.

He glimpsed Elsa in the doorway. She must have been standing there for a while.

"I've got to go," Victor said. "To Dresden."

"I'll wait here," she said. "In the hope they come back. Or perhaps one of them. So the one will have someone to return to."

Arrests

Peace never comes peacefully.

A white truck was parked in the parsonage forecourt. Two young boys in windcheaters sat in the back, each with a British military rifle by their knees. The front door was wide open. Screams could be heard from the kitchen. Two men wearing white armbands came out with Fru Røhme between them. Her hair, which had been like golden corn in her youth, and a well-kempt silver grey in old age, was now hacked off in uneven tufts, and there were cuts in her scalp. It had started, the public shaming of women who had associated with the Germans.

As Kristine ran towards her, she smelled liquor on the breath of her captors.

"Old for a German whore, but a German whore alright," a man muttered.

From another door the grandchildren came running, half dressed. They disappeared towards the parsonage's tenant farm. Soon afterwards Herr Røhme was brought out. Behind him were two Butangen men who had never done anything useful during the war, but who had also been given white armbands.

"Stop," said Kristine. "Stop this at once."

"We has our orders," said one.

"Orders, my foot!" Kristine said. "Who gave thee such orders? Who has been made general for the day?"

"Nazis are t' be interned. All Nazis are to be taken in. We has our orders, I say! They're to be interned in the townhall in Ringebu."

Fru Røhme tore herself free and screamed: "Ye mun let us talk with our grandbairns! They canna' understand! All this war they has been tormented. The littlest believes we shall be shot!"

"The Røhme family in't Nazis," said Kristine. "They never has been. Nor has they ever been members of the NS."

She was wasting her time. Already by May 7 Major Sprockhoff and his soldiers had lowered the war flag and left. Norwegian flags climbed up the flagpoles that day, and villagers who had barely been on greeting terms embraced. Cheers rang out across the village.

The parsonage lay abandoned with its floors unwashed, and revenge-lust festered. Soon the men from Milorg came with trucks to raid the house of Ola Mossen's widow, where they found the membership lists for the NS Party. Each and every collaborator was to be arrested and have their weapons confiscated.

The villagers had been cheated out of an arrest of the Mossens, so now the Røhmes were first in their index box of resentment. Since the start of the war the Røhmes had, they said, served the Germans with lavish meals and bent over backwards for them. With diligent haste the truck drove up to the parsonage. Barely anyone remembered it as the home of their old pastor, and, worse, the arresting officers were assisted by non-villagers who had never known the couple previously and who had been celebrating Norway's liberation by drinking.

Kai Schweigaard was in no state to come to anyone's defence. He was in bed at Hekne, dosed up on morphine. They had expected him to slip away quickly, but instead they had watched him defeat death every day, and he seemed in his mute perseverance to be waiting for something.

The quarrel in the forecourt grew more heated. Kristine tried to get them to understand that Fru Røhme had helped Astrid escape.

"Escape?" said a man. "Naybody escaped. Astrid died in t' church fire."

"We made out she were dead," said Kristine. "So the Nazis

wouldna' look for her. Both Astrid and Fru Røhme worked against the Germans."

A man with a pistol on his hip strode forward. "With Milorg? Neither of them ever worked with Milorg. I'd have known."

Jehans tried to explain that his wife was not talking about Milorg, but an organisation so secret it barely had a name.

One of the strangers burst into drunken laughter.

"No name, eh?" he said, leaping into the middle of the forecourt to put on a show. "I were spying on the enemy, honest, judge! I were out spying, and I saw a German tie his bootlaces! But the fellow I reported it to, he had no name!"

"Nay, for the pastor forgot t' baptise him!" his comrade scoffed, brandishing his sub-machine gun.

"Stop waving that thing about," said Jehans. "The safety catch isna' on. Nay, ye mun turn the knob upwards!"

A Butangen man came down.

"Ye can all shut yer traps now, all o' ye graspers from up at Hekne. Who supplied the Germans wi' electricity and traded food wi' them right inside their camp! Those be punishable acts. Whether ye were wi' the NS Party or nay."

Everything in the villagers' little black books came out now. The sale of Sunbeam. Tarald's poster. The mystery that Svarten, of all the Døla horses taken, had been the only one to return. The fact that Kristine was back serving in the shop the day after Astrid had supposedly been arrested.

The quarrel continued. It was a hot day in May and the wind brought the smell of the burnt-out church.

A car entered the gates at top speed and stopped, making the mud spatter. A clean-shaven young man in a light windcheater stepped from the passenger side. He had a pistol in his belt. Another man ran over to him and explained something. The young man took some papers from his inside pocket and looked around. Nobody had introduced themselves.

Night of Nights

"Take those two away," he said, pointing past Jehans. The men who had brought out Fru Røhme were stripped of their weapons and bundled into a car. Jehans tried to engage the man in conversation, but he said he had to drive on.

"I shall call the sheriff," said Jehans.

"You do that. We arrested him yesterday."

Again Jehans tried to make him understand what had actually happened.

"Listen," the man said. "I'm a pretty reasonable fellow. But . . ." He shook his head. "You must see for yourself that this isn't the place for defence speeches. This must be put before the courts. The woman can report the man who cut off her hair. But right now we have to move on."

He folded the papers and shouted out for the truck to follow him.

The last thing they saw was the Røhmes being driven away on the back of the truck. Dust sticking to the blood on Fru Røhme's scalp.

Necropolis Dresden

Victor Harrison could already smell the smoke from a height of 1,200 feet. He tried to look for Albertstadt and Antonstadt, but Albertstadt and Antonstadt were nowhere to be seen, since both had been erased along with the rest of Dresden.

He could hardly believe that this was the city he had known so well. The buildings were recognisable, as a loved one's skeletal form might be recognisable. Where the fire had been at its most intense, everything was burned white. On the outer edges the remains were blackened and gnarled. A stamped-out campfire that extended kilometre upon kilometre.

Three days it had taken him and the Fokker to get here. Pit stops, long waits for fuel, repeated inspections of his authorisation documents from the RAF.

He brought the plane lower. Saw people below. They seemed to be searching for something. Nobody looked up.

They had probably seen too many planes.

But their search seemed incomprehensible. Like a search for something other than rock in a quarry. As incomprehensible as his own search.

The Hurricane fighter came alongside him. It had escorted him for two hours. The pilot waved, turned and was gone.

In the hold Victor had various gifts he knew would appeal to soldiers. Pre-war whisky and cigarettes. Under these boxes lay the bribe he hoped some high-ranking officer would appreciate: a leather case with two handmade shotguns.

It had been honoured now, the debt Arthur Harris, the chief of Bomber Command, had owed Victor since 1917.

"Dresden?" Arthur had said. "No plane can land near Dresden now. It's all been destroyed. Every road, every runway."

"There's always a runway," Victor had replied. "The runway that repairs itself. On which a seaplane can land."

He could see the curves in the Elbe now. It was the only thing that had kept its shape and smooth surface. Every river's blessing: a new supply of water each day. Every exploded brick, every warped iron strut and every corpse had sunk, and any broken timber had been carried away by the current.

"I don't understand you, Victor old boy," Arthur Harris said. "Never have. You'll never find them. And, just so it's said, this raid could not be avoided. But, that aside, my word is my word."

It was sealed. The Fokker's range was eight hundred kilometres, and he would be permitted to buy three refills of fuel

Night of Nights

from RAF bases in Germany. Arthur Harris had got a commitment from a Soviet general that Victor would be allowed to land on the Elbe.

Victor had seen the numbers. Seven hundred bombers had dropped sixty thousand tons of bombs on Dresden. The following night, seven hundred more bombers had come in from another angle and released a further sixty thousand tons.

The aim had not been to bomb Dresden, but to obliterate Dresden.

Somewhere down there was his father's grave. Somewhere down there was Galerie Apfelbaum, where he had met Elsa. Nothing he saw had roofs or windows. Following a bend in the river he flew past some twisted statues on a roof and realised that he was looking at the remains of the Dresden Art Academy, where his father had been an architecture student.

The arranged meeting place was just below the Academy, between the Albert Bridge and Carola Bridge. Victor flew past them, turned, assessed the distance and guided the Fokker down, landing once again on what he viewed as life's great mystery. The surface that was hard at first, then soft. Like a headwind in fast form.

He pushed the throttle in, the engine slowed and soon he could see each separate blade in his propeller. Then the plane came to a standstill and rocked on the river's gentle current.

The air was even more pungent down here. Its odour like the smell of welding, but mixed with the heavier fumes of burnt oil, burnt asphalt, scorched stone and burnt humans too, no doubt.

There had been a promenade along the river here. An elegant example of garden design, with old beech trees and Japanese cherry trees that blossomed with pink flowers. Now just black stumps. The Elbe below lapped around capsized and burnt-out cargo boats. The wooden piers were gone, their charred posts protruding from the water.

He saw the Soviet soldiers on the riverbank.

Victor lowered his left ailerons and steered towards them, checking all the while for driftwood that might damage his floats. A rowing boat was put out. He stopped, walked out onto the float and cast anchor.

Armed with machine pistols, the soldiers were far from friendly. One of them had a dent from a bullet in his helmet. Victor gave them a large box of cigarettes, and they were still unfriendly, but lowered their machine guns. He showed them the letter in Cyrillic script, with its many stamp marks.

Back on the riverbank they gave instructions to a fellow soldier with a field radio. Half an hour passed without anything happening or being said.

It was hot, and the smells came and went.

A city this big must contain nearly every material known to man, thought Victor. Metals, cotton, wool, stone, petrol, oil, coal, rubber, Bakelite, wood, every kind of foodstuff.

He sat and waited, knowing his nose would never get used to this myriad of smells. Nor should it. This was the stench of an incinerated world.

Two men stood before him. One was of high rank. The other wore threadbare civilian trousers, but had apparently been given a soldier's shirt.

Victor stood up and explained his mission.

A smirk formed on the officer's lips. Interrupting Victor, he said something in Russian to the man in the tatty trousers, who only now introduced himself as the interpreter.

"What is he saying?" Victor said to the interpreter, interrupting the officer sharply.

"He asks what the planes were made of," he said in German.

Victor looked at the officer, replying that they were naturally made of aluminium.

"And how hot, he asks, must it be for aluminium to melt?"

Night of Nights

Victor did not answer.

"He tries to make you understand that if the planes crashed here they would have melted," said the interpreter. "And not just melted, perhaps. In many places it got so hot that even some metals caught fire."

"I had two sons in the raid over Dresden," Victor said. "Tell him that."

"It was you British that sent them here."

"They were sent to destroy the supply lines, so you Soviets could enter the city."

"You could have done that with a tenth of the bombs."

It was unclear whether the interpreter was speaking on his own behalf or the officer's. But whatever the case, he was right. It was pointless to look for a crashed Lancaster in Dresden. It was like looking for a particular piece of ash in a whole hearthful.

"Could someone escort me to Großer Garten?" said Victor. "It's just a couple of kilometres away."

The interpreter said something to the officer, who turned and left. Victor knew they could take his bribes, his plane and his life without anyone ever knowing.

An hour later a truck arrived. The soldiers pointed towards the tailgate, he climbed up and sat there alone.

The truck zigzagged between collapsed walls and bomb craters filled with rainwater. All the gates and tramrails and anything made of iron were brown with rust. They drove so recklessly he almost fell off. Some minutes later the truck stopped. Using sign language, the soldiers told him that he must climb over what had, from a distance, looked like a hill, but which turned out to be a collapsed apartment block. Behind it another truck was waiting.

An old man and a little boy were standing next to the pile of rubble. The boy wore an adult's coat and no shoes. Victor could not look at them. He started to climb. The apartment block had not been completely burned out before its collapse, and he picked through mattress springs and the remains of a pair of pyjamas.

There was a different smell here, and now he understood why. The building had been so completely flattened that the rescue teams had not even come here. What he could smell were the cellars where people had gone to hide, which had turned into incinerators that had not finished the job.

He reached the top of the mound and looked out. In a side street, men were at work with shovels and wheelbarrows. It seemed an impossible task. A shot from a rifle rang out in the distance. Victor scrambled down the rubble to the next truck, which continued to zigzag through the few drivable streets to Großer Garten.

The park was a scorched wasteland. Despite it already being May, the grass showed no sign of return. He assumed the soil was dead to a depth of two metres. They passed a tent camp whose bedraggled inhabitants turned and stared. Then they were back on what had once been an elegant avenue of trees. They constantly had to swerve to avoid the bomb craters.

The truck stopped. He had clearly pointed to Lake Carola on the map, but the landscape he saw now from this small hillside was unrecognisable.

He felt faint. The damage of the city had got to him. He stood up on the cargo bed, then slowly he realised that he was indeed looking down at Lake Carola. There was so much soot and ash floating on the water's surface that it blended in seamlessly with the ground.

Contours of a cruciform rose from the charred landscape.

The foundation walls of the stave church.

Victor jumped down. The soldiers stayed in the driver's cab.

He climbed the old church steps and looked around. He walked along the foundation walls and found somewhere to climb down. With the wall reaching his shoulders here, he looked up at the sky and noted that he had not seen a single bird. The sky was leaden, the sun reluctant.

His shoes were covered in ash as he walked through the nave to the spot where he and Elsa had been married in 1919.

He knelt on the scorched earth and banished his hope of emergency landings, of opened parachutes, of faces behind the barbed-wire fence of a prison camp. He directed his trust towards the heavens that at least *one* son was alive, in the knowledge that there was only one power great enough to hear him, and were his wish granted it would already have happened long before this prayer was sent.

He climbed back onto the wall. Below him, in the monotone, scorched landscape, he spied a crooked woman in old-fashioned clothes. She was going towards Lake Carola. She turned midway and looked up at him before walking on. Her face was somehow ageless.

Victor looked over at the soldiers on the truck. They were sitting on the cargo bed, legs swinging, having a smoke. When he turned back, the woman had vanished. He had no idea where she had gone.

He walked down to the edge of Lake Carola. Some way out in the swelling slush of ashes and soot, his eyes were drawn to a strange shape. Something big was floating out there. It looked like a strange sea creature in a black swamp. It was the giant mythical serpent from the portal of the stave church. He put one foot in the water and stepped out into the lake. It was like breaking up soft, noiseless ice floes. He took another step, and another, until he was waist-high in water. Just as he reached out and caught hold of the serpent, the water got even deeper. And as he struggled back to the shore with it, he was as black as the soot he waded in.

He dragged the serpent up onto land. It was charred, and there was little left of the slanted, angry eyes or the jaws with bared teeth. But it was still recognisable. And in a way it was still alive.

Some metres from the shore his movements had disturbed the black coating on the lake. A yellow object was bobbing on the surface. The first bright colour he had seen all day. At first he thought it was a waterlily flowering in this sea of ashes, but then saw it was a rocking horse. It floated up, tilted, then it appeared to nod its head towards something.

Right in front of the rocking horse two rotund shapes took form in the slush, like boulders in a river. He waded in again and swished his hands back and forth until clear water came to the surface. He glimpsed a ring of script that came and went in wavelets of slush.

The same inscribed letters he had seen out on Lake Løsnes in 1918.

...HER MOTHER ASTRID. IN LOVING MEMORIE...

The bell was lying at a strange tilt, and, as he waded more closely, the grey-black layer parted and he could see deeper into the water.

The church bells.

Both.

He looked back over at the scorched wall of the stave church. Trying to make sense of what had happened. Then realised that the equally big question was how the second bell came to be in Dresden.

For it *was* them.

This was Gunhild.

This was Halfrid.

Two copper-brown domes, in a burnt-out land, in a burnt-out time.

It occurred to him that the bells were lying very close and at a peculiar angle to each other. As though suspended in an eternal ringing motion. He stood there in Lake Carola surrounded by soot and ashes, and it was some time before he saw that his sons had brought the Sister Bells together.

I Thought It Was the May Wind

When Astrid Hekne returned home, Jehans and Kristine barely recognised their daughter. Her face was the same. Her gestures were as fleet as ever. But they were drained of vivacity. A strange sort of calm surrounded her, a measured candour reminiscent of Adolf and Ingeborg, and other old folk in Butangen. To hide the bare patches and scars on her scalp, she wore an old-fashioned scarf she had been given, white with blue checks, and when little Eirik flung his arms about her, they could see that she flinched with pain but said nothing.

What she told them was that she had woken up in Lillehammer Hospital to the news that she had undergone an operation. She had stayed there under a false name until she was able to walk independently.

Later she had gone into hiding.

What she did not tell them was that the doctors had saved both her kidneys but removed her uterus and spleen.

The Røhmes were still under arrest. Rumours still festered around Kristine, Ada Borgen and Widow Fløter. Tarald sat in jail along with his colleagues from the Herold Advertising Bureau. Kai had moved back into his old bedroom in the parsonage, and they took turns watching over him.

Astrid disentangled herself from Eirik, saying she'd be back

I Thought It Was the May Wind

but had something urgent to do, yes, even though it was late evening.

She went down through the woods so nobody would see her. The parsonage front door was unlocked. She paused in the hallway to gather herself. The floor was scuffed, the living room door hung askew on its hinges, furniture was missing. She noted the acrid smell of gun oil, leather polish, tobacco and sweat.

A flag lay folded on a chest of drawers. The evening smell of new-sprung leaves diffused the one left by the soldiers.

She came to the cellar door. Opened it and looked down. The odours from below brought back a set of memories, and she stood there battling with them for a long time before firmly shutting the door.

His bedroom window was open. She saw him there in the twilight, and when she stepped forward, he lifted his head. "I thought it was the May breeze," he said. "So gentle and warm. But it was you. Really you."

A long night was followed by good omens. Morning would come and he would live another day. She touched his arm and understood he had been awake the whole time. The burns covered his face, upper body and arms. She knew he suffered pain at every touch, but also that he endured it because the joy outweighed the pain.

He gestured towards the cemetery.

"Their grave," he said. "The sisters. Their grave is unharmed. And now – now it is touched by the sun."

In the growing dawn Astrid heard an engine's hum. It did not come from the road, because the sound did not shift on varying terrain. Instead, it was even in tone, and seemed to come from above.

Kai heard it too. Astrid rose from her stool and went over to the window. He managed to raise his head a little, and when

Night of Nights

she drew back the curtains they both saw a tiny speck in the sky. The sound seemed to lag oddly behind it, as though it came from a place where sight and hearing, light and sound, did not agree, and then it burst into view in front of the low sun.

A plane. Coming from the south. Kai tried to haul himself further up on the bed and strained to see. She put her face close to the window and followed it with her gaze until it disappeared.

"Was . . ." Kai said, weakly, "was it yellow?"

Astrid looked at him. "Aye. Or, happen it was yellow at one time. Have ye seen it before?"

"The Golden Raven," he murmured.

"Kai. It was a plane. A seaplane."

He fell back on his pillow. Astrid walked down the stairs, heard her own footsteps echo in the unpeopled parsonage, and put on her shoes. The dawn she walked out into was hushed. As hushed as if there had never been a war.

The engine's drone and the propeller's drag in the air increased. The plane came back into view and passed right above her. Its belly was noticeably dark in colour. Overgrown with something, like the underside of a boat.

She limped down towards Lake Løsnes, filled with the sight and sound of the plane. It sloped its wings down towards the south end of the lake, skimmed the water's surface and lifted again, and she thought the pilot might be doing this to ensure there were no ice floes in the water.

But there are no ice floes now. It is May. It is May 1945, and a seaplane is landing on Lake Løsnes.

Astrid passed the fire site in the cemetery, single-handedly cleared by Herr Røhme with his shovel and wheelbarrow. It still smelled burnt from a long way off, and the grass between the gravestones was dead.

As she reached the mist-covered lake, she saw the plane approach again. And now the noise no longer lagged behind, it came *from* the plane, and hope floated together with reality and assumed its final form.

The water was still and the reflection sharp, so that the plane seemed to both descend from the sky and rise from the depths of Lake Løsnes, and for a split second everything stood still. And as the floats and their mirrored image touched, it was as though the plane met itself.

An instant later, the water grew choppy. The plane turned, and now Astrid saw how dirty and worn it was.

The engine stopped, the plane rocked, and the waves became calmer and ready to mirror the vision again.

A weary old aircraft. Behind the window, an equally weary man.

Astrid untied the Priest Boat and rowed up alongside the plane. Her uncle had already opened the door and stepped out, and soon they stood beside each other on the float, swaying with Lake Løsnes.

They had not seen each other since she was small, but there was no need for her to say who she was. He thanked her for her letters and messages before he pointed up the hill and asked: "What happened to the church?"

When she had told him everything, he asked if they knew about the bombing of Dresden. He told her that both his sons had been reported missing, and that the soot under his plane came from Lake Carola.

"The stave church is gone, Astrid. As is Dresden."

On the slope at the top of the village, Astrid saw four figures. A little boy was running ahead, and she knew it was Eirik, with her father and mother, and Esther.

Then he explained why the plane lay so heavy in the water.

"What I don't understand," he said, "is that they were both there. Halfrid *and* Gunhild."

Astrid told him about Tarald.

Night of Nights

Her uncle gazed out over Lake Løsnes. His eyes came to rest on a spot on the opposite bank, at the outlet of a stream. He nodded slowly.

"Go on in to them, Astrid," he said, opening the hold.

It was dark and wet inside, and the smell of petrol and lubricating oil and rope rose towards her. The only light crept in through the gap into the cockpit, and in this light she saw the outline of two church bells. They were covered in faded sailcloth, and she could not understand how they could stand in this shape without falling over. She pulled off the sailcloth.

The Sister Bells were melted into one another.

Halfrid lay next to Gunhild at the angle church bells have when they swing in opposite directions. Along the join in the melted and solidified bronze the words IN LOVING MEMORIE ran into each other.

How long Astrid knelt before the Sister Bells, she had no idea. As in that timeless moment up in the belfry so many years ago. A breath of the undead. A witness or a guardian. The trace of a stranger's will that quickly found peace as it slid together with her will.

Outside she heard the voices of her father and Victor, and noticed how alike they sounded. Only their accents made it possible to distinguish who was who.

She came out, saw them in the rowing boat together, and tried to imagine how these two men might have looked when they raised Gunhild in 1918. It was surprisingly easy.

Her uncle was talking about the air currents drawn into firestorms. He thought the stave church's tower had burned with such intensity that the Sister Bells glowed red, until they were sucked out by the maelstrom of the burning city, and flung into Lake Carola, where the water saved them from melting completely. The Soviets had helped him to get the bells into the plane. But not before he had offered a general his most precious

I Thought It Was the May Wind

bribe. A pair of handcrafted shotguns, their stocks carved from the wood of a single walnut tree.

There was a crowd on the shoreline now, and several boats were launched in the dawn light. Down in the Priest Boat, her uncle Victor leaned over and told Jehans something that made him shake his head in sympathy. Somebody rowed close to them, but nobody disturbed the Hekne brothers' reunion.

Sitting in one boat were the tenant farmers from Romsås and Hjelle, another was so full that the water nearly came over the side. In it were folk from Dokken and Fjellstad, in others sat folk from Flyen, Norddølum, Kinn and Spangrud, and over by the boatyard Ole Asmund Gildevollen was instructing a farmhand to row him over.

For the first time in years, Astrid felt the mood lighten. She thought she glimpsed the old curiosity, the good humour, the character. Butangen folk as Butangen folk ought to be.

As they could perhaps be again.

The boats circled them. There was no reason to keep the cargo a secret, and Jehans was soon swamped by wishes and suggestions from excited villagers, for whom this was now Butangen's only shared asset. Later, when Astrid limped back up to Kai, discussions were underway about how to transport the Sister Bells from the plane and up to the bell tower. Some thought that for the last stretch up the slopes, it would be best to carry them on the milk truck's cargo bed.

"Nay," said Jehans. "This in't a job for a truck. Not even for the Reo. Send for Svarten and Giant Isum."

The Last Piece on the Sledge

"Do ye wish t' see the bells?" Jehans said. "Have ye the strength?"

Kai shook his head. "I shall probably have to be content with hearing them when the time comes."

It was a hot day, and Kai had refused any morphine so he could listen properly and speak clearly. The two brothers were at his bedside, and at Kai's request they sat so he could hold hands with both of them.

"I fear they may crack when we ring them," said Jehans.

"They won't crack," Kai said. "Just as the ice didn't crack when I brought your mother home in 1881."

He lay there and gathered his strength. "I have a wish for you both. That you should go with that plane, Jehans. Now or later. And visit your brother's house."

They tried to leave him an hour later. But only when Victor took his brother by the shoulder did they manage to go, and they stood in the doorway and looked at him, searching for a few last words.

Then they closed the door.

Schweigaard slept deeply. When he awoke, he saw a giant figure at his bedside.

"Is't so," Giant Isum began. "Is't so, that . . . Herr Pastor shall pass from us?"

"I'm afraid so, Isum," said Kai Schweigaard.

Isum sat down on a stool, but immediately got up again.

"There were sommat I be thinking about for a while now. I in't never been one t' brood upon things, so I mun ask Herr Pastor afore he – well, do horses go t' heaven?"

Schweigaard tried to sit up.

"Not as reward for good behaviour, for a horse mainly does what a horse be told. But I be trying t' ask Herr Pastor whether there be horses up in heaven. So that folks that goes there has horses? How else shall they get owt done?"

"Otherwise, you don't want to go to heaven. Is that it?"

Isum wiped away an Arctic drip with the back of his hand. "I know I mun accept it, where'er I be sent. But I should like it to be a place wi' horses, Herr Pastor. Or I shall be awful lonesome."

Schweigaard turned, gathered his strength and said that he must consider the matter.

"Are there still lots of people down by Lake Løsnes?" he said.

"Oh aye. They wants t' see the plane, ye understand. Hear the news about the Sister Bells. We dragged them up to the bell tower. Jehans were a bit surprised when I told him I knew how the bells mun be hanged."

Out of habit Schweigaard stretched up to look out, but he was unable to sit upright, and then something strange happened, though it was not really so strange. Without giving it a second thought, Giant Isum crouched low and lifted the bed with Schweigaard in it, and carried him like a child in a cradle over to the window. Then, still holding the bed off the floor, he lowered the foot end slightly, giving Schweigaard a good view of the crowd around the seaplane below, and they commented about the conduct of this person and that.

Schweigaard looked up.

"Do you remember our sledge trip with the church bell, Herr Isum?"

"That were the most wond'rous thing I ever did in my life, Herr Pastor."

Isum laughed a little and cried a little, and Schweigaard made the effort to laugh. He took one last look at Lake Løsnes and the villagers of Butangen, and said: "I think you'd better put me down now, Isum."

"Oh, aye!"

Isum carried the bed back to the corner and set it gently down,

Night of Nights

and Schweigaard said: "I've been thinking, Herr Isum, I would presume that there are indeed horses in heaven. But just in case, I think I've got quite a good scoresheet with Our Lord, so I'll ask Him to make an exception for Svarten. And, Herr Isum, I'll try to meet you at heaven's gates. If there's snow when your time comes, I should like to pull you the last stretch by sledge."

Schweigaard thanked Isum once again for having saved his life, and nodded off, and when he opened his eyes, Isum was still standing there. He bowed, and they made their final farewells.

The Dead Say *Come*

A grey light played over the curtains. A gentle shifting. The first transition from absolute night to dawn. He had slept a little during the night, and she had got him to take a couple of spoons of porridge and a little water. She continually dampened cloths and laid them on his skin. Slowly the room brightened.

The sun began, with great tenderness, to model the features of the burnt man. The skin that before the war had hung slightly loose around his cheekbones and chin was taut after the fire. His hair had grown slightly and become soft and downy, as if he had been clipped for the summer. The faint, grey-blue light smoothed out the wrinkled burns, and in the forgiving semi-darkness, the young Kai Schweigaard stepped forward. The vision lasted some minutes. Then daylight entered and offered the reality: that he was wounded by fire and would soon die.

"Ye were pretending to sleep, Kai, so I wouldna' feel pity for thee," said Astrid.

Seconds passed.

"You're right, Astrid," he said. "I was pretending to sleep."

She lit the candle on the bedside table. In the glow of the flame, she placed a gold ring in her palm and held out her hand. His scarred fingers took it, and she moved the candle closer so he could read the inscription.

1881. *Eternally yours.*

He gathered his strength, and when he had gathered strength enough, he said: "Is that it? Is that *really* it?"

She said yes.

"So, it didn't disappear."

"Nothing disappears," Astrid Hekne said.

The sounds and smells of Butangen streamed in through his window.

He had rallied in the past hour, and they understood this would be his last burst of strength. The pain returned and took hold. The monstrous burning and itching that crawled and nipped and tore through his whole body. When the agony began to ease its grip, he said: "It will happen quickly. I shan't drag it out. It's not a pleasant sight."

"When ye die," Astrid said, "the Sister Bells—"

"No, Astrid – don't ring them then. Wait – for my funeral. Listen to the hymn."

Taking a deep breath, he said it was an old custom to ring the church bells at the moment of death, to help lead the soul to heaven.

"But I shall find my own way," he said. "I've instructed Jehans as to how I want things. I have left two letters."

"It shall be as ye wish," said Astrid.

He squeezed his scorched hand round hers, and she thought that the pain had either gone or was worth it.

"Kai. D'ye remember what we talked about before the seaplane landed?"

Night of Nights

"About the Hekne Weave."

"Aye, and how happiness is like a fire."

"Yes. So sudden. So big. But it burns itself out, Astrid."

"The happiness we talked of is right here," said Astrid. "And 'tis good. And so big it can never burn out."

The grip on her hand grew looser. "They're calling me," he said.

She asked if he could see anyone.

"No. Nothing but grey."

His body twitched, and he said that he heard them call again. She asked what they said.

"I think . . . the dead are saying *come*. And the living are saying *go*."

"Then ye mun go, Kai. But wait for me."

"I don't need to wait. I already see you."

"Ye can see me?"

"Yes."

"Where?"

"I see you there, and I see you here."

Her tears fell on his wounds and brought colour and life to the thin skin, and she continued to weep and asked once again if he was sure they shouldn't ring the bells, and he said no.

"I'll hear them," Kai said. "I shall hear the Sister Bells. Then I shall think it again, what I'm going to tell you now."

"Tell me, Kai," Astrid said slowly, as though every word might keep him alive a little longer. "When ye hear the Sister Bells, what shall ye think?"

"That what God has joined together, no man shall part."

She kissed him on the forehead, and he put his hands in hers. She held him until she could hold him no longer and the candle on the bedside table burned out on its own. Then Astrid had to get up and lay his arms in a cross and understood that Kai Schweigaard was dead.

Wishing the World Goodnight

They had no church. No pastor. No organ.

But they had the Sister Bells in the bell tower, though nobody knew how they would sound. What the villagers also had was the scorched foundation walls of an ancient stave church. And a special day in the Norwegian calendar, which had been granted them again. May 17. Independence Day.

When Schweigaard died on the morning of May 15, Astrid sat with him until the sun filled the room. Barefooted she went downstairs, and found the flag that Major Sprockhoff had placed on the chest of drawers, and hoisted it at half-mast. Eventually she saw the same on flagpole after flagpole throughout the village. The flag they had barely seen in five years fluttered between fresh green birches, announcing the death.

That afternoon brought something to celebrate at last. The sheriff arrived with Herr and Fru Røhme. The couple had been released on bail. It transpired that, before they had taken Schweigaard to the parsonage from Hekne, he had picked up the telephone and told the new sheriff that if he failed to get Herr Røhme out to arrange his funeral, a sheriff's badge wouldn't cut the mustard when he stood at Heaven's gates.

Schweigaard's plan for his funeral contained significant departures from the norm. It would take place after just two days, the bishop would not be notified of his death, and the undertaker would follow the church's simplified rules for emergency burials.

Jehans and Herr Røhme were unsure how many people would come, since the village was still far from united. After those first jubilant days, and then the excitement of seeing a plane on the lake and the Sister Bells' return, the distrust of the war years was still manifest. Gossip that had once been forgivable in its colourful extravagancies, the goading and snide insinuations that had always been Butangen's preferred form of greeting (indeed, it was rude not to offend somebody you met) – these rituals had slipped into something poisonous and ugly.

So, when the day came and Herr Røhme stood in the bell tower contemplating two bell ropes and his most difficult bell-ringing assignment to date, he was still uncertain of what the turnout would be. But they had, it seemed, underestimated what sixty-five years of ministry meant.

Because everyone came.

They came from Fjellstad and from Solfritt. They came from Arnemoen and from Gildevollen. From every farmstead and house in the village, each and every one, old folk, little children, grim-faced women, stolid men. No matter what part they had played in the war, they set out towards the church, along main roads, farm roads and byways, and yes, they even came through the forest, in the best clothes they could find after five years of war. They rowed across Lake Løsnes, they came on foot from Imsdalen, they arrived in *knott*-fuelled cars from Fåvang. And all the way from Dovre, an elderly and arthritic but most elegantly attired woman arrived in a taxicab.

The first thing attendees saw was that a set of newly carpentered steps led up to the top of the stave church's foundation wall, and a second led down to the earthen floor within.

Everything in sight was black. The mourning dress, the charred remains of timbers that had evaded Herr Røhme's fine-toothed rake, the ash on the rocks in the church wall, the soot on the tombstones, the scorched grass in the cemetery. The only thing that caught the sunlight in the darkness was a golden coffin made of flame birch by Borgedal the Younger's son and treated with linseed oil, and scattered on its lid yellow Stars-of-Bethlehem and blue pennywort, and a wreath of barely sprung birch leaves.

Within the cruciform-shaped wall, the mourners arranged themselves with surprising ease, creating an invisible aisle and facing an invisible chancel. They stood, as the custom was in the ancient times of the stave church, and right at the front were the pious, hymn-loving widows. Old and bedridden folk had been carried here, and were ensconced on top of the old foundation wall as though in a church gallery, with the welcome privilege of lying beneath sheepskins, toothless and watery-eyed.

Even though folk stood tightly packed, there was only room for a third of the mourners within the walls. The others had to spread out among the gravestones on the surrounding slopes.

The assembly was not, however, quite at peace. Eyes roamed with suspicion, memories nursed pre-war grudges. The Røhme family were glowered at, as were the womenfolk from the dairy.

But all that must wait. This was, after all, a funeral. Yes, the Sister Bells were back in the tower, and it was certain they would be rung, but what were all these rumours that something unexpected was going to happen?

The first surprise was when old Mons Flyen – the local hero who had in his time led the sledge team that transported the stave church from Butangen, and who thus awakened memories of a very different era – mounted the church wall. He announced that he had been selected by Schweigaard to officiate at his funeral, and that they should begin by singing the popular hymn, "Herre Gud, ditt navn or ære". It was the deceased's wish that the hymn be well known, so it could be sung without any of the usual mumbling!

Flyen led the singing, which was loud and unrestrained, and then began the eulogy. This was agreeably short, and anyone with an interest in liturgy would have realised that Mons Flyen was using the service order for a burial at sea, which concluded with the words from the old Altar Book: *And God shall wipe away all tears from their eyes; and there shall be no more death, neither sorrow, nor crying.*

They had come to the part of the ceremony where the Altar Book allowed for personal prayer or a homily on a suitable Bible passage. It was here that the deceased interjected in his own funeral.

"I shall now read sommat from Kai Schweigaard," said Mons Flyen. "Written over the last month. He were unable t' manage more than one sentence each day. And some o' it were written on the night afore he died."

My dear parishioners. I have presided over many funerals, in fact I have buried nearly everyone who has departed from Butangen since 1879. But I am, for obvious reasons, prevented from presiding over my own committal to the earth.

Mons Flyen cleared his throat, and took a few steps along the church wall to be sure his voice carried to everyone standing on the slope. He went on:

Certain punishments should be meted out by the Law. Other punishments must be meted out by God. Throughout the war, and in particular from 1944, suspicion has reigned among us. Many have fought bravely against the enemy. Strong resistance may also be made without weapons. Some have made great sacrifices for our country, under the guise of helping the enemy. So important was their work, they could not, and never can, tell anyone what they did.

A breeze travelled through the birch trees, bringing the fragrance of sun-warmed tar from the bell tower. Flyen breathed in and continued:

Long ago this village had a tradition that was known as skussmål. *It protected people from slander, from accusations that were impossible to prove wrong. People gathered in the church, and those who could vouch for the accused would stand and raise their hands. I now vouch for those who shall carry me to my grave. They have my hand held over them, now and forever, as does the man who will make our old bells ring again. The church bells have been absent for a long time, because of an error I committed decades ago. Now they are here once more, together, and they allow me at last to say good night to the world and place my soul in God's hands.*

Over the rustling of birch leaves, the Sister Bells rang out.

First with a fragile, almost youthful tone, and they rang in an uncertain rhythm as they gathered confidence. Then the hammers seemed to strike both bells simultaneously, releasing a spectrum of deeper resonances. Neither menacing nor unfriendly. And over these lower base notes, free and unforced tones sparkled with the sound of spring sunlight. And with each stroke the ringing increased its strength until it had the power of a mountain. Only then, with the harmony of something united and reunited, was it audible that the bells were bound together, as something in their double chime disclosed their inability to ring freely of each other, so that each chime gradually petered out with a gently muted sound, so that its wildness possessed a kernel of humble renunciation, quickly dispelled by the next chime.

As the bells rang, five women walked towards the coffin, shoes crunching on charred wood.

Widow Fløter. Ada Borgen. Fru Røhme. Kristine Hekne. Astrid Hekne.

They exchanged glances and took a coffin handle each. In a single heave they lifted the coffin up from the ashes and onto their shoulders. Eirik Hekne, now seven years old, was standing beside his mother, but dashed forward and reached up so his hands touched the bottom of the coffin.

Fru Røhme led the way. She had refused to put on a scarf, and after her public shaming, she wore her iron-grey hair short like a man's. Her gaze was so hard that nobody could catch it as she passed by with the coffin.

But there was no reason for her to have such a hard gaze as she passed through the congregation.

For one by one they bowed their heads. Not just for the man in the coffin.

But for her. For the five women who carried him.

A hand was raised to vouch for the honour of the pallbearers. Then another. A hunting team raised their hands. Then another. And as the coffin moved on, one hand after the other was raised. The five women climbed the makeshift steps onto the church wall and out into the crowd, where the black-clad mourners in the burnt landscape moved aside for them, like a prayer of black on black, and behind them came Isum, planting great footprints.

At the grave Kai Schweigaard's memorial stone was already in place.

Long before the war, Jehans had known that the only fitting gravestone was the one that had torn itself free from the mountainside when the road to the seters had been built, breaking trees and sweeping away smaller rocks in its wake. The terrain was so steep and the rock so huge that it had taken two hundred metres of rope, four Døla horses and twelve men to fetch it up. The Breia had washed it clean, and it was now a spray of colour, a whirl of cobalt blue and grey. The rock was of Schweigaard's height, and its shape bore a similarity to him too. It leaned a little, not much, just as the pastor had done when he rested on his walking stick and gazed out over the lake and fields.

Herr Røhme had spent the night working on the rock, grinding an area smooth for the inscription, carving the pastor's name and dates, and filling each letter and numeral with gold leaf. Those closest to the graveside noticed there was something unusual about the epitaph, but it was hard to see with the jostling crowd, and everyone's eyes were fixed on the five women and little boy as they came with the coffin. Anyone up on Hellorn that day would have observed that the honey-gold coffin that proceeded through the black-clad sea of mourners looked like a newly carpentered boat moving through dark, shifting waters.

His grave was at the top of the cemetery, overlooking Lake Løsnes and the memorial stones of all those he had buried. The coffin was set down with care. Astrid Hekne stepped forward and on its lid she placed a bouquet of white wood anemones. On her hands she wore delicate, white, fingerless gloves.

And Flyen introduced the hymn.

A final hymn.

Flyen announced that it had been Schweigaard's wish that this should not be a hymn for a funeral, but a wedding hymn. A hymn to joy.

Flyen gave the starting note for "Love from God" and the singing was tuneful and sincere, the only fault being that it had only three verses and when it ended an unbearable silence descended, together with a sense that a unique moment had passed.

The Sister Bells rang again.

Then, on the last chime, it happened.

Somebody, a very old woman to judge by her old Butangen dialect, started to sing a hymn. Folk stared around, but it was impossible to see who it was in the crowd, so her identity remained a mystery. She continued, in a frail but determined voice, then some children joined in, then the adults and old folk, and the hymn sung by the grave on this morning of May 17, 1945 was old Klara's favourite: "Thy little ones are we".

Final Story

Where the Ancestors Tread

A Profusion of Thistles and Brambles

A CEMETERY IS WHERE ALL THINGS END, EVEN STORIES that stretch over four hundred years.

The church was never rebuilt in Butangen. In the thick layer of consecrated earth and ash within the old stave church walls, two species of plants began to grow. Both were unusual for the area, but they took root and spread quickly. The first was thistle, the plant of longing and stubbornness. The second was rose madder, the weavers' plant, known to very few despite it being cultivated in ancient times throughout the valley because a coveted dye was extracted from its roots. This dye produced such a beautiful deep red that its Latin name was *rubia tinctorum*.

Nobody had a good explanation for this sudden phenomenon, other than that, long ago, some of Butangen's dead must have been buried under the stave church floor with bouquets of wildflowers in their hands, flowers with ripened seeds which had lain dormant in the cool darkness down below.

The plants thrived because nothing else had grown in this soil for eight hundred years and it was enriched by ash. Meeting with rainwater and sunlight, the thistles and rose madder soon seeded themselves from wall to wall. Close up, the profusion of flowers was like a spring meadow, but from the slopes above the village, and probably from heaven, the spot where the stave church had once stood was now a cross filled with green and yellow and violet.

The Sister Bells hung untouched in the bell tower, the key for which dangled from Our Saviour's big toe. Kai Schweigaard's archive of newspapers lay yellowing in the attic, a slumbering memento of the years 1879 to 1945. The living room floor retained the marks left by the soldiers' hobnail boots. Fru Røhme furnished the pastor's study as it had been before the war, put his old typewriter on the desk and closed the door.

Herr Røhme continued to make headstones until someone else had to make his, and then he took a secret with him, namely why Kai Schweigaard's was as it was.

Its strangeness did not lie in the fact that the rock was unhewn. It had taken its form when it blasted free from the mountainside, when the sharpest and most rugged edges had been knocked off by the terrain it stormed through, before being scoured for years by the sand in the Breia. This was as it should be. What was strange was that the pastor's name had been carved so high on the smoothly polished area, as if it were made for the addition of another name, as is usual for the first deceased in a married couple who will later share a grave: *Here I wait, in the hope that you'll join me, or it'll be plain for all the world to see that you chose otherwise.*

But surely Schweigaard had been a bachelor all his life?

True, rumours had circulated about him, most unsensational, and almost all connected to Widow Stueflaaten. But when she died in 1948, she was buried with her husband up in Dovre.

Curious elders cast their memories back to the Silver Winter, to those fatal months between 1880 and 1881, and to Astrid Hekne's gravestone. With the ground thaw in 1945, Herr Røhme had lifted her stone back into place, but found to his horror that the gold leaf was stuck in the grass. Her name and dates stared back at him in mirror reverse, and they were visible for a few days before they crumbled away. After that it was only with good will and a slanting sun that you could see whose gravestone it was. It stood veiled in darkness, something Herr Røhme said was in accordance with "someone's will", but whose will nobody ever knew, and at the top of the cemetery a leaning figure stood watching:

KAI SCHWEIGAARD
PASTOR OF BUTANGEN
1856–1945

Weeks turned to months, months to years, years to decades, and decades are the building blocks of centuries, and also of forgetting.

There were fewer and fewer burials in Butangen. Folk opted for convenience. It was easier to lay your dead beneath the earth close to where the ceremony took place, or it was back and forth by car, and coffee and pastries were a must at the memorial reception, so throughout the fifties and sixties most of Butangen's inhabitants were buried at Fåvang church. The gates of Butangen's cemetery grew rusty, and the grass was allowed to grow high. The hanging birches outside the cemetery walls grew tall, and the bell tower's shutters were always closed. In the semi-darkness within, the Sister Bells kept watch.

There is one thing about church bells. They are always prepared. They have a vigilance within them that makes itself felt by everyone in their proximity, for it takes so little for them to ring and spread warning of something that will happen.

Which was why the cemetery at Butangen always had an expectant tranquillity about it, as if someone were observing it from a distance. Those who came in and tended the graves did not experience this vigilance as alarming or even unsettling, but they sensed some sort of expectation, perhaps an unfulfilled will or resolve. So much had happened here, so much sacrifice and devotion had been upended, and the peace of 1945 had come so abruptly. It seemed impossible it should all end like a candle being blown out. It was as though the dead themselves and the earth in which they rested were not completely satisfied, nor were the few visitors, for they surely hoped there was more to come, if only a little.

The Promise

They are patient, the dead. There is a hush there, among the gravestones, but never silence. The dead are the best of listeners, and it is possible to imagine that they are happy whenever somebody comes, and that, through the consecrated ground, they notice the footsteps from the world of light above. On the whole they must know that these footsteps will fade into the distance. A cemetery is so big, most visitors will head for another grave, and those who visit the dead die too, so that fewer and fewer stop to say a few words.

But hope lingers on the air. Hope that the gates will open and the peace and tranquillity shift, but never break.

One evening in mid-May, a few decades after the war, the sound of car wheels could be heard in the gravel outside the cemetery in Butangen. The car stopped, not in the usual place, but in front of the tethering post for horses, which nobody had ever had the heart to remove. It was a midnight-blue Jaguar, and out of it stepped Astrid Hekne. She leaned over and put her National Intelligence name badge in the glove compartment. Then from the trunk she took a basket of compost and plants, and soon the unique squeak of a rusty cemetery gate sounded.

She filled a watering can and walked up towards the foundation wall of the stave church, knelt by a gravestone, and cleared it of twigs and leaves.

Ingeborg. Always in her striped dress and work apron. Adolf, thoughtful and gentle, staunch in his admiration of what Astrid's parents accomplished, staunch in the belief that everything would work itself out. Always glad to share stories of the past, about weather signs and reindeer paths, about the Golden Raven and Lightning Horn, about everything that was no longer, but yet was.

Widow Framstad's gravestone had virtually disappeared under a juniper thicket, just as her knowledge of the crossbar and other old customs had vanished. Nobody ever touched this thicket, because it bore berries, berries bursting with seeds, which the birds gobbled up with the fruit and then dropped in another area, where a new bush would grow. Hence, there could be no plant more fitting for the grave of an old midwife.

A white wagtail hopped from the gravestone of Simen Røhme. Herr and Fru Røhme lay beside him, and Astrid stayed with them for a good while before she walked on and laid a bunch of heather under the little wooden cross that was Klara Mytting's. She laid flowers on Mari Slåen's grave and on the graves of Widow Fløter, Fløteren and Ada Borgen. As usual Margit Bressum's grave demanded proper care, and Astrid's back was getting stiff.

Giant Isum lay at the edge of the cemetery, overlooking the forests he had worked in. He and Svarten had continued together until the late winter of 1953. By then decades had passed since the last auction of *vonapjank*, and all his colourful knitwear, apart from his yellow wool hat with a red pompom, was long since worn out. He had been felling trees at the top of the village, with an axe of course, since he hated the new chainsaws as much as any tractor. Later they discovered that Isum had felled a massive silver birch, and concluded that his heart had failed as he lifted it, but that he had managed to collapse onto his sledge. Svarten had taken him down to Hekne, where he stopped outside the farmhouse and whinnied. Kristine came out and saw Giant Isum lying dead in a yellow bobble hat. They made a coffin from the birch he had felled, and after his funeral in Fåvang church, where the floor creaked worryingly as he was carried out, he was put on the timber sledge and pulled back up the slopes to Butangen. There, they tethered Svarten to the gate, and ten men carried the coffin to the massive hole into which he was to be lowered. Then Eirik and Jehans looked at each other.

"Nay," Eirik said. "Fair is fair."

He went back to fetch Svarten and led him between the gravestones to where mourners and pastor were waiting. It was the first and only time a horse attended a funeral in Butangen.

Astrid laid a wreath of young pine on Isum's grave now, straightened up and looked out over Lake Løsnes. A gust of wind streamed through the birches. It had been a sunny spring morning, and the mild wind carried with it the scent of bird cherry and warm tar from the bell tower. They were ploughing the fields at Hekne, and she could hear the sound of the tractor.

In 1946, Jehans had finally visited Finlaggan and had the pleasure of meeting Victor's family, including Edgar, the nephew who had survived the bombing of Dresden. On his return home, Jehans had taken his grandson by the hand and walked to the edge of Storjordet. Ten years later Eirik had turned into a pretty decent farmer, but the war had made him unsure of himself. Concerned he might be too much of a homebody, Esther had persuaded him to start at Klones agricultural college. By the end of his first week he was smitten by Rønnaug Einarsvoll, a statuesque girl from Glimsdal in Bøverdalen. She coldshouldered him, but, as she perhaps hoped, this only made Eirik keener. He proposed that Christmas, they walked down the aisle in Lom stave church two weeks after the end of college, and their girls were born in the spring of 1960.

Eirik and Rønnaug now lived in a newly built farmhouse. In an overgrown flower bed were found twelve stones bored with holes. Rønnaug thought they were the weights for an old upright loom, and carried them down to the corner room in the old farmhouse, alongside an old, wooden chest with an H carved on the lid.

Their daughters were still too young at the time to understand.

They had grown beautiful. Not so that their looks got in their way, but they had a beauty that could be seen from thirty metres away. A beauty that seemed just and fitting.

On their sixteenth birthday, Astrid had taken the girls aside and unlocked the corner room door. She showed them the weave, the pillows and the black knife, and was herself surprised on seeing these old heirlooms. They felt spent somehow. Obsolete. Before she looked more closely and saw that what seemed spent was in truth complete, and what was obsolete was at peace.

The sisters accepted their heirlooms rather too unthinkingly and slipped back out, free as playful cats let out through a gap in the door. They are too young, she thought, the day will come when they'll understand the gravity of all this.

Until she wondered if that day wasn't already past.

Astrid put down her basket and trowel, and brushed the earth from her hands.

She had been staying at Hekne for a couple of days. Esther liked the smell and sound of her new car, and they drove it up to the seters despite the road being muddy.

But Astrid always came here alone. Always in May. Come sun or rain, wind or snow. It was good when it was cold, it was good when it was warm. For May was the youngster among the months of the year, and then the weather meant nothing.

She climbed onto the foundation wall of the old stave church. The sea of rose madder and thistles had just begun to turn green.

From here she could see her parents' grave.

The two of you. Father. Mother.

She thought of the year 1967. Her father had turned eighty-six, but still wanted to go out on a reindeer hunt with the Hekne Krag, which had turned up at the bailiff's office in 1945, battered and scratched. A road had been built to Imsdal, and Astrid, Esther, Jehans and Kristine had driven there in Eirik's beige Cortina.

Astrid had woken to the smell of coffee and roast pork. It was pitch dark outside the window, but Jehans had been dressed for some time. He sat preparing the gun sight of the Hekne Krag, smoke rising from his fists from the soot. At first light they came across a small herd of reindeer below Hemfjellet. Astrid and Eirik lay on the ground, watching through their binoculars while Jehans crept towards the herd.

The old reindeer hunter took his time so as not to startle them. Through her binoculars, Astrid could see him lie down with the Hekne Krag. She scanned back and forth between her father and the herd.

Waited and waited.

Asked herself why he didn't shoot.

A young bull stood up and shook his antlers. It turned in the sunlight and looked at Jehans, who still did not release the shot. That's the one Father has his sights on, Astrid thought.

Then she saw that the bull had her father in its sights.

It walked in an arc towards Jehans, who lay with his cheek against the stock of the Krag. The young reindeer stopped for a moment, then turned and bounded calmly away. The other reindeer took off with the old matriarch leading. The young bull caught up with them, and in an instant the herd was one with the mountain.

They came forward and found Jehans dead.

Astrid bent down and drew his finger gently out of the trigger guard. Then they sat a while looking at the mountains.

It was not yet ten when Jehans was carried down to Orm seter on a stretcher they made of birch, with the Krag laid on his chest. Kristine was already standing outside the old seter hut waiting for them. She knew. Her thoughts must have returned to a morning in 1903 when she gave shelter to a wet and freezing-cold young reindeer hunter, because she lit the stove before which she had thawed him that night, and when they carried him in, she demanded he be laid on a certain bench, certainly not on the floor, and she added more logs and chased Astrid and Eirik out of the hut. But as they closed the door gently behind them, they caught sight of Kristine sitting up close to him, saying: "My daftish old reindeer hunter, ye."

Kristine made less of a fuss over her own death. She finished her workday just as she always had, with a sigh and a good stretch. She had continued working at the dairy without break or rest. Three years after Jehans' death, in October 1970, she put on a windproof jacket and took a lift in the milk truck up to Saubua. She wanted to revisit the mountain pass she had walked so many times. The pass that had led her as a young woman to Butangen from Imsdalen, and very nearly back again, and which offered such fine views of the mountain and its riches. When the milk truck returned to fetch her, she was not at the turning point as agreed. She was soon found, sitting with her back against a rock further along the path. A rock from which Saubua could be seen if you were sitting on somebody's shoulders.

*

The graveyard was so easy to draw into conversation. But with dusk closing in now, it was doubtless the graveyard itself that wanted to get Astrid Hekne into conversation.

At the very top, beneath a flicker of shadows from the leaves of the silver birches, lay the grave of Kai Schweigaard. During the fifties the ground had battled with the frost. The gravestone had leaned forward a little more with each year that passed, as if to reflect how Schweigaard had changed over time, putting more weight on his walking stick. Herr Røhme had then straightened it, and it now stood as tall as Kai in his younger years.

Astrid walked down to the car and came back with a wrought-iron key and some lilies.

She went to the bell tower.

It was as cold and dark in there as ever. The smell of tar and eternity. In the middle of the room hung the bell ropes.

She climbed up to the Sister Bells. They were just as they had been found after the fire in Dresden. A play of verdigris green and copper brown. Discoloured by shooting flames, warped and stretched, locked in the ringing position in which the glowing metal had hardened. In the narrow shards of light from the hatches, she could see that Halfrid had more verdigris. Gunhild was slightly shinier from so many years under water. The birds must have kept them company, as white dirt dripped down over the bronze. The letters in the inscriptions were distorted and melted together, but the sisters' names were legible.

Outside it had grown a touch darker. A wind carried the smell of evening towards her. It was going to be one of those violet Gudbrandsdal nights when love rose and love was reciprocated.

There was nobody about. The only sounds were the wind in the leaves and her footsteps on the gravel. The low sun rendered her a silhouette as she walked up the shadow-ribbed path towards him.

She had reached him again across time. When she too met her end, those who still wondered would understand why there was space for an extra name on Kai Schweigaard's gravestone.

Astrid Hekne pulled her travel rug tight about her and stood looking out over Lake Løsnes, where the water's surface collected the evening light. The same light that touched the gold ring she held between her forefinger and thumb.

And standing there she remembered an old, old promise.

She looked at her bouquet.

From the bell tower came a soft, warm chime.

Followed by other bolder and more uplifting chimes. A tingling sifted through her, a tingling that shifted into a ringing, ringing twinned with the ringing of the Sister Bells.

Astrid Hekne moved on, past the gravestones and the stave church's foundation walls, across the fields and over Lake Løsnes and then over the mountains.

Up and over, over and up, to the highest place of all, where the ancestors tread.

Those who Lived
and Those who Live On

An overview of the most important people, animals, weapons and fishing rods in the Sister Bells trilogy.

The order follows family ties or year of birth, and often differs from the chronology in the books. The symbol ≠ means that the person actually lived at some point, or that the object actually existed, although the events described are mainly made up.

The stave church Church in Butangen, completed in 1170. In 1880 dismantled, moved to Dresden and given the name Carolakirche. Called the Nordenkirche by the Nazi regime.

Astrid Hekne b. *c.*1570 † 1595. The mother of the Hekne sisters.

Eirik Hekne b. *c.*1565. Father of the Hekne sisters.

Gunhild Hekne b. 1595 † *c.*1625. The sister who, according to local folklore, should *shuttle close*. The bell cast in her name sank in Lake Løsnes in December 1880, and was raised by Jehans Hekne and Victor Harrison in 1918.

Halfrid Hekne b. 1595 † *c.*1625. In love with a young Scottish soldier who fought in the Battle of Kringen, 1612. According to the local legend, the sister who was supposed to *shuttle wide*.

The Night of the Scourge

The bell cast in her name sank in Lake Løsnes in 1880, but was found and sent to Dresden that same year.

Leaf Drifter The "winter lamb" found in the mountains in 1617. Hand-reared by the Hekne sisters.

Archibald Harrison Oldest known ancestor of the Harrison family. Probably born at the end of the sixteenth century. Originally from the area near Loch Finlaggan on Islay in the Hebrides. Little else is known about his life.

Mats Nielssøn ≠ Bailiff in Gudbrandsdalen in the years 1619–27. Condemned five women to burn at the stake, 1619–21.

Jens Mortensen ≠ Priest in Fron, 1602–25. Contributed to the prosecution in several local witchcraft cases.

Sigvard C. Krafft Priest in Butangen in the Hekne sisters' lifetime. Fell out of favour with the bishop *c.*1620, but continued as priest until he was dismissed in 1626. Probably lived in hiding for several years in Butangen or up in the mountains.

Lightning Horn Breeding bull at Hekne that covered only one cow. Was struck by lightning and left behind two magnificent calves that would found a lineage. The origin of Hekne's emblem is a lightning-shaped horn.

Golden Raven A raven with pale yellow plumage, known from the legend of Butangen. Fell from its nest and taken into the house by a young boy from the village. Disappeared, but was said to return when its rescuer was buried.

Those who Lived and Those who Live On

Kai Schweigaard b. 1856 † 1945. Parish priest in Butangen 1879–1945.

Astrid Hekne b. 1859 † 1881. Oldest girl of seven siblings in the Hekne family. Married Gerhard Schönauer just before he travelled to Dresden to rebuild the stave church. Died in childbirth at the Birthing Institute in Kristiania (now Oslo) after giving birth to two sons.

Gerhard Schönauer b. 1858 † 1881. Born in Memel, East Prussia. Student at the Art Academy in Dresden. Died of pneumonia during the stave church's rebuilding.

Sabinka Gerhard's first lover in Dresden.

Dahl, J.C. ≠ Norwegian painter. Professor at the Art Academy in Dresden 1824–57. The first to draw greater attention to Norwegian stave churches, and in 1840 oversaw the transport of a stave church from Vang in Valdres to present-day Poland.

Professor Ulbricht Professor at the Art Academy in Dresden 1858–1902. Took over J.C. Dahl's office and field of interest. Leader of the consortium that had the stave church moved from Butangen to Dresden, a task he chose Gerhard Schönauer to carry out. Visited Butangen in the winter of 1880.

Carola von Wasa ≠ Queen Carola of Saxony, resident in Dresden. Born and raised in Sweden. Several landmarks are named after her, including Carolasee (Lake Carola) and Carolabrücke (Carola Bridge). Funded the relocation of the Butangen stave church to Dresden.

The Night of the Scourge

Courtier Kastler Queen Carola's envoy to Butangen in the winter of 1880.

Emort Hekne Originally the Hekne *odelsgutt*: the oldest boy, expected to inherit the farm. Astrid's closest brother and friend. Moved to America in 1890. Paid a visit to Butangen in 1947.

Osvald Hekne Astrid's younger brother. Took over the Hekne farmstead in 1890. Lost Hekne at a forced auction in 1917.

Klara Mytting b. ? † 1880. Pauper woman given shelter and alms by the Hekne family. Froze to death in the stave church during the New Year Mass of 1880. Later known in Dresden as Mystische Clara.

The Door Serpent The largest of the ornamental carvings around the stave church's original portal.

Margit Bressum Housekeeper at the rectory 1850–1917. Known by her preferred title of Oldfrue Bressum.

Halvor Folkestad ≠ Bishop of Hamar. The Norwegian bishop who had the most churches demolished, and built, during his tenure. Schweigaard's first superior.

Ida Calmeyer Kai Schweigaard's fiancée. Their engagement was broken off in 1880.

I. Kveilen Local historian who recorded the first written accounts of the Sister Bells and Hekne Weave. His unpublished manuscript – *Witness accounts and apocryphal reports from legends and folklore, including personal experiences of a metaphysical nature, linked to the oldest church buildings from the most remote landscapes* *in Norway* – was later found in Dresden, and probably caused several misconceptions about the Sister Bells.

Jehans "up at Hekne" Farm labourer and reindeer hunter who lived in Hekne from *c.*1840 until his death in 1875. Astrid named one of her sons after him.

Borgedal the Elder Carpenter in Butangen. Responsible for the first attempt at demolishing the stave church, as well as for the construction of the new church.

Borgedal the Younger, Son of Borgedal the Elder. Carpenter in Butangen. Oversaw, among other things, the construction of the one-room palace during the establishment of Hellorn farmstead.

Borgedal the Younger's son. Carpenter in Butangen. Restored the new church and made Kai Schweigaard's coffin.

Ole Asmund Gildevollen Wealthy and powerful farmer in Butangen. Invested in the establishment of Hellorn power station and other progressive projects in the village.

Vasslos Mythological creature from Butangen legend. Varying significance in local folklore, but said to lead spawning fish up rivers. Older men often put out porridge or cured meat on rocks in the riverbed to keep Vasslos satisfied.

The Silver Winter The winter when the Sister Bells, which had been cast using the Hekne family's heirloom silver, were bound for Dresden. Folk beliefs in Butangen added greater weight to the strange events of this time.

The Night of the Scourge

The Bell Witness A ghostly spirit dressed in red who is said to have been seen on the ice on Lake Løsnes during the Silver Winter. Also called the Woman in Red and the Lake Spirit. Bore a likeness to a figure that, according to popular belief, lived in the bell tower of the stave church tower and guarded the Sister Bells. These stories had died out in the village by the turn of the century.

Arvid Halle A village simpleton. Saved Gerhard Schönauer's life. The first to meet the Bell Witness on the ice of Lake Løsnes.

Gyda Braastad Quick-witted village girl. Heard the Bell Witness whispering the prophecy that only chain-brothers could reunite the Sister Bells.

Michelsen Master builder from Bergen. Oversaw the demolition of the Butangen stave church, and was employed, for a large payment, to solve the unforeseen problems of erecting it in Dresden.

Mons Flyen Foreman of the sledge drivers. Responsible for the transport of the stave church. Presided over Kai Schweigaard's funeral.

Widow Framstad Midwife in Butangen who maintained many ancient customs, including a ritual that was said to give mothers visions of their unborn children.

Karl Gustav Emmerich b. 1865 † 1945. Carpenter's assistant who took part in the erection of the stave church in Dresden. Served as its churchwarden until his death. Unmarried.

Those who Lived and Those who Live On

Max Sänger ≠ German obstetrician living in Leipzig. Collaborated closely with Norwegian doctors. Considered the father of the modern caesarean section. Married a Norwegian.

Oddny Spangrud Midwife in Butangen from 1890. Called the "new midwife" until Widow Framstad's death in 1903.

The Priest Boat Kai Schweigaard's rowing boat. Clinker-built from spruce in the summer of 1884. Disappeared in strange and unexplained circumstances in late autumn 1945. Possibly sank in Lake Løsnes.

Ada Borgen Single mother who made her living from odd jobs and as a maid until she was employed at the dairy, where she worked until her death. Worked during World War II for the resistance intelligence network XU.

Widow Fløter Widow of a logger who drowned in the Laugen while working. Originally a crofter, later employed at the dairy factory, became manager of the Colonial (the dairy shop). Fløteren's mother. Worked in the resistance for XU.

Fløteren Widow Fløter's son and Jehans' closest, lifelong friend. Telegraph operator at Ringebu railway station. Contact person 1942–5 for the resistance intelligence network XU.

Adolf and Ingeborg Jehans' foster parents. Crofters on Halvfarelia farm. Were given refuge in the old midwife's cottage after being evicted by Osvald Hekne. Lived at the end of their lives on the Hekne estate, where they looked after the Hekne siblings: Astrid, Tarald and Esther.

Jehans Hekne b. 1881 † 1967. Son of Astrid Hekne and Gerhard Schönauer. Grew up on Halvfarelia, established small farm and power plant at Hellorn. Bought Hekne at a forced auction in 1917.

Kristine Messelt b. 1884 † 1970. Youngest daughter from a farm in Imsdalen. Original under-dairymaid at Orm seter. Married Jehans. Founded the Butangen Dairy and the Colonial. Her vision and determination would contribute hugely to the modernisation of the village.

Victor Harrison b. 1881 † 1951. Jehans' twin brother. Originally named Edgar by his birth mother, Astrid Hekne. Grew up on Finlaggan, a country estate in Northumberland, with Elisabeth and Cyrus Harrison. He believed for a long time that he was their natural son.

Elisabeth Harrison Magistrate's daughter from Møre, married to Cyrus Harrison, owner of Finlaggan country estate in Northumberland. Lost a child in childbirth and adopted one of Astrid's twin sons immediately after his birth. Later moved to Italy with her and Cyrus' natural-born son and lived on the interest from the sale of a tea plantation.

Ragna Elisabeth Harrison's Norwegian maid. Lived at Finlaggan, Victor Harrison's nanny. Sent home to Norway when Victor was nine. On leaving, she gave Victor the little jacket that Astrid Hekne had knitted for him as a baby.

Cyrus Harrison Victor's foster father. Was tacitly aware that Victor was not his rightful son and heir, but always insisted that Victor should inherit Finlaggan.

Joseph Harrison b. 1885. Cyrus and Elisabeth Harrison's natural-born son. Lived his teenage years in Italy with his mother. He never made a claim on Finlaggan and never wanted close contact with Victor Harrison.

Kumara Foreman of the Harrison family's plantation in Ceylon. Resident at Finlaggan from 1899.

The Smuggler Gerhard Schönauer's fishing rod. Made of split cane by the Hardy brothers in Alnwick. Probably the prototype for the travel fishing rods that were launched many decades later under the same designation.

The Chamber Charger (Kammerladeren) Military rifle made by Kongsberg weapons factory, in 1848, for 16.8 mm bullets (the so-called 18 calibre). Adolf found this gun in a pine forest in 1865 and gave it to Jehans, his foster son, in 1896. Still extant at Hekne.

The Hekne Krag A Krag-Jørgensen rifle, model 1894 (long barrel), calibre 6.5 × 55 mm. Bought by Jehans Hekne in 1903 for 54 kroner and 60 øre. Originally with a notch sight, exchanged for a diopter sight in 1922. Hanging now in the drawing room at Hekne under a reindeer antler.

The Rigby One of Victor Harrison's hunting rifles. Calibre .256 Mannlicher (6.5 × 54 mm). Built on an Austrian Mannlicher-Schönauer action. Still used by Victor Harrison's son Edgar for deer hunting.

The Bleriot Victor Harrison's first airplane. Type XI-2. Used on the journey to Norway in November 1918. Disassembled and shipped to Finlaggan in 1919, but important parts went missing and it was sold to a French museum.

The Fokker Universal Victor Harrison's last aircraft. Used for the transport of the Sister Bells in 1945. Sold in 1949.

Botulven ≠ Scythe belonging to a legendary, highly skilled scytheman from Butangen. It received its name – the Patched Wolf – because it had been repaired so many times. Used by Jehans Hekne during the scythe chase by Osvald Hekne in 1903. (In reality, Botulven was a scythe used by scytheman at Kjønås in Ringebu at the end of the nineteenth century.)

Tailor Konow Kai Schweigaard's tailor. Had a tailor's shop in the main town square in Lillehammer before it was ransacked in 1944 by the local Hirdmen. He attended the inaugural meeting of the Forbundet av 1948: the Association for Homosexual Rights.

Jenny Stueflaaten (Widow Stueflaaten) Owner of a large farm in Dovre, women's rights advocate and textiles expert. Formed a close friendship with Kai Schweigaard.

Varsimla A matriarch reindeer that Jehans encounters on two occasions. Local folklore assigns varsimlas a role in "soul wandering", an intermediate state for a human between death and rebirth.

Elsa Rathenau b. 1886 † 1970. Daughter of an art dealer and the owner of Galerie Apfelbaum in Dresden. Married Eugen Kreis in 1913 and was widowed in 1914. Married Victor Harrison in 1919.

Those who Lived and Those who Live On

Eugen Kreis Elsa's first husband. Died in the Battle of the Marne in 1914.

Gisela Harrison b. 1914 (née Kreis). Elsa and Eugen Kreis' daughter, later Victor Harrison's stepdaughter. Worked in her father's company, Harrison Air Lift, from 1932, becoming its manager in 1946.

Arthur Harris ≠ War pilot 1915–18. Served for a time with Victor Harrison. In 1942–5 was chief of RAF Bomber Command and Commander-in-Chief of the bombing raids on Dresden.

Kåre Røhme (Herr Røhme) b. 1879 † 1961. Churchwarden in Butangen from 1898. Severe stutterer until he met Gyda Lilleseter in 1903.

Gyda Lilleseter (Fru Røhme) b. 1880 † 1962. Originally a cook in Widow Stueflaaten's household, later housekeeper at the Butangen parsonage 1904–45. Worked for the resistance in XU from 1942.

Simen Røhme b. 1904 † 1918. Herr and Fru Røhme's firstborn son. Died of the Spanish flu aged 14.

Lilly Røhme Daughter of Herr and Fru Røhme. Moved to Oslo as an adult. Sent her children away to live in the relative safety of the Butangen parsonage during the Nazi occupation in 1940.

Johan Røhme Youngest son of Herr and Fru Røhme. Later became district doctor.

Astrid Regine Hekne b. 1919. Jehans and Kristine's daughter. Never used her middle name.

The Night of the Scourge

Tarald Hekne b. 1919. Astrid's twin brother. Having served his time for treason after the war, he studied architecture in Sweden. Devoted the rest of his life to finding someone to build the modern stave church (the Astridkirche) which his grandfather had designed in 1880.

Esther Hekne b. 1921. Born blind. Jehans' and Kristine's younger daughter, and mother to Eirik Hekne. Remained at Hekne and lived up at the winter seter every summer until her death.

Giant Isum Originally from Hundorp, he was arrested in 1919 for breaking the vagrancy law and sent to Hekne as a farmhand. Had a drink problem, but was famed locally for his amazing strength. Teetotal from spring 1940. Died in March 1953.

Svarten ≠ Workhorse at Hekne. Died in June 1953. Lies under a rock at the top of Storjordet in Hekne.

The Reo A Reo Speedwagon, 1924 model. The dairy factory's truck. In use until 1958, when it was replaced by a Dodge D400. Said to be in a barn in Brekkom.

Sunbeam Two cows of the same name. Both said to be descendants of Lightning Horn (see above). The first was Adolf and Ingeborg's cow in Halvfarelia. The second was the Hekne cow, shot by a German soldier.

Mari Slåen Astrid's childhood friend and classmate at the teacher training school.

Kåre Karlsen Young chaplain who was supposed to have taken office as a priest at Butangen in May 1940.

Henrik Hille ≠ Bishop of Hamar. Kai Schweigaard's last clerical superior.

Arnoldus Hille ≠ Editor of the 1939 *Russeavis* in Hamar, the satirical student graduating publication. Secretary of the home front leadership during the war, later an academic.

Edgar Harrison b. 1924. War pilot, later postal flight pilot. Victor and Elsa Harrison's eldest son. Named Edgar as a gesture to Astrid Hekne and Gerhard Schönauer, who had wanted Victor Harrison to bear this name.

Alastair Harrison b. 1925 † 1945. War pilot. Edgar's brother. Died during the bombing raid on Dresden, February 13, 1945.

Hans F.K. Günther ≠ German writer and advocate of racialist thought and *Nordicism*. Lived in Skien for two years.

Maggen Blom ≠ Günther's Norwegian-born wife.

Herbert Jankuhn ≠ German archaeologist who became the Ahnenerbe's most influential prehistorian. A keen advocate for the protection of antiquities in occupied territories, but confiscated a number of priceless objects with the help of the Waffen-SS.

Otto Sprockhoff Infantry officer (Major) who led the German station in Butangen throughout the war. Revisited Butangen in 1951 incognito.

Ola Mossen Small farmer and local politician. Team leader in Butangen's Nasjonal Samling Party. Died in the fire in 1945.

Jon Mossen Son of Ola Mossen. Milk truck driver until 1940. Died in the fire in 1945.

Odd Mossen Son of Ola Mossen. Survived the fire in 1945, but lost his sight.

Ole Haffergård ≠ NS pastor in Ringebu and visiting pastor to Butangen.

Eirik Hekne b. 1938. Esther's son. Father unknown.

Rønnaug Einarsvoll b. 1937. Born on Glimsdal Farm in Bøverdalen. Married Eirik Hekne in 1958.

Halfrid Hekne b. 1960. Daughter of Rønnaug Einarsvoll and Eirik Hekne.

Gunhild Hekne b. 1960. Daughter of Rønnaug Einarsvoll and Eirik Hekne.

Acknowledgements

A BIG THANK YOU TO THE DEAD OF UVDAL, AND TO Marianne Vedeler, Anette Storeide, Asbjørn Fretheim, Inger Karin Martinsen, Ole Kristian Bonden, Kristin Fridtun, Inge Asphoug, Kirsti Krekling, Arild Teigen, Lord James Percy, Bjørn Lindstad, Lars Syversen, Marius Emanuelsen, Jørg Lian, Maria Zoéga, Arvid Nordquist, Elverum Car and Tyre, Siko and everyone at Gyldendal, Gudrun Hebel, Hedvig, Selma and my mother Randi. A very special thank you goes to Tuva, who has supported and advised me through these many years of writing. In addition, a special greeting is sent to the publisher's editor Oddvar Aurstad, as well as to the many good helpers who are not mentioned, but know who they are.

Books and texts by the following authors have been particularly important: Einar Hovdhaugen, Ingar Sletten Kolloen, Jon Vegard Lunde, Terje Emberland, Vegard Sæther, Tore Fevolden, Oddbjørn Evenshaug, Gunnar W. Knutsen, Alan W.H. Bates and Svein Sæter.

As in the previous volumes in this trilogy, farm names and surnames are used without regard to reality and geography. The descriptions of the witch trials in Gudbrandsdalen in 1619–32 are based in reality, but there are no local stories that connect the Hekne sisters to any such persecution, except for accounts from Møre of two weavers moving to Virumdalen to live in hiding. Many of the wartime events in this novel are based on fact, including the fighting at Tretten and the subsequent collection by Norwegians of abandoned military weapons. For reasons of narrative, some stories have been shifted in time. For example, the XU's discovery of torpedoes occurred on November 28, 1944, and close readers will find that the Colonial had, in one case, Sunday opening. The forced requisition of horses for the Eastern Front took place as described, and it is true that a horse named Svarten managed to escape and get back to his farm. But in reality this farm is located in Brekkom and is called Mytting. My mother told me this and many other stories, and without such stories and the villagers' encouragement to retell them freely, this trilogy would never have come about.